congratulations?

scott spinelli

ISBN: 148001818X
ISBN-13: 978-1480018181

for my grandma and mom

1 notre dame, before school

"Why don't we just run there? It'll take the same amount of time."

"Don't come if you're going to bitch the whole time. Seriously, I'd rather go by myself."

I wasn't happy about it. Not really at all. Then again, why would I be? Who on earth wanted to drive to Notre Dame? From Syracuse. Sure, I'd get to sit courtside to watch the basketball game on Sunday. I'd get to go on the air after talking with the coach and players (hell, sportscasting was only my career dream and nearly two-hundred-thousand-dollar major). But still, who wanted to drive to Notre Dame?

The only good news from the whole lot was that Chris Gordon, my Chicago-born friend since freshman year and roommate for the upcoming semester, had been assigned by the radio station to call the men's basketball game that Sunday at Notre Dame. His color guy was already there, but at least we'd have each other on the nine-hour drive to South Bend.

I liked to think of myself as a *real* asshole. The kind of kid that interrupted his friends, the kind of kid that didn't give a damn about anything. But that was only my on-stage persona. In real life, I couldn't let Chris go down there by himself. I couldn't. But, that wouldn't stop me from complaining about it.

I emerged from my first-floor room to see him watching television in the living room while working on his laptop. "I can't *believe* I have to go down to South Bend," I lamented. "Eddie, how come we're driving? When we went to Louisville last year, we flew, didn't we?"

"Umm...yeah, I believe so," Chris answered. I had nicknamed him Eddie. The path to that final resting point as a nickname was a winding one, but like most other names I came up with, it stuck. Chris had started out as just Gordon, which morphed to Gordo, which then transformed to Eddie Gordo, my favorite character from *Tekken*. Finally, it was shortened to simply Eddie, or even Ed. Chris, not one to care about these things, responded to just about anything.

"But, come on! This really, really sucks," I continued to whine. I was beginning to get annoying.

"Honestly, if you're going to act like such a sissy about it, then just stay home," Chris said flatly, barely looking away from his computer screen.

I took a shortened breath. Chris was right. *Just get over yourself, and quit acting like such a woman,* I thought. Surprisingly, I was a sexist even in my inner thoughts. Without saying another word, I headed back into my room. I had to pack.

***

Traveling almost always turned the trick for me. Then again, maybe it was the open road. I'm not entirely sure, but something about just getting your stuff together and hitting the pavement put me at ease. Possibly it had something to do with the promise of what lay ahead. The upcoming semester and the impending basketball game were certainly enough to get excited about, but this happened every time I traveled.

We loaded up Chris's blue SUV (shockingly, the car bore a striking resemblance to the blue found in the Chicago Cubs' logo) and we were out of Syracuse by 7:30 Saturday morning. We'd anticipated that the ride would take at least eight or nine hours. What we hadn't anticipated was what we'd talk about, what we'd do for those hours. Before we could go anywhere, Chris stopped at the gas station to fill up for the ride. It didn't matter how many times we filled up, since the radio station was paying for all gas expenses. There was also a ten-dollar allowance for food, which was fine if you planned on skipping one or two meals a day.

It took about an hour and a half. Maybe that's not entirely fair; it was closer to a full two hours. Regardless, we had exhausted all sports conversation. It was at this point that we reached a rare silent moment. Neither of us had anything to say.

After what seemed like an eternity, I finally had to break the silence.

"You know what this is like?" I asked. My voice clearly lacked a sense of interest. I couldn't have cared less if Chris even answered.

Which he did. "What's that?" Chris didn't care much about what I was about to say, either. Unless I had just invented a time machine or some sort of car that could travel at the speed of sound, he wasn't interested.

"This is like when you're on one of those long flights, cross-country or something. You eat the shit meal they give you, watch two full-length feature films, listen to every song on your iPod, and still have five hours left on the trip. If only we had *Schindler's List*...we could watch it twice, and by the time it was over, we'd be there."

"Now that would be a fun way to spend nine hours."

Another pause. This was becoming unbearable, despite how tired of talking we actually were. Our whole existence together had been filled with conversation, literally from its very start. I could still hear our freshman RA barking at us, "Honestly, please shut the hell up for two whole minutes!" during the first floor-wide meeting. Man, that was an awkward time. Angst hung in the air – it was apparent that no one knew how to act in the college setting just yet. People were still feeling the whole thing out.

...this guy seems pretty cool...that girl is fucking smokin'...did it hurt when he got that enormous hole punched in his earlobe?...I'll bet that kid smells....

Then there were Chris and me. We'd known each other for a total of four and a half minutes. The meeting was in its sixth minute. Chris had been talking with someone about baseball – more specifically, the Cubs.

"Come on, you can't seriously think the Cubs are going to lose a hundred games," I interjected. I rattled off the star players from their lineup, along with a few well-placed stats, and my thesis was complete.

Not at all impressed and feeling well at home after my purging of knowledge, Chris rebutted and soon after that the previous members of the conversation had exited stage left. Too nerdy, too *much* for their taste. They were hoping for generic sports banter – the sort of talk that all men fall back on to relieve tension at awkward times. Almost like comments about the weather the first time you meet a girlfriend's father, it's idle chatter to fill time.

What soon developed was a full-on war. A statistically intense but friendly conversation on all things in the world of sports, where taking a breath signaled the other person to pick up the dead air.

At first, we were pretty quiet. Only half the room could hear us blatantly carrying on our own conversation with complete disregard for the meeting. *Can you believe how well he's playing? How about this team? Could he be any worse? Is there a better player in the league? I think that he stinks, just terrible, the worst....*

Football. Basketball. Baseball. It was as if we'd been waiting the past seventeen years to have this conversation, and all the pent-up information came gushing out like word vomit. From that point forward, to this car ride, there hadn't been much conversational downtime. I had to break the silence again.

"I've been thinking about this semester. What is there to look forward to? I mean, what are we, two single men, looking for?"

"I'm not really sure what you're getting at," Chris responded, slightly puzzled. He wasn't paying full attention, plus he had the slight task of driving the car for nine hours along a four-lane high way in the middle of Pennsylvania. "Are you talking about having a good last semester, about graduation?"

"Well, in a way, yes. But, what I'm talking about is one thing – women. What female prospects do we have? I don't have anything. Nothing. I thought writing that column might help....I've had enough of women saying they like funny men. There's no one funnier than me. I should have closets and drawers filled with pussy."

"And so modest! How do they resist you?" Chris said. A smile crept across his face, but he knew exactly what I was referring to. A dust bowl-esque drought, at least as far as women were concerned. It had certainly been a while. A long, drawn-out while. Neither of us really had any prospects, but I had to make it seem like I was worse off.

"Am I an ugly man? Do I not attract members of the opposite sex?"

"I hate when you ask questions like that."

"What do we have going on, female-wise, on the horizon? Don't even answer that; let me tell you. We've got one more semester left. This is when all the girls are supposed to be wild. Matter of fact, that was supposed to be college, right? Crazy parties and tons of girls, tons of sex. Maybe we just went to the wrong school, I don't know. I do know that going to the bar with all you guys should be a help. But – I don't even know how to approach a girl. I don't know what to say to them. I think that's because I just don't get one thing about women. Not one."

"Yeah, me either. Me either," Chris replied.

"There are some guys, like Matt, that can just go up to random girls and talk to them. I can't do that. Just can't. I doubt being able to go to a bar will change that much. I mean, I don't even know what girls I have 'on deck.' I'm praying that there's some girl in one of my classes that I've never met before, some girl that somehow has slipped through the cracks for four years. What the hell are the odds of that, after four years of classes at the same school? A hot single girl I haven't already failed or even tried with?"

"I'd say, honestly, zero."

"Thanks for the vote of confidence."

"Sorry, but it's true. I'm in the same boat, unfortunately. Same boat...." Chris trailed off. "Well, what about that girl from freshman year...Lauren?"

"Parker?"

"Is there another Lauren you've been obsessing over for the last three and a half years?"

I paused before speaking, a rarity. "Obsession isn't that bad, though, is it? A lot of famous people and things have involved obsession. James Earl Ray is pretty famous, and I'm sure he was obsessed with Martin Luther King, Jr. Same with Mark David Chapman and John Lennon. Wasn't there a cologne by Calvin Klein called Obsession?"

"What is wrong with you? Those two guys were assassins. They killed people. They were delusional obsessives. You're not that bad...yet," Chris reasoned. "And I have no idea if that was a cologne."

Again, we had exhausted a topic. First, all things athletic. Now, in a matter of mere minutes, all things female. There was only one option remaining.

"I'm going to take a nap," I said.

"Thanks for the company."

"Not a problem, pal. Remember, I'm here for you." Five minutes later, I was fast asleep.

When I woke up, we realized there was still one level of recourse left. The always prolonged, always challenging Name Game. Only athletes, of course. But, considering we had at least another three or four hours to kill, the pool was open to anyone that had ever played any sport at any time in history. The only prerequisite was that they had to have a last name, so ancient Greek and Roman athletes didn't count.

"Jackie Joyner-Kersee," I started off with. I thought I'd give him an easy one to start with, while showing off with my choice.

"You are such a dick. 'Y'? That's what I have to start with? I haven't even got one name and I have to think of a 'Y'. Real nice."

Asshole that I am, I let him think his letter was Y.

"I play to win, fella. Get to thinking."

The game ping-ponged back and forth, but I would ultimately get my comeuppance. A last name ending in 'Y' came back my way. After a while of making funny 'y' sounds aloud, I ultimately offered a last gasp effort.

"Yul Brynner?"

"Is that a question, or a guess?" Chris asked.

"That is a guess. Yul Brynner. He was a boxer, right? Or an Olympian of some kind."

"I don't think so. Sorry."

"That's not good enough. I think he was a boxer, so why can't I be right? Why do you have to be right?" I was competitive. Clearly, I wasn't going to just let this go.

Then again, neither was Chris.

"Okay, what do I have to do to prove that he wasn't an athlete? Would you like me to call my father? He would know what Yul Brynner did. I don't know for certain, but I do know that he wasn't an athlete."

"Fine, go ahead and call your dad."

A phone call later, the game was settled. Yul Brynner, the bald Broadway and Hollywood actor, didn't count. I lost.

***

By the time we got settled at our hotel, all we wanted was their version of Chuck's. I'd been able to go to the campus bar only once, as my twenty-first birthday had just passed and the semester had just ended. The bar we stumbled towards was called The Blarney Stone.

"You've got to be kidding me. That's the name of this bar? On the campus of Notre Dame? Jesus Christ," I said. I hated Notre Dame with a passion that ran deep, but that I couldn't fully call my own. My father hated two things: Notre Dame and the Red Sox. I picked up both hatreds. There was something extremely pretentious about the whole thing, at least as far as I was concerned. Why this was ignorant, beyond the obvious reasons, was that neither my father nor I had ever been to Notre Dame nor knew anyone, beyond a passing acquaintance, that had actually attended the school.

"Aye, mate," the bouncer said to me. "You have ID on ya?"

"What? What is this?"

"ID. Identification, mate. Need to see it if you're going to come in."

I showed my license, with a look that screamed, *"What the fuck was that accent?"*

As if I'd said it aloud, Chris answered, "Don't even worry about it. I'm sure he's just playing around."

Once inside the bar, we found it was surprisingly quiet for what was described to us as a college bar on a Saturday, when it should have been packed. Tacky wouldn't have even begun to describe this place. Everything in the bar was green, from the suspenders the waiters and waitresses wore, to the seat covers, to the bar itself (a lighter shade, of course). Fightin' Irish pennants and leprechaun cut-outs adorned the four walls. It was like an Irish Applebee's, enough to make you want to puke.

There were people in the place, but we had no difficulty getting a booth where we were soon approached by a waitress.

"Hi, guys! My name is Michelle, and I'll be your server

tonight! What can I get you guys?!" She truly was as bubbly as that reads. Rare is the case where the "?!" is an accurate representation of the level of excitement in someone's voice. This was one of those cases.

"Hey there, Michelle," Chris said, his excitement level rising with hers, "We'll have two car bombs! You can put this round on this card! Thank you so much!"

"Okay! Thanks, guys!" she said, flitting back towards the bar.

"Thanks for the drink, dude," I said. "Do you find this place absolutely revolting?"

"It's a bit," Chris said, choosing his words carefully, "much."

"Guys," Michelle said, returning to the table empty-handed, "I'm so sorry, but we don't have any Guinness. We can't do car bombs."

"You mean you ran out?" I said.

"No, I'm sorry. We just don't have it. We have Miller and Bud on draft, and a bunch of other stuff. I could check? Would you like that?"

"You are serious? You really don't have Guinness?" I asked, just to make sure I had heard her correctly. At the most Irish school in the country, at its most Irish bar, there wasn't any Guinness. They didn't carry it in stock. Simply stunning.

"No, sir, no Guinness."

"This is too good to be true," I laughed.

"Can we just have two Buds?" Chris asked.

"Sure. Sorry for the confusion about the Guinness. I wasn't sure what was in a car bomb at first," Michelle said before leaving.

"The hits just keep coming," I said, now hysterical. "I hope Chuck's isn't like this. You guys have been hyping that place up for so long that—"

"It's not like this dump, trust me," Chris smiled.

After the game... which Syracuse lost, 97-78

My lone job, on this and every other radio station-sponsored trip, was to go into the locker room after the game and talk to the players and coaches. Get some sound to use for the rest of the week, try to gain some insight into what had just happened, and then call into the post-game show and report it all back. Not too difficult.

Of course, when the team got trounced by nearly twenty points by a conference rival, it wasn't as simple. Throw on top of that the fact that the locker room would have been more aptly described as a locker closet, and it made for an uncomfortable situation.

The coach's press conference was short, curt, and near an eruption at every turn. That, sadly, wasn't odd. Jim Boeheim, coach of the men's basketball team, rarely seemed content. Win by twenty, lose by twenty, he never seemed too happy. Questions he deemed inferior weren't simply cast aside, they were amplified for the room to hear again.

Afterwards, I followed the herd into the locker room. Usually I'd go and talk to whichever player wasn't being swarmed, so I could ask my own questions. That typically meant I'd be asking the best players questions on the second go-round, but I'd dealt with most of these guys before. They were cool. They were usually happy to talk to the media, even the student media.

A couple of players in, I finally got the star of the game (if you can even call someone that leads the team with twelve points a star) in point guard Jonny Flynn. Jonny was a nice kid. He had NBA written all over him (solely a matter of when, not if) and yet it didn't affect his attitude. Always smiling, always polite in victory or defeat. Not to mention, despite his dominance on the court, he was hardly imposing off it. At around 5'11" or so I actually stood even with Flynn, with a possible slight height advantage. So it came as no surprise that I felt on his level, even though in a short while I would be an unemployed college grad and Jonny would be a multi-millionaire college dropout playing in the NBA.

"Jonny, got a few minutes?"

Sitting down at his makeshift locker with ice on his knees, Flynn looked up and gave a smile indicating that it was okay for me to sit with him.

"Notre Dame really gave you guys a hard time out there today. You guys haven't struggled like that all season, especially with a man-to-man defense like the one they had out there. Any feelings as to what happened today?"

He answered with something about how the quickness of the perimeter players and length of the big guys gave them trouble, now standing, getting changed, and putting his stuff away into his bag.

"You still managed to nearly rack up a double-double. That's what, five or six impressive performances in a row now? You have thoughts about going to the League after this year?"

"You know I can't talk about that stuff, man," Flynn smiled, finally looking at me.

"No, I know, I know. It's just—"

"Yo, aren't you the dude that writes that thing in the paper?" Flynn interrupted.

I paused, unsure if he was even talking to me. Looking around, I realized he had to be.

"I do. I don't write for the sports section, though," I said, immediately regretting how condescending that sounded. *You're an athlete, it's a wonder you can read, and we all know you don't read anything other than your own press clippings...Jeez, what century do I live in?*

"Nah, I know that. You write that funny column. On Wednesdays. Or Thursdays?"

"Thursdays," I said quietly.

"That shit is hilarious, dude. Honest, keep that up. I love reading it," he said, resuming his packing.

"Thanks a lot," I said trying to keep my erection hidden. *Jonny Flynn, star point guard, reads my column? The one where I whine about not being able to get girls or the value of destroying your three-year old niece in board games? No way.*

"Yeah, man, we all read it. We want a shout out in that shit!" he laughed.

"I guess I can see what I can...."

"I'm fuckin' with you, dude," Flynn said. "For real, though, it's funny. We like it. What's your name again?"

"Nick. Nick Alexander," I said, still amazed at what had just transpired. People like me were supposed to know who Jonny Flynn was. People like me enjoyed people like Jonny Flynn's work, followed them. Not the other way around. At least, I didn't think.

"All right, Nick, I'ma get outta here. Bus is leaving in a bit. You have anything else you need to ask about the game before we head out? Basically, we got our ass kicked today. Plain and simple," he chuckled. "We're going to make a note of this, practice harder, and come out strong next game at home. Believe that."

"Thanks, Jonny," I said.

"No doubt. See you around," he said, heading out.

***

If there was one lasting thing that came out of that brief weekend in South Bend, it was an idea. During the whole visit, concluding with the incident with Jonny Flynn, I gradually hatched an idea. Rightfully, it should have been detailed in previous pages, but seeing as how we're past that, it'll do here.

The campus of Notre Dame is indeed very beautiful and historic (if a bit repetitive architecturally). Old buildings and churches seemed to pop up around every corner. In front of one of these, the idea was conceived.

"Yo, take a picture of this!" I said, kneeling down in front of the doors of a random church. I had one knee on the ground, the other bent, with both hands meeting in a prayer position as I looked towards the sky. I had to get a good shot to send to my dad. "Make sure you get the stuff at the top, too."

That stuff at the top was the following words, engraved in stone: "God. Country. Notre Dame. In Glory Everlasting."

Looking at the picture later, Chris said, "You know what?

This would be a hysterical poster or cover for a CD." He was kidding. I took it seriously.

"You know what, you might be onto something," I said back.

"What, are you going to record a CD now? Make this your cover art?" he laughed.

I wasn't even sure exactly what I meant. I just knew, looking at that raw picture taken from a simple digital camera, that I might be able to use it for something larger.

If the conception of the idea was that picture, the birth occurred shortly after the encounter with Flynn. There was something about recognition by a nationally-known college basketball superstar that pushed me over the edge.

"I've got it!" I shouted on the drive back.

"No need to shout, just me and you in here," Chris said.

"Remember that picture we took of me kneeling in front of the church?"

"Yeah, what about it?"

"I know what I can use that for!" I said, expecting him to ask, *What for, Nick?* He didn't, though, so I continued, "I'm going to put on my own comedy show."

"Cut it out," he said, now taking his eyes off the road and looking at me in a manner that made it seem like he really had a ripping session in mind.

"No, I'm dead serious. I've got the name and everything. It's going to be called 'I Hope God's Wearing Earmuffs.' Get it? The church thing and the fact that I'm a filthy comic? Yeah, well anyway, that's the title, and all the proceeds are going to go to cystic fibrosis."

That last part, it should be clarified, wasn't as random as it might appear. My cousin of the same age, Brooke, had the disease, and I'd always been very conscious (as much as a conceited twenty-something could be) of trying to help out.

"You cannot be serious," Chris said, apparently unsatisfied with anything he'd just heard.

"What's wrong with that idea?"

"Are you really that delusional? You really think people

are going to pay to see you? I know you are *buddies* with Jonny Flynn and you've got your little column, doing your stand-up for a year now, but come on."

"They're not paying to see me. I mean, I guess indirectly they are. But it's for charity, you douche. It's not like I'm pocketing the money."

"What about getting a place to do it in? That's not free. How about advertising, what about anyone else in the show? Don't forget—"

"Easy," I said, cutting him off. "I just thought of it now. I haven't ironed out all the details. But I know some people and I think I can make this a reality. You watch, this is going to happen."

"I doubt it. I think you're underestimating how hard these things are to pull off. I'm not rooting against you, but...."

"It sure fucking sounds like it," I laughed. I knew what was going on. Chris wasn't angry; he just tended to get worked up over things. He also was a meticulous planner, not the sort of kid who often did things without thinking them through. I often did. As such, I knew I had work ahead.

***

We finally arrived back in Syracuse just a shade after two a.m. I crept through the house, snuck into my room for a brief second to put my bags down, emerged to take the step across the hall to the bathroom to brush my teeth, and then immediately went back into my room. Pushing my bags aside, I collapsed on the bed. I didn't feel like chit-chatting with my roommates; that could wait.

I'd be heading home for winter break in a few days, and all I could think about was the upcoming semester. I'd be twenty-one for a full semester. I looked at it as my rebirth. A second-semester renaissance. I sort of felt like my whole life had been building up to the coming four months, though I had no solid reason to believe that was the case.

2 the drive to school

"You know the 'Niners set themselves back years, maybe even decades, when they drafted that bum," Lotfi Bougherra said as he wolfed down his eighth White Castle burger.

"Decades, hell—maybe even centuries," I smarted back. "Why stop there, maybe millennia?"

"Very funny."

Lotfi Bougherra was, and still is, a San Francisco 49ers fan. No one knew for sure why, but then again, no one really knew why Lotfi did any of the things he did. For instance, we all pronounced his name Loat-*fee*. After a few years at school without correction from the burly Algerian transfer student by way of Michigan State, we assumed there wasn't an issue. Turns out, Lotfi was pronounced Luht-*fee*. He never said a thing when people were constantly getting it wrong. For years. That's the kind of guy he was, whatever that says about him.

We both lived in New Jersey and only one of us had a car. As such, I drove Lotfi up to school with me after every break or solstice or holiday or what have you that caused us to be spending time with family in the Garden State.

There was a certain routine to this whole thing. Lotfi showed up within a few minutes of when I had asked him to be at my house. We loaded up the back of my car with all our stuff. We left the house, headed to White Castle for a Crave Case of burgers, and then hopped onto Route 287, only ten to fifteen miles detoured from the original beginning of the nearly four-hour trek back to Syracuse.

So, at around 11:30 on this brisk Wednesday morning in January, we had hit the road to begin the last semester of our college careers.

We'd be arriving half a week early to cover for the radio station we worked for at school, WAER. The basketball team was playing Cincinnati, and someone needed to be there to host "The Double Overtime," which was easily the peak of my social life: talking with older men about a basketball team that seemed incapable of getting out of its own proverbial way, chattering with recluses about why a head coach of thirty-plus years deserved to keep his job, and just generally pandering to the random queries of the small population (if you can even call it a population) listening to nearly commercial-free, NPR, student-run radio. Half of the time, callers to the show were the sort of guys you prayed were calling from a home phone. The other half was friends of people on the staff, pretending to be that first half.

"No, no, no. Take it easy, now, with that....You've got to actually listen to the program every once in a while, Floyd. You can't just come on here and tell me I'm terrible at what I do, and call me Andrew. Get rid of this guy. The name's Nick...Alexander, and yes, maybe I am terrible at this, but at least I know your name...Floyd. Next caller...."

Something about it we enjoyed. You'd think we were starved for similar conversation in our normal lives, but a simple ride back up to school disproved that theory.

"Come on, man, I know Alex Smith stinks. You know he stinks, how could they have taken him?"

"I don't know," I answered, generally disinterested. I had other pressing matters: shoving down as many hamburgers as my gullet could logistically handle, watching the road, trying not to vomit, trying not to get pulled over for speeding.

"Listen, I've never run a football team, professionally or

otherwise. But I could've told you not to draft this guy. He's the worst quarterback in the whole league!" Lotfi had a tendency to make outrageous claims that seemed to be thrown out against the wall to either incite further argument or prove the theory that if you throw enough shit, some of it will eventually stick. This one didn't.

"I guess."

"You guess? That's it?"

"I don't know. Haven't we had this exact same fucking conversation a thousand times?" I wasn't remotely angry, but I'm Italian, from New Jersey, and as such, I speak with my hands and use the F-word like it's a required part of speech. Subject, expletive, predicate.

One of Lotfi's favorite songs came blaring out of the stereo of my Infiniti hand-me-down car—a Jennifer Lopez ditty that all 240 pounds of the man to my right jiggled along to. He wasn't a fat 240, but he wasn't a muscular 240 either. He had one of the most strangely proportioned bodies I had ever seen and I made that clear to him the first second I laid eyes on him.

"Holy shit! Your head is fucking huge!" I had nearly shrieked in a mix somewhere between absolute fright and shock. It was, without doubt, the biggest head I had ever seen. It was the sort of head that, if Lotfi closed his eyes for a few hours, could double as a movie projection screen.

The block-shaped, gargantuan melon (imagine the top half of an hour glass) sat atop a fireplug of a body, with broad shoulders adorned usually with either a football jersey or overused fleece of some kind. He never wore pants and made a point of letting everyone know about it, despite going to school in Syracuse. Often jorts, or jeans shorts, were the undergarment of choice.

As it turns out, there was reason for his strange shape— his family did look quite normal upon initial glance. Lotfi had a spinal condition so rare that not even his local doctors knew what to call it. By the time he was eleven years old, he had already had five back surgeries and no one was sure when the next problem would arise, though he had been issue-free for quite some time.

His demeanor, despite his overwhelming size, was that of a puppy. He never stopped smiling, revealing almost every single white tooth when he did. Hell, his face had enough room to stretch a full smile on it, so why not? Many people preferred a simple "high five", hand-pound, or hand wave when meeting someone. Not Lotfi. He went for a full-fledged, arms-extended, near-suffocating grip of a hug. Usually it was followed with something generic in tone.

"You, you're pretty. You're a good man, you." Lotfi had a deep-throated voice and sounded like a badly impersonated Robert De Niro, though he looked more like a well-drawn Quasimodo.

Driving up to Syracuse was usually a four-hour trip, plus one stop to throw away the White Castle trash (which was stenching the entire car at this point). The drive had three legs on three separate highways, none of which looked any different from the others.

And so the trip continued, with the weather as bleak as it was likely to be for the remainder of January and most of February and probably a good portion of March. Music blasted nearly the entire time. Sports talk seemingly never ceased and despite being on constant loop, neither of us got sick of the other. We hadn't known each other for a lifetime, or even been the closest of friends up until the previous semester. But Lotfi, unlike me, could get along with anyone or anything. He was a top-heavy, energy-drink-obsessed, jean-shorts-wearing Algerian. I was a skinny, slightly neurotic, Sour Patch Kid-addicted, arrogant Italian. Match made in heaven.

.

3 more of the drive

As Lotfi and I cruised up I-81, now only fifteen to twenty miles from campus, we quickly remembered what we loved so much about school.

"Can you believe all this fucking snow? Jesus, I will tell you this, I won't miss this crap at all. Not one bit."

"You, you," Lotfi started up. "You're pretty. You're special."

We cruised on. I told him about the comedy show I had planned and he supported the cause as I knew he would, saying he'd help with whatever I needed. The trip had taken about four hours and forty-five minutes by my count, with the stop to throw away the White Castle. The one thing we hadn't really counted on was how amazingly empty the campus would be when we got there. Classes weren't starting up until the following week, and it was Wednesday. Around Friday or so, the legions of youth fed up with the stress of living the same lives as their parents for a month would invade the school, and normalcy would be restored.

Lotfi and I were there exceedingly early, but I enjoyed the advance time. I liked getting everything straightened out, everything cleaned. Clorox-wipe my desk and dresser. Wipe down the night table. Vacuum the bedroom. Wash and change the bedspread. Once I was done with all that, I'd clean my computer screen and clean out my desk drawers. Buy new pens, a package in black and blue. Wipe down the dry-erase board in my room (clean slate for the new semester, of course).

"Can you believe this, just walking down the middle of the street like this? I don't think I've ever seen the place this empty," I said.

"Yeah, this is strange. No one is here, not a soul," Lotfi responded, as a tumbleweed actually danced down the street.

"I feel like we're on a campus-wide Candid Camera show. I kinda half-expect everyone to pop out from behind trees and out of their dorms in about ten minutes. Either that or the world is about to end, and no one told us to flee the village."

"You're a strange man."

Lacking better ideas, Lotfi and I took a leisurely stroll through the barren campus. Barren, actually, in two senses. There wasn't anyone there, nor were there any leaves on the trees. The rectangular quad we had left a lush shade of green last semester had aged in the past two months to a blinding white. Snow, though not nearly in what would be considered Syracuse abundance, clung to every tree, bush, and rooftop.

A slight breeze ran through the quad, which was fenced in by school buildings I rarely if ever entered. The biology, engineering, physics, and art buildings made up the border. These weren't "my" buildings. "My" building was the journalism school and that was about it. I felt comfortable there, not totally at ease, but comfortable. For some reason, I had a deep-seated, nonsensical fear that as soon as I'd enter a building I really didn't *belong* in, I'd be caught. As if there were engineering-department police officers.

Either way, we were used to the cold. Neither of us wore more than t-shirts covered by hooded sweatshirts. Snow and a breeze weren't a big deal, plain and simple.

Walking along the sidewalk that split the quad in half, I came to a sudden stop, halting a retread sports conversation.

"So, this is the end. The beginning of the end, I mean," I

said. My gaze was unfixed, darting back and forth between the buildings and the looming on-campus chapel.

"What are you talking about?" Lotfi asked, sighing. He was actually a little annoyed—he was just about to drop a killer statistic regarding the school's basketball team, proving why he was right and I was wrong about the team's success, or lack thereof, on the road this season. That discussion would have to wait.

"This is it. This is supposed to be the beginning of the last part, of the best part, of our lives. How does that make you feel? Like you wasted it? Like it's just...gone?"

"I don't know. To be honest, I've never really thought about it."

"Well, neither have I, really. But it just seems like I need to let this whole thing soak in. I mean, I look back on the past few years, and...man, what the hell have I done? College was supposed to be a time where you get with a million girls, get drunk at all these parties. Whatever. And how many girls have I been with? One. And that was almost a year and a half ago."

"I wouldn't base everything on how many women you've been with," Lotfi said, and then, under his breath, "though I know you do."

"No, no. I know what you mean. But what prospects do I have? Don't even bother answering. The number's zero. None."

"All right, now you're just being ridiculous. Calm down," Lotfi tried to reason.

"Yeah, yeah, you're right. Sorry. Anyway, like I was saying, I want to take this all in. And I don't mean it like when I've said every semester that I'm going to start taking more pictures or use—"

"That video camera you bought, but never used?" Lotfi interjected.

"Thank you for that three-hundred-dollar reminder," I said curtly.

"What I'm here for," Lotfi shot back. He might not have gotten to win the sports argument, but at least he got in that minor ribbing.

"*Any*way," I said, stretching the word out, "you know, just try to really enjoy this. Girls or not. Just be me, and leave with no regrets—"

"You know me," Lotfi interjected again. "And you know I've never been one to interrupt you that often, but we've got to talk about something else. This is depressing the hell out of me."

"Yeah, you're right. Fuck this. Let's go get something to eat? Wingz?"

Dinner was patently average: fried chicken with French fries. Nothing too fancy; we wanted to go back to the house and crash. There wasn't energy left for anything other than going to sleep. Lotfi lived a block away from me, and could've easily gone back to his own place. But he ended up staying with me until the rest of my roommates returned to Syracuse at various points towards the end of the week.

"You sure you don't want me to just sleep at my own apartment?" he asked, often enough that it almost became a nuisance.

"No, no," I reassured. "Why not just hang here? There's no one else in this zip code not playing for the basketball team. We might as well chill here."

That was all I wanted. To be around a friend, or two or three. Give me that, and I was content. Living at 125 Clarendon gave me that opportunity every day of the week. Rare was the instance when there wasn't anyone else home. That was the beauty of college, the immediacy of like-minded souls. How much I'd miss it, I had no idea.

Often, in fact, I would sit out on the porch whenever the weather would allow for it. I'd bring a friend, a drink, a chair, and maybe some music or something to eat. The first time I asked a roommate to join me, I was met with confusion.

"Go outside and sit, and do what?" Matt asked incredulously. "Just sit there?"

"Yeah. Just sit. If your schedule allows for it, maybe we can talk, but we don't have to. Nothing big."

And from there it was birthed. People walking back from class on a day that was even remotely warm would inevitably find me (with or without a friend) sitting out on my porch. The space itself couldn't have been more than four feet by seven feet. If that. It was enough for two or three lawn chairs, and that was enough for me.

The house itself had a chipped white exterior—Victorian-style with two staircases, one at the front of the house and the other in back. Matt, Colin, Chris, and Natalie all had their rooms on the second floor. I lived alone, in the biggest room of the house, on the first floor. An immediate left out my door would take you into the kitchen, centered by an island countertop—a frequent spot for chatting, eating, and general congregation. Two steps forward from my door, and you'd be in the bathroom. An immediate right led into the dining room and living room area—a space mostly reserved for watching television, hanging out, and drinking assorted alcoholic beverages.

There wasn't anything outrageously cozy about the place, especially not when we moved in last August. The walls were a bare white and revealed obvious attempts, weak at best, to cover various holes and patches with paint. There weren't even shades on the windows. Yet, after a trip to the depot of all depots (Home Depot) and a few months of general decoration, the house began to develop its own character. Movie posters (I framed mine, definitely makes it much more "adult") adorned the walls of the living room. Matt built shelves in the living room atop the windows to house a project he had been working on over the past year: the beer wall. There were a few simple rules as to what could be added to the wall:

1. Only bottles.
2. Only beers or ales, none of that "fruity shit," as per Matt's declaration.
3. Nothing that was a variation of something else up there. For instance, once you had one type of Sam

Adams, the other 87 weren't allowed.

Natalie, the only and requisite female of the group, did her part. Her room easily smelled the best, candles going nearly all the time, which helped keep the house from completely smelling like old socks. She also bought some of those plug-in scents for the rooms her candles couldn't cover. Matt rigged up the kitchen refrigerator, which didn't come with shelves, so that everyone could keep what they bought cold without much hassle. Chris and Colin took care of the electronics department—a TV, from back when it was a big deal to have a color TV, sat in the living room. Colin also brought a small refrigerator that hung out in the middle of that room, an appliance that came to be used as "the beer fridge." It wasn't going to win an award in *House and Garden*, but it fit the descriptions of its inhabitants.

4 the man i am

To get a full understanding of the kind of man I am, one would have to truly understand how important women are to me

That's not to say—not at all, in fact—that I was a knight in shining armor, every woman's chivalrous dream. Far from it, actually. Though, in fairness, I wasn't a womanizer, either. Somewhere hopelessly and pathetically in the middle.

I was obsessed. Not with what one would normally figure as the stereotypical virtuous female partner: kind, a confidante, a best friend. No, I figured I had all of these—in my mother and male friends. I wanted what all heterosexual men wanted to varying degrees from women: sex. Though I would just as gladly take oral sex. I certainly wasn't picky; no one would ever say that of me.

There was one girl, one single, perfect girl, whom I'd been in love with since my freshman year: Lauren Parker. Well, "in love with" is a bit strong, considering that I'd only spoken to her a few times.

My freshman-year room was a floor above hers—that was how the infatuation began. Still, I never mustered up enough courage throughout the whole year even to talk to her. I just prayed that she wouldn't transfer, and by some miracle I'd get another shot at some point in the next three years.

The first time I'd actually met her was just outside of my dorm during sophomore year. I had fantasized about what it would finally be like to actually meet this blonde, fair-skinned beauty. I'd pictured her as...well, I pictured her naked, that was about as far as my mind had wandered.

The conversation we had, if you could even call it that, was at best was brief and entirely forgettable. Unless, of course, you were me. In which case, this moment was a watershed mark in the "relationship." Being from Minnesota, Lauren shrieked when she saw me wearing a Twins jersey around campus. I wish I had more to say about it, and frankly, I'm not sure it even qualifies as a conversation when both parties aren't actively involved.

Make no mistake: I was well aware of my shortcomings in these areas and I had no delusions about there being any semblance of a relationship of any kind between us. It wasn't as if I'd memorized her routine the second semester of sophomore year so I could "accidentally" run into her. Nothing crazy like that.

From that point on, I saw her only in passing, here and there. Maybe at the gym, maybe on Marshall Street, the only worthwhile street on campus, getting food. Never at a party, never "out." But I knew—or, more accurately, I dreamed— that I'd get one final shot even though I knew in the back of my mind that I'd screw it up somehow.

What made me different was the amount of energy I expended. The extreme amount of real estate these thoughts occupied in my brain could simply be described as remarkable. At one point last semester, Matt and Chris actually made a bet, challenging those overcrowded thoughts.

"Okay, what's the bet?" I pleaded with them. Grinning, they looked like they had been hatching a plot to take over the western hemisphere.

Chris began. "Well, we've decided—"

"Both of us. And Colin. And Natalie," Matt interjected.

"Yes, all of us. We've *all* decided that we want to make a bet with you that you can't go two weeks without talking about women."

There was silence. Matt and Chris wanted to let the bomb fully drop. I let it all hit me. Initially, my brain couldn't comprehend the concept...

No talking about women? Not at all? Can I think about them? I thought.

"Well, whaddya say?" Matt asked. He and Chris leaned with their forearms against the rectangular island dividing the small kitchen. Knocked away by the proposed wager, I rested on the laundry machine opposite the window side of the room.

Propping myself up a bit, I began my inquisition. "Okay, so who can I not talk about women to? Sorry, does that even make sense?"

"Anyone."

"No one?"

"No one."

"Okay, can I talk to women?" I asked.

"Uh...." the two said together, each one's mind clearly sprinting towards the easiest punch line. Matt got to it first.

"Sure, you can talk to women, but at your current rate, that wouldn't make much of a difference, now, would it?"

"Hyuck, hyuck," I said, feigning laughter. "Okay, what about if I don't make it the two weeks? What happens then?"

"Well, here's the thing," Chris began. By this point, the noise and topic of the conversation had brought Natalie and Colin out of their second-floor rooms and down into the kitchen. "We figure that you likely won't be able to make it forty-eight hours. So, if that's the case and you crap out before two days, you owe us lunch. If, by some miracle, you make it past that point but then crap out, you've got to go up to a random girl—who we'll pick out for you—in the quad, and ask her out, right then and there."

"Is she going to be hot?" I asked. It was clear where my mind was and that I had basically conceded defeat already.

"I guess, but that's not really the point, though. If you do make it those two weeks, we'll each give you"—Chris paused—"twenty-five bucks." A look of satisfaction settled on his face.

"Fuck that shit. You can keep your fifty," I said, interrupting Chris's brief delight.

Realizing that it would take more than fifty dollars to get me to essentially not speak for two weeks, Matt took it upon himself to up the ante.

"Fine, fifty," he said, briefly pausing. "Each."

Before I could answer, Colin chimed in, "I'm in for that, too," as a look of confidence took over his face. If there had been a competition to see who was the stingiest, Colin would definitely place first. Thus, with his entry into the bet, he shocked even himself. "I know, I know," he muttered.

"Make it two hundred," Natalie finished. That decided it: fifty from each roommate if only I could simply not talk about women for two weeks. Seemed easy enough.

Twenty-seven hours and thirty-five minutes later....

"I love basketball so much... I think I'd actually watch the WNBA if the NBA was abolished," I said. "Well, not a full game, but one of those things where they wrap up a whole game in sixty minutes. That can't be so bad, can it? And some of the girls on the team aren't so bad looking. That Becky Hammon has a nice—"

"Oh! Oh! Oh!" Chris shrieked. He couldn't contain his laughter, almost falling out of his chair on the porch.

"Shit." I realized that I had officially blown it. I was certainly disappointed, but on the other hand, I felt a definite sense of relief. Those past twenty-seven hours had been some of the most taxing of my whole life. Never before had I put such thought into everything I said. Even when I was on stage doing comedy. Even when I was with a girlfriend who was looking for a reason to break up with me.

Regardless, I'd have to buy lunch but I could live with that. Chris, still unable to contain his laughter, had managed to get all the roommates up to speed on what had just transpired, either via phone or by shouting up the stairs.

"I knew this would be hard for you," Chris began, in between fits of laughter, "but barely over a day? Come on, you're better than that. At least I thought you were. I guess not." He cracked himself up with that one, nearly falling off the chair again.

"What was I saying?"

"I think you were talking about...Becky Hammon's ass?"

And so we continued our conversation, in a seemingly perpetual loop. From the merits of WNBA players' sexiness (if we dated, was it an issue they were better athletes than we were?), we ultimately settled on the familiar topic of picking up girls at school. I couldn't figure how girls didn't like me, or more accurately, why it wasn't easier to just find out when they did. I hated the whole game that always had to be played between men and women. The texts and Facebook messages. The reading into every single move, every meaningless action (or, in many instances, the lack thereof). It's exhausting just writing about it.

I was, some might say, a late bloomer. I didn't have a girlfriend until the very end of my junior year in high school. I didn't have sex until the summer after my freshman year. And my first real relationship, my first real foray into the world of consistent male-female interaction, would come a month into my sophomore year of college.

Fresh off reading a disturbing message left by my ex-girlfriend on Facebook, I was feeling like I was in a bit of a sexual rut. Despite its harsh tone, there wasn't much in the message that I could honestly object to. I had slept with her all summer. I had sworn that I'd call. I never actually did, and never planned to. It wasn't a premeditated plan; I wasn't intentionally vicious. Would I have preferred that she thought of me as a sugar plum fairy? Probably, but minus the homosexual undertones.

I wondered, at the time, about a few things. First of all, how could I take a message like that seriously when right next to it was her smiling face? The picture she wanted to attract other men with was the same one she was using to curse the man that had fucked her over. Quite literally, in this instance. Secondly, what sort of person uses Facebook to tell someone that they hate them? Then again, if she'd called, I likely wouldn't have answered.

Later on, I'd rationalize my lack of response to her in the first few months by imagining that the busyness of classes and a new semester simply occupied too much of my mind. That wasn't even close to true.

The truth was, I wanted to hook up with this gorgeous red-headed girl from one of my classes. When I discovered that Katie lived in my building, I was almost overcome with horror.

"Should I go out there and talk to her?" I asked nervously. I had been practically bouncing off the walls of the first-floor dorm room I shared with Matt. Looking outside our window into the enclosed courtyard, Matt and I saw her sitting there, by herself.

My mind wandered...she was almost like a gazelle unsuspectingly drinking out of the lake, with that alligator obviously and shadily lurking a few feet yonder. Just as teeth sink into the gazelle's neck, she has to be wondering: *Where are all of my friends, and why didn't I listen to them when they said not to come here alone?*

"Jesus Christ, dude. You've been debating this for hours now. She's going to go inside pretty soon...the semester's nearly over," Matt joked, a smile slipping onto his face. It was the first week of October. After being paired together randomly freshman year, Matt and I decided to room together sophomore year as well.

It wasn't so much that he and I were similar as that we simply *fit* together. Matt knew how to handle me: laugh at my jokes only when he really thought they were funny, keep my ego in check, and deal with my random neuroses. Conversely, I knew when Matt needed calming down (he once smashed an Xbox controller after losing a video game), when to let Matt explode, and to trust Matt when it came to dealing with members of the opposite sex.

"Yeah, yeah...but what do I say to her? Maybe I should just go up and say…'Hello?'"

"Well, first of all, 'Hello' is not a question. Second of all, you're not a cyborg. I wouldn't greet her like you want to know if she'll sign a treaty allowing for physical contact. Be a person. Be yourself."

I hated that piece of advice. "Just be yourself," people always said. Somehow, I doubted that that would work. I'd been being myself for the past nineteen years and I'd only had one girlfriend. Maybe just being yourself wasn't enough. I often wondered how long ago people started saying "be yourself" when they could no longer give advice in a situation they knew wasn't fixable.

Still, I realized I had to either do something about it, or shut the hell up. I'd been fretting back and forth, peppering Matt with questions, for the last twenty-five minutes. Without another word, I left the room.

Matt knew what was going down. "Go get 'er!" he shouted, watching his friend leave the room. He was praying this would work out, or at the very least wouldn't be catastrophically bad. He wanted to graduate in two years, and if this went poorly, he knew my complaining wouldn't allow him to get to that point.

The fifty feet from the room to the grassy spot on the courtyard where she sat reading gave me ample time to think of the first thing I'd say.

"Hello!" I shouted. *Why am I shouting?* "I mean, hi...uh...hello."

"Hey," she chuckled, her fiery red hair blazing in the sunlight. "Took you long enough."

"What?" I gasped. *How did she....*

"You live on the first floor, right over there," she said, pointing in the direction of my room. "Your window was wide open. You were practically shouting."

"Wow." It was all I could say. "Wow," I repeated.

And so I sat. And we started talking. Outside of silly class interaction, this was the first time we actually spoke. I had thought about this moment (and other future moments with her) all the time, but my paralyzing fear of rejection often led me to pay her no mind, giving the impression that I wasn't interested at all. I'd rather play it safe and not get embarrassed than show interest and risk it.

We talked for quite some time. About three hours into our conversation, the sun having already vanished behind the four-story dorm, we decided to go get something to eat and somehow continue talking. There was that initial ease that comes with talking to a new person, especially when attraction exists. It was the sort of conversation that left me scratching my head the next day, wondering what else I'd ever say to her. All my old stories, my "go-tos," had been used. I had essentially blown my storytelling "load" all in one night.

Only a week later, we were dating. On a night when things couldn't get any worse (the Yankees, in three embarrassing games, were eliminated in the first round of the playoffs), we kissed for the first time. I knew she liked me when she actually wanted to come to watch the Yankee game with me. It wasn't that women couldn't like sports, but even after I had repeatedly made clear my psychotic tendencies (often, I'd mute the game if my favorite team was on the road because I hated to hear opposing fans enjoying themselves), she still showed up. That had to be a good sign, right?

We dated for nearly nine months, a new high for me. Unfortunately, the shine of the relationship wore off before the end of those nine months.

I didn't like it that she drank so much. Ironic, considering how much I would be drinking in just two short years. Katie didn't like the lack of affection I showed her in public. Behind closed doors, I'd cuddle, even hold hands sometimes (gasp!). I was, for all intents and purposes, a gentleman. Outside was a different story. For whatever reason, I couldn't let other people see me acting like that. Maybe I felt it emasculated me. Maybe I just didn't like her that much. Maybe, just maybe, the behind-closed-doors me was the real acting job.

What wasn't an act was my new-found sex life. Never in

my life had I had the ability to get "it" nearly as often as I liked. My mind struggled to fully embrace the reality of the situation. Blow jobs? Sex? Whenever I wanted? Surely there must be some sort of a catch to this. A monthly fee, at least.

Obviously, though, I didn't put too much thought into it. I simply enjoyed my new-found, albeit admittedly undeserved, sex life. Selfishly, I figured that I made her laugh and that was enough compensation on my end. Later on, Matt would point out that problematic exchange as a likely reason for the crumbling relationship.

Regardless, this was my first true test. My first time dealing with a girlfriend that lived close, that could (and often did) stop by whenever she felt like it. My first time dealing with bad moods and good moods and mood swings and the always fun "a mood" (as in "no, I am *not* in 'a mood'"). My first time with, for lack of a better phrase, a full-time girlfriend. A year later, I graded myself a "C/C-" for how I handled my first round.

From that point forward, women became even more elusive and mysterious. I barely spoke to any not named Mom or Grandma or Natalie. I was clearly a beaten man. My "sexless" streak was getting to the point where it teetered dangerously close to not being funny even to joke about in public anymore. And, as every man knows, a right hand can only grant comfort for so long.

5 wednesday, january 16th

Surprisingly, it was sunny outside. I wasn't surprised by the weather, though. I was surprised that I noticed it at all. Today I had too many other things going on. My first column of the semester would be coming out—I was convinced this one was a definite winner. If the columns went well and people continued to enjoy them, that could only mean good things for the comedy show I wanted to put on. I also looked forward, perhaps a bit too eagerly, to my final class in broadcast journalism. My only other class that was even related to journalism was a required law class which would normally take place on Tuesdays and Thursdays, but had been cancelled for the week. I didn't mind.

If my track record was any indication, meeting girls in class was a serious weapon for me. In fact, it may have been the only option I had left in my arsenal. A semester with ugly girls in this class would definitely spell trouble. Or, at the least, it could spell sexual disappointment. Would there be any new girls I had somehow never met, in four years of classes with the same women who were previously taken or unavailable to me for a variety of reasons (I "wasn't their type," my paralyzing fear of being rejected, friend zone, etc.)?

But, before I did any of that, I had to wake up Colin, a task I was already becoming sick of now three days into the semester.

"Hey, wake the fuck up!" I shouted, rapping on the door to Colin's room, which was atop the stairs and overlooking the front of the house. Colin's room would make sardines feel like they had it good. His bed, barely small enough to fit into the room, was wedged up against the far side wall and the room had a slight downward slope to boot so his feet were always above his head when he slept. Not that any of that mattered to me at this point. My concern was getting my friend up for class.

"Come on already, don't make me come in there and sit on your face," I threatened. The scary part? I actually would do that to him. For whatever reason, I truly enjoyed torturing Colin. He had a small, almost prepubescent body shape and a face that made you want to grab both cheeks and squeeze for dear life. Colin never enjoyed the constant harassment, but he never hated it and for that reason I kept it up.

Still, there was no answer. Usually, at this point, I would hear an "Unnnnnhhhhhh," or something similarly lagoon-creature-esque to signify that my friend was actually alive and would momentarily be waking from his slumber. This time, though, no answer. I had knocked, I had banged, I had even threatened physical harm. Nothing.

Turning around, I began muttering to myself, "Fuck this kid...what a fucking pain in the ass he is...if he thinks I'm going to...."

"...wake him up every day, he has another thing coming?" Colin finished. He had been in the shower downstairs, and was on his way back up to his room. He passed me without stopping. "I'll be ready in a minute. Gotta change and find my iPod."

My relationship with Colin was, by far, the strangest I had with any of my roommates. The two of us, prior to this point, hadn't had many classes together despite having the same major. We hated each other's favorite sports cities (Boston was his, New York was mine). And, before the previous semester in the house, we never really hung out together on our own. With Chris, sure. In a group, definitely. But rarely ever just the two of us. Sure, there were moments (read: hours) that we spent watching mindless television together without saying more than a few words, one hand in a bag of chips, the other wrapped around a soda (or beer, depending on whether or not it was past three in the afternoon). But there wasn't any quality time. We didn't "hang out." This could be blamed almost entirely on Colin's alarming indifference to basically everything and everyone. He didn't seem to care about a thing. Even when he was really upset about something serious, say, a Red Sox game, it didn't seem like he was truly angry. He was content to go along and didn't often put up much of a fuss.

"Colin, we're going to head down to Chuck's in about fifteen minutes. That okay with you?" someone might say.

"Yeah, that's fine."

"Hey, Colin, we decided we're not going to Chuck's tonight, just hang here, all right?"

"Yeah, whatever."

"Colin, your sister is really hot. When's she coming up to visit again? Matt and I wanted to take turns, have some fun."

"Not sure, I'll ask her."

(Entirely kidding about that last one; we'd usually just go ahead and do it without asking.)

The closer pairing, from Jump Street, had been Colin and Chris. Those two were inseparable from early in freshman year. They lived together sophomore and junior years, they both worked for the radio station, they both had Broadcast Journalism majors, and they even had the same useless minor: Psychology.

"Are you kidding me, psychology? Why? Do you plan on becoming a psychologist?" I asked, unable to resist shoving my nose into Chris and Colin's business. Why they'd pick this as their minor, I couldn't possibly understand.

"No, I plan on becoming a psycho. And killing you once I get my certification, for asking these annoying questions," Chris remarked.

The clearest indicator that we got along well? Colin and I rarely talked about women together. There were, oddly enough for me, just too many other things to chat about with Colin. Based on all that, one would think I would hang out with Colin more simply because of what a good time we had together. But it just never happened. There wasn't any rhyme or reason to it.

That would change, of course, with the coming semester. I was taking four classes and Colin was in three with me. One was a byproduct of having the same major and having to complete requirements. The other two came about due to a mutual aversion to hard work.

Last semester...

"Heyyyyyyyyyyy!!!" I shouted from the couch in the living room up to Colin's bedroom. "What classes did you say you had signed up for?" It was the infamous registration time, essentially tax season for students campus-wide.

All throughout Syracuse University, worried, sleep-deprived students would be pacing around asking anyone they could find, "What day is your registration day?! I don't even know when mine is! I think I have class! Oh my God!" Almost as a prize for remaining calm, I never seemed to get screwed out of my classes of choice. I got into the recitations I wanted and usually had the schedule I had planned for.

Further, I wasn't one of those kids who would sit on the wait-list for a class, even if it would prevent me from graduating.

"Fuck that," I said to Chris once, who was notorious for not getting into the classes he wanted and making a stink about it. "If I don't get into a class, I'm not wait-listing. I'll just go somewhere else."

"You mean, like a different section of the class?" he asked, not sure where I was going.

"No, I mean, like, Ithaca."

In typical nothing-has-gone-my-way-in-a-while fashion, all of my desired classes were already filled up by the time I got to my sign-up date. Beer and Wine Appreciation, Cooking, Basketball 304, History of Dinosaurs. All gone.

"I'm screwed, the good ones are all gone!" I yelled to Colin across the room. "What are you taking?"

"It's called Introduction to Coaching!" Colin shouted back. "I had this teacher for something else last semester. She's soooo easy. It says there are classes on Friday, but last semester we were supposed to have them on Fridays, too, and she always gave us off. And all the football players are in these classes, so if they can do it, there's no way it's hard."

And so I signed up for a class about coaching. I didn't want to be a coach, but I also didn't want to do any real work. So it was as close to a win-win as I could think of, unless of course there was a class on Drinking that met Mondays and Wednesdays from 1:25 to 1:40.

"Anything else?" I ventured. I hoped Colin had at least one more up his sleeve. My well of classes officially dry (it turned out that MAG 205 wasn't a class on magic, but instead a magazine class), my last chance at doing no work was through Colin.

"Hmmm...." Colin said, thinking aloud. "How about this one, Sports and the Media? We like athletics...should be easy enough, no?"

"Eh, that sounds a bit too scholarly to me. I don't know. Anything else?" I asked, looking down at the course book on my lap. "Wait, I found it! Get the hell out of here! History of Baseball Cards! Oh my God, are you kidding?!"

"Just saw that. I'm in."

And so that was our schedule. One class in broadcasting, one in coaching, and another in collectibles.

Back to Wednesday...

We wound up leaving the house for class by 9:20 a.m.,

giving us just enough time to make it to class at exactly the 9:30 start time. For me and Colin showing up on time meant literally that: 9:30:00. Maybe even a few minutes later. Never early, especially not for a class. I rarely was early to anything. I figured that so long as I was there around when it started, what was the difference between fifteen minutes to spare and fifteen seconds?

As we strolled towards the building that had eaten up all of our class time since freshman year, I couldn't help but comment on the weather.

"Can you believe this weather? I know, I know, who cares? And I know how I always say I hate people talking about the weather, but this is just great, isn't it?"

It was actually amazingly nice. Sunny, not a cloud in the sky. The temperature was a happy medium between summer and fall, the sort of weather where you could get away with wearing shorts, or feel comfortable in pants. Slightly breezy, but not enough to necessitate a jacket. In short, comfortable.

"Yeah, I'm glad we get to go to class for three hours," Colin said, still looking half asleep. A Red Sox hat perched upon his short, cropped brown hair, he wore a brown suede jacket atop a green polo shirt. I decided I wasn't going to wear sweatpants to class for the first time this year. I wore jeans and a t-shirt, plain red. What I considered my "Wednesday best."

Just before stepping into our classroom, I picked up a copy of the *Daily Orange*. One of my pet peeves was when the paper would over-edit my columns, taking out what I thought were the funniest parts. At one point last semester, I nearly overstepped my bounds after seeing that my piece in the paper contained jokes I knew I didn't write.

"What the hell is this?" I demanded. I had barged into an early meeting amongst the editors of the paper, all fellow students. No one answered; obviously, they didn't know what I was talking about. "Why the hell were there new jokes in my column? Who said it was okay to put someone else's jokes in there?" My voice rose, actual anger clear in my tone.

"I did," said Andrew McAllarney, editor of the features section, in

which my column appeared. Andy was a cool customer, someone I had come to be friendly with. But I wouldn't stand for this.

"Well, cut that shit out. Listen, you want to edit it, do it while I'm sitting here with you guys for a fucking hour. Don't let me read this shit the next day again and see jokes I didn't write in it like some jerkoff," I barked.

Andy didn't respond. He just looked at me as I continued.

"Listen, you let me handle the 'funny'; you guys handle the rest. Don't tell me how to do my fucking job," I said, inhaling deeply.

After Andy took a breath of his own, he finally spoke up. "And if you want to keep this column, don't tell me how to do mine."

So I toned down my rants and eventually the paper let me do my thing. People seemed to really like the column, despite the internal disdain for it at the paper. The jealousy was easy to figure. I was a kid with no newspaper training, skipping onto the scene, cranking out a few nonsensical columns about playing the game of hearts and pitting Christmas against Hanukah, and—poof!—I was getting more reads than the rest of the writers at the paper. I never did any reporting, I never sourced anything. I only took thirty minutes to write the column (and bragged about it). This sudden, and in some people's minds undeserved, popularity rubbed people the wrong way at the paper. But I was getting people to read it and as long as that kept up, there wasn't much they could do to me.

I sat down, to my surprise, an entire minute before the class was supposed to start. Just enough time to start reading the column.

First Day of Classes Always Stressful; Better to Just Make It Up

Though this is my final go-around for "first days" in college, the procedure hasn't gotten any easier. For some reason, the small ritual that is the introduction scares the bejesus out of me. I can get in front of a crowd of 100 people and (try to) tell jokes, but saying my name in front of 15 strangers is simply terrifying.

First, the teacher has to go around the room and ask the class to talk about themselves in the most embarrassing of fashions.

"All right, I'd like you each to say your name, where you're from, and what your major is." Then comes the pause, as if the teacher is just thinking of this for the very first time: "and actually, say something interesting about yourself."

My real heart-attack moment comes when it's finally time to say my major. Heartbeat rapidly skyrocketing, I've often thought about lying and saying "math," because it's got fewer syllables than "broadcast journalism." I doubt that simply "math" is an actual major, but whenever this time of year comes around, I can't think of anything other than that.

However, once my moment of despair has passed, I truly enjoy hearing some of the other majors this university has cooked up. I've actually heard a kid say his major was gym. What does it take to qualify for a gym major, I wonder? Classes like "Living in Your Office 132," "Wearing Air Pants to Work Every Day for the Rest of Eternity 255" and "How to Hang Up Stupid Posters Such As 'Your Altitude Reflects Your Attitude' 482."

Then comes the kicker. Something interesting? Come on, I'm not interesting. That's the thought that goes through basically everyone's mind. I've actually said, as embarrassing as this is, that I play basketball a lot, as my interesting fact. Like I'm the only one who does that.

More humorously, when truly bored, I've even lied. In one class last year I was the son of a mechanic, so naturally I was very good at working with cars. In another I won a state championship in basketball while in high school. Not only did I never play a second of basketball in high school, but I can barely tell you what kind of car I drive.

Once the introductory shenanigans have mercifully concluded, the only thing left for the heterosexual male to do is scope out the room for the smoking hot girls. God help you if you're in a class with only

```
15 people in it. Your chances just went down about
25 percent. A note to the ladies out there: if you
see a guy writing furiously on a sheet of paper
during the introductions, he's probably writing your
name. Sorry, but that's just the truth. Facebook is
a scary mother.

Luckily, it all goes downhill from there.
Assignments to ignore, books to buy to collect dust,
chapters to "read," etc. God, I love school.
```

Not bad, I thought. Not bad at all. Not much had been changed, and I was happy about that.

Folding my paper once over itself, I set it down on the table in front of me. Looking up, I realized for the first time that there wasn't much noise.

In fact, there wasn't any noise.

And…everyone was staring right at me.

"Nick, nice of you to join us," Professor Phillips said. He was a goofy-looking man, one of those 1970s news-anchor types that hadn't ditched the porn-star mustache or Lego lift-and-drop pompadour hairstyle. His forehead had deep wrinkles running through it, as if he'd been doing something stressful for quite some time—maybe just basic thinking. Lawrence Phillips stood as a prime example of why tenure was a bad idea. Having received the gift of untouchability, Larry had given up on actually "teaching," or even appearing not to be on the verge of senility, quite some time ago.

Having had Phillips before, I knew how to handle the old professor. Clearing my throat, adjusting my paper again unnecessarily: "Well, it sure is nice to be here. Thanks for waiting."

And that was it. There were a few scattered laughs; Phillips barely paid me any mind. It was almost as if he simply delighted in making the witless remark to his students, and anything that normally would follow (such as a possible rebuke for a smart-ass answer) required more energy than he cared to put in. Sad thing for the state of education, but a great thing for Colin and I. We both knew, right away, that minimal effort would be all that was necessary.

A few minutes later, I found myself already drifting off....

...How am I going to be able to work if I can't even pay attention for more than five minutes?...Does he think he looks good with that haircut?...How the hell am I going to pull off my own comedy show?...How hot are the girls in this class?...If Phillips took out a gun and forced each of the girls in the class to have sex with either me, Colin, or Will, how many would choose me?...

"—Hey, you gonna come with?" Colin asked. There wasn't anyone in the room; apparently we were on a break. Though I had started taking mine, albeit mentally, a few minutes in, I joined Colin for a jaunt to the building's cafe.

"How fucking hot are the girls in this class?" I asked, in a half-whisper.

"They're something," Colin said back, clearly understating his enthusiasm. He didn't feel as comfortable as I did shouting openly about how good-looking the girls were in the class. They could have been anywhere; what if one of them heard him talking about them? He might actually have to talk to her (Oh, no!).

"Good Lord," I exclaimed, hands on my head. I couldn't get over it; there were too many good-looking girls in the class. "Have you ever even seen some of these girls? I mean, ever? Not only that, but I think, unless someone's not here for the first day, that you, me, and Will are the only three dudes in the whole class. How 'bout them odds?"

"Pretty good."

"O-R-G. Why? Because I can," I jokingly shouted. Dancing down the hall, I continued, "And I will—"

"Real nice, Nick," Katie said. I hadn't seen her coming up in front of us. The ex was in the class too, but in my glee I had conveniently forgotten that point. I wasn't discouraged.

"You can still get in on it, if you like," I joked. I didn't care about her any longer and I didn't really think I was going to have an orgy. Matter of fact, I didn't anticipate myself even talking to any of these girls outside of class. I was just happy that I'd have something to fantasize about during class. That, sadly, was enough for me.

After Colin bought a yogurt and two orange juices, we headed back to class. Neither of us was in a big hurry to get back, but then again, neither was our professor. By the time we'd returned, he still hadn't. A "break" originally slated for fifteen minutes had turned into twenty and counting.

I sat down, still chatting with Colin, now on a more PG subject.

"I just don't understand who would ever choose regular orange juice when the Immunity Defense orange juice is right next to it for the exact same price. Who out there doesn't want immunity defense? It's just stupidity...."

"So, how is this class?" Heather Murphy interrupted. A sly smile crept up the side of her face. She was, far and away by my estimation, the sexiest girl in the class. Not the prettiest, no, that award could go to a number of different ladies, depending on who was asked. But, amongst popular voters (me, Will, and Colin), Heather had the best body. Slim, with curves and a pretty smile, she never wore anything that didn't highlight each and every feature.

As far as her interruption was concerned, I had no idea what she was talking about.

"I'm sorry?"

"How is this class?" she repeated, folding the paper. It hit me then.

"Ahhhhhh," I smiled, leaning back in my chair. "I'd say pretty good...." I couldn't think of anything cute, clever, or humorous. I have no charm.

"Well, I'm Heather Murphy," she said, sticking out her slender right hand, "and you can masturbate to pictures of me on Facebook any time you want," she finished, leaning in real close. *Did she just lick her lips?* I wondered

"Uh, what was that?" I couldn't believe what I had just heard. This smoking-hot girl read my article, was using it in a conversation with me, and, unless my penis was so out of practice it no longer functioned, I thought she was flirting with me.

"I said, I'm Heather Murphy. That Facebook joke was

funny. I always wondered how some guys get to finding me or my friends."

"Oh, oh, of course. Thanks, glad you liked it," I choked out. For a second, I really had myself convinced that she had said that first bit to me.

A few minutes later, five to be precise, Phillips re-entered the room. The wiseass in me wouldn't let it go.

"Nice of *you* to join us," I muttered under my breath, laughing.

"What was that, Nick?" he said, barely making the effort to look up from the paperwork he had brought into the room.

"Nothing, Professor Phillips," I said, speaking up now. Putting on my best good-student accent, I added, "I just can't wait to get started with learning again."

"Great to hear," he answered, still not looking up. Finally, after clearing his throat, he addressed the class: "All right, class, for next Monday, we're going to have a news analysis project due. On the sheet that's getting passed around are the teams."

The actual details of the project I had missed completely. I was focused on one thing: who was in this group? Would I get Heather? How about Sophia? Or maybe Erin, or Sarah, or Courtney, or Denise? I could barely contain my excitement.

Soon, though, it was quashed.

"Fuck!" I actually said, aloud.

"What?" Colin asked.

"What, what?" I answered. I didn't realize that I had voiced my frustration with my group-mates aloud. I did luck out a little, since Heather would be in the group. That was it, though. There were fifteen girls in the class. My group had four, three of them being the only three that weren't attractive.

More, with this? Can't I get a break? I thought.

My head down like I'd just gotten a phone call with bad news about my new puppy, I left the classroom that day in a dejected mood. Colin brightened it soon thereafter.

"You're right, that's got to be the hottest class I've ever been in," he said, now safely away from any of the girls in question, on the walk back towards the house. "You know, it could be the hottest class ever assembled...anywhere."

"Somehow, I doubt that," I responded. I was still pissed off about my group assignment.

"What's your deal? Is it the groups? It's really not that big of a deal. You weren't going to have sex with these girls during a group meeting."

I shot him a look that said, *Hey, you never know....*

"Okay, maybe, but still...."

"Well, who's in your group?" I asked, fearing the worst.

"Denise, Erin, and...I think Courtney. Yeah, Courtney. Not bad, huh?"

I didn't answer, just punched him in the arm.

"Okay, let's just get it out there. I know you were thinking about it the whole time. What's your top three?" I asked. I was strangely curious, because I couldn't wait to share my gold, silver, and bronze.

"Hmm. It depends. What are we talking about? Like, which girls are the hottest, just plain hottest? Or the prettiest, or what?"

"Come on, cut the shit," I deadpanned. "Who would you fuck? If every girl would, which three would you fuckin' just take outside and just tear it up?"

Laughing at the incredible bluntness, Colin said, "Okay, let's see...My number one would have to be Heather. She's just...." He was at a loss for how to describe her. "Yeah, she's number one. After her, I'd say Denise and then Courtney. Courtney's real pretty, but I don't love her face."

"I'm not asking you to marry these girls, just to have sex with them. Can you handle that? Even so, you wouldn't have to look at her face if you didn't want to."

"All right, that's fine there," Colin said, sounding uncomfortable once again. He wasn't an awkward kid, not by a long shot. More accurately, he'd be described as quiet by those who didn't really know him. Still, he just didn't love talking about women. No one knew exactly how to account for the aversion. "I'm assuming you have yours set up already?"

"Hell, yes," I quickly answered back. I'd been ready to answer this question since twenty minutes into the class. "Courtney, Heather, and Sophia...."

We strolled the rest of the way back to our house, debating the various merits of each girl in the class. Ass, tits, face, the whole deal. I used a system for rating girls I had gotten from my brother; he called it the Area Code. Three numbers to describe a girl. First, 1-10 for her face. Second, 0 or 1, with one being yes, you would have sex with her. And third, 1-10 for the body. Honestly, it's a ridiculous system and not because it's incredibly demeaning. My home area code was 908. Who the hell is a 908? *Dude, this chick's gorgeous. Great body, total smoke show. I'm sorry, what did you ask? No, I wouldn't have sex with her.* The only way that would happen is if Scarlett Johansson had an STD and even then there'd still be guys willing to risk it.

A few minutes later, with the walk back already done, Colin crashed onto the well-worn couch in the living room. It couldn't be any less inviting, as far as couches go, with a fabric that would make steel wool seem cozy, but he had a Donkey Kong game he had to finish. I opted to head to my room. I had some girls to look up on Facebook.

6 friday, january 18th

"What the hell is instant pudding?" The incredible amount of variety at grocery stores always pissed me off.

"What?" Natalie responded, only vaguely interested. She was more concerned with trying to remember whether or not there was still enough brown sugar left in the house for her oatmeal cookie recipe. She usually didn't even get to eat the cookies. Matt and I would normally eat, out of the thirty she would make, at least fifteen to twenty. Such was life of a girl living with four guys.

"C'mere, take a look at this." I had a point I wanted to make, regardless of how little Natalie actually cared. I read the label directly: "INSTANT PUDDING. Well?"

"Well, what?" she asked raspily. Natalie was just starting to get over a cold that had basically robbed her of her ability to vocalize her thoughts the last two weeks of the previous semester.

"Well, what I'm saying is, how instant could this pudding be? If it really was instant pudding, I could just look at it," I said, folding my hands over one another, *I Dream of Jeanie*-style, blinking, "and instantly, we'd have some damn pudding."

After her courtesy laugh, Natalie grabbed the shopping cart from behind me. "Come on, let's just get going, okay?"

"Yeah, sure.   I still think there's too many types of pudding.   Banana, mint Oreo.   Instant, regular, al dente, strawberry, pesto. When I was a kid, pudding was drawn along racial lines—black and white.   That was it."   I was clearly kidding around, but I refused to smile.   Not only was I trying to get a rise out of Natalie, but I was also hoping some random strangers had heard me, too.   I found it amusing to leave random people with strange bits and pieces of my conversations.   *Did that kid just make a racist remark about pudding?...*

In an effort to reduce refrigerator chaos, the five housemates had decided back in August that splitting up for grocery shopping was the best plan of action. Partnering was done, in large part, by similarity in eating habits. Chris and Colin, naturally, had similar patterns. Matt ate healthy food, protein shakes and all that nonsense, so he took care of himself. That left Natalie and me. Nat, from Florida, loved fruits and vegetables. I did, too, but would usually forget unless she reminded me. It seemed to be a good pairing.

And so we strolled through the local grocery store. It was approximately one p.m. and I had already finished my morning class and taken a nap, but I had forgotten to do one important thing.

"This is a huge mistake," I said.

"What? Coming here? I thought *you* were the one who liked this place," Natalie responded. She preferred Wegmans, a specialty grocery store, but recognized the unnecessary purchases that almost always accompanied a trip there.

"No. Coming here hungry. How many times do I have to make this mistake before I learn?" Looking down at our cart, I continued, "Seriously, do we really need chocolate, peanut butter, and chocolate peanut butter Oreos? All three? Three roasted chickens? What is this, *Cheaper by the Dozen*?"

"Oooh, nice reference, Nick," Natalie said. Her voice had a crackling innocence to it. Something about it that made you think she meant what she said. She, more than anyone else in the house, also had a habit of actually referring to people by their first names. Might not seem like much, but it was definitely noticeable. "Great book, terrible movie. Or, movies? Did they wind up making the second one?"

"Unfortunately, yes," I replied, placing the chocolate Oreos back on the shelf. Two packages of Oreos I could deal with. Three was just plain ridiculous.

Three and a half years ago, Natalie Vaughn lived in the room immediately next to the one I shared with Matt. Natalie and I met under odd circumstances, a week or so into the semester. Neither of us had any clothes on, it was just around noon, and we were both in the hallway.

"LET ME IN! COME ON, WAKE UP ALREADY!" I shouted, banging on the door to my room. I was wearing this enormous white robe that my parents had bought for me. Never having had to shower in a community setting aside from my stint in prison, I figured I'd give the robe look a shot. If nothing else, I could have dressed up as a boxer for Halloween.

"You all right?" Natalie asked. I hadn't even noticed her there I was so angry about being locked out.

She, too, was wearing a robe, appropriately pink and not dragging on the floor.

Glorious, I thought, *she probably thinks I'm a psycho.*

"I'm fine, it's just my roommate. He locked me out and he's not waking up. How deep a sleeper could this kid possibly be?"

Chuckling, Natalie said, "Sorry, that sucks. I'm not laughing at you, but...actually, I guess I am. You can stay in here 'til he gets back, if you like." She kept laughing.

"Well, let me try for a minute more. If you notice the screaming stopping, I'm probably a step away."

"Okay, sure."

As it turned out, Matt wasn't asleep. He was actually down at the dining hall and returned from his unannounced trip a minute or so later.

At 5'4", Natalie wasn't going to physically wow anyone with her athletic ability, at least at first glance. But it was this ability that initially caught my attention. That and a cute, squared jaw, a soft smile, and a rush of blonde hair of the kind I hadn't seen in its honest form since I was six. Girls in New Jersey just didn't have light hair. Something about the negativity that hung like a dark cloud around the area.

She actually had an opportunity to play softball at Syracuse but an ankle injury in her junior year of high school, the height of scouting, hobbled both her and her chances. The school, still mildly interested and now financially uninvested, told her they'd give her a tryout if she liked. She decided that club softball and club soccer were enough athletic fulfillment.

For a short while, Matt and I had a bit of a crush on our Floridian neighbor. Unfortunately (or fortunately, depending on whose point of view you were taking), she had a boyfriend. And, as time would reveal, it wasn't one of those "let's see how the long-distance thing works out" relationships. No, they'd been together (and stayed together) for the duration of college.

What made it incalculably worse for Matt and me was that, despite our best efforts, we couldn't help but love her boyfriend, Kent. In some ways, namely that he was a guy, he was cooler than she was. Of course, we'd never tell her that.

With the secret crush firmly in the rear-view mirror, Natalie and I became fast friends. It was clear that we bonded on an athletic level—we played whiffle ball with Chris and Colin whenever we could. Yet it was a bit more than that. I enjoyed the nuances of having a female friend, something that had previously been outside my grasp. This was largely because I just didn't see many women I'd want to spend more time with than my guy friends, unless of course I was sexually attracted to them. Even then, I wasn't sure I wanted to evenly divide my time. But Natalie seemed to care about what I said—she actually listened to me. On top of this, we had similar frivolous interests: rap music, cursing, baseball. Most importantly, Natalie never got self-righteous when I would go on one of my anti-women rants. In other words, she was one of the guys. But better.

For her part, Natalie didn't much mind being the only girl in a house littered with boys, at one point all single. The question "How is it, living with all those guys?" would come up quite frequently. Tactfully and politely, she'd answer with some variant of "Oh, not that bad," which for anyone wearing their decoder ring meant "It's fine! Leave me the fuck alone." She'd usually give a half-smile, implying that there was some sort of detail or shenanigan that she'd kept from the person asking.

As we left the store, Natalie had to ask the inevitable question that was burning a hole through her brain: "So, you excited about tonight?"

"What's tonight?" I asked, playing coy.

"Come on, Nick. Chuck's? You're going, right? First week of school? Your first real bar trip at school? How's it feel?"

"Nah, it's no big deal," I answered, not fooling even myself.

"Oh, shut up," she joked.

In a sudden change of emotion, I burst out, "Hell, yeah! Shit, yeah, I'm excited! This is the beginning for me."

"That's it, there's the Nicky I know," she said, steering the full shopping cart through the iced parking lot.

"And you know what I'm going to start up again?"

"Oh God, what do you plan on doing now?" she said, sounding worried, not for my physical safety but more for my emotional safety. She knew that, more often than not, when I was cooking up a scheme it had something to do with a woman.

"A certain Lau-rennn Parrr-kerr," I said, purposely dramatizing the pronunciation of her name for no apparent reason.

"Not her again, Nick!" Natalie pleaded. Nat didn't even know Lauren personally, but she knew enough. She knew about how obsessive I was about her. About how I had invested so much effort into thinking about and hoping for this girl, but had never had done anything about her. It bothered her that I couldn't have the same confidence with a girl like Lauren that I seemed to have around nearly everyone else.

"What do you see in this girl, anyway? Matt's got bigger tits than she does."

"Real nice, Nat. Real nice. And don't talk about her like that, okay? She's a nice girl."

"A nice girl?" she said, pausing in the middle of the parking lot. She'd heard some doozies in her day, but this one took the cake. "This nice girl, this great girl....Is this the same one that you've talked about bending over the kitchen island and—"

"All right, all right. Got the picture. Maybe, maybe I did say that. Either way, I'm going to give her one more shot. That's it. Just one more. Don't roll your eyes at me, I mean it this time. I hear she's single. Even if not, it's about time I make a real, human move. You guys were always telling me that you saw her at Chuck's, no? So, if she's there tonight, I'll just have to make my move."

"Fat chance of that," Natalie mumbled.

I heard her, but didn't care to respond. I was envisioning the possibilities of the night. All last semester, my roommates had regaled me with fabulous tales of the night that was at Chuck's: *Remember Colleen, the redhead from freshman year?....Lindsay was there last night, and not with any guys, either....Jessica looked so hot last night, she was there too, man, should've seen her....*These stories had taken on such a majestic quality that, by the end of the semester, I half-expected Chuck's to resemble Narnia.

I knew Lauren would be there. And Natalie's crude remark was on point. I was a "tits guy," and made no bones about it, pardon the pun. Lauren wasn't a buxom girl, by any stretch. In fact, she didn't fit any of my stereotypes. She wasn't particularly curvy, and she had blonde hair. I'd made a habit of falling for redheads and brunettes. She was beautiful, though.

Her face was more oblong than circular, with smooth, high cheekbones so unpronounced that everyone else's faces looked wrong by comparison. Lauren had long eyelashes, batting constantly over her deep blue eyes. As it was, she could've been a card-carrying Nazi (as if they needed ID cards) and I likely wouldn't have cared. And, though I hadn't done much talking with her, I'd seen her smile. It was wide and white and full, and I couldn't get enough of it. If I remembered nothing else about a girl, it was her smile. Maybe it was because I spent more time making girls laugh than in bed with them, but a good smile was something that never really left me.

I had no idea what my plan of action would be, at least as far as Lauren was concerned. Assuming she was there, which was the fact that would swing the balance of the entire night, I'd probably wind up "accidentally bumping into" her at some point. Literally. And, from there, it'd be up to me to strike up further conversation.

Since sophomore year, I'd seen her only sporadically. First semester of senior year, I thought I'd been graced by God when I saw her working out one early Monday morning. My class schedule had me up for an 8:30 class Mondays, Wednesdays, and Fridays, so I'd head to the gym at around 9:30 on those days. I never figured I'd see anyone there, let alone Lauren. Because, you see, at this point she'd become nearly a figment of my imagination. I'd been crazy for her, or the idea of her, since freshman year. Once I'd reconciled myself to the pathetic reality that I'd never get a chance with a beautiful blonde girl, I settled for the random glimpse of her.

When I saw her at the gym, and then again the next Monday, I'd realized we were on similar schedules. From afar, I'd watch her on the elliptical, turning "creeper mode" into full gear. I dreamed of being able to have the confidence in myself to just go up to her and introduce myself.

What would I say? I could never figure out the opening. The middle, even the closing, I figured I'd be able to handle. That jumping-off point, though—that was the toughie.

"Um...hello, my parents named me Nick." No, that sounded

idiotic. And, could I approach her in the gym? She probably thought she looked terrible, as most girls think at the gym and didn't want to be talked to. What was I going to do, ask her if she needed a spotter? I didn't want to be A.C. Slater, but I couldn't figure a way to be Zack Morris. So, it seemed I settled for a less nerdy Screech.

This whole process was just a major psych-out. All I did was convince myself, without any real proof, that I couldn't do it. I never really even failed, I just didn't try.

I loved this girl, or to be accurate, I lusted for this girl and confused the latter with the former. Either way, I was content with seeing her there, if only a day or two a week. I dreaded my new schedule, knowing that the odds of running into each other regularly again were almost as slim as the odds of me actually taking on a chance on her.

7 fridays at school

Seventeen. That's how many Fridays there were in the semester. Actually, sixteen, if you took away the one during Spring Break. On its face, it doesn't seem like that much time, does it? Yet, at this moment, I felt as if there were an entirely new frontier awaiting me, just begging to be explored.

Sixteen happy hours. Sixteen chances to get that girl to come home. Sixteen chances to go out, the group of us. It would be gone, forever, in just sixteen short Fridays, but no one was looking that far ahead. I, especially, had only uncomplicated, loosely-connected thoughts bouncing around my mind: ...*three-dollar pitchers of beer...Lauren Parker...pitchers of beer that only cost three dollars.....* Anything else was cast aside as either superfluous or only worth caring about later.

Direct proof that college doesn't prepare you for the real world could be found in Chuck's Friday happy-hour deal. First of all, there wasn't a greater misleader than this "hour." Most bars stretched the titular sixty-minute span to two, three, maybe even four hours. Chuck's, in blatant disregard for the rules (and in a desperate need to pander to the alcoholic needs of its student population), extended happy hour to all of Friday, making it more appropriate to call it a Happy Day.

As Natalie had said to me earlier, this was a big day, a first. I'd been drooling over my first true Chuck's happy hour since the first day that Colin turned twenty-one, leaving me as the only one unable to go to the bars.

Many a night last semester, I'd watch as three, four, or five of my friends would head for the bar. I'd put on a happy face for them.

"No, no. You guys go out and have a good time," I'd say, lying through my teeth. I prayed they'd have an awful time. *"Thanks a lot for leaving me at home again, you fucking inconsiderate asshole motherfuck...."*

"What?" a roommate would ask, thinking they had heard something.

"Nothing, nothing. Have a good time."

One Friday night last semester, as they headed out to make the ten- to fifteen-minute walk down to the bar, I realized that I desperately needed an activity for the night. I wasn't going to go to another house party and I wasn't a fake ID-type guy. First off, I wasn't a good-looking girl or scholarship athlete—so I'd get no special treatment. Second, I looked young. Facial hair, while fairly consistent, looked more like decoration than true aging. I just had a young face. Not a baby face. That would be too much. I was on that annoying cusp. Definitely old enough to buy cigarettes, but certainly *not* old enough to buy alcohol. And that presented a problem. My younger friends were kind enough to keep inviting me to their parties every weekend. But after a while, I started to feel like the old creepy guy at a girls' youth soccer tournament. So I stopped going. Plus, I couldn't stand to play even one more game of beer pong.

I never understood the idea of drinking games. Drinking itself was enough of a game. How many can I have before I throw up? Does a cranberry vodka sit well in a stomach filled with beer after eating fried chicken all night? I didn't see the need to play additional games. The way I saw it, if there wasn't any chance to come home with a girl, there wasn't much reason to play any games.

"Matt!" I shouted out the door at the one kid who actually knew how to work the Nintendo in the living room. "Before you go, can you set me up with this?"

I wanted to play Mortal Kombat, see how far I could get in one-player mode. Almost exclusively, this game was played in two-player mode, one on one. Tonight, I'd be flying solo. Time to play against the computer, that old friend.

Now I really felt like a fourth-grader. I couldn't hang out with my friends because I wasn't old enough and my activity for the evening had to be set up for me.

Matt came back into the house and showed me how to do it. As I sat down, I thought, *This has to be the lowest point. It can't get any more pathetic than this.*

No, that point would come a few minutes later—once I realized, after getting myself a non-alcoholic beverage, that I didn't have the television set up properly. Now I couldn't even play video games. Immediately, I felt better once I remembered Chris had recently DVRed a *Full House* marathon. However, even that was short lived because after some fidgeting and a strange *phhhhhhttttt* sound from the monitor—*hmmm, that's not a normal sound,* my inner electrician opined—I discovered I couldn't watch TV at all. *That* was rock bottom.

Now, within the confines of my room getting ready to finally go out, I thought about how much I needed this semester to work out for me. It had been, honestly, a rough road since coming back from London the first semester of junior year. In the weeks between fall and spring semester that year, I tore my ACL off the bone playing football, which shot the upcoming semester as well as the summer. Then there was the fun semester of being the only young guy in the house. Now, though, there was hope: living with all my friends, being able to go out to the bars, having my column. If things weren't going to turn around soon, maybe it just wasn't meant to be.

"HEY!" Matt shouted over my blaring stereo, interrupting the musically induced reverie, "WE'RE LEAVing in...thank you. We're leaving at five-thirty. You going to be ready?"

Would I be ready? That wasn't even worth answering, as

far as I was concerned.

"Yo, you there? You going to be ready, or what?"

Unfortunately, this wasn't a TV show. "Yes, yes, I'll be ready, no problem."

While on other days the group might begin to head out to the bar at around eight or eight-thirty, the start time was advanced on Fridays to a more AA-friendly five p.m. Well, in fairness, we never got down to the bars by five, but we tried to and usually wound up showing by around five forty-five or six. Matt, king of the procrastinators with his plans, usually wouldn't decide what he wanted to do until the half hour before we'd leave. Natalie, like most girls, took longer than the five seconds it took the rest of the house to get ready. Colin usually had a video game he had to finish. As for Chris and me, well, we were the only ones who would be ready and raring to go at five o'clock sharp.

Of major import to the whole evening was what I was going to wear. It may sound effeminate for a man to admit to spending time considering his outfit for the night (editor's note: you could argue that even using the word "outfit" would qualify as effeminate). But what is little known about men is that we often put significant amounts of time and effort into what we eventually wind up dressing ourselves in. A striped button-down shirt with jeans may appear casual and just "thrown on," but you can rest assured that more often than not, it wasn't some accidental coincidence.

What lay ahead of me was an arduous task. This was my coming-out party, a moment I'd been eagerly anticipating. So, for those reasons alone, it would seem obvious that I would want to look nice. But the real question was how nice. Too nice and I looked pathetic. Like the guy at a bar who wore a Polo shirt buttoned all the way to the top. That kind of pathetic. As important as the evening was to me, and as desperately as I wanted to make a good impression on Lauren, I also wanted to be able to blend in. Make it look like I'd done it before, appear casually attractive. Stand out without calling attention to myself, if that was even possible. Imagine the

Marlboro man, in less cowboy-specific attire.

My style was part wannabe thug, part bohemian, part GAP advertisement, and part hobo. Often I'd go to class wearing oversized sweatpants, a sweatshirt that would more appropriately fit someone in the NBA, and a winter hat barely resting atop my head, generally tilted to the side. Rarely did I shave, based on a combination of laziness and an entirely misplaced notion that women somehow liked the scruffy, unkempt hobo look. On another night, I would have no issue wearing a v-neck sweater with a yellow button-down collared shirt underneath.

Turning up my music once again, I saw that I really needed to focus on getting ready. I wasn't exactly sure what to wear. There were the choices of button-down shirts I had, and there was a white Oxford my mom said I looked "cute" in. That had to count for something. There was also a group of sweaters. Practical, at least as far as the walk to the bar was concerned. But would I be too hot once I was at the bar? How about just a plain t-shirt, accompanied by my black jacket? No, too casual. Of course, none of my friends would ever come anywhere near the level of analysis I was putting into my outfit at this point, but I still couldn't *not* care. Finally, I settled on what it would be. I found a brown hooded zip-up sweater I had purchased at the GAP (as a white man, I was actually allowed to write off shopping there on my taxes). Imagine a trendier Obi-Wan Kenobi. Under the sweater, a crisp white t-shirt. Dark blue jeans, and I'd messily mix up my hair. I hadn't truly "styled' my hair since my eighth grade dance eight years ago, when the gelled flip-up look was in style. Then again, the Macarena was in style for a while there, too.

I put the different parts of this near-perfect (in my mind) outfit on in front of the mirror, taking time to admire each. For the first time in a long time I liked what I saw, staring at my reflection in the mirror. With my acne beginning to clear up, facial hair coming in evenly, I felt happy with how I looked. No one really suspected that I doubted myself, at least not physically, and that was the way I wanted it. Truth was, I was extremely self-conscious about my looks, specifically my acne, because I assumed, for whatever reason, that it was my fault. Did I shower enough? Too much greasy food? I didn't know, but still figured it had to be my fault. My mom, dad, and brothers didn't have acne. I'd been told I had a cute smile, pretty eyes, and even a nice nose. But my skin worried me constantly. Whenever a pimple would show up, I'd feel like I was a unicorn sprouting a horn on the center of my forehead. Any time I was in a conversation with a girl I was attracted to, I wondered at some point, "Does she notice my acne? Does she care?" I put myself, in those situations, at an immediate self-imposed disadvantage. I didn't talk about the acne (which I suspected wasn't nearly as bad as I imagined it to be) and so it didn't get talked about.

"I'm ready!" I announced, bounding out of my room. I knew that at least a few of the housemates were in the living room, by the nature of the noise. I soon realized I'd have to bring my enthusiasm down a notch.

No one turned.

"I'm…ready!" I said in a sing-song voice.

Still, no notice.

"Fuck you guys, do you want to go or what?" I said. How quickly I'd given up on "cool and collected."

Nothing.

I stared at Matt, Chris, and Colin, fixated on the TV. I couldn't tell exactly from the angle I had, but it sounded like the History Channel, something on the Second World War. None of my friends even so much as tilted their heads towards me. Then, almost like a synchronized swimming event, they all got up. Still not turning around, they exited the living room, Chris first, Colin second, and Matt the last to go through the saloon doors (yes, saloon doors—he had designed them in his spare time) separating the living room from the small entrance parlor.

I stood still just outside my door, in shock.

Muttering, I complained, "What the f—"

"Yo, d-bag!" Matt's head reappeared in the living room.

"You coming, or what?!"

"Oh, oh, you're a funny guy now, huh?" I said, realizing the joke was on me. I could hear Chris and Colin laughing hysterically from the porch. That Matt was the one making the jokes really showed how far we had come in our relationship.

The summer before freshman year, shockingly, I had made no attempt to get in contact with my future roommate, a Matt Reilly from Pennsylvania. My parents would bug me incessantly to get in touch with him, but I simply refused. I had no interest in talking to him; I figured we'd get to do enough of that all year.

The phone rang one day and my dad answered. He seemed to be doing something other than chatting with the person on the other end. I turned my head back to whatever I was reading. A minute later, I was interrupted by the sound of my dad's voice.

"Hey, Nick," my dad said, doing his best Mr. Cleaver impersonation, "It's your roommate, Matt."

I frantically waved my hands to indicate I didn't want to talk.

"Hold on, Matt, he's right here," my dad continued.

Even more frantically now, waving, hopping, and mouthing so vehemently it almost was audible: *"I'm! Not! Here!"*

"Okay, here he is. Nice to talk with you, Matt." And then he simply handed me the phone. Game over.

I waited for Matt to say something. Finally, he filled the void.

"Hi, my name is Matt Reilly, I'm going to be your roommate next year, and I wanted to know if you had any time to talk about what we were going to bring up to the room for this year." It was harmless, honest, and helpful. There wasn't anything wrong with the content. It wasn't that, no. It was his voice. He sounded like a lost member of the Supremes, before going through puberty. His voice had a sort of lisp, and a high-pitched quality that couldn't fully be defined but that certainly sent shivers up my spine. Immediately, all I could think of was having the most stereotypically gay roommate. Lisp *obviously* meant gay, and gay *obviously* meant he didn't like sports. Not to mention, would a straight roommate call to ask about decorating the dorm room? I didn't think so.

As it would turn out, my ignorance couldn't have been more misplaced. Matt, at 5'11," was a statue built of muscles that I could barely pronounce and definitely not identify. He had the option of playing Division II football at a few schools, but turned them down to come to Syracuse to pursue a degree in a real pushover of a major: aerospace engineering. I would later joke that if you could somehow combine the two of us, you'd have a perfect person. Matt wasn't what you'd refer to as poetic with the language (I sometimes called him Thor, in reference to the horrific spelling and grammar in his papers which I corrected freshman year), and I needed an abacus to count to anything over ten.

"Oh, shut up, you love it," Matt said, putting his arm around my shoulders. "You ready to go? Good, good. All right, men, move out."

On his orders, the four of us headed out. Matt, the sharpest dresser of the quartet, wore what had been dubbed his grilling shirt, as he'd worn it once to a barbecue where everyone else was wearing t-shirts, and the shirt never lost the nickname. It was just a button-down shirt with a hint of purple in it. It was the sort of purple that made me think, "Wow, purple might not be *that* gay." Colin hadn't changed since earlier in the day, and still had on his Red Sox cap. Chris never dressed without stripes or the color blue. And you know what I was wearing. Four studs, or so we thought.

It wasn't yet fully dark out, and it wasn't even five-thirty. But four friends, four men, were on a mission. Beer and women, our targets in that order, were the game of the day. If the latter didn't pan out, at least we'd get drunk. And we'd get to do it again next Friday.

8 the first friday

I wasn't sure, but I thought that was what I heard. No, no way. Could it be? I hadn't heard that since...well, in at least ten years.

Were they really playing Blues Traveler? Get out of here. I hadn't heard Blues Traveler since I bought the cassette, maybe twelve years ago. It was going to be a good night.

The walk to Chuck's had been a relatively quick one. Sure, it was unimaginably cold but the conversation, paired with the anticipation, distracted the minds of the group. The bar offered little true attraction in and of itself. Dimly lit, poorly set up, it was the honest embodiment of what a college bar should be. Nineties music blasted from the speakers in a seemingly continuous loop. No one ever seemed to mind. There were two pool tables, one on each side of the space, which was cut in half by the bar itself. There never were enough tables, and if by some Virgin Mary-esque miracle you happened to snag a table, the odds that you would have enough chairs were just as slim. But, this aside, the beer was cheap and all the girls went there.

"First round's on me," Chris, giddy as a schoolboy, had exclaimed. His AOL Instant Messenger screen name was

Pitcher922, he claimed because he was a pitcher in high school. However, his track record at Chuck's might suggest that the name more appropriately described his affinity for the three-dollar pitchers at happy hour.

We all knew a few commonly-accepted truths (the other guys from experience, me from hearing the lore). We'd all be buying rounds. We'd all be drinking well into the night, likely on a consistent basis until a quarter to one, maybe one-thirty, depending on the night. And at some point, we'd all split up to hunt. The time-tested expression "bros over hos" took a back seat on Fridays.

The whole experience for me could be likened to a young child's first time at a carnival. Bright lights, lots of people, music blaring. Money being spent at a rapid rate, all for the professed purpose of "having a good time." As we had approached the bar, I saw its sign looming ahead. A yellow square hung over the entranceway, decorated with the words "Hungry Chuck's" scrawled around a screaming clown face. There was a slight line, maybe eight or nine people out the door, but it moved fast enough.

An enormous wall of a man stood in the door way. I would later find out that this man was referred to as "Big Steve," "big" being the operative and understated term. Steve was so large, he could easily have submitted a petition to the government to qualify as the planet to replace Pluto. He checked IDs at the door, with a slow precision that indicated one of two things: either he was extremely serious about his job and approached it with military execution, or he wasn't that bright and couldn't do it much faster. We all knew it had to be the latter.

The first few times I'd gone to a bar after turning twenty-one, I'd gotten that cute half-smile from some of the bouncers. Maybe even a half-hearted "Happy Birthday." I was special. Now I was just another college kid, old enough to get in, old enough to get drunk with my friends. I was happy with that.

With the music absolutely blaring, I headed past the bouncer, paid my three-dollar cover, and made my way towards the bar where Matt, Colin, and Chris had grabbed seats. What better way to kick off a night of drinking than with a greasy hamburger and French fries?

I had to shout to get the bartender's attention, "I'LL HAVE A HAMBURGER—NO, SORRY, A CHEESEBURG—"

The bartender, uninterested in my order and my indecisiveness, simply pointed to the right.

ORDER FOOD HERE, the sign said. Okay, one minute in, one mistake. Matt saw the gaffe and didn't feel like letting me off the hook. He knew how nervous I really was, whether or not I showed it. Matt figured someone had to try to calm me down.

"The bathroom's that way, before you go pissing in the bartender's mouth," Matt shouted at me.

I couldn't even think of a response, I could only laugh. I knew it was stupid. Finally I answered Matt, "Hey, would you mind getting me a glass of milk with my burger?"

"Yeah, no problem, ma'am. Chris, Colin? Milk?"

They weren't listening; ESPN on the flat-screens above the bar had their attention. "Sure, sure," both answered, without turning.

Whether or not the food was actually any good was a subject of true debate. It certainly wasn't bad, that much was for sure. But, when looking back on Friday nights later on in the semester it was hard to separate the drunken haze of the rest of the night from the taste of the burger at the beginning of the evening.

"Doesn't seem like there's that many people here yet, huh?" I said, in between mouthfuls of burger.

"Take it easy," Chris said, noting the worried tone in my voice. If there was one person that could out-worry me, it was Chris. In his mind, nothing had ever gone his way. Having his health, getting into school, doing well in school, having friends: these were all fortunate accidents that he felt would later come back to bite him, as his luck was bound to run out. "This is how it usually is. People start to really show up around seven or so, so just chill out."

"Yeah, take a sip of your beer, why don't ya?" Colin chided. "Does your husband drink beer?"

I took a big gulp of the pitcher-poured beer. Slightly warm, slightly flat, and slightly tasteless. Entirely perfect.

"And," Chris continued, "She'll be here, don't worry about that."

"Who? Who is 'she'?" I asked. I continued to play this ridiculous game of pretending not to care about Lauren, pretending I wasn't thinking only about her, and it quickly became tiresome.

An hour or so having gone by, only a few things had changed. We'd moved from the bar to a table just a few feet away. A more relaxed atmosphere, for sure. Actually, that was all that had changed. We still were drinking. Heavily.

Either "Breakfast at Tiffany's" or something by the Goo Goo Dolls was booming throughout the bar. I couldn't tell for certain which it was; I was more of a hip-hip and rap fan by nature. My older brother liked rap, so as a kid, I did too. My older brother also got a Wu-Tang tattoo on his bicep. Fortunately, I didn't follow him blindly.

By near ten o'clock, I'd passed buzzed quite some time ago and was rapidly approaching drunk. The final station stop, "blackout," wasn't too far off.

For those of you scoring at home, the group was on pitcher number nine. Fear not, it still was a group at this point. We'd pretty much stayed together thus far, though it was expected that at some point we'd probably split. I might see someone from class, Chris and Colin would wander off somewhere. Matt, at all events, usually went off and did his own thing. He was a social butterfly, you might say. Legend had it (actually, I was there and saw the whole thing, so more accurately, I had it) that Matt, in the social scene that is the dining hall, went up to a gorgeous girl he had never talked to before and got her phone number. He bought himself, with the superhero effort, the ability to say or do pretty much whatever he wanted when it came to social affairs.

The room itself was now officially crowded. There were no open spaces at the bar. There were no tables or chairs available. There was a small wait at the pool table in the far corner and a slightly longer wait at the bathrooms.

I still hadn't seen her. I'd had some stupid, meaningless conversation with a friend from class, both parties trying desperately to not sound drunk. Almost as if there was some sort of shame attached to being drunk at ten o'clock, especially after drinking for five straight hours.

Matt continued, "Chris is right. Just chill out. She'll be here. Where else does she have to go? Where else does anyone on this campus have to go?"

"Good point. Sad," I said, taking a massive gulp of beer, belching. "But, good point."

Then it happened. She entered the bar, with a friend, and was doing the typical "look-around" to find her other friends or anyone else she could talk to. No one wanted to be there by themselves, alone in a sea of people.

I whacked Chris's arm. "Check it out. She's here."

Looking, briefly. "Yeah, so? Told you, first of all. Second, you're not gonna do anything about it anyway. I'm not trying to bring you down, but let's be honest."

"Nice, real nice. That's exactly what I didn't fucking need," I pleaded. "I needed positivity, a yes-man, not a Debbie Downer."

"Okay, okay. You're the man. You're going to go talk to her, you're going to fuck her tonight. You're money," he said, obviously faking it.

We laughed at Chris's calculated insincerity, but I never broke away from looking at least towards Lauren's vicinity.

I couldn't stare directly, at least not for long. She was wearing some sort of florally patterned dress, from what I jokingly termed the maternity collection. You know, that dress with its front seam right under the bra, at times making the rest of the dress flow outwards. Either way, I wasn't focused too much on her dress. I had two things on my mind.

First, was there a guy with her? The answer there was no,

at least not at the moment.

Second, what was my next move? Would I just go up to her, like a normal human? Maybe I'd wait until she came up to me? I quickly shot that idea down, remembering that the bar closed before Never O'clock.

My plan, I decided, was just to wait and see where the night took me. Technically, it was still early, only a bit after ten. I had begun to get officially drunk and now had to officially break the seal. The line for the bathroom wasn't terrible, so I hopped on. The other alternative, going outside and pissing behind the dumpster, was only a last resort.

I made my way around the bar, through the various crowds, between the tables playing flip cup. When did all these people get here? It seemed like a minute ago, the place was a warehouse. Now I could barely get to the bathroom. Each step I took, my bladder stabbed harder. That first bathroom trip was really some kind of experience. Each time I'd been drunk in my short life, I was convinced that the first piss was easily the longest, most relieving one ever.

Finally at the bathroom, I had to get in the line. There was something strangely social about being in that line. No one wanted to be there, no one really wanted to talk. At this point in the night, no one really knew exactly what was going on, except for the fact that they had to piss like their life depended on it. Jokes that weren't even funny (or jokes at all) were laughed at. High fives, hand pounds were exchanged amongst friends that weren't even friends. All commonplace in the bathroom line.

"FUCKKKKKKKK!!!!!" some guy exhaled. He wasn't hurt, he wasn't in trouble, he was just shouting for sheer joy about getting to go to the bathroom. No one seemed to notice.

I turned to the guy behind me, an enormous, rugby-player-looking fella wearing a flannel shirt. "Did you hear what that—" I started, before realizing the sheer girth of the man I was talking to. "Never mind," I finished, facing frontwards once again.

The walls in the bathroom, more so than even the dirtiest truck stop, had nonsense written all over them.

jimmy loves sucking cock (no, I don't!)

all these bitches are coming home wit me!

fuck bitches! bro's over ho's

fuck you!

It went on like this for a while, in all directions, in all colors and styles of handwriting.

How do these people have the time to do all this writing while they're going to the bathroom? And where are they getting Sharpies from? Are they bringing pens to the bathroom with them? Should I have? How did they get up high enough to write that one?

I was having enough of a time maintaining my own balance, swaying back and forth while I was going. The idea of writing while doing this was completely out of the question. I would've preferred the stall, where I could take my time. Maybe pour some of my beer out without anyone seeing? No, I wouldn't do that. But I was drunk enough to consider it.

The first available urinal was where I had to go, though. Standing there, I could feel everyone's eyes glaring at me.

HURRY UP AND FINISH PISSING ALREADY!!! I could hear them thinking, apparently at a high volume.

Once I'd finished washing my hands, something practically everyone else had neglected to do, I left the bathroom and headed back into the mass of life in the bar. I was determined. Maybe I wouldn't talk to her, at least not yet. But I'd get close enough that I could possibly bump into her. Then I'd *have* to say something.

If I couldn't talk to her after I'd "accidentally" bumped into her, would I have to wait until I "accidentally" hit her with my car?

No, I can do this, I thought.

Peering into the crowd, I couldn't find her. Actually, I couldn't even find my friends. They weren't sitting at the table any longer, which made me slightly nervous. As I went over to make sure my jacket was still at the table, I felt someone tap my back. *Please be her!*

"Nick, what's up, broseph?"

Ugh. It was Jeremy. Jeremy Stetson. Or Jetson, as he wanted to be called. "My friends from high school call me that," he'd say. And I would laugh to myself, knowing he hadn't had any friends in high school. No one on Earth called him Jetson, J-Stet, or anything else, really. He was the kind of kid who wanted to have his own nickname and because no one gave him one, he decided he'd come up with it on his own.

Jeremy and I shared majors. He was a well-meaning kid, but he was without question one of the most annoying people I knew.

"What's going on, Jeremy?"

"Come on, man, it's Jetson," he said.

"Sure, *Jetson*. Anyway, how are things?" I asked, doing my best to appear uninterested. I was looking around the bar like someone was drowning and I was the only one there who knew how to swim.

"Well, not much, pal," Jeremy started. He always used words like that. Pal, buddy, boss, chief. We weren't anything. I wasn't friends with Jeremy. We weren't co-workers or members of the same tribe. "Had a good break, good solid break. How about you, how was yours?"

I knew this line of questioning. I knew, from years of experience at this point, that people like Jeremy only asked how breaks went so that they could tell me how great theirs were. Normally I wouldn't say much and let the other person hurry up and get their story started. Quicker it started, quicker it was over, I figured.

But this time, I decided to take a different path.

"Well, my parents wanted to take me to Spain for the month, but I told them I'd been there before, when I went abroad, so they left it up to me," I began, lying so forcefully I could barely look Jeremy in the eyes. "I wasn't sure. Africa? I do have friends there, but Africa is sooo lame in late December. Long story short, I spun a globe and landed on Hawaii. So we went there. That was fucking nuts, dude. Just got bombed every night with my boys down there. Fucked some chick that went to USC, she was slammin'. Real fun. How about you, what were you up to?"

"Uh...well, not much, really. I mean, my brother and I went skiing in Vermont. Nothing special, I guess," he said, clearly deflated. I knew that Jeremy had some sort of killer story prepared, about how he and his brother probably stayed up past eleven one evening watching Nick at Nite. But my powerful lie diverted that story. I thought I'd crushed Jeremy's spirit so much that I'd actually gotten myself out of the conversation entirely.

"All right, dude, I'm gonna go and—"

Paying no attention to that, Jeremy interrupted, "Come on, let's go get a drink. My treat." He put his arm around my shoulders. *What a pal*, I thought.

"So, how's 565 treating ya?" Jeremy shouted above the noise at the bar. He really thought he was being conversational, that was the sad part. Why he wanted to talk about school, about classes (especially those that were one week old), I could never figure. I'd rather be silent than talk about either the weather or school. Still, I couldn't avoid either when I came to the bar. People just can't handle any pause in conversation.

"It's fine," I said, purposely brief.

"Yeah, man, that's good to hear," Jeremy said.

He's not even listening to me, this jackass! I could've told him that Phillips threatened to rape me in front of the whole class, and he wouldn't have reacted differently. What a clown....

"So, do you have something lined up for after school?"

"What do you mean?" I asked, actually not sure what Jeremy meant. I assumed he was talking about jobs, but seeing as how we were only a week into the semester, maybe he meant something else.

But, sure enough: "Jobs, prospects. Anything cooking, boss?"

"Nah, not really. Nothing yet," I said. Worn out from my previous lie, I didn't feel like making up a story about how the President had asked me to work for him in a covert effort to plan a mission to Saturn.

"Yeah, man, I hear ya. I've got a few things lined up, nothing definite yet, I guess," he started.

"Oh."

Oblivious, Jeremy continued, "Yeah, I interned at CNN last summer, nothing big. Talked with a producer there about doing something for them come May. Who knows though, right?"

"Right."

"When are you performing next?"

"You know, I'm not really sure," I said, again lying. I knew my next show was a week from that Saturday, and I had no desire to tell him about my plans for the *Earmuffs* show. Scanning the room intensely for anyone I even remotely knew, I said, with as much insincerity as I could muster, "But when I find out, I'll let you know."

"Yeah, man, please do. I'd love to come, definitely."

"Of course."

Throughout my scanning, I did find Matt. He was talking to this girl he was kind of dating, kind of having sex with, kind of avoiding. Her name was Jessica, or Jackie, or Jillian, or Jamie. Something with a J. Either way, I wasn't about to interrupt him; things hadn't gotten that bad yet on my home front.

I checked my cell phone and to my absolute shock, it was almost midnight. Had I been in the bathroom and talking to this kid for that long? Was I so drunk that I'd completely lost control of the night?

"Jeremy, great catching up with you. I'll see you around. Thanks for the beer. Next one on me," I said. I had no intention whatsoever of either seeing him around or buying him a beer.

Leaving before I could get *Jetson'd* again, I hurried back to what at one point in the night had been our table. Somehow, despite my friends having left the spot for a while, all of our jackets were still on the seat backs.

Colin and Chris were in the area, talking with kids from

the radio station. I sauntered over there, a beaten man. Drunk, tired, and a bit depressed that I didn't get to talk to a girl (Lauren or otherwise) and instead spent the whole night talking with Jeremy Stetson. I didn't want to talk about sports; but standing alone was worse, so I headed over. Reviewing the evening in my head, I knew I hadn't really even seen much of Lauren, let alone gotten anywhere near close enough to talk to her. Matter of fact, where was she? Had she left yet? At this point, I really didn't care all that much.

The walk home was a generally quiet one; the real review of the night would come the next morning. Some nights, of course, we'd stay up even later, eating or just bullshitting. I wasn't going to be around for much of that tonight. I was falling asleep walking home.

Unlike some people, who tended to get belligerent when drunk, or Chris, who tended to get miserable when drunk, I just got more relaxed, and more tired. And so, once the walk home had concluded, I headed straight for my room. Chris started to ask something about Lauren, but I cut him off.

"Tomorrow," I groused out. I couldn't keep my eyes open another second and each step I took felt like I had just gotten off one of those Tilt-A-Whirls at a carnival. I needed to go to bed. Lauren or no Lauren, my night was over.

9 saturday, january 19th

    The first thing I made out upon waking was the number eight. Everything else was still really loud, and really blurry. And really, really thirsty.

    Could it only be eight a.m.? No way, I thought. I went to bed at almost three in the morning, how could it be that early? Don't drunk people normally pass out and then sleep for long periods of time?

    Well, as it turns out, some do. But not me. I would gradually discover that I woke up even earlier than usual when I was drunk. It likely had something to do with a combination of factors, including the fact that someone, in the middle of the night, had replaced my tongue and mouth lining with sand paper, and the fact that I'd take a bullet to the back of my brain to ease the throbbing.

    Sitting up in bed, I realized I was still drunk. The room was still swirling and unless we'd moved to the San Fernando Valley in the middle of the night, I had to rule out an earthquake. Looking around the room, I saw my clothes scattered about like evidence at a crime scene.

    Boots, step forward. Socks, another step. Pants, step forward. Sweater, final step. I had no recollection of putting on my Syracuse sweatpants or even of getting into bed—and certainly not of putting my retainer in. How did I remember to do that?

My hand began to search the multi-tiered plastic stand that stood next to my bed. I was fumbling for my glasses, which I rarely wore but found to be necessary at this point, if only to attempt to restore some bit of normalcy. Finally I found the glasses, took out my retainer, and got out of bed.

The floor was freezing, but my feet and body weren't surprised. It was always cold in Syracuse, and it was always cold in our house because A) we didn't have insulation in Syracuse and B) Matt was basically the Heat Miser. I thought I heard some noise from outside my room, but I figured someone must've left the TV on.

After checking my e-mail and Facebook, I resigned myself to a shower. Wrapped up in a towel, I braved the expedition out the door for the two-step walk to the bathroom. In between steps one and two, I looked to the right and saw Matt and Colin, sitting like zombies in front of the TV.

"Yooooo," I let out.

"Mgmhhhh," Matt responded. Colin kept staring ahead. I wasn't sure if they were conscious, so I headed over, and sat down in between the pair.

"Some night last night, huh?"

No one bit.

"Matt, what happened with you and that girl Jackie?"

"Jamie, dude. It's fucking Jamie. How can't you remember that?" he said, not nearly as mad as this may read.

"Fine, Jamie, whatever. What went down with her? You hold her hand this time?"

"Nah, man, I got her number, we're going to hang out next week or something. She's cool, but she's got this thing going on with some ex-boyfriend or something. I don't really know....And you're one to talk."

"Hell's that supposed to mean?" I asked.

"Yeah, you know exactly what that's supposed to mean. What'd you do last night? You talk to Lauren? How about...anyone with a vagina? Oh, that's right, I saw you talking to your best buddy Jeremy," Matt said, jokingly shoving me.

"Listen, it was the first time. I don't want to make a move out of desperation. It's still January. My time will come; I've got a plan."

"Yeah, a plan to do nothing," Matt said.

"How long did it take you to think of that one? Is that why you're down here so early? You been scheming all night, writing that little joke?"

"Go take your fucking shower," Matt said, laughing.

After what felt like thirty minutes of waiting for the shower water to heat up, I stepped in and let the scalding water burn my skin. Normally I was in and out. Real quick. Other people needed hot water, I was sensitive to that. Normally. Today, this early, I couldn't move.

Thinking back, I reviewed the previous night. The more I thought about it, the more I realized I wasn't upset about not talking to Lauren. Really, I never was going to. Just because I was suddenly able to go to bars, I'd be able to have confidence and bravado and self-esteem? Don't be ridiculous.

Fact was, Lauren existed for me almost like a movie star. I knew her about as well as someone knows a star on their favorite soap opera. I knew what she looked like, things she could be found doing or wearing, but never got close enough to actually talk with her. It was almost as if she truly did exist on television for me and after that glass wall had been in place for so long between us (evidence suggested that only I knew of this wall; as far as anyone could tell, there was no *real* proof she'd ever known of my existence), it wasn't going to come crashing down in one night. No matter how much beer was consumed. And, as pathetic as it seemed, I was comfortable on my side of the glass. I'd grown accustomed to it. Actually, that's a horrible lie. I hated being on the side of the glass that she wasn't on. I wanted to make a cameo in the show, and then, once the fans had decided they couldn't do without me, have myself written into the script for the rest of the series and on into reruns. But enough of the TV analogy.

Drying myself off as best I could, I still couldn't shake the thought of her. Even my thoughts were getting annoyed by her presence.

That's enough, I thought. *Just because you went out last night and yeah, sure, you could've gone up to her and talked to her, you didn't. That's not the end of the world. You'll get another chance. Seeing her there doesn't change how things have been the past three years, and things have been okay the way they've been. Have they? You've had one girlfriend, been with two girls during school? How good could it be? Fuck!! Stop thinking. Go and do something constructive!*

This wasn't working, mentally or physically (I'd stopped drying myself for some reason, as if I needed my body's full attention in order to think). I finished up, got back into my room, and put on an extremely oversized (but wonderfully comfortable) pair of Nike sweatpants in Syracuse Orange and Blue.

The rest of the day was filled with nothing. Nothing in the form of eating crappy fried chicken, nothing in the form of mindless television and mindless conversation. The evening prior was reviewed, and, as was customary, Chris came down the stairs wearing nothing but a t-shirt and boxers that seemed tenuously (at best) to be covering his genitals. It was a sight we all dreaded but, strangely, also took comfort in if only because of its implicit reassurance of normality. Had he come down one morning after a Friday night at Chuck's wearing jeans, or looking fairly put-together, it just wouldn't have made sense.

I wound up getting some work done on Sunday, once my headache had subsided fully and my vision had returned to its normal functioning capacity. School had just picked up again, and already I had readings to do, work to finish, and projects to worry about.

I couldn't wait for next Friday.

10 tuesday, january 22nd

Tuesdays were the only days when I wasn't with Colin the whole day. Today, I'd have my first meeting of the dreaded Com Law class, short for Communications Law. It was the final course in my major and everyone that wanted to graduate from Syracuse with a degree from the journalism school had to take the class. No way around it. Before I got ready for that misery, I headed down for lunch with my friend Aaron at Panda West, the campus Chinese restaurant, which was the only Chinese food place you could eat in without needing a tetanus shot beforehand.

"You know what? I don't think I'm going to miss college all that much." I think, frankly, that there must have been a point somewhere between complete self-denial and partial realization at which even I became aware of how full of shit I sounded. "Yeah, I mean, I guess I'll miss it at least a little bit," I blurted between slurps of chow mein. "But you know my theory," I went on (editor's note: Nick often inserts his theories as if A) anyone cares, or B) they are actually something more than his own uninformed opinion). "I'm ready to get back to real life. Getting paid instead of paying. I'm ready."

Aaron wasn't convinced at all. Aaron was a junior—he

wasn't up for parole for another year. But a friend he was, so he didn't push me on it. "Hell, you're a better man than I am. I'm holding on to every second I have here."

Obviously not too convinced myself, I looked to change the topic. Not that anyone would notice. This random quality to my thoughts and speech was something my friends had come to expect, not as a sign that something was wrong but rather as an accepted character defect.

"Why does it seem like all Chinese restaurants have something distinctly Chinese in their titles?" I pointed up at the sign. "Panda West? Back home we have Lotus House and Lotus Tea Garden. I don't know too many other countries associated with the lotus flower. Or is it the lotus plant?"

"Not sure."

"I think it's the lotus plant," I quickly answered.

"What about Taiwan, the Koreas, Myanmar, Thailand—"

"Wait a minute, did you just make a Myanmar reference?" I asked.

"Yeah. Myanmar, formerly Burma, or was it formerly Laos? Or was it formerly Myanmar and it's now Burma? Forget it. Point is, how do you know the lotus *plant* doesn't grow there?" Aaron asked.

"I don't."

"Well, there you go," Aaron said.

"Let's put it this way," I began, a wise-ass remark clear in my mind. "Next time I find myself eating Myanmar...ese food or, for that matter, locating it on a fucking map, I'll give you a call."

As I walked up Marshall Street to meet Natalie before class, my brain raced with the horror stories I'd heard about this 500-level course. Awful stories, of pain and anguish and murder and treachery. Okay, the last two are exaggerations. But I'd definitely heard some awful things.

I held open the door for Natalie, entering the amphitheater-style classroom. It was half-filled by the time we decided we would sit on the far left side of the room.

As was my custom, I sat down, unloaded all I had for the

class on the desk in front of me (at this point that was only a notebook, as I hadn't yet gone to the bookstore), and began to take stock of the class.

Scanning, I saw a few of the hot girls from my other journalism class. *Good, good*, I thought. In the back row, both on the far right and behind me, I saw a bunch of guys I didn't recognize. Judging by their age (a few of them were bald) and the fact that a few had wedding rings on, I assumed that they were either ridiculous student impostors or Army students. Turns out, it was the latter.

Towards the middle, a few rows down, I spotted a few friends from the radio station. A quick "what's up," and back to scanning.

Sadly, nothing too exciting. There were the girls from the other class, but they were sitting in a bad spot for me to do any staring. In fact, as I sat there, I realized that Natalie and I had accidentally made a tactical error in choosing our seats. By sitting all the way on the left-hand side of the room, I wouldn't be able to look at any girls immediately to my right. Then again, this was only a problem because the only five or six good-looking girls in the class were sitting in that exact blind spot. Everyone else I had a pretty clear view of, from my three-row-up, stage-right seat.

As John Edington, the professor, showed up, I realized how much I hated a few small arrogances about college life.

When the hell did teachers become professors? Why do I have to call him Professor Edington, not Mr. Edington? Also: syllabuses. And when they call them syllabi, how annoying is that? It can't just be syllabuses, or how about just class outlines*? It's all bullshit; fuck this....*

"Are you all right? You're breathing kinda heavy," Natalie said to me in a hushed tone during the professor's introduction.

"Yeah, yeah, fine," I said.

Edington had already begun his lecture. He was an odd guy, no doubt about it. Part of the time, he made you want to rip your eyes out and put them in the sink disposal, he was so boring. Then, just when you were about to flick the switch, post-eye-ripping-out, he'd say something completely off the wall and you'd be right back to involved. Other times, of course, he was the most fun, interesting, and wildly informative professor I'd ever had. But, of all the things John Edington was, he was most certainly prompt. When I'd had him before in previous classes, whatever time it said on the syllabus was exactly when he started talking.

"This is a serious class on law, but it's going to be fun. I'm going to make it fun for you guys, for us....much you get out of this class depends on how much work you guys put into this class....been teaching law for....two papers, one midterm and one final, all of which will be....everything you learn in this class will truly prepare you for...."

You can see how it was hard to pay attention sometimes.

Then it happened. The break of all breaks. With my head resting in the palms of my hands, elbows on my desk, I saw a streak of blonde down the aisle to my right. My field of vision, which had previously been on auto-pilot, was briefly interrupted. Now ten minutes into class, I had been staring straight ahead, almost like I was sleeping with my eyes open. Every once in a while I'd nod, maybe even write something down. All to give the appearance that I was fully paying attention.

But this blonde streak, it turned out to be a girl. I thought I recognized the back of her head, but it was confirmed when she announced to the professor who she was and that she was sorry for being late.

She turned back from the front of the room, now facing in my general direction, though it was clear she too was scanning the room, desperate, now fifteen minutes into the class, to just find a seat and bury her head.

Intuitively, I began to search the room as well. She wouldn't sit next to me, unless she had a thing about sitting right next to the wall. Again, damn that left side decision, I thought. There was some space on the right side of the room, but since she'd come in on the left, it didn't seem likely that she'd go up the right side.

At this point, it felt like either time had stopped or the room had entirely filled with water, because she was moving incredibly slowly. *God, could this take any longer? Right or left!!*

YESSSS!!! She was coming towards me. I was excited, but immediately the excitement turned to freakish nerves.

What if she sits behind me? Now I'm going to have to worry about her staring at the back of me all day? And I won't see her? Fuck!

For whatever reason, the fates aligned and she picked a seat directly in front of me.

Three and a half years You made me wait for this? I thought, looking up towards the ceiling.

And so, for the remaining hour of the class, I was content. I stared now not at the teacher, but at the back of my dream girl's head. Any time there was a break in the action from the professor, I'd say something witty or sarcastic to Natalie with purposeful volume, hoping Lauren would hear me. It was a pathetic move, no doubt, but what else could I do?

"You know why I hate Mentos?" I started up to Natalie, completely randomly, in an effort to get this girl's attention. "Because of those commercials. That one with the guy with the blue suit who sits on the park bench, the one that was just painted. He looks at the painter, who gives him one of those stupid nods, and then this guy, in a Mentos-induced frenzy, decides to roll around on the bench, turning his blue suit into a pinstriped suit. All the painter does is smile at this fuckin' guy's *ingenious* plan. Like that crap would ever work," I finished, popping a Mentos into my mouth.

She didn't turn around, and, so far as I could tell, she didn't even hear it. Okay, strike one. The way I looked at it, though, I had as many strikes as there were days over the course of the semester, so I was nowhere near finished.

The rest of the class passed without much more of an attempt. I knew I'd tried and that was somewhat comforting. It was only Day One, so I'd have to build up from here.

Once the class ended, Natalie and I headed to our next

class together, the baseball card class, where we'd be meeting Colin.

"How about that, huh, Nick?" Natalie asked, sounding nearly as excited as I felt but didn't act.

"Yeah, amazing, right? I couldn't believe that it was her. I'd just about given up hope on that class. It was boring as fuck today," I said.

"Yes, and we all know how boring 'fuck' is," Natalie joked.

"No, but seriously, I was losing my mind. I can't believe we have to do that twice a week until we graduate. That sucks huge," I said, pausing. Reminding myself that I was talking to a girl, even if it was just Natalie, I finished, "huge, well, you know."

"Yes, dick. It sucks huge dick. What, are you afraid?"

"No, come on. I just thought that...well, sometimes I try to at least *act* like a gentleman."

"Yeah, some act," Natalie laughed.

As we sat down inside the classroom for what promised to be at the very least an enjoyable class, I knew there wouldn't be much scanning to be done in here. Come on, a class on baseball cards *and* hot girls? That's getting greedy, wouldn't you say?

There's a thin line in the class dynamic. Too boring, too easy and it's awful. Too stimulating, too challenging and it's too hard. The ideal class found itself somewhere in the middle, where effort was decidedly only half necessary, conversation at least mildly entertaining, and grades easily achieved. Minimal amounts of papers and projects, but enough to make you feel like you were doing something. In retrospect, as I thought back on my time at SU, I realized that I probably had only one or two courses that truly fit this description. Also, a cool teacher that preferably cursed often and made snide remarks about kids in the class when they would say stupid things was a bonus.

I'll spare you the time and say, simply, that this class had none of that.

"You wanna stop at the bookstore?" I asked Colin and Natalie on the walk back to our house. The building our previous class was in was located on the farthest corner of the campus. Walking back across campus, we'd pass the bookstore without a detour on the way to the house. Natalie said she couldn't; she had a meeting for some "magazine major bullshit." Colin had nothing else to do, surprisingly.

"Yeah, I don't plan on reading, but sure, I'll go," Colin said.

Going to buy books was easily the biggest rip-off in the whole process. Sure, one could argue that charging nearly fifty grand a year for schooling was a bigger rip-off, but at least in that situation, you weren't so blatantly aware of how much you were getting screwed.

"Colin, come here and look at this," I said, struggling to even lift my Law book. "Holy shit, ninety-five dollars?"

"Yeah, man, mine was that much last semester. Who wrote it?"

"Uh...Jay Wright. Why?"

"Same guy, same book as last semester. What edition?"

"Fourth, I think. Yes, fourth. My professor said we had to buy this year's edition, that we couldn't buy the previous editions," I said.

"Yeah, you know why he says that, right? So that you have to spend more on the 'newer' book, which isn't newer at all, really. And that Wright guy? He's a teacher here, made it mandatory for the other professors to use his book," Colin said, a look of disgust on his face.

Truth be told, it was surprising that any of the kids here were actually annoyed by the prices of the books, as most of them weren't paying for them on their own anyway. Still, it was the principle of the thing.

The final tally for our books was a combined $275—we decided to share most of the books, as we were in nearly every class together and didn't plan on reading the books anyway. Having at least one copy in the house made us feel like we weren't completely wasting our time (just our parent's money).

"You want to hear something unbelievable?" I asked Colin, as we turned the corner off Ostrom and onto Clarendon Street.

"Sure," Colin said.

"Try to contain yourself," I said. "In my Com Law class, guess who was sitting right fucking in front of me!"

"Denzel Washington."

"No, no," I said, at first not realizing what Colin had said. "Wait, what? Denzel Washington? Where the hell's that come from?"

"I don't know. You seemed really excited about it. I know you love him. Who was it?"

"Uh, well, now that you ruined that surprise, it was just that girl, Lauren. The blonde girl?"

"You don't have to refer to her like you haven't been talking to everyone about her for four years. I know who she is, maybe as well as you do at this point," Colin said.

"Here's the problem with this, though," I started.

"Of course, you'd find a problem with your dream girl sitting right in front of you all semester. Out with it; let's hear it."

"The problem is," I continued, "now I definitely won't be able to get her out of my mind. It used to just be whenever I'd randomly see her, or now with the bar, on Friday nights. But that was it. Listen, I'm not complaining, really. Just mentioning that my neurosis won't be able to handle all of this."

"I'm sure you'll deal," Colin said as he headed upstairs to check on his Fantasy Football team. No one else was home, or at least no one was in the living room watching TV. I wasn't going to just watch television by myself, for the same reason that many people fear being called an alcoholic for drinking by themselves. No, those two things weren't on the same level, but that's just how I thought. I retired to my room, ready to reorganize everything, get all of my books and binders and pens and notebooks, and all the jazz I bought from the store, in order for class.

Father's Cellular **is calling....**

I didn't hear the ring. I could feel the vibration of my phone somewhere on my desk. Shuffling around, searching, I knew my time was running out. Finally, I found it underneath two notebooks and a stack of pencils.

"Hey," I huffed.

"What are you, out of breath? What's wrong?" my dad asked. Charles Alexander was a worrier. In many ways, my personality closely resembled my father's. Both of us loved being the center of attention in a group, telling stories, making people laugh. Both of us were good at it and both of us knew it. We'd convinced ourselves that we didn't have egos. Everyone else we knew did, of course.

My dad hadn't gone to college. As he'd told me many times, "Nana and Pop, they didn't give a shit if I went to college, they didn't care about my grades, so I didn't care." And for this reason, among others, I was under careful (if not vicarious) watch by my father.

My older siblings, Jason and Ashley, hadn't gone to college, either. My younger brother, Rich, wasn't going to set the world on fire when he went, in all likelihood. My mom finished school, but did it by going at night to a local community school six years after she'd started. This wasn't to say these people weren't successful. Somehow, the less schooling they'd each had, the more they'd accomplished.

"No, not out of breath—" I started, taking another inhale.

"Well, you sound like it. What are you doing up there?" my dad said. He wasn't questioning in the way that a parent might in trying to catch a child doing something wrong. Say, underage drinking or smoking pot, for example. No, I had gained their trust to this point. This was just how Charles interacted with his children.

One day in high school, at the dinner table....

"Dad, you'll never guess what happened at school today," I had said, sounding excited.

"What did you get in trouble for, hmm?" my dad said.

I looked at my dad with this shitty little teenager look that said two things: 1) Why would you assume I did something wrong? and 2) I know more than you do about high school and life in general.

"Charles, take it easy," my mom laughed. My worst case of "trouble" was when I got lunch detention for showing up late for class in the sixth grade. My best friend Patrick had gotten a bloody nose en route and I took him to the nurse. Real troublemaker.

"Well, now that we've officially taken the fun out of this announcement," I began, the wiseass gearing up, "all I was going to say was that I finally asked out Beth. I think we're going to go out to a movie this weekend."

On a dime, my dad had changed expression and tone. "That's great!" he said, sounding easily more excited than me.

"Nothing, Dad. I'm not doing anything up here. I mean, I am doing something, but nothing bad. I was just putting all the shit from the bookstore away in my room, the pens and the books and all that stuff," I said.

"And I'll be seeing that charge soon? Just don't tell your mother how much the books wound up costing. You know how much she goes nuts over that."

"Yeah, no, I know. So, yeah, I was just doing that, and I couldn't find my phone and started looking for it, and—"

"And that got you out of breath?" my dad interrupted.

"You want to let me finish? Yes, that was it. I heard the phone, but I couldn't find it, and then I looked....Actually, who gives a shit? What's going on?"

"Nothing much. Wanted to know how you're liking your classes thus far."

This was a regular phone call at the beginning of each semester. My dad just wanted to make sure I wasn't unhappy. If I was also enjoying the classes and learning, well, that was a bonus far as my dad was concerned. My mom was more of an idealistic intellectual and wanted me to be sucking the last bit of juice out of every academic opportunity I had while at school. So sometimes I lied. White, polite lies.

"Loving them, actually. Interesting, good kids in the classes. All pretty good," I said, purposely glossing over a few important details, such as how the classes weren't that great, and how the only "good kids" were the hot girls in the classes. I was bored in my classes, and really, I was tired of going to school. I'd put in my sixteen years and that was about enough. Time for something new. What exactly that something would be, I didn't know at this point but I knew that the routine of going to class and doing work and getting stressed (if even mildly) over papers and such was just tired. I was ready to move on, or so I had convinced myself.

"That's it? You've got to tell me a bit more, just so I don't have to make stuff up to Mom," my dad said. It may seem like my dad and I were in some sort of collusion against Stacy Alexander. That was hardly the case. We just both knew that there were things better done the way she wanted them and if that meant bending the truth at times without her knowing, so be it.

"Yeah, I don't know. The classes, they're classes. What do you want me to say? It's early; I've really only had each class once or twice. My professors all seem nice; the work load doesn't seem too heavy. They seem fine to me."

For the next fifteen minutes, my dad and I went back and forth about the merits of the Yankees acquiring a new second baseman. Who would be the best guy to fill that spot? What happened to that scrappy kid from Oakland? We always talked sports and while it used to be more one-sided, I had begun to close the gap in sports knowledge between the two of us. This was something my father obviously appreciated, as neither of my brothers was nearly as interested in sports, and all he wanted was someone to talk to about what he spent a large portion of his free time watching and reading about.

"All right, I'm going to get going, gotta eat some dinner," I said, signaling the end.

"Okay, I'll let you go. Say hello to everyone for us."

In all the years of "Say hello to X for us," I've likely relayed the message under five percent of the time. Maybe even less. Why people insisted on saying that made absolutely no sense to me and I'd long since given up trying to convince people of how truly stupid I felt it was.

11 why college was fun

There was a certain liberation in going to college. I wasn't fully aware of it, but it was there.

A certain freedom implicit in being a student at a university. You could have no job and do nothing but drink or bullshit with your friends, and that was pretty much standard operating procedure. Anyone who did that outside of college, even a few months after graduation, might be considered a bum. Unemployed, even.

No, here at school, within the comfortable confines of college life, this sort of activity, or more precisely a lack thereof, was not only common but encouraged. The whole point was to somehow figure out how to minimize the amount of time spent in class, or worrying about or working on things related to class, and to maximize the amount of time spent outside of class either hanging out or drinking or eating, or doing any combination.

Not ones to skip class, my housemates and I handled the minimization of class time challenge by continuing to attend, but checking out mentally. For instance, the previous semester Colin had devised an in-class game that had proven to take up at least twenty to twenty-five minutes of class time. Best yet, it was nearly impossible to be spotted playing it.

"All right, here's how it works," Colin said one morning in October. He was handing out strips of paper, talking in front of his exhausted friends, almost like a commander before his chiefs. "Each week we'll all pick a word to be used...this week, how about 'rhombus'?"

"What the fuck are you talking about?" I asked.

Not acknowledging, Colin continued, "So, you'll write 'rhombus' vertically down the side of your paper. Then, whatever the topic is, you've gotta think of something that starts with each letter."

"You mean like Scattergories?" Natalie asked.

"Yeah, like that."

Everyone agreed that Scattergories was a fun game.

"I like Yahtzee," I said, "I don't think that game gets enough play. Am I wrong?" It was way too early in the morning (10:30 a.m.) for anyone to even begin to feign interest in a discussion about the merits of Yahtzee.

Score was rarely kept, tallies never checked. The game merely served as something to do instead of paying attention during class. An example of one such game follows:

Video Games

Returns, Batman

Hirby's Adventure

O

Mario Brothers

Brothers, Mario

Underground Racing

Street Fighter

It would turn out that I was actually thinking of Kirby's Adventure, and Hirby's Adventure didn't exist. Also, simply rearranging the name of the game to fit your letter wasn't allowed either, so R and B were duds. Needless to say, I wasn't good.

The other beautiful thing about college life was its immediacy. If I wanted to go and hang out with a friend of mine who didn't live in the house, I didn't have to walk more than ten minutes. The radio station? Five-minute walk. Class? Eight-minute walk. Meet some girl for a date somewhere on Marshall Street? No more than ten minutes.

Everything was close. It was just another one of the beauties of college that I took for granted. Then again, it wasn't as if the rest of my friends took time out each day to thank God for college. We all took it for granted, unaware not of how great it was (that, we definitely knew) but of how difficult such contentment was to find once out of the college scene.

12 friday, february 1st

This was a Friday, and as such was cause for celebration. The previous Friday hadn't gone extremely well. The group of us had headed down to Chuck's last week and fun was still had, no doubt about that.

It was on this second Friday that I realized what it was that I in fact loved about these nights. There was a completely carefree attitude draped over the entire evening and all of its participants. No one had anything to do that night, or the next morning. At least, not something that couldn't be pushed back until Sunday. No one cared about how many empty calories were in the pitchers of beer they'd down at an otherwise frightening rate, or the pizza they'd eat around three in the morning after the bars had been closed for a bit. No, these issues would be saved for later. Now, Friday night, wasn't the time for such concerns, for such worries.

So, on those levels, the past Fridays were fun. Drinking, general merriment. The occasional piss outside, around back near the dumpsters instead of waiting in line inside. All the markers of a familiar and fun Friday.

Again though, I'd struck out on the female front.

"I don't know, nothing really happened, not much new to

report," I would say at some point in one of the weekend wrap-ups in the living room. The words began to carry the air of a pro-athlete tired of answering the same questions about using steroids.

And while I certainly wasn't using any sort of performance-enhancing drugs, I was cheating myself. At least that's what Natalie told me on the way to the grocery store that Friday morning.

"I can never figure out why you struggle so much with women," Natalie remarked, sitting passenger-side in my car.

"Where's that come from?"

"Nowhere specific, really. You're just always," she paused, searching for the right word, "talking about women...."

"You mean, complaining."

"You said it."

"I call it like it is," I laughed.

"Well, whatever it is, it never seems to work out for you. When was the last time you even had sex?" Natalie had an obvious way of being quite blunt.

I didn't answer at first, pretending to be concentrating extra hard on the road ahead, even going so far as to bob my head particularly noticeably, as if this was a part of the song playing that I really enjoyed.

"Answer the question," Natalie said, shutting off the radio and ending my charade.

"It has been a while," I said, my voice discernibly lower.

"A while...as in, not since Katie, sophomore year?" She wasn't trying to make me feel bad. She was just curious. And I didn't feel bad so much as I felt reminded. Ignoring my sexual failures, I could live contently. Brought to attention, I was back to being a bit annoyed at myself. I chose ignorance more often than not.

"Yeah."

"And you know, I just don't get that, Nick. You should be out boning all day and all night, just getting cooter."

Laughing, I said, "I love that one, cooter. I've never heard that term before you said it. Cooter. Real pretty, real nice."

We laughed over Natalie's mouth, the ridiculousness of the curse. There was a pause as we arrived at the store. I got the cart, Natalie started in on the produce aisle. A few minutes later, inspecting the merits of a cucumber, Natalie continued.

"You're funny. You *can* be a gentleman, a nice guy, even though you wouldn't let anyone think that. You have personality. You're cute—"

"Listen, you want to go, let's go. Right now. I'll push the seats up in my car. I've told you how I feel about you, deal always stands."

Laughing, Natalie pressed forward. "I mean, you're pretty normal...physically appealing. You can go out in public and not scare any kids."

"Thank you."

"Of course," she said. Putting down the cucumber. Apparently it wasn't dense enough, didn't have a sturdy enough center, or something like that. "So, where I always get stuck is why it doesn't work out in real life, which is I guess where you come into play and fuck it all up."

"Thank you again."

"No, come on, Nick," Natalie said, her voice cracking a bit at the end there. "That's not what I mean, you know that."

"Nah, I know what you mean," I said, bringing about visible relief on Natalie's face. "I do fuck it all up. I psyche myself out, is what it is. You put me in front of a group of people, tell me, do funny stuff and tell jokes. I can do that. Put me in a room with my friends, I'm in my element, telling stories, joking. But when it comes to girls I'm really attracted to, I completely freeze up. It's like there's some sort of inverse equation, where the hotter I think a girl is, the more of a wuss I become, and the less attracted I am to the person, the more confident I get. See, like with you, when I'm around ugly girls, I don't lose any confidence at all...."

She punched me on the arm.

We walked on, discussing other things. In the junk food aisle, I decided I wanted to try every kind of Teddy Grahams, so I bought them all. *All* really only consisted of four, but it was still a gratuitous purchase. When we had finished unloading the cart into the car, I picked up the conversation from before as if we were still inspecting cantaloupes, not one to let it drop.

"Thing is," I started, pulling out of the parking lot. "It's confidence. Some guys have it with girls, some don't. Like Matt. He's got it. Colin, sadly, doesn't. If Colin had Matt's confidence, he'd get women all the time, too."

"Yeah, I guess, but how do you not have this *confidence*? Did your parents beat you up when you were a kid?"

"Yes, actually."

She looked over at me and I wasn't smiling.

"I'm fucking with you," I said. "Wouldn't have been such a funny joke if I was serious, huh?" Truly, the more curious conversation would be why I thought it was funny to joke about parental violence. But Natalie didn't want to talk about the vagaries of my mind. So the women talk continued.

"I always think to myself, I'm ready to be a better boyfriend this time around. I'm ready now. I think I can do it," I said.

"Well, you certainly couldn't get any worse," Natalie said, half-joking, half-kidding. Sophomore year, obsessed with my new girlfriend, I had barely spent time with the rest of my friends on Friday and Saturday nights the whole year. They'd all be at Natalie's off-campus apartment, barbequing and drinking. I'd stay on campus, hanging out with Katie. As Natalie would later jokingly tell me, that was my "douche bag year." As always, she was direct.

"But then I see Matt having to call a girl back all the time and do all that lovey-dovey shit, and I just can't stand that crap."

"Lovey-dovey?" Natalie asked.

"Yeah, you know. Holding hands, calling her every single day to ask how her day went...I don't know, shit like that."

"Ah, normal dating, male-female stuff. Sure, you're right. That is awful. How *does* anyone stand it?"

Pretending her sarcasm would cease if I answered her straight, "I have no idea," I said.

"You know what you need to do?" Natalie asked, intoning that she'd be telling me regardless of whether or not I wanted to hear it. "You need to just move on past this obsession with Lauren. I'm not saying give up, I'm just saying leave yourself open to someone else. You're not going to believe me when I say this and I know what you're going to say, but when you're not trying so hard and worrying so much about getting a girl, that's when these sorts of things happen."

I wondered, internally, how it was she spoke so definitively about relationships and picking up women when she'd been with the same guy since the middle of high school. The more I thought about it, the more I reasoned that even if she was way off base (which I didn't think she was), it was better to just let the comments slide. Maybe there was some truth to just relaxing, letting it come to me.

"Yeah, that's easy for you to say. You're telling me that all this time I've been going out looking for girls and haven't been coming home with any of them, but if I went out not looking for anything, then I would get something? Not to be rude, but that sounds fucking ridiculous."

Natalie laughed, "I know, I know. And what do I know about this type of stuff, right?" *How did she know that I...* "But, trust me, if you just chill out a little bit, you'll do fine. I'm not saying it's a guarantee, but look at it another way: your current strategy hasn't really worked, has it?"

"Good point."

"So, all I'm saying is, just relax. Don't totally give up on Lauren; that could work itself out at some point if it's meant to be. I've seen you, you sly dog. Talking real loud in class, making funny comments to me, hoping she'll notice, getting into little quick conversations with her." *How did she...* "Who knows, maybe that could be an opening down at Chuck's one weekend. But for now, I'm just saying, play the field. And relax."

"Got it. More women. Less concentration. Calming

down, now."

Later that day

It was around five-thirty, and I was starving. I hadn't started drinking yet and no one besides Chris was home. Quite honestly, I wasn't quite sure what to do with myself. Friday afternoon, no one to talk to, no one to go down to Chuck's with.

"Yo Eddie, you want to get some food!" I shouted up the stairs at Chris's room.

"What?"

"Do you...want...to get...some food!" I shouted, again.

"I'm sorry," Chris said, stepping out of his room, from which the TV was blaring. "What are you saying?"

"DO YOU WANT TO GET SOME FUCKING FOOD?!" I said.

"Yeah, sure. Give me a minute?" Chris said, pausing as he looked down. He wasn't wearing any pants, so the minute to change wasn't so much a question as it was a statement.

There wasn't too much discussion about where we were headed; that was pretty much already decided. We had a favorite spot, Delmonico's, an Italian restaurant (or at least the closest thing to it in Syracuse by my snobbish standards). The only thing he and I did more than eat/drink together was play baseball (or whiffle ball) together.

I was actually the one who introduced Chris to the other two guys who would become part of the quintet in the senior-year house—Matt and Colin. As I recall it, there wasn't a cloud in the sky on that particular early September day. I wasn't fully aware of how bad the weather was and how quickly it could change. My first few experiences with Syracuse weather were, quite honestly, entirely positive. The initial visit to the school must have been the nicest, sunniest day Syracuse had ever seen. Chris and I developed a theory that the University had some sort of contract with the people who controlled the weather to make every fall Friday and spring Monday that prospective students came to visit a gorgeous, sun-drenched day. The other six days of those weeks? Miserable. But what the hell did those young kids know?

And so, with the weather so nice, I strolled into Chris's room and politely asked him to stop doing his work and play catch.

"Come on, you loser, stop doing all your work, and let's go and play catch," I said, not really raising my voice as much as the words might suggest.

Not yet bothering to look up from his work, Chris responded, "Ehhh...I can't. I really need to finish reading this psychology article."

"Oh, come on, quit being such a pussy," I said courteously, leaning up against the door frame. I ambled towards Chris's closet, took out his glove, and gently tossed it onto the desk. "Let's go. I promise you, the electricity isn't going to go anywhere. You can read about Sigmund freaking Freud when it's dark out."

Chris may have taken studying seriously, but he never was hard to convince. He put the book down and we began the walk down the hall towards the stairs that would take us the four floors down to the courtyard. Once there, we began discussing how things were going early on with school and, more importantly, friends.

"You liking your roommate?" Chris asked.

Thwwwwaattt.

"Yeah, he's a pretty cool dude. Gotta admit, I was a bit nervous about it at first, but he's real cool," I said, firing back another ball at Chris.

"Oh, yeah, that's good. What's his name again?"

"Matt. Matt Reilly. You meet him yet?"

"Nope, don't think so. I haven't really been introduced to a lot of people on the floor yet, besides my roommate Dan."

Thhhhhhhhwwwwwwwwwwwwack.

This one came in seemingly harder than the other throws. "Yeah, I take it that's going swimmingly...." I said, trying not to let my voice be too rife with sarcasm.

With a grunt, Chris explained, "I don't know. He and I just don't get along. We don't really talk much at all and his side of the room is a fucking pigsty."

"Well, I know I've only known you for a little bit, but from what I've seen, you do happen to keep your room like an army barracks. Don't you think you're being a little judgmental?"

"No. Not at all. He paints in his bed for class, he eats in his bed. He has showered....twice...I believe...and I may be gifting him one shower. I'm not sure."

"Okay, that is gross. Good point," I concluded. "Well, I need to introduce you to Matt. He's a good dude. Kind of looks like Jeremy Shockey; the kid is built like a linebacker. But he's got the voice of a cartoon. Not as silly, but not as serious as his body looks. You'll see what I mean right away."

Laughing, Chris caught my next toss.

I continued. "Also, this kid Colin, he's British, or Scottish, or Welsh, or some shit. I don't know, exactly." I paused to consider. "How would I describe Colin? Let me put it to you this way: he looks like one of those kids that was a brainiac in high school and skipped a bunch of grades and is now in college when in reality he's only twelve and should still be in the sixth grade. Kind of like Doogie Howser, I guess."

Laughing again, Chris nearly dropped my throw this time. The toss continued for a bit longer, nothing of any importance happened the whole time. To this day, I can't say for sure what it was about this moment that made it memorable. Many of my memories with Chris, Matt, Colin, and Natalie were just as simple, just as humdrum. Maybe it was the mundane nature of the memory that kept it so relevant. Or, more likely, maybe the rest of my life was so pathetic that even the seemingly insignificant stuck out as the most important.

Walking towards Chris's Cubby-blue Jeep Wrangler, we saw Lotfi heading back to his house from campus. The people in my life outside of those who lived in the house floated in and out without any real pattern. Lotfi was a prime example. Sometimes I would see him several times a day, other times I'd go a week without even so much as seeing the back of his gargantuan melon.

"Lotus!" I shouted. That was my nickname for Lotfi, as if a name (or, to be honest, a person) like that really needed a nickname anyway.

"Yo, yo," he said, in a more subdued way than usual. Something had to be going on. To anyone else, this would have sounded incessantly (even annoyingly) upbeat. I knew better than that.

"What's goin' on? You doing anything?"

"Nope," Lotfi said again, sounding unusually down, and particularly curt.

"You feeling all right?" Chris and I asked.

"Fine, fine," Lotfi said. We looked at him, as if to say *Bullshit, fine. Tell us what's going on.* "Just my back again, been acting up, 's all. I'll be fine."

I knew that Lotfi had had issues with his neck and his back in the past, but I didn't really know the severity. With Lotfi, though, I realized I'd never get a straight answer. So I continued. "You have plans for dinner? We're going to—"

"Sure," he said, already sounding more upbeat. He enjoyed company, pure, plain and simple. He was from the same school of thought as most grandpas come from, in that they are too tough to tell you when something is wrong. And he was also from the grandparent school in that he was generally the friendliest person you could run into. I could have said that Chris and I were going to go do anything short of bomb a mosque and he'd have tagged along. Had I said we were going to go eat at the abandoned Arthur Treacher's on Erie Boulevard, he'd have come.

The twosome having grown into a threesome, Lotfi hopped into the back of the car, tossing his enormous backpack onto the unoccupied seat to his right. I was convinced that Lotfi was the last college student on planet Earth to have a backpack that heavy and soon would be the last college student to have a backpack at all.

A few minutes into the ride, I got a phone call from a

number I didn't recognize. Some people had issues about picking up these phone calls. *Should I get this, does anyone know this (insert random) area code?* Why does it matter? Who do you think is calling, I often would say to these people. In this one area, I wasn't a hypocrite.

"Hello?" I said, in a tone that sounded as if I was asking the word more than saying it.

"Hi, is this Nick Alexander?" a female voice asked.

"Yes, this is he," I started hesitantly. *This is he*, my brain mocked. "Who am I speaking to?"

"This is Mary Pulanski. I got your number from Leah?"

Again, with these declarative sentences sounding like questions.

"Leah," I said, clearly forgetting the one Leah I knew. Then it hit me. Leah Higgins, the girl that ran Woo Hoo Comedy every two weeks in the Student Center. "Yeah, Leah, okay...."

"Anyway, I'm a TRF student here at Syracuse, and I'm directing a TV show this semester for the local channel, OrangeTV? Each week we do something different and this week we're starting with a comedian. Basically, we do a talk show and we need someone to do a five-or-so-minute set, or bit, or whatever."

"Okay," I said, not sure what to make of any of this.

"Well, would you be interested?"

"Uh, yeah, sure. When would this be? I mean, where? Actually, when and where?"

"Next Friday, you could probably show up around three-thirty. Would that work? We could move the time a bit if you needed it."

"No, no, that's fine," I said. Leah must have picked me out of the rest of the Woo Hoo Comedians, so that felt good. I'd get to pretend to be on TV, so that was good, too. "That sounds great. Do I need to do it on anything specific? Can I promote a charity show I'm planning?"

"This may sound a little ridiculous, but if you had anything on classes or school or teachers or anything like that,

that would fit perfectly. Far as the rest, we'll plug whatever you like and I'd say just don't curse too much."

"Okay...." I said, trailing off.

"Just don't say fuck, that's about all. And try not to say shit. Actually, don't say shit. Actually, sorry, if you could, try not to curse really at all. You can be dirty, just don't curse too, too much. I don't know, I guess we'll see your act and let you know. I'm sorry if that doesn't answer your question."

"No, got it," I lied.

"All right then, next Friday?"

"Yes, thanks again. I'll be there. Glad to help."

"Good. See you then," Mary said.

I hung up the phone, and it all hit me, right there. This was it. I was officially a big deal. Well, maybe not just yet, but at least on my way. Someone, somewhere, must have thought I was at least mildly funny, outside of my small group of friends. And she was a girl. Two steps in the right direction.

"Who was that on the phone on the way over here?" Chris asked as we sat down inside the restaurant. The walls were decorated with caricatures of seemingly every important Italian figure, real or imagined. Everyone from Rocky Balboa to Robert De Niro to Joe DiMaggio.

"Let me put it to you this way," I began. "I'm blowin' up like you thought I would."

"What does that even mean?" Chris asked.

"It's a line from a Jay-Z song," Lotfi started to say.

"Biggie," I corrected.

"Whatever. You do realize you can't just quote the Notorious B.I.G. like he's Ralph Waldo Emerson. You do realize that, right?"

"Whoa. All three names, Ed, congratulations," I joked. "Listen, make fun if you like. But they needed someone to do something for their show on—"

"So, *naturally*, they contacted you," Chris interrupted. "When is this happening?"

"If you'd have let me finish...next Friday. Should be pretty fun. Do the show, be a big shot, and get shitfaced afterwards. I'll be right near Chuck's anyway, by the time the taping ends."

"And what *would* you do if you couldn't get down there right away?" Lotfi said. The sarcasm oozed.

"Okay, dicks. What are we going to have to eat? Lotfi, I assume you'll be having the pork chops?" Lotfi stuck up his middle finger. He was a practicing Muslim. "Edward, you want to go halves on some East Utica Greens?" He did. The greens were basically the most delicious appetizer I had ever had. Escarole, bread crumbs, peppers, and small pieces of fried Italian meat. Then the whole thing was baked. Wowsers.

All the waitresses were dressed in pinstriped vests, white button-down shirts, short black skirts, and black hats. It looked like something from a Janet Jackson music video.

After a particularly bubbly waitress named Christy took our order, the conversation returned to its normal course. Female frustrations on the part of Chris and me, sports frustrations on the part of Lotfi and Chris, general frustrations on my part. Back and forth it would go, waffling between the ridiculousness that was going to classes with only three months left before we graduated, to the idiocy that was the last possession in the basketball game the previous night.

"You know what I can't stand?" I interrupted. "When people use the expression 'shit hits the fan.' Or 'bull in a china shop.' Or 'long story short.'"

"Who says 'bull in a china shop'?" Lotfi asked, honestly curious.

"*That's when the shit hit the fan,*'" I said in a mocking voice, ignoring Lotfi's question. "You know what, I've yet to hear a story where whatever was happening would actually be worse than shit literally hitting a fan. Can you imagine how much of mess that would make?"

"What is wrong with you?" Chris asked.

"And don't get me started on 'long story short.' *Long story short, blah blah blah.* When people say that, you know they're just making the story longer. Just once, I'd like to hear it actually be shorter. You want a long story short?"

Lotfi and Chris inhaled, ready to say *not really*, but they couldn't get it out in time.

"A while ago, a bearded guy died for your sins. Thus, Christianity. That's a long fucking story, short."

"Okay," Chris said, pausing. "Anyway, I just think Devendorf should've passed the ball at the end. He was open, sure, but not as open as Harris under the rim. He never passes the ball, though, so I'm not really surprised."

By the time we'd gotten home from dinner, everyone in the house had already left for Chuck's. Lotfi went back to his apartment, saying he'd meet up with us later. We knew Lotfi wouldn't be joining us at any point, but if it made him feel better to leave the door open than to just be honest, it didn't really bother us.

It was just after seven-thirty when Chris and I bought our first pitcher of the night. Splitting the drum of beer, we went over our respective plans for the evening.

"I think I'm actually going to talk to her!" I shouted.

Chris didn't even respond. He just smiled.

"Yeah, I know, I know," I started, "you don't have to tell me."

We both knew how many times I had said that. And we both knew that the whole "talking to her" thing (that little issue) was really the only step left.

Taking a big swig from my plastic pint thing (glass wouldn't be the right word and it was more than a cup), I wheeled around to find the nearest bartender and ordered two more, signaling we would soon be splitting up. Usually, there would be some more conversation, some more drinking before this occurred, but we both knew the night wasn't as young as it was on Fridays past. We had moves to make (or at least pretend to make).

I refilled Chris's cup, which had barely gone down at all since the first pour of the first pitcher. Something was up.

"What's wrong with you, Ed," I asked.

"Nothing, really," Chris said, again lying and using the familiar tactic of pretending nothing was wrong when, in fact, everything was. I knew just what the problem was, or at least the general gist. Essentially, there was a girl from class (the name escaped me at the moment; I was sure it was the same name as Matt's girl, but seeing as how I couldn't ever remember her name, I was at a loss here as well) that Chris had the eye for. They'd spoken a few times, but nothing had really come of it. All Chris *really* knew, from what he'd told me in prior conversations, was that this girl was a junior and that she seemed pretty strait-laced. But she had a passable fake ID and could get into the bars without much issue.

This was the first time we found ourselves actively involved in a discussion with each other about this sort of thing. For whatever reason, Chris's main sexual conquests came while I was abroad in London. For me, my dominance came sophomore year, when we lived in different buildings.

"Do you have her number?" I asked.

"I don't," Chris said flatly. He wasn't a happy camper and it was starting to bring me down. Just an hour or so ago we were eating and drinking and being merry, but now he had a sourpuss look on his face. Not a bitter beer face, or the kind of face you make when you have too many Sour Patch Kids in your mouth. Somewhere in the middle, but with a distinct tinge of disappointment. I watched Chris looking about the room, as almost all the men were doing (constantly on the lookout for more women). But something was different in Chris's gaze. He seemed above it all on this night, like he couldn't care any less about what was going on.

As I watched Chris looking through almost everyone and everything, I knew it was only a matter of time before one of two things happened. I knew Chris was going to wind up leaving Chuck's at some point; it was just a matter of when and in what state. The first option had him leaving fairly soon, depressed but not too drunk. The second possibility had him drinking all night, then leaving even more depressed and telling anyone who would listen how bad his life was. I (and all my roommates) prayed for the former.

"I know I'm not one to really talk," I said, searching for

something to cheer up my friend, "but you just need to be aggressive with this whole thing. I know that's way, way easier to say than do. But, like you guys say to me, what's the worst that can happen?"

"We never say that to you," Chris said, sipping.

"Maybe not in those exact words," I said, putting my arm around Chris, "but the point's the same. You won't know until she says no and that's really the worst possible thing that could happen. Not that bad if you think about it. I know this is going to sound really fucking pathetic, but I would say to just Facebook her." I had tried Facebook in the past, with limited (read: absolutely no) success. But I continued to encourage.

"I guess I could do that," Chris said, not sold.

"Well, what other choices do you really have? You don't have her number. You're not going to ask her in person. You don't really see her that much outside of class. This is really the only option."

"I guess you're right."

"I am. Just keep it simple. Something like, 'Hey, I'm out at Chuck's right now, I never see you out that much. I'm sure you do things other than class....' I don't fucking know, something like that. Keep it light, make it something present, so that it's clear you aren't doing this instead of talking to her in person. Like, you wouldn't want to leave her a message during the week, when you could see her the next day in class. That's *way* more pathetic than what we're talking about here."

I waited for Chris to nod in agreement, which he did, and I continued.

"So, just make it like, 'I'm here, where the fuck are you, and something cute or witty,'" I said, pleased with myself.

"That's not bad. I mean, minus the cursing, I like that idea."

"Of course you do," I said, beer arrogance kicking in.

"I think I'm going to do it."

"You should," I responded. Another refill.

"I will," Chris answered, as he took out his iPhone. "Okay. Sent."

"Now, we wait," I said. I added, under my breath, "And pray."

"You know, for someone without any testicles and who hasn't actually spoken to a woman not named Stacy Alexander in two or three years, that was pretty impressive. Not bad work."

"Just because I'm extremely flawed with women doesn't mean I can't see what I'm doing wrong. I know what I do wrong, or I guess, more accurately, what I don't do at all. I know it, trust me. I just can't actually fix it." For some reason, I remained fairly lucid the more I drank. This wasn't just my opinion, because most people think they're Rhodes Scholars after a few beers. Other people had noted that they rarely saw me drunk, but really, it was that they never heard me "talk drunk." Using phrases like "more accurately" tended to aid that impression.

And so it was: Chris would be set up with Erica (I stole a glance at Chris's screen while he was messaging. And I was way off about her name being the same as Matt's girl's). The two would wind up going out for dinner the following week after a few messages and soon thereafter would have hooked up. School would end and the two would still be together. Besides one Cubs victory during freshman year where they'd hit a walk-off grand slam to win a very important playoff-race-implicating game, I hadn't seen Chris nearly as happy as when he was with Erica. Chris's girl issues had been solved.

But, at the present time, none of this had occurred, aside from the fact that Chris's misery was averted for the time being. I knew I had lost even more time. It was now close to ten and I was drunk. No questions asked, definitely drunk. I'd gone to the bathroom twice (once outside by the dumpsters, for those keeping track), and felt a third trip coming on. The seal, as they say, had been broken.

By the time I noticed the time again, I'd been on a whirlwind tour of the bar. I'd run into Matt, Natalie, and Colin. The four of us had sat down at a table for a bit, then taken a stroll around the bar: "the walk," as Matt called it. He was truly an Aerospace Engineering student, literary creativity not his strongest suit. Natalie and Colin were deeply engaged in some sort of card game that I couldn't really understand. Kings, it might have been called; I wasn't sure. I was too drunk to learn any new games at this point and besides that fact, I was mesmerized by the cards themselves. Natalie had bought a pack of plastic playing cards that were designed to be used on wet surfaces, so as not to get ruined by liquids. Say, for instance, beer.

"But they're not made of paper?" I asked incredulously.

"No, they're not," Natalie laughed. I had asked some variation of that question four times now.

From my seat, even walking around, I came very close to Lauren. I saw her, many times, in very approachable situations. She normally didn't have a whole pack of friends (guys or girls) around her, which would make it easier for the normal male. Honestly, she didn't seem like the kind of girl who was *really* that hard to approach.

Maybe it was a fear of rejection that served as my roadblock. Though, don't most people fear rejection? I really could only think of two times in my whole life when I'd been patently rejected by someone or something. Both came during my first two years of high school. Freshman year I was rejected by the basketball team and sophomore year by a blonde-haired girl named Elaine. Though I got over those two specific instances soon enough, I never was able to mentally get over the hurdle of "What if she says no?"

Something in me made me think women didn't want to talk to me. I figured if an ugly girl came up to me, I'd try to get out of it at all costs; and I simply flipped that situation on its head, figuring most women wouldn't want to talk to me. Now, this isn't to say that I was a stud lacking only in confidence. Far from it. Yet I also wasn't the physical reject I imagined myself to be. I was somewhere in the middle, like most people.

Sitting there watching Colin and Natalie play cards, I desperately wanted to do something proactive. *I'll go and get a beer*, I thought, *and I'll "run into" her on my way up there. Yeah, that'll work.* So I got up without saying anything. I was on a mission.

She was standing near a corner of the bar, not by herself, but not really talking to anyone specific. It was clear that she could be taken away from the "group" she was standing with. All I had to do was continue on my natural path towards the bar. If things worked according to my plan, I'd buy her a drink. People had always told me that the whole "can I buy you a drink?" line was completely played out, but I didn't care. I was desperate and I needed something to break the ice.

As I got closer I realized that, for the life of me, I couldn't figure out how I could have nothing to say to her. Of all people, Nick Alexander, the comedian, the talkative, chatty one in the group, had nothing to say. I couldn't think of a thing.

I can't do this. I can't fucking doing this. I was still a decent distance away in terms of bar-measurement (which factors in music volume, crowd density, and open walking lanes).

Looking around the bar again, I caught Matt's eye. Matt saw where I was heading and pumped his fist in the air, mouthing something to the effect of *Yes! Go get her!*

Still, I was having second thoughts. Well, not really second thoughts so much as a recurring attack of "vaginitis," as Matt had termed my condition. Symptoms of vaginitis included inability to talk to women, "pussing out in social situations around females," and generally acting like a wuss. Maybe it was the air in the bar, but for whatever reason, my vaginitis seemed to really act up when I was at Chuck's.

Now I was only three feet away from her. My heartbeat was off the charts. *Calm the fuck down. Jesus Christ. What is wrong with you?!*

Rethinking my idea of buying her a drink, I decided I'd call an audible. I'd head to the bar first, buy myself a drink, and *then* on my way back, run into her. That was what I'd do. I was sure of it.

Signaling with my hands, I asked for a bottle of Bud Light. I was in such a rush that I paid with a ten, leaving a nine-dollar tip.

When I turned around, I lost my breath for a moment. *Where'd she go?* I wondered, scanning the bar. Maybe I'd just misremembered where she was standing...no, that wasn't it. *Where the hell did she go?* I couldn't find her anywhere. Instinctively, I looked towards the exits. Sure enough, there she was, her back to the bar with a coat on. She was leaving.

"Well, I screwed it up again," I said as I got back to the table.

Not looking at me because of the game he was engrossed in, Colin responded half-heartedly with a "Yeah?"

"Yeah, I was going to go up and talk to her. At first, before I got my beer. Then I was like, no, wait 'til *after* you get your beer. And then I turn around, after I got my beer, and she's gone. Just like that. Gone."

"How do you know that she....Game! Game!" he shouted, slamming his remaining cards down on the table. "Sorry. How do you know she left? She's probably still here."

"Nah, I saw her actually leave."

"Well, that about solves that, doesn't it?" Colin said.

"I'd say so," I said. "How the hell do you do it? How do you pick up women? I mean, not you, Colin. I know you can't and don't pick up women, but how does anyone do it? How do you, er...how does *one* go up to any old woman and just strike up conversation?"

"Well, for starters, not by talking to another dude at a bar when most of the girls here are already half in the bag," Natalie piped up. She was right: if there was such a time as was ripe for the picking, this eleven-thirtyish window was it. Shuffling the cards, she asked, "Colin, you want to play again?"

"Yeah, deal me up again," he said. Looking towards me, he continued, "I can't be of much help here. I have no idea. Equally as clueless about women. I can pick them out of a group. That right *there*. That's a woman. And that one there; that one, too. After that, I'm as lost as you."

I laughed, not only at the joke, but at the odd significance in the humor. Freshman year, at some point very early in the fall semester, Colin and I had crossed paths on the quad. We were at a point in our fledgling friendship where we would typically give a head nod in these situations. I wasn't sold on Colin yet. I found him odd, to be honest. Maybe it was his silence, or his Red Sox hat. There was a bit of awkwardness between us. Nothing bad, only the normal awkwardness that comes from being forced to live in a close environment with seventy-five strangers.

Either way, I was walking back to the dorm when I saw Colin coming towards me. Normally, I'd have waved or maybe fist-pounded, or something to that effect. But not after what I'd just seen.

"Hey," I said with a bit of urgency, enough to get Colin to take his headphones off his ears and stop for a second. "Three o'clock. No, sorry, your nine o'clock. What is that? I just saw it coming out of Maxwell. Is that a dude or a chick? I can't tell."

It was a game I would often play, one I'd come to call "What Are You?" Funny to those guessing, offensive to those in the game. Certainly, it was an odd and forward game to play with someone you'd known for no more than a week or two.

"Uh, what?" Colin said. He had no idea what the hell I was talking about. So I repeated the question. Basically, I just wanted to know if he was looking at a man or a woman. There were breasts, a short hair cut, earrings, and an amorphous body shape. I'm sure if I'd dug deeper, I'd have found a name like Terry.

Whether or not Colin had gotten it right that time, I couldn't remember, especially in the impaired mental state I was in at the moment. But I took comfort in the fact that one of the first jokes we had shared was still funny four years later.

"Didn't we talk about this?" Natalie asked. "I thought we agreed you'd wait, relax, and let all this stuff come to you. Let it go, and let it flow."

"Why are you rhyming?" I asked.

"Don't sass me. You said you were going to relax. Going up there and pussying out and then freaking out about it doesn't seem like relaxing to me."

"I'm not freaking out," I said.

"Whatever. Just let it come to you. That's how it goes, that's how I've seen it work best. Trust me." Natalie now sounded almost like she was begging me. She probably was, if only so she wouldn't have to act as a counselor for me anymore that night.

For the rest of the night, I was only half there. I drank a little bit more and tried to learn how to play the game (again to no avail). All in all, I was stymied. I had tried, that was for sure, but even my best effort thus far this semester had left me wondering how the hell I'd ever pull something like this off.

13 thursday, february 7th

In need of an idea, I had only one place to turn for my fourth column of the semester: how to pick up women. I had no idea how to do it, but after talking to several other men (Colin, Chris, and Lotfi, namely), I guessed that most men had very little idea what they were doing.

Pick-up lines: for the not-so-confident guy

I want to put a question to any woman reading this right now. Single, not single. Whatever. At this point, I'm not going to make distinctions.

How is it that you'd like to be approached in public places?

Everyone knows those stupid pick-up lines, that Fresh Prince-style garbage.

Girl, you must be tired, cuz you been running through my mind all day.

Just this past weekend, my lack of confidence stymied me again. The lucky gal was left to her own devices. It turns out she was lucky in more ways than she could have even imagined.

You see, the truth, at least as far as I see it, is that there really are no good pick-up lines. The men who have to use pick-up lines (uh, me) are the ones who aren't good enough at anything else to get the woman in the first place.

Do you think any of the guys on the basketball team go up to women and say, "Excuse me, young lady, but I would like to let you know that I play for the inter-collegiate basketball squad here on campus. May I purchase you an adult beverage?"

No, they don't have to do that. Simply being alive and enormous is enough. Yet the rest of us mere humans don't have that luxury.

Contrary to what you might imagine, I absolutely clam up. I have nothing to say to this person, nor can I think of any reason I'd ever have anything to say to her, ever. I actually, and I swear this is true, almost went up to a girl and told her that I couldn't think of anything to say to her, but would still like to buy her a drink. Talk about being a quitter.

I obviously don't have enough confidence to try even that.

People like that belong in the hall of fame. Can you imagine that, a hall of fame for men? No athletes, no musicians. Just regular men.

A gold plaque for John Q. Pimp: Career Highlights: More than 125 random women picked up at bars, saloons, socials, etc. Has been with women between 5'2" and 6'7". Favorite Line: "Girl, you must be a ticket, because you've got fine written all over you."

Essentially, ladies, consider pick-up lines to be a fairly harmless trap. We're the Elmer Fudds of the world, desperately searching for you, the Bugs Bunnies of the world, if you follow the metaphor. Really, all the effort we put into those lines are just to trick you into speaking with us for a few minutes more, and we'll do anything to try and see that through to the end.

I had to say, I was pretty happy with the column. Not too many e-mails this time around, but a few kids in my class thought it would be *just hysterical* to start giving me advice. Any time a column of mine had some sort of question in it, anyone who read it would find it a truly hysterical (and, of course, original) opportunity to needle me with responses.

Later that night, back in my room, I stowed myself away. I had a routine to practice. Friday was my television debut. Closed circuit for student television, that is. But television, nonetheless.

14 friday, february 8th

What should I wear? I couldn't dodge the question all day. In fact, at this point, it was starting to cause a problem.

"When's that stand-up thing?" Natalie asked from the kitchen into my open room. She could hear me shuffling around, opening and closing drawers.

"What was that?" I asked back. I was in my walk-in closet at the time. (Yes, I had a walk-in closet. The room was a woman's a year back.)

"I said," Natalie began, walking into my room, "when is your stand-up thing today? You're still going to be able to come out tonight, right?"

"Yeah, no doubt. I'll be there," I said. I was wearing a button-down shirt that was supposed to have that worn-out look. The kind of look that was a bit rumpled, but with a sort of sexy disorganization. "It's at...holy shit. It's in ten minutes! I've got to get moving. Thank you."

Hurrying out of my room while she was still in it, I paused in the hallway between my room and the bathroom.

"Looks great. I'd consider zipping up, but other than that, you're fine."

I hadn't zipped up my fly. She was right. Doing that

quickly, I thanked her again and bolted out of the house. This was the first time I'd been asked to do something like this, and I was going to be late? Great first impression.

How had I even gotten to the point where I was cutting it this close, anyway? I wasn't sure. I had hopped into the shower about an hour ago. Then I got into a conversation on Instant Messenger with a friend from back home. Checked my e-mail and saw I had something in it from a few professors. I didn't bother reading any of them, as the first e-mail I'd clicked on was a Facebook notification. Someone had written on my wall. Naturally, that took precedence.

Jogging towards the building that held the TV studio, I figured that in all that excitement, I'd lost track of time. All said and done, I was only a minute or so late. No one even seemed to notice me when I walked into the room.

In the far corner of the room was a lit TV studio that looked surprisingly professional for a class project. Camera people and assorted crew members were scattered about, everyone's attention focused on the action taking place on the set.

That set consisted of a two-person green sofa, a desk made of what looked like fake wood, and a maroon background. A tall black guy sat on the desk, apparently interviewing a cute blonde-haired girl sitting in the closest seat on the couch. I assumed the black guy was the host. He had jet-black hair that looked like it was overly styled, but he was dressed extremely sharply, wearing a charcoal gray sweater, white button-down, and matching gray pants. The girl I couldn't see quite as well, but she looked very cheerful, smiling broadly.

I stood in the back of the studio for a few minutes, wondering where to go. To my left I saw a control room, where I guessed the director and the other technical people were working. I decided I'd take a seat in a chair that was about ten feet ahead of me.

"Can I help you?" a voice asked, accompanied by what felt like a small hand tapping me on the shoulder. I almost fell out of my chair.

Turning around, I saw a girl with a headset on, wearing nondescript clothing and a facial expression to match. I couldn't tell if she really wanted to help me, was annoyed that she didn't know why a stranger was in the studio, or just generally had a dour personality.

"*Can I help you?*" she repeated, this time actually sounding a little pissed off.

"I'm sorry?" I wasn't exactly sure why she was giving me an attitude. I returned it in kind.

"Excuse me, but we're taping a show for a class here and unless you're in the class, you can't be here right now."

"But I was told by Mary to be here," I paused to look at my cell phone, "at three-thirty. This is Studio A, right?"

"Yes, it is. Mary told you to come?" She sounded as if she didn't believe the words she was saying. "Who are you?"

"I'm Nick Alexander. I'm here to do a stand-up bit for the show, at least that's what Mary Pulan..."

"Lanski. Mary Pulanski. She's the director."

"Yes, her. That's what she told me. So I just wanted to know where I had to go or what I needed to do or when you guys would need me. Just let me know what I need to do to get out of your hair."

"Let me ask her," she said, seeming almost annoyed that *the comedian* was here. Pushing a button on the device resting on her belt loop, she asked, "Can I get a hold of Mary? Anyone know where she is?" Waiting for an answer, she held up a finger at me, giving me a look like *Just a minute, big shot.*

I had no idea what I'd done to have her acting like this. All I'd done is what I was told. They wanted me to come, so I showed up. This girl had something up her ass, I was certain of it.

Just then, I heard something come through this girl's headset.

"Okay, okay. Sorry, I'll send him there...okay, got it. All right, already—he's on his way." Taking her finger off the button, she said, "Jesus. All right, go back in that room over there. She's waiting for you." She was pointing at what I had rightly assumed was the control room.

Mary was waiting for me in the room, but didn't turn as I entered.

"Let me apologize for her, first off," she said. "That girl's a massive bitch. Don't let her bother you."

"Well, no, she's just—" I started.

"A bitch," Mary said flatly. "She's like that with all our guests. The only reason she's still the floor manager is that no one else in the class wants the job. For some reason, she still wants to do it. Whatever."

"Well, okay. I, uh...I'm sorry for being a little late. I...."

"You were late? Don't worry about it. We'll be ready for you in about fifteen minutes. Is that going to be enough time? If not, let us know; we can move it back."

"No, no. That's fine; whatever you guys want," I answered. This girl didn't sound at all like the passive person I'd spoken to on the phone a week prior. *This* Mary was a high-powered, wheelin'-and-dealin' director. It was a turn-on. So was her ass, but that's really neither here nor there.

She still had barely even turned to face me; she was so focused on watching all the screens directly in front of her or shouting into her headset for this person to do that and that person to do this. I figured my debriefing was finished, so I turned towards the door, still not exactly sure where to sit until I was needed.

As I placed my hand on the doorknob, Mary shouted out after me, "Don't go back out there. From that door you came in, go out that door. Make a right, and the second room down the hall on your left, go in there. That's the green room we've had set up for you."

I was sure she was fucking with me. A green room? For me? Get the hell out of here. I didn't even think those things actually existed. As I was about to stutter out something like *Are you serious?,* she cut me off. "I'll have someone come and check on you in a bit. Give you a heads-up when we'll be needing you. Go relax. Thanks again for showing up on time."

"But I wasn't...." I stopped. A green room? I couldn't get over it. *Snap out of it, you idiot,* I thought. *It's probably just a small room, that happens to have green wallpaper.*

When I walked into the room a moment later, I nearly lost my breath. The room wasn't much bigger than my room at home (which wasn't big at all), but there were two leather recliners pushed up against the far corners of the room. On the wall opposite the chairs hung a flat-screen television. A table with bottles of water, cans of soda and energy drinks, and a few bags of candy (*were those Sour Patch Kids?*) lined the other wall.

What the hell is going on here? This can't be for me. No way. I'm just going to sit down and watch whatever is on this gorgeous, enormous, beautiful television. Okay, Sports Center. Just a coincidence. Every guy likes ESPN, not a big deal...Those are Sour Patch Kids. Again, has to be a coincidence. Ginger ale, too? Bottled water? Okay, stop it. No way on earth this shit is for you. Just sit down, watch TV, and practice your routine.

Trying to concentrate over the drone of reports on the Dallas Cowboys' upcoming game against the Redskins, I stared deeply into my red spiral notebook. This notebook had pages and pages of anything even remotely funny that I'd thought of over the past two years. Ideas, observations, full bits: they were all in here. For this show, I went back and found some material I'd written about classes and teachers.

I had a bit about choosing classes. That one had gone over well the time I'd first done it. Unlike real comedians, I didn't often repeat material. It wasn't a show-off move. I didn't do it to prove to people that I could think of new stuff all the time. Rather, I didn't want to let my friends down. They weren't paying to see me, but I appreciated them coming to my shows and I wanted to give them the best show I could. And I knew that not repeating myself went a long way towards that. Would it have been more beneficial to my comedic development to be able to craft jokes and refine them on stage via trial and error? Sure, but I put that aside because I didn't want to disappoint anyone in the audience.

As I was going over the bit in my head, thinking of exactly how to place that punch line of thinking MAG 205 was a class on magic and not magazine journalism, there was a knock at the door.

I looked up, assuming that whoever was knocking would come in. They didn't.

"Uh, come in," I said.

"Nick, how are you? Everything okay in here?" a short, square-faced girl said. She seemed pleasant. At least compared to the first girl.

I wasn't sure how to answer. "Yeah, everything's fine. Is this," I said, pointing to the table of drinks and candy, "for me?"

"Yes," she chuckled. "Of course. I see you haven't had anything yet. Please, take whatever you want. If there's anything else you need, just pick up the phone and ask for Meghan. Mary said to tell you that we're going to be needing you in about five minutes or so. That okay? Also, what is the information for your show? The one you had said you wanted to promote?"

"Yeah," I said, trying to hide my deer-in-headlights confusion. I hadn't even noticed the phone mounted on the wall to my right. Not that I *needed* anything anyway, but still. "It's called...well, I think I'm going to call it *I Hope God's Wearing Earmuffs*. Now that I think about it, I don't have a date for it. Or a venue. That could be an issue."

"No, no, Trevor's great," she said, referring to the show's host. "I'll tell him the name of the show and we can just have it as something people can keep their eyes open for."

I cleared my throat to indicate that I was fine with that, but without a word she was gone.

I glanced at the table and though I didn't want any of the soda, I felt like I could go for a bottle of water and some candy. After I polished off one of the former and two of the latter while rehearsing what I'd say, Meghan came back into the room.

"We're ready for you, Nick."

Getting up from my seat, my only actual fear of the day hit me right away: makeup. This, for some reason, scared me more than doing standup comedy on television. The thought of makeup. Unbelievable.

"Why, is that a problem?"

"No, no problem. It's just, Mary never really said anything about it, that's all," I said sheepishly.

"Well, it is television. So I'm afraid you're going to have to have some makeup put on you. I'll tell the makeup artist to go easy on the rouge, okay?"

I puffed out a chuckle. My mind wasn't fully with her, walking back towards the studio. Even as I was getting makeup applied, I still couldn't believe what was going on. Half of my brain thought I was dreaming. The other half was certain I was dreaming. A green room filled with stuff for me, a personal assistant/liaison for the day, and the general idea that whatever I wanted was what was going to happen. I got the impression that if I wasn't ready when they asked, they'd wait.

"Where's the talent?!" I heard Mary shout. She was glancing around, then turned to look in my general direction. "Oh, okay, there you are," she was saying. I turned around to look behind me, curious to see who the talent was. Mary went on, "Nick, are you ready? Makeup almost good to go? Ready here?"

She was talking to me. *Did she just call me "the talent"? That's pretty cool*, I thought. I hopped onto the stage, still not 100% sure what the hell was going on. Was I going to sit at the couch, where that blonde had sat when I came in? Would I be doing a standup bit somewhere else?

As if she were listening to my thoughts, Mary answered all of my questions at once. "All right, Nick, here's how it's going to go. We'll have Trevor—this is Trevor—we'll have Trevor introduce you. He'll be standing in front of the desk and you'll be over here, in front of the brick backdrop with a microphone. The mic isn't turned on; you'll be wearing this clip-on. But still pick up the mic and use it like it's live. You'll do your set and when the time is up, someone will be giving you time cues to get out. At that point, Trevor will come over, say something to you, and send it to commercial. And that's that."

"Okay," I said, stunned at the depth of her description. "What happens if I mess something up—do you want me to keep going? Should I be pausing as if there are people in the audience that might be laughing?"

"Just do it like you'd normally do a show. If you pause a lot normally, do it that way. If not, then don't. As far as screwing up, don't worry about that. We'll do as many takes as you need to get it the way you want it."

Once "action" was called, Trevor started right up: All right, next up on the show is a local comedian. He's performed all over New York City and Syracuse and has a charity show coming up later in the semester, "I Hope God's Wearing Headphones." He's a really funny dude. My man, Nick Alexander.

Thanks, Trevor. Great to be here. I'm feeling great, I've got to tell you. Last semester here at school, and that means no more struggling to get into classes. I was awful at that. One year, I really thought I lucked out, running into a course MAG 205. I thought it was about....

Later that day

Sitting down for a beer with my housemates at the Sheraton Hotel, I couldn't believe what had transpired over the previous few hours at the TV station. The Sheraton, located almost right in the center of campus, was the only major hotel located around the University, but more importantly for me and my friends, they had free food from six to eight on Fridays. The drinks there were more expensive than at Chuck's or any other campus bar, but you didn't really go to get drunk. It wasn't as if you had to stay there the whole night.

In front of me I had a plate piled with complimentary Buffalo wings, two slices of pizza, and a $4.50 Bud Light.

"Can you believe how fucking expensive this is?" I said as

I took a sip from my beer. My roommates nodded in agreement. We had no idea about the price of beer in the real world.

Almost as if I were still taking mental inventory of what had happened, I told the bunch about the green room, the free candy, and the free soda and free water. How Mary had called me "the talent," how I was treated like a big deal, how Mary had a nice ass.

"The strangest thing about it, though," I said, "was that when I actually did the set, there wasn't really an audience."

"What do you mean, there wasn't an audience?" Colin asked, mouth full of pizza.

"I mean, there wasn't anyone there listening. There were a few techies, and the camera people, and that's about it. No one was there to really laugh or anything," I said.

"Not that they would have anyway," Matt said.

"Maybe not, but it's still odd not having an audience. Or just someone to play off of. Like, I'm saying something that I'd usually wait for someone to laugh at before I continue on. But when no one laughs, or is even there to laugh at all, it kind of screws with your pacing."

They all agreed that it sounded *awful*.

"But then I'm going through that joke about your first day of classes and looking for all the hot girls in your classes so you can stalk them on Facebook. Know what I'm talking about?

They did.

"Well, yeah, so I'm halfway through that, and I fuck something up. And she goes, don't worry, pick it up from the beginning of that joke. So I just start back up again. She had told me, take as many tries as you need. I was sort of hoping they'd bring one of those scene chopper things. But they didn't.

"And they fucked up the name of my show," I laughed. "I think he said 'headphones' instead of 'earmuffs.'"

"Unc, you don't even have a date, a time, or a place for it yet," Chris said, "So, really, there's nothing to mess up." He called me the Uncle because I would fall into calling everyone "cousin" from time to time. People constantly had to remind me that just because I watched the NBA and listened to rap, it didn't mean I was black.

"So do you think you want to do something more in TV, now that you did this?" Natalie asked. She seemed legitimately curious.

"You know, I'm not so sure. I had to get makeup put on me and that was awful. It took forever and it was hot on my face. Other than that, I still don't know how much I loved the actual television aspect of it. But I did like how much of a big shot they made me out to be. That I could get used to," I said, smiling.

After I had finished wrapping up my story about the day, we finished eating, emptied our one drink apiece, and headed down to the real bar. As far as we knew, Syracuse was the only place in the continental United States where it was cheaper to get drunk at the bars than at home.

Though I appeared exactly the same, I felt a new confidence heading into the bar this Friday night. Maybe it was because I was already a little buzzed from a brew at the Sheraton. Maybe it was because I always felt confident going in, and wound up finding new ways to screw it up each week. And maybe it was my fifteen minutes of fame on the TV show earlier in the day.

I was well aware of what had happened. I had no illusions that I'd be on Jay Leno any time soon, or even that anyone would ever see the show. It was closed-circuit dorm television. And it wasn't of very good quality, either.

I didn't care. I felt important, even if there wasn't a person at the bar that would ever see the show or know I had done it earlier in the day. There is something about being called "talent" and being pampered that made a person feel an inflated sense of self.

Queen's "Fat Bottomed Girls" was blasting as we entered Chuck's. It was around nine, way later than we normally got there. As such, the place was already packed. Tables and seats were a thing of the past. It was stand in a crowd or go home.

But, in a way, the delayed start time was actually a good thing.

Normally, we would get there so early that we would have our own table or corner of the bar. We'd socialize within our group wherever we were and occasionally one of us would take "the walk" or go to the bathroom. But, by and large, it made the evening more exclusive than we probably intended it to be.

"Mind Erasers?!" Natalie asked, trying her best to shout over the thunderous noise. Mind Erasers did exactly what their name suggested, since a combination of Kahlua, rum, and Sprite, drunk as fast as possible, tends to rock your world. Truth be told, one of them didn't do too much. It was when we'd each have three or four or five that the actual neurological erasing came into play. This night seemed like it had the potential to be one of those nights. We'd gotten a late start and when the evening began with these things, it usually continued with them.

"Yes!" Chris shouted. He loved the drink—so much that he ordered another round right on top of Natalie's.

"We have to do this, I guess," Colin laughed.

Through a straw, the first round went down. Same for the second. I bought a pitcher, Colin bought another, and the rest took from those. We were set up.

By this point, we'd made it to the far section of the bar, opposite the entrance. It was a bit calmer, a few less people there. You could actually turn around without hitting someone, which was a plus.

"Yo, I'm going to the bathroom," Matt said. He wouldn't wind up coming back, as he'd run into Jamie on the way back from the bar.

"Uh, okay. See you in a bit, dude," I said. I resumed a conversation with Colin about the upcoming Super Bowl. As I turned to my left to see what Chris might have to say about it, I discovered that Chris, too, had disappeared.

"Where's Chris?" I asked, looking around the dimly-lit bar. "Or Natalie? What happened?"

"I think they're erasing their minds," Colin said, pointing towards a section of the bar about ten feet away. There, sure enough, were Chris and Natalie in a mass of people piled up at the bar.

By the time Colin and I got up to them, they still hadn't ordered.

"You guys want another round of Erasers?" Natalie said.

Chris was clearly excited. "Yeah, come on, you girls! Let's go!"

Round three, down. The first two had just started to hit me, so I was already feeling it. I bought a pitcher for Natalie and Chris. This was starting to get ridiculous already. Granted, the drinks weren't much more than three or four dollars a pop, but still, I did have some pride.

"All right, fuck it," I said. "One more. Colin, Nat, Ed?"

No one actually said no, though the look on Colin's face definitely said, "No fucking way." Still, he didn't speak up, so it was too late. Four more ordered, four more slurped up. Four rounds, two pitchers. It was now just after eleven. We were golden.

"All right, I'm going to the bathroom," I said.

"Dumpster or inside?" Natalie said.

"I'm gonna reserve the right to call an audible at the line," I said. *Reserve the right?* I thought. Maybe my vocabulary really did improve with the consumption of alcohol.

As I headed back from my dumpster trip, I had renewed focus. Immediately, I caught Lauren in my gaze. She was straight ahead of the entrance, at the far wall. Before I did anything, though, I had to go and get a drink. It wasn't that I felt I needed another drink. No, not at all. Rather, when you go outside to go the bathroom, you have to leave your drink in the bar which is as good as throwing it out. Going over to talk to her without a drink in my hand this late in the night at a bar would be like wearing jeans without pockets. I needed something to occupy my hands and a cup would do the job admirably.

There weren't many people lined up in the spot where I had gotten through to the bar, so I felt fairly confident about my ability to get the bartender's attention.

"Uh, can I have a bottle of...Miller Lite?" I wasn't pausing to go through my mental Rolodex of personal favorites. No, I was just trying to think of any kind of beer. Far as I was concerned, they mostly tasted the same and they all did the same thing. If there was one thing I hated, it was when people were beer or wine connoisseurs, giving human traits to alcohol.

This wine has a witty, dark aroma, more pungent than strange. It's best with steak, fish, and a good movie....It starts out tasting nutty, but finishes with a sinister punch, something more romantic than decadent.

Fuck those people, I thought. *I can't stand here getting annoyed at them; I've got shit to do.*

And so I left, beer in hand, dollar tip on the bar. As I looked towards where I'd seen her, I realized she wasn't there any longer. Her friends, or at least the people I'd assumed were her friends since I'd always seen her come in with them, were all still here. She had to be here.

And just as I was going to go searching, I found her. By the grace of God, she was alone, or at least as alone as you can be in a packed house. Between a floor beam and the opposite corner of the actual bar, not more than an NBA player away from me.

Approaching, all I could think about was how I'd strike up a conversation. I could talk to someone right near where she was standing and work her in. I could also grow a pair of testicles and simply do what most men have been doing for years and years: say hello. Oh, how much harder it was to say than to do. Even when drunk.

"Hey, Nick Alexander!"

What the fu—

"Nick!" she shouted again. Yes, my eyes confirmed that my brain wasn't playing tricks on me. Lauren was yelling at me. Why was she calling me by my first and last name? How did she know my first and last name?

"Uh, hey," I said, in a mix of confusion, embarrassment, and a completely obvious attempt to appear cool. "What's going on?"

"Nothing much," she said cheerily. She looked great, I

thought. She was wearing something that, even if sober, I'd have had trouble describing. It was a white and black one-piece, dress-type thing. Imagine a white undershirt with a black dress sewn on top of it. Despite the oddity of the outfit, I was stunned by her. Her hair was slightly matted from the humidity in the bar, but it still shone bright and blonde. As always, her rounded face appeared full, vibrant, and seemingly devoid of any makeup or other enhancements.

"How long have you been here?" I asked. *Stupid, stupid! How long have you been here? What kind of question is that?*

"Uh, pretty much all night," she said, sipping from a straw out of a plastic cup filled with ice and some drink I couldn't identify.

"What are you drinking?" *Okay, not bad. Getting better....*

"Vodka and Sprite. I know, pathetic, right? Beer's so cheap here, why not that? It's my drink, so sue me," Lauren said.

"I don't mean to be awkward," I started, "but I'm curious. How'd you know what my last name was?"

"Oh," she said, laughing. Her smile was wide and white. *Say you read my column religiously, say you read my column religiously.* "I think I heard Edington call you by your last name at some point during class."

"Ah," I said, a layer of disappointment hanging over my tone.

"And I've read a few of your columns," she said. "Not bad."

"Not bad, huh? Tell me how you really feel," I laughed. "I can handle it, trust me."

"Well, to be honest, I think you make fun of women too much," she said.

"Oh, no, come on. That was just a few articles."

"Yeah, a few in which women were the central targets. Seems like you've got some issues with women, and with confidence, Mr. Alexander. Every column, or at least every other one," she said, a wry smile creeping over her face. Was she flirting with me, or just acting that way because it was near midnight and had been drinking for quite a while? I couldn't even say whether or not this was how she normally acted. I'd never had any real conversation with her before.

"Okay," I said, mockingly raising both arms in the air, "You caught me. I have a few issues. Don't we all? I'd say so."

Taking a big sip from her cup, she said, "Definitely. Take me right now, for instance. I have an issue. I just finished my drink and I need to go get another one," she laughed.

"Let me get it. What was it again? Vodka, Sprite? Come on," I said, holding out my hand. She grabbed it, following me towards the bar.

We talked for the next forty-five minutes, discussing everything from our families to how often we went out during the week to what we had in mind for after graduation. All of a sudden, I was in the zone. I was making jokes, I wasn't holding onto any story too long, I was asking enough questions, appearing to listen to the answers (as if I could honestly be bothered about what her oldest sister out of four was doing now, five years out of college). Sitting down at a table, I found myself side by side with the girl I'd been obsessing over for four years.

It was near one-thirty in the morning and I was exhausted. I had felt her leg rubbing up against mine for a bit now, her hand on my shoulder every so often. We'd been energetically talking for a while. The Mind Erasers and all the beer and all the conversation were wearing me down. I decided to go in for the kill.

"Listen, I'm really tired. I think I'm going to go home in a bit. You want to come with?" *Oh my God, no! No, no! I didn't just say that! That was the best I could come up with?*

"What?" she said, not in a "no way" tone but in a legitimate "I didn't hear what you just said" tone. I'd gotten a second chance. I had to think quickly. This girl wasn't going to come home with me, but I needed to get something out of this evening. A phone number, future date, something.

"You like basketball?"

"Yeah, I guess so. Where does that come from?"

"I have two tickets to the Villanova game tomorrow afternoon, but I need someone to come with me. If I can't get anyone to come with me, I'm probably going to wind up just wasting the tickets. You wouldn't want that, would you?"

"I would love to come, really, I would. I just don't know if I can tomorrow. I have a study group thing at four-thirty in the afternoon, so I don't know. What time does the game start?"

"Oh, that's no problem. Game's at noon, so you'll have plenty of time," I said. I couldn't decide if she looked like she was telling the truth. Women, it seemed to me, were just busier than men. When it came to making time for a girl I found attractive, I figured that there were probably only five or six hours out of the one-hundred-and-sixty-eight-hour week that I was not available. The rest were on notice, or already free.

Her expression of concern seemed to lift a bit. I thought I might have her convinced.

"Well, come on, what do you say? The tickets aren't that good, but we'll be there and it's a big game. And, to be honest, I don't even really want to go with you, but it'd be a sin to waste the tickets."

"Oh, well, if you put it that way...." she said, her arm playfully extending to push me away.

"Why don't you just say yes, already? Come on."

"Okay, yes. Here's my number," she said, reaching for my phone and entering it on my keypad. "I live at the corner of Ostrom and Euclid. Call me when you're on your way to the game, okay?"

"Sounds good, sounds great," I said, still in absolute awe. I not only got a date with this girl, but I got her number and was playfully flirting and being cute and all that crap. Where had this been?

"I'm going to get going. I'm getting really tired. Thanks for the drink. See you tomorrow?" she said. She put her hand on my shoulder, got up, and grabbed a jacket from behind her.

Just like that, she was gone.

A few minutes later, I spotted Colin, Natalie, and Chris. They were all huddled up at the bar, staring in my direction.

"Nicky!!" Natalie said.

Chris, smiling, simply stuck out his hand for a shake. Colin gave me a hug.

"Look at you! Getting numbers, making plans. Making some moves. Good for you! Look at this kid!" Natalie said. Her excitement couldn't be contained. "She was *so* into you. So, so into you."

"You think?" I said, coming back to reality.

"Oh, no doubt about it," Chris chimed in. "She was all over you, touching. Not to mention, she was with you for what? Over an hour."

"That's true. That is true," I said, half-smiling.

"What's wrong? What did you say to her?"

"No, nothing's wrong, per se. I just, I may have promised something that I might not be able to deliver on," I said.

No one responded. They had no idea what I could be talking about.

"I asked her to go to the game with me tomorrow."

"Yeah, so?" Colin asked. "What's the problem with that?"

"Well, nothing, really. Except I told her I had two tickets that would go to waste if she didn't come with me. But I actually don't have any tickets for tomorrow's game."

Chris and Colin lost it, laughing uncontrollably.

"Why would you do that?" Colin asked.

I didn't answer. Why did I lie like that? I began to laugh, a mixture of confusion at my own lie and chagrin at my own stupidity. The game was in approximately ten hours. When was I going to be able to get tickets?

"Well, you can just get up early, buy the tickets tomorrow morning, and pretend like you aren't actually a jackass when you pick her up tomorrow," Chris said, reading my mind.

"You know what's weird, at no point while I was going on with her was I concerned about the fact that my whole premise for this date was false. Here I am, just plain lying through my teeth, and it never hit me. Wow."

The lot of us left the bar, laughing at my lie. Snow flurried outside as we hit the pavement, heading back towards the house. It didn't feel nearly as cold outside to us as it might to anyone who hadn't been drinking for hours in a hot bar. Fortunately for our body temperatures, we had been.

15 saturday, february 9th

The only tickets left cost $65 apiece, an amazing rip-off considering they were in the upper deck and that I hadn't even been planning on going to begin with.

Walking back from the ticket office, I took the long way through campus so as not to pass her apartment on my route back to the house. I couldn't get the idea of lying about this whole thing out of my mind. It wasn't because I was disgusted. No, far from it. And it wasn't because I'd never done something like this before. It was more how random and completely unprovoked it was.

She'd really given me no reason to lie, no sign that I had to stoop or get desperate. But I had lied anyway and unless she turned into Tom Brokaw, I wasn't likely to get grilled about where and when I got the tickets. Still, I couldn't help but smile at the ridiculousness of it all. Never mind the sheer absurdity that I actually had a date with Lauren Parker. Never mind that she seemed to actually like me at least a little bit, on some level, for some reason. I was somehow more amazed that I felt compelled, in the midst of all the good things swirling around the previous night, to lie. And to do so quite aggressively.

"*If I can't get anyone to come with me, I'm probably going to wind up just wasting the tickets,*" I said to myself in a mocking tone. I could only laugh.

A few hours later...

I knew for sure that I didn't want to knock on her door. That I was definitely not going to do. I could text when I was outside, or when I was close. That wouldn't be so bad.

No, I would call, I decided. Calling was the most mature way to handle this. I'd call and I'd simply announce I was outside.

All I could think about was whether or not the previous night was alcohol-induced. Was she being that friendly and flirty just because she'd been drinking for so long? Was she normally that friendly? Was this a date?

Of course, not even I could be so forward as to ask her those questions.

She came out of her apartment after making me wait for a few minutes: not much of a surprise. *She is a girl*, I thought. She had on a dark blue sweater and faded jeans, all of which added up to the colors of the opponent.

"You're kidding, right?" I said, smiling. I was trying to break the tension on the first bit of the walk to the Dome. Nothing outside of general pleasantries had been exchanged up to this point: how do you feel today, some night last night, etc.

"Kidding about what?" Lauren asked. She legitimately had no idea.

"You're wearing Nova's colors, you know that, right?" I laughed.

"Really?"

"Yes, they're blue and white. We're—"

"Orange and blue," she interrupted. "Ha ha, smart guy."

"Just thought you'd like to know. So when some drunken kid in the student section wants to beat you up and I have to defend your honor, you'll know why."

"Glad to hear chivalry still exists," she said.

I did love this girl, I was convinced. Since my last girlfriend, I'd been looking for a girl who actually had something to say. A witty remark, some sarcasm, a little spunk. Lauren seemed to have it. Early returns suggested as much.

The one thing I'd yet to figure out about her, though, was whether or not she was seeing someone. She couldn't have a serious boyfriend, could she? Wouldn't he have been there with her last night, at some point? Would she just go out with some random guy when she had a serious boyfriend?

Syracuse wound up getting destroyed by Villanova. It wasn't really close after the first fifteen minutes of the game, from which point the Wildcats led by at least 18 points. Our respective hangovers (we both mentioned quite a few times that we wouldn't have been up this early had the game not been going on) got me off the hook from having to make any real food purchases, aside from an old, dry pretzel we picked on.

With about five minutes left in the game, it dawned on me that I'd yet to encounter the most awkward part of the day. Sure, our conversation had dried a bit, but that was only natural since we'd talked for an hour the night before, were both hung over, and were both at least attempting to watch the game. I realized that I'd have to do something when I "dropped her off." Hug? Kiss? Maybe a handshake?

"I can't believe we got beat that badly," Lauren said, head down as we walked back towards her apartment. It wasn't in disappointment; she just happened to be looking towards the pavement.

"Yeah, that was a whooping," I said. "I'm sure what they did to us has to be considered illegal in at least a few states, no?"

"It has to be," she said.

We walked at a slow gait, side by side, but not touching. Every once in a while, our hands swinging at our sides would touch and one of us might make a recycled joke about holding hands or something similarly stupid. We'd both laugh, regardless. The walk back had all the makings of two people trying to feel each other out, trying to gauge how the "date" (if it even was that) went; was there interest on the other person's part? As far as I was concerned, I couldn't see how Lauren could confuse my interest for anything else. Why else would I take her, and just her, to the game?

We'd been in front of her apartment talking for a few minutes now, both clearly stalling for the eventual departure. She was going to let me handle this one, or so it seemed.

"Okay, I guess I'm going to get going," Lauren said. "Thank you again, very much, for the tickets."

"Oh, no problem. My pleasure. I'm glad you had a good time," I said.

"I did, thank you."

"All right," I said. I decided a hug was the way to go. Facing her, I leaned closer, right hand in the air in front of me extending behind her. As the hand hung there in a time warp, I imperceptibly pulled it back. *No*, I thought, *go for it.* So I pushed forward and just did it. I hugged her—so what?

We left on what I saw as a fairly solid note. It seemed like she really did have a good time and it couldn't have been because the seats were any good. I wished one of us had said something fairly concrete regarding a future meeting. In fact, that bothered me quite a bit. Did she not want to see me again? Was she waiting or hoping I'd make a move like that? When could I get in touch with her again to do something? My head felt like it was going to explode.

I went about all this stuff too much like a woman, Matt had told me. Just stop thinking and be yourself, Natalie had advised. Still, I couldn't help it. These thoughts all swished around in my brain, and began, almost immediately, to cloud any positive thoughts I might have had about the previous night or that day's date. *Yes, it was a date*, I finally decided.

16 wednesday, february 13th

"Why haven't you tried to get in touch with her?" Natalie begged. She couldn't understand how four days had gone by and I hadn't even once tried to make contact with Lauren. We were assuming a fairly regular position in the living room: computers on laps, television on even though neither of us was really watching it, discussing my failed relationships.

"Well, first of all, it hasn't been four days. Today's Wednesday. That would be," I said, counting on my fingers, "one...two...three days."

"No, four. Today is Wednesday, and it's, what, five o'clock? And you still haven't called or texted her or anything. So today's over. That's four days."

"Okay, fine."

"And you barely said a word to her yesterday in class," Natalie said.

She was right; I hadn't said anything. Well, barely anything. I didn't even try my ridiculous tactic of talking louder than necessary to see if she'd volunteer herself into the conversation. Why *was* I acting like this?

"I don't know, I don't know. I probably should have said something."

"Ya think?" Lotfi laughed. Apparently he'd been in the kitchen, listening to the conversation going on between Natalie and me in the living room.

"When did you even get here?" I said, not looking up as Lotfi sat down in the faded flannel recliner to my right.

"A minute ago, came in through the back door. You should lock that, you know."

"I guess so. What, did you need a cup of sugar?" I said.

"No, just came to butt my nose into your business, is all."

"Lotus," Natalie said. "Don't you think Nick is acting like a raging pussy?"

Laughing at her candor, Lotfi answered, "I don't know if I'd have worded it the same way, but yes. I'd say he is acting like a raging pussy."

"Enough. Jesus! Why couldn't she be the one to contact me? Would that be so much to ask? If she's interested in me, how come she can't just come up to me and talk to me or ask me to do something?"

The groans elicited by this remark probably could be heard for miles.

"You can't be serious," they both said.

"What? What's wrong with that? She can't get in touch with me?"

"Oh my God, what is wrong with you? What are we going to do with him, Lotfi?" Natalie asked. "I really don't know how you ever got a woman to begin with. Ever. You've got to call her. Come on! You have to. Now it's been four days and she hasn't so much as gotten a hello from you. What do you think she's thinking?"

"I don't really know. I guess I never thought about it like that," I said. I lifted my head up from my screen, tearing myself away from my e-mail. For some reason, I was always checking my e-mail. It wasn't as if anyone ever sent me anything important, or more accurately, as if people were so constantly sending me anything important. More often, it was a Facebook e-mail or some sort of spam my computer might have picked up after I'd gone to a porn site.

"I'll tell you what she's thinking," Natalie bullishly continued, "She's thinking, 'Well, I guess this kid doesn't like me all that much, because...HE HASN'T CALLED ME!' Jeez, Louise."

"I'm not so sure she's thinking that, to be honest," I answered.

Natalie looked back at me, waiting for me to continue.

"She just didn't seem like it was anything other than two humans going to a basketball game together. She might as well have been my sister."

"Oh, come on. What gave you that impression?" Natalie asked.

"I don't know, exactly. I'm not allowed to just have a feeling anymore? She just seemed oddly uninterested while still being friendly."

"The old friend zone, eh?" Lotfi chimed in.

"Possibly. I guess it's too early to say for sure. Being her friend would be better than nothing. Then again, not too many friends have sex. So that would likely be out...."

"'Fraid so," Lotfi said. He had an odd habit of taking letters off words and talking like he was a cowboy from the early 1800s. Somehow, no one made fun of it.

There was a pause in the conversation. I broke the silence.

"Well, as much as I've enjoyed this grilling, I must be off."

"Where the hell are you going?" Natalie asked.

"Gotta go to this extra credit thing, down at Maxwell," I mumbled.

"You? Extra credit?" Natalie asked. She knew how much I avoided any extra work, even that of the compensated variety.

"Yeah, Colin and I are going. Some guy from ESPN is going to be speaking, I'm not really sure," I said.

That wasn't the entire truth. It was close, though. An employee of ESPN would be in a building in Syracuse talking to the people in the audience. That part, quite literally, was true. Also, Colin was going.

What wasn't true was why I was going. There was extra credit on the line, but I wasn't going to do it. I was going because the girl who would be interviewing Mr. ESPN was really attractive. Not my typical girl, Sophia Velazquez was half-Colombian, half-Dominican, born and raised in the Bronx. She had attitude, was a Yankees fan, and was the proud owner of one of the curviest bodies I'd ever seen.

Despite our having the same major and taking the same courses for four years, our Tuesday class with Phillips was our first encounter. And even there, we hadn't spoken much. Shockingly, I didn't really talk to any of the good number of gorgeous girls in that class. So my brilliant, multi-staged plan was to go to her event, show my face, and pretty much see what happened.

As for Colin, he was simply coming along for the ride.

"Why do I have to come with you?" he had said when I told him about it the day before.

"Because I can't go by myself. That would look ridiculous. Just me, showing up there alone? Come on," I said.

"As opposed to you showing up with a friend to something you clearly would never have gone to otherwise? No, you're right—that's much different."

"What the hell else are you doing? Honestly," I asked.

"Well, I—"

"Don't even fucking say playing Nintendo. That's all you do. I promise you, you can come right back and play when we're done. Just come," I pleaded. It wasn't really necessary; Colin was coming anyway. That's not meant to be insulting; he really didn't have anything else to do.

"What's this guy's name, do you even know?" Colin asked.

"Nope. I probably was told a few times, but I wasn't listening. I honestly don't care who it is. I care more about how long it is. I plan on just walking to the back, sitting there, maybe taking a little nap depending on the lighting, who knows," I said.

"You really are a classy kid, you know that?" Colin

laughed.

"Look at it like this: tonight's an investment. Show our faces, well, my face. She sees that I came to something of hers, and then maybe this weekend, maybe next, at some point, it could pay off. I mean, it's not like I'm going with the intent of hooking up with this girl on a Wednesday night."

"Who are you?"

"What's that supposed to mean?"

"Well, the Nick I thought I knew never made these sorts of little power plays. Making moves, and not just that, but making moves that are setting up future moves. Impressive, but you've got to admit that it's a little odd, for you at least."

"Well, yeah. I guess so, I mean, I don't think it's that amazing, what I'm doing. If I had any backbone, I'd have asked her out to do something, straight up. Matter of fact, I'd have done that with Lauren a while ago. So I'm not that different."

"What ever happened with that?"

"With what? Lauren?" I said. Colin nodded, as if to say *Who else would I be talking about?* "Jeez, everyone's asking me about that. I don't know dude, I just don't know. We had a great time at that game, but then I didn't really call her, and we didn't talk much during class, and all of a sudden it's weird. I have no idea what the hell happened. I'm not done, but I'm fucking confused."

After walking in the back entrance so as to easily grab a seat in the depths of the auditorium, Colin and I settled in. A few minutes later, Melissa, a friend of mine since freshman year, sat down next to us.

I asked her what the hell she was doing there, and she responded with something about extra credit. When she asked me, I answered: same. No need to get into it with her.

"So, what's your deal with women these days? You always seem to have a few lined up, a few schemes," Melissa giggled. Okay, maybe there was a need to get into it. The ESPN guy wasn't yet at the stage, so we continued our conversation. Then again, I'd have kept talking even if the interview had already started.

Why is she asking me this? I wondered. The two of us had never been anything other than friends, so it was clear she wasn't coming on to me. I couldn't figure it out.

"Why do you ask?" I said, figuring that playing it close to the vest to start would probably be the best option.

"No reason," she came back with.

"Oh, come on, what the hell does that mean?" I laughed. Maybe she was asking for a friend. But which one? She wasn't friends with Lauren, so far as I knew.

"Oh, nothing. I'll tell you later; it's about to start."

"No. Tell me now. Come on."

We bickered back and forth. I stole the notebook she was furiously taking down notes in. She smacked me on the head.

There was something about overachiever types that bothered me. That "worker-bee" type, buzzing around, taking down notes on everything, asking a zillion questions, always early to class. *Fuck these people*, I said as I looked down from my white horse on the rest of the kids in the auditorium taking notes.

It was this ridiculous duality that I worked hard to maintain. I wanted to appear, at least to those who only knew me casually, as if I were a slacker. The kind of kid that didn't really give a damn about anything or anyone. On the other hand, those who knew me, such as my roommates, knew that I was quite possibly one of the most neurotic people on the planet. While I reveled in being a dick, I'd immediately feel remorse for it. While I'd show up for class ten minutes late and then talk the entire time, I worried about what effect it might have on my grade.

"So, are you seeing anyone?" Melissa said, interrupting our silence. The speaker was droning on about something regarding the importance of Nielson ratings.

Leaning in close to her, I put my arm around her and cooed, "No, are you?"

"Nick, stop it," she laughed. "I'm serious, what's your

deal?"

"My deal? Come on, you know my deal. I've been complaining about two things since I met you. Women and sports. Neither has really changed. What's with the sudden curiosity?"

"No reason, really," she said, trailing off.

"Can I ask you a question?"

"Sure."

"How long do you want to play this game?"

"Do you know who Allison Goldin is?"

I thought for a second. *Allison Goldin, Allison...Goldin.* Yes, I knew who she was. Skinny Jewish girl from New Jersey. She, too, was a Yankee fan; we'd chatted about that before. She was in a sorority and was not the sharpest knife. I'd never really given her much thought.

"Yeah," I said, keeping the rest of it to myself.

"Well...?" She was trying to lead me on. I wasn't having any of it.

"Well, what? What do you want me to say?"

"Do you like her?" The bluntness of the statement hung in the air for a second, smacking me in the face. *Wow, do I like her? I guess I do. I like people who like me, people who are female who are attractive. I think I like them...*

"Yeah, I'd say I do. I hadn't really thought about it much."

"Sorry for being so weird about all this. It's just that I've heard you were with some girl from the tennis team, that's all."

"What the," I started. There was a rumor about me and a girl on the tennis team? There was a rumor about me? What was this? Where did this come from? Not that I minded at all, but I couldn't remember the last time I'd known of a rumor spreading about me. I wasn't important enough.

"Tennis team? Where'd you hear that?"

"A bunch of people in class were talking about it. Hold on for a second, don't let your head get too big, it was just a few people and it came up randomly once. Maybe twice. It wasn't like class was stopped to talk about you."

People were talking about me when I wasn't around?

Wow. It was a pretty odd thing to think about. I knew it went on, but never really thought that it actually happened to me. And to think, people seemed to be under the impression that I was with a girl.

The only girl I knew from the tennis team was a girl I'd spoken to a few times that semester, from the baseball card class. Amanda, or Ainsley, or something with an A. Either way, I'd asked her to do something once or twice, she'd been largely unavailable because of tennis commitments, and that was pretty much that. Who had I told about that? Who would know? I laughed to myself; the whole thing was simultaneously amazing and hysterical.

"What were people saying? Who was it that was even talking?" I obviously couldn't let it go.

"I don't know," she started. It was clear that she was already tired of feeding my ego. "I'm not just saying that; I really don't know exactly who it was. I'd just heard that you two were getting kinda serious and that's why I asked, that's all. You're saying you're single, so I believe you. No need to get defensive."

"Trust me, I'm not defensive. I'm amazed."

"Amazed at what?"

"Amazed that people are talking about me. Amazed that there's a rumor that I'm with a girl from the tennis team—a generally well-regarded group of girls. I mean, if the rumor was that I was with some girl from the lacrosse team, ehhh...."

"You're crazy, you know that?" she laughed. "You mind if I give Allison your phone number?"

"Yeah, that's fine by me. She seems cool."

So, on the night that I went to plant seeds with Sophia, I was approached by a fully-grown tree in the form of Allison. Who, as it happened, was in the same class as Sophia and me on Tuesdays. I didn't really let that small realization bother me much. The idea that I was desired by someone—that was just too much for me.

In my entire life, this was the first time a girl who I found out was attracted to me didn't make me want to throw up.

Harsh, sure. But most of the girls who had ever come up to me, or sent friends to do the dirty work, weren't my type. The girls I'd been with—high school girlfriend, college girlfriend, scattered randoms—were all my doing. And not by some amazing breath of suave air. No, usually by pleading and pathetic attempts to ask them out, which ultimately led to a yes (even if it was a pity yes). Ultimately, I'd win because of my sense of humor, but these women were rarely interested in me first.

There wasn't much else to consider, so far as Allison was concerned. Melissa assured me that she was interested and I did my best to play it cool, as if women were always fawning over me. Of course, no one was fooled. She knew me too well.

"Wild, isn't it?" she said, getting up from her chair as people began filing out. The lecture had ended, apparently. I had completely zoned out. I'd missed everything ESPN had said, had forgotten Colin was even there, hadn't taken a single note (not that I could have, if I'd wanted to—I didn't bring a pen or pad).

I laughed, unsure of exactly what she was talking about, hoping my laughter would mask my confusion.

"I know, I'm just as confused as you are as to how it is anyone could actually stomach you," Melissa said, laughing. She was having a good time with this. Getting up, she said good-bye, and I sat in my chair, dumbfounded.

Colin smacked me on the arm. "You want to get out of here tonight, or what?"

"Yes, I want to go down there and tell Sophia how much I enjoyed this."

"But you didn't listen to a single word. What if she asks you something? Anything?"

"She's not going to ask me anything, don't worry," I said, looking through the crowd exiting the auditorium for my target.

"It's not me I'm worried about," Colin mumbled.

A few minutes later, we scrummed through the pack to

find Sophia still talking to a few people who came to congratulate her on a job well done. I stood with Colin at the base of the stage where the interview had been conducted.

Looking over at her, I was impressed. She cleaned up nice, I noticed. In class, I'd known her as the girl who wore yoga pants and t-shirts, and if it was a really special day, maybe a pair of jeans instead.

Talking to a professor, she looked my way and I caught her glance. There was a glint in her eye, as if she were happy to see me. Calming myself, I realized that in all likelihood the look derived from the fact that she was stuck in a long conversation with a professor. She shot me another look, this one accompanied by a sly smile.

I took the hint, at least as to what I thought it meant and hopped onto the stage, interrupting the professor to say hello as if I hadn't even seen the old man there in the first place.

"Hey!" I said, faking surprise.

She moved in for a hug, looked back at the professor and said something like, "Hold on—I'll be right back."

Just out of earshot of the professor and now with Colin between her and the stage, she exhaled, clearly exhausted from all the work she had put into the interview and even more from all the well-wishers mobbing her afterwards.

"Saw you were dying there a little bit, figured I'd lend a hand," I began.

"Yeah, definitely. Wow, he could've gone on forever. Anyway, what are you guys doing here?"

We looked at each other, but Colin spoke up first. "I'm just here with Nick. He was the one who really wanted to go."

"Word?" Sophia said.

"Yeah, I just wasn't going to miss this. Circled this one on my calendar months...no, years ago," I said. She laughed; I had dodged that one.

"Well, thank you for coming, either way. That's really nice of you guys. I mean it," she said, smiling.

"No, no, not a problem. We really liked it," I said.

"Did you? I can't tell. There's too many fake-ass people,

ya know?" She had a way of talking that, at times, was so Bronx, New York, it was remarkable.

"No, we both said to each other, several times, as a matter of fact, that we thought it was well done."

"You mean it? Was there anything in particular that you liked?" she asked. It wasn't an inquisition, just an insecure girl wondering if people liked her work.

I thought I heard Colin laugh, but trudged ahead, hoping to do my best bullshitting. "There wasn't anything *specific* that I can point to that I really liked. I just thought it was very...very provocative."

"Good, that was part of the point. I mean, it's cool that he works for ESPN and has interviewed all these famous dudes, but I wanted to get people thinking. So if it did that for *you*, I guess it worked," she chuckled, play-punching me on the arm.

"Ha," I gasped nervously. I was just happy that she didn't question me further.

There was an awkward pause amongst us. I looked at Sophia, who looked at Colin, who looked back at me.

"Well, all right, then," I broke in, "I guess we're gonna get going. Colin and I have to go home and fill out our Valentine's Day cards." I didn't smile. Sophia clearly wasn't sure if I was kidding or not. "Joke," I said, smiling. "Wow, annnyyywayyy, this was fun. Maybe I'll see you out this weekend?"

"Yeah, maybe," she said, blankly. It wasn't angry, it wasn't leading, it just *was*.

Hugs exchanged, Colin and I left the auditorium and walked back to the house.

"'Provocative'?" Colin laughed. He could barely contain himself.

"Yeah, I fuckin' blanked. I don't think I've ever actually said that word before. Provocative? Jeez. She seemed to buy it, though, right?"

"Yeah, I guess. She's not an easy read, that's for sure. She seemed like she was happy we were there, that we liked it.

That's good, I guess," Colin said.

We concluded that nothing tangible had been accomplished, though I didn't expect anything, either. I realized, heading home, that I'd yet to write my column for the week and it was due to be in the paper the next day. I'd completely forgotten about it, consumed with Sophia and Allison and Lauren. Women. Ironic, considering that tomorrow would be Valentine's Day, a day I never liked, even when I had women.

I had my idea.

17 thursday, february 14th

Forget the fun and romance: Valentine's Day a no-win situation for guys

And so it comes, and hopefully, so it goes. Another Valentine's Day spent alone. Sound the violins, cue up the world's smallest tear. Though, if you don't mind, I think I'd rather keep the extra money in my pocket this year.

I don't know why it is, but for some reason, women think that they're entitled to something on Valentine's Day. Why is that? At what point did having a birthday, or simply being the one that gets showered with "just-because" gifts in exchange for sexual favors, cease to be enough?

Let's be honest about those "just-because" gifts. Not that they all result in immediate bang for the buck, but we can all agree that they work at least like a point system. 50 points for flowers, 35 for a card, etc. If you get to 100, who knows what you could exchange them for?

Anyway, I could never quite wrap my mind around Valentine's Day. Maybe it's because I'm a miserable cynic who was raised by a man who hated Halloween (his reason largely draws from how much fun other people were having). Maybe it's because I eat candy every day of the year instead of just on holidays.

Thing is, there are two types of women when it comes to February 14. There's the type that really do want a celebration thrown in their honor, and there's the type that say they want nothing, but really would love anything more than nothing.

The former want streamers, balloons, dinner, candy, cards, gifts and roses. A breakfast in bed, a singing telegram delivery and two solid "I Love Yous" from that special guy. Not the kind of "I Love You" that's said to make her happy, but one that you really mean. Or at least have gotten adept enough at faking.

Cards are easily the biggest cop-out. What says "I Love You" better than generic writing from a stranger on a folded piece of thick paper?

The latter kind of girl is the biggest pain.

"No, no. I don't want anything special. Just your company, and that'll do it for me."

The interesting thing, as far as I'm concerned, is how utterly simple V-Day is for men. On my end, there are only a few things I would like to make me happy. Sour Patch Kids, sports on television and maybe something else that can't be said in these pages.

If you're curious, I did get one gift for Valentine's Day this year. Sadly, it was from a male friend of mine who, as salt on the proverbial wound, happens to have a girlfriend. Funny, yes. A painful reminder also, yes.

Despite my cynicism, I recognize the aspect of Valentine's Day that doesn't have to do with Hallmark. Love for that special someone and significant amounts of gifts for that person, too.

I guess I can afford a few extra Sour Patch bags after all. Nothing says "I Love Me" and gluttony like a self-purchased 5-pound bag of candy from the bookstore.

There were nerves associated with this particular column. Not that I said anything so racy or offensive. No, I'd certainly said and printed worse. This column made me nervous because, while reading it in the student center later that day, I realized that the people I was trying to attract (women) were the ones who most often read my column and also happened to be my subject of scorn. Whereas my other "anti-women" columns came off as glib and musing ("how do you pick up a girl in a public place?," "women confuse me," etc.), this one might have gone a bit too far. I did try to end it by painting myself as the cynical ass, lonely and confined to my own sad Valentine's Day.

The truth, though, wasn't as grim. Sure, I didn't have a girlfriend, or a girl of any kind. But I didn't mind it specifically on this day. I had a few girls in mind and that was enough to keep me going. There was Sophia, there was Allison. There was the problem that they were friends, at least casually, with each other and were in the same class with me twice a week. And, of course, there was Lauren, whom I had barely spoken to since our basketball game date. Time having passed, I wasn't sure if I was the one who wasn't talking to her, or the other way around. The development of Sophia and Allison allowed my mind, thankfully, to move on for a bit.

The plan, advanced for this week because of the "holiday," was to head to down to Chuck's tonight. We got there earlier than most to assure ourselves a table.

"See, this place is so much better like this," I said.

Chris agreed. "I hate having to sit at the bar. Too loud, too hard to talk to each other."

"Shut up and just grab a chair, you babies," Matt said.

Walking towards the other end of the bar to get chairs, I said to Chris, "Guess who I got an e-mail from the other day...."

"I...I don't know, who?" he responded. He wasn't much for guessing games. Chris was the kind of kid who, when playing the "guess-the-check" game at dinner, would guess something like thirty-eight dollars even. Invariably, I would snap back with something like, "When the hell, in your life, has a check ever, ever come out to an exactly even total? Has it ever?" And in turn, used to my biting style, Chris would feign naïveté, knowing it would piss me off even more. "It actually has a few times and don't ask me to say exactly when, because I know that's what you're going to ask next."

So I didn't exactly pause when Chris didn't guess. "Professor Johnny Edington, that's who." No one had ever called him Johnny, but I felt it made it funnier. More appropriate, even. You see, Chris and I had both had Edington as a professor at least once over the years at Syracuse. But, while I had developed something of a relationship with the surly professor, it certainly didn't start off that way.

I had heard about him, how he was a bit of a loose cannon, how he could be extremely difficult. I'd also heard that there was a cool side to him, but I never thought I'd be able to connect with it.

It was first semester of sophomore year and I had a question about a grade I'd gotten. I felt I deserved better than the C-, and at that point in my college career, I still cared about my grades. So I felt it was my duty to bring the issue up with the person who gave me the grade. That person was John Edington.

As has been mentioned, he didn't waste time and when it came to his class time, he didn't let you waste it, either. I was slightly aware of this, if only by way of legend, of those who'd dared waste in the past and lived to tell; yet I still raised my hand to ask a question after the papers had been passed out. Mid-sentence, Edington stopped and looked right at my raised hand.

"Alexander, what do you want?"

"Well, I wanted to, I mean, I would like to, if you had a minute, I was hoping to—". For clarification purposes, besides his demeanor, Edington was an imposing individual. He was nearly 6'4", with a long, drawn face that only rarely showed anything other than a blank expression.

"Are you going to be wasting my time? Because that's what this sounds like."

"No. I mean, I don't think so? No, I just have a quick question."

"You're already wasting my time," Edington said, turning back towards the rest of the class dismissively. As he began to continue with the lecture, I interrupted him.

"You know, I could also just talk to you about it after class," I sniped in a hushed tone, pissed off because I'd been embarrassed.

"No, now you can't."

"What?"

The room fell silent; no one knew quite what was going on.

"Pack up your shit and get the fuck out of my class right now. You want to know why you got a C- on that project? Is that what you're curious about? Your stand-up in front of the school parking lot was terrible. Your nat sound was barely audible, interviews were dull, and your subject material failed to intrigue. Maybe if you stopped worrying so much about grades and talking while I'm talking, and instead paid attention, you might not have bad grades to worry about."

I didn't say anything. I just sat there, stunned.

"Did you hear what I said?" Edington barked. "Get the hell out of here. Now!"

I packed up my things, clumsily shoving them and whatever was left of my dignity into my bag. For nearly the rest of the semester, I'd barely speak a word to Edington. Stubborn and stupid, I couldn't see how it was possible that I was wrong. Instead, I focused my energies on doing even less in class and being even angrier at him.

A week prior to the finals, I got an e-mail from him asking me to meet in his office later that day.

"You hate my fucking guts, don't you?" he said after I'd sat down.

Though I completely agreed, I was surprised by the

statement and didn't say anything. Instead, I shifted my gaze from the floor to make direct eye contact.

"You don't have to say anything. I know you do. And, quite frankly, I'd hate me, too, if I were you. What I did was a little over the top, but I had to make my point."

Still, I said nothing.

"You're a bright kid, Alexander. I like you—I do. But you needed to learn to shut your mouth during my class. These grades, all this run-around bullshit, you think that's important? Let me tell you something. I graduated from here about twenty-five years ago with a C average, and I worked in the business for twenty years. If you're good, you're good. Don't let pricks like me get in the way of your success. Take the criticism, take the hits. And instead of being a wiseass, instead of hating the person for it, try to make yourself better. You've got potential; you and I both know it. I wouldn't be wasting my time sitting here talking to you if I didn't think you did. You don't have to like me. Matter of fact, I don't give a damn if any of my students like me. It's not my job to be your friend. But it is my job to prepare you for that shitty world out there once you graduate. So again, I'll say it to you: You hate my fucking guts? Fine. But don't let it get in the way of making yourself better. I'll see you in class."

I left the room without having said a single word. But my entire perspective had changed. I went from hating every fiber of this man's being to completely and totally respecting him. The honesty, the foul language, the trust, the message. Everything he'd said that day truly resonated with me. From that point forward, I got along with John Edington. Sometimes I'd even stop by his office to chat during semesters when I didn't have him for a class. I even began to look to take sections of courses that he taught, so I could have him again.

"What the fuck did he want?" Chris asked, interrupting my reverie. He'd had a few beers back at the house; otherwise, he'd have simply asked, *What did he want?*

"Well, he didn't actually *want* anything from me, per se.

He wanted to know if I'd be interested in talking with someone about a job in Los Angeles after school."

The weight of the news must have hit Chris like waves crashing down, as he almost staggered back a bit. "You're a lucky sonofabitch," drunk Chris said. Once more for clarification, sober Chris would have said something to the effect of "You're a lucky guy."

"It was about how he thought I might be interested in talking with some guy he knew about a job opportunity—production?—for the NFL Network. Which, as it turns out, is out in L.A."

"What did you say?"

"Nothing, yet. I just read it, and then I checked the Facebook e-mails I'd gotten."

Chris launched into an even-more-dramatic-than-usual tirade about how much he hated Facebook and how he never went on and how he barely knew how to use it and all this nonsense, when in reality, everyone knew he went on it just as often as everyone else.

"So that's it, huh?" Chris said, with a tone of either annoyance at the opportunity or annoyance at my blasé attitude towards the opportunity.

"That is it. I'm going to get back to him on Monday," I said, as we lifted some chairs back towards the group table.

"That's so you, you know that?" Chris said, and without waiting for me to answer, he continued. "Someone you barely know, someone you made no effort to network with or butter up to, just out and out offers you a job. Some people have it all, don't they?"

"The fuck is that supposed to mean?" I prided myself on not buttering up to professors just for their potential future help. I'd become friendly with Edington on odd terms and I enjoyed staying in general contact with the man. That was all there was to it.

"Nothing. I'm kidding," Chris said, smiling. I could tell that he was kidding about the "have it all" remark, but not as much with his bitterness about the minimal effort it seemed like I put out. That was exactly as I wanted it. But when things went my way, it could rankle people like Chris, who worked much harder.

"Listen, it's not like he's offering me a job, so cool it with that, okay? He just said he wanted to put me in touch with someone who might possibly help me get a job. That's all."

We left it at that, sitting down to a table filled with pitchers and friends. Life, I thought, couldn't get much better. Slowly but surely, the place became packed to the gills. Thursday nights were dollar draft nights, so naturally there was a crowd. Add to that Valentine's Day and you had yourself a scene. It seemed like everyone in the bar—even men, surprisingly—was wearing some shade of red.

By around ten p.m., the whole lot of us was drunk. The milling-about process had begun, but the communal table and coat-resting spot had remained. I sat with Natalie and Colin on my left and right respectively, the flat-screen television and assorted tables in front of me. Chris, at the moment, had gone MIA. Last anyone had heard from him, he'd announced his intention, boldly, to "go and take a fucking piss outside." Matt was playing pool; he'd won four games in a row at this point. The only reason I knew that was because every time I'd look over in that direction, he would hold up a number of fingers to brag about how many people he'd beaten.

Some sort of amped version of a Beatles song ("Lonely People," maybe?) was blasting through the speakers. It was the sort of song that annoyed real Beatles fans and even bothered the casual ones, because it just sounded stupid to make techno remixes of classic songs.

"Why do people do this? Why do they butcher songs like this?" Natalie said in my direction.

"I have no idea, but I was thinking the same exact thing. These people should be routinely taken from their homes and executed."

"Might be a bit harsh," Colin chimed in.

"Maybe so, but that's just how I feel," I laughed. "Do we need another pitcher?" I surveyed the table, which had now grown to two tables, with the second circular one joined right up against the first. A whole other group of people who were in some way loosely connected to Natalie occupied that section. Empty pitchers stacked upon empty pitchers filled the tables, so it was easy to think that another might be necessary.

"I think...I think we're good," Natalie said, reaching for a previously hidden, near-full pitcher.

"Excuse me, sorry to bother y'all, but I wanted to ask you a question," an average-looking girl said to the group. She stood in front of the television, blocking out basically everything other than Colin and Natalie. No one really who she was speaking to, so no one answered.

"Sorry, can I ask you a question?" she repeated, this time leaning in on the table, getting a bit closer to me.

"Me?" I said, looking around. I'd never seen this girl before. She had brown hair and very forgettable features.

"Yes, you. Are you Nick Alexander?"

I broke out laughing.

"What's so funny?"

"Did he pay you to say this?" I said, looking to point out Matt.

"Who? No, no one paid me. I want to know if you're Nick Alexander. I read your column in the newspaper all the time. It's hysterical."

"I...thanks. Thank you." That was all I could say.

"Well, like I said, I'm sorry to bother you, but my friends told me that I had to come over here and tell you how great we think your writing is."

"I can't say enough how flattering that is. Your friends?" I said, again simply floored. I noticed out of the corner of my eye that both Natalie and Colin had big grins on their faces.

"Yeah, they wanted to know if we could buy you a drink."

"No, no, that's quite all right, but tell them I said thank you, anyway."

"Well, if you find yourself thirsty, let us know," she said, turning back towards her table. As she walked away, I realized what it was that Natalie and Colin were laughing about.

A group of guys, stuffed into a booth on the far wall, welcomed the girl back to their table. Catching my gaze, they all raised their cups in salute.

"You're fucking awesome, dude!" they shouted.

Ducking my head from morbid embarrassment, I grunted out something sounding like a combination of "Hey" and "Thanks."

Natalie and Colin could barely contain themselves. Colin laughed so hard he nearly toppled over the pitcher as he slapped the table in pure jubilation. They'd seen it all. They'd seen the shock, the sudden realization, the questioning. It was all written right on my face as each second passed. *Was this girl really looking for me? She loves my column? She's not that bad looking, is she? She has friends?*

Then, of course, they saw the final realization, that the friends this girl was talking about, and I was busying dreaming of drunken orgies with, were just a bunch of not-so-frat guys.

As the laughing subsided to a dull roar, I filled my cup with beer, took a gigantic swig. Burping, I looked at Natalie and Colin. A smile creeping across my face, I said, "Hey, I don't see any men...or women…coming up to you two losers. So fuck you. You just wish you could be as popular as me."

"Eyooooooo!" someone shouted from behind me, tapping me on my left shoulder. For some reason, I turned right. I didn't see anyone that would be calling my name. I looked left, and there she was. Not *her,* but Sophia. She was drunk.

"Hey there, you," I said. I was drunk as well, I realized. But she was absolutely gone. Regardless, I'd completely forgotten about her. I'd been more interested in trying to rekindle something (anything) with Lauren and secondarily in trying to figure out the whole Allison situation. Was I interested in her? How did that tennis girl rumor start? Were there other cool rumors about me?

Giving her a once-over, I noticed that she looked sexier than I'd remembered from the night in the auditorium. That could have been because she dressed like a fifty-six-year old professor that night, but still. She wore tight-fitting dark blue jeans, a pair of wildly colored Nike Air sneakers, and a crisp white t-shirt with some kind of trendy vest-looking thing.

"What's good, homey?" she shouted.

"Oh, we're friends now?" I mocked back at her. I got up from my seat, now standing right next to her. I felt a sudden need to be close to her, to feel her. She didn't seem to resist.

"Shut up," she smiled. "You okay? You looked like you were lonely over here. Figured I'd come and say hello."

That had to be a lie, I reasoned. I looked lonely? The place is absolutely packed, and I'm sitting with a bunch of my friends; how lonely could I be?

"You been here the whole night? I don't think I've seen you at all. Actually, I don't think I ever really see you here."

"Nah, I've been at Lucy's for a minute," she said. "I figured I'd come and hang here with you losers for a bit, let you guys in on all this fly-ness."

"Wow, so thoughtful," I said.

A smile spread across her face as she sat down on the nearest seat. Instinctively, I followed suit, making sure to push my chair as close to hers as possible without turning it into a bunk bed.

We continued a conversation, ranging from rap to basketball to broadcast class. I found I really had an easy time talking with her. That could have been because she was drunk and I was too. It also could have been because she had the interests of a 14-year old boy. Really, if I had a difficult time relating to a girl that loved my favorite type of music and favorite sport, I was pretty much doomed.

Ultimately, as the night wore on, a conclusion loomed in both our minds, no doubt. I knew from about fifteen minutes into the conversation that I'd have to come up with something. Anything would be better than "Listen, I'm really tired, I think I'm going to go home in a bit. You want to come with?" I couldn't lie about tickets to a basketball game, as there wasn't a game the following day. So, instead, I used the oldest move in the college book: the old "let's get food" so I can buy myself some more time to think of a better way to get you back to my place. Classic maneuver.

The destination was Augie's, the dollar-slice pizza joint around the block. Walking there, I thought about holding her hand, or putting my arm around her. We were doing that drunken walk that found us bumping into each other quite often. But, ultimately, I decided to hang back on any public displays. I knew someone from class might very well be out and around, and I didn't want any of this stuff spreading.

There were two reasons for that. First was the simple issue of privacy. The second reason was that I realized any publication of details with Sophia could easily lower chances with other girls, from that class or otherwise. In short, it was an extremely self-centered, conniving move.

"So, how are you getting home tonight?" I asked.

Furiously punching away at her Blackberry, she didn't look up when she said, "Not sure. Anna is supposed to pick me up, I can't get in touch with this bitch."

"You want to cool it with the cursing? You sound like a sailor." I knew I probably sounded like her mother, but there was something in me that hated the sound of a woman cursing. It was incredibly sexist, but it struck my ears the wrong way.

She didn't bother answering the sailor remark, as she was too busy demolishing the pizza she refused to let me pay for. "What a gentleman, offering to pay for a pair of dollar slices," she'd said.

Finished, she spoke up. "You know, I think I'm just gonna take the bus home, cool?"

"Yeah," I said. I couldn't believe I'd just said yes to that being okay. Thinking quickly, I replied, "I can walk you to the bus; it's on the way."

About a block from the where the bus stop was, her phone went off. The ring grew louder and louder. It was some sort of Notorious B.I.G. instrumental. She couldn't find the phone anywhere, in her enormous red leather purse or in her boots, as we trudged through the now mounting snow. We could both hear the ring, but couldn't locate it. Finally, it stopped.

"Super Nintendo, Sega Genesis, man, when I was dead broke I couldn't picture this," I rapped, doing my best Biggie impression.

"You're playin', cut that out," Sophia laughed.

"What, a white guy from the suburbs can't like rap? Huh? Only you hoods from the big, bad Bronx can like it?"

"Nah, you just don't do it right," she said.

"Oh, yeah?" I said, stopping dead in my tracks. My plan had worked. We had now walked several blocks past the bus stop and were only a minute or so away from my house. "How exactly is it done?"

She stopped, turned back a few steps, getting right next to my face. "Not...like...that...." she said, jogging away, laughing.

Catching up, I grabbed her by the waist and we finished the walk back to my house.

Once inside the house, we sat down in the kitchen, an arm's length away from the final destination (read: bed, my room). A few things sank in. One, I was at my house with a girl I found attractive. Two, that girl wasn't Lauren. Three, I was really, really drunk. Four, I was really, really tired.

"You gotta see this dry-erase board I've got in my room," I said. That was *it*. That, pathetically, was my close. Hell, she was already in the house. But still, the dry-erase board? Granted, the rest of the house loved this thing. It was a see-through piece of glass that you could write on with markers. Natalie would leave rap quotes on it, Matt math problems, and Colin and I kept our Mortal Kombat standings on it.

As she looked at the board, starting to make a remark about how much she missed playing Mortal Kombat, I put my arms on her shoulders, and turned her to face me.

Moving my hands down to the small of her back, I moved closer and kissed her. I hadn't kissed a woman not named Mom or Grandma or Abbey in about a year. Like riding a bike, it came back to me. We started off slow, making out in a very nice, respectable way. That quickly deteriorated, as I took off the Yankees sweatshirt I'd given her to wear and almost as suddenly as it had started, we were in my bed, wearing nothing but underwear.

As we fooled around, I began to realize the reality of what was actually going on: I was with a woman. Sure, she wasn't my first choice. Maybe not even someone I'd given much thought to a week or so prior. But she was a good-looking, sexy girl. Woman, whatever. Point is, I was actually able to keep my mind off of Lauren, for at least one night.

18 friday, february 15th

"So how'd last night go, Mr. Stud?" Natalie asked. She came into the living room from the kitchen with a cup of coffee. It was around two in the afternoon on Friday

"That's rich, me a stud," I joked back.

She chuckled, but held firm. I had brought home a girl, and a pretty good-looking one at that. She wanted details.

"Well, we didn't have sex," I opened up, "if that's what you're wondering."

"Noooo," she cooed. It was clear that that was *exactly* what she was wondering. "Well, what are we talking about? Make-out sesh? Some boobies?"

"Jesus, do I need to give you some money to have Kent fly up here?"

"Shut up and just tell me what went down. I want to know because I hope you had a good night, is all."

"Well, if that's the only reason....Yeah, it was just a make-out fest. I actually got so tired of it that I said to her, 'Are we going to do anything else?'"

"Nick! You did not say that!" she laughed.

"Yeah, I was tired. It was, like, four in the morning. I wanted to either...you know, or just go to bed. I had had enough. So she said, 'What do you mean?' To which I said, 'Nothing,' and rolled over. That was pretty much that."

"You're a real romantic, you know that?" Natalie said.

"And you're some kind of lady."

"Touché."

"You want to go food shopping?" I asked. We usually went on Fridays, I figured. Also, Natalie and I had eaten rice for two days in a row. It was time to restock.

"I thought you'd never ask. Let me go change."

"For P&C Foods?" She was a woman after all. For all the cursing and crassness, there was an essential femininity to her. Somewhere, if even only deep down.

As Gym Class Heroes blared from my speakers, I looked over at Natalie and asked, "At what point do we have to grow up?"

"What do you mean," she said, leaning in to lower the music, "*grow up*? Like married, kids?"

"No, more like...I don't know. I mean, look at me; I'm still wearing 'They're Grrrrreat!' t-shirts with Tony the Tiger on them. I eat the food I cook out of enormous bowls. My favorite things to do are drink, play basketball, and eat Sour Patch Kids. Not in that order, or concurrently...you get the point."

"What's wrong with enormous bowls?"

"You're missing the point. I'm saying, when does this...this all have to end? At some point, we can't live like this; we have to become our parents, don't we?"

"Jesus, I hope not. Don't tell my folks I said that, but damn! I hope that's not the case. I'm really hoping it's not. And thanks for the positive talk. Here we are, jamming to some good tunes, you just hooked up with a hot girl and you're talking like this?" Natalie said.

"I don't know, to tell the truth. I'm not upset, just curious. I'm going to be seeing Sophia tonight, or at least that's the plan, but I'm not even excited about it. How can it be that after one extremely uneventful evening with a girl, I'm already tired of her?"

"Because you're a piece of shit?" Natalie said, laughing.

"You've got jokes?" I said, a wry smile on my face. We moved on to greener subjects, like whether or not we'd be purchasing any more Teddy Grahams this time. Fact was, I was still concerned, but it wasn't something I'd openly share. I talked more about these things with Natalie than anyone else. Maybe it was because she was the only girl in the house, or just a better listener than the rest. Whatever the reason, I only really let this side out, as infrequently as I did, to her.

Still, though, conversations like that rarely lasted long. It was just too likely that someone (often me) would make some sort of wisecrack that would make the other person laugh. And, almost before it had begun, the negativity, the pensive and somewhat deep conversation, had ended.

19 fuck valentine's day (that saturday)

"Valentine's Day is such bullshit," I said.

"What's that supposed to mean?" Natalie asked in a motherly tone. You could tell there was a hint of defensiveness in there.

"It means that Valentine's Day is ridiculous. You can't win. Some girls want everything, and you can't get them enough. Other girls don't want—"

"We all read your column, big shot," Matt said from the other room. He loved to bust on me when it seemed like I was using material on them.

Matt walked into the living room where Natalie and I sat watching TV. He tossed us both bottles of Bud Light. Almost as if they were triggered by the sound of the beer being opened, Chris and Colin came downstairs, headed for the beer fridge located to the right of the main sofa in the TV room, and sat down.

"I don't *hate* Valentine's Day," Colin said.

"You would fucking say that," I said, throwing a nearby

bottle cap in his direction.

"Leave him alone, you no-love-having motherfucker," Matt said.

"Oh, here we go," I laughed.

"What?"

"You? I know you. You love Valentine's Day. Go ahead, tell them the story."

"What story?" Matt asked.

"You know…"

"Oh. Freshman year? They have to know that one by now," Matt said.

No one said anything. They hadn't heard it.

"You tell it," Matt said to me.

"Listen, we both know I tell it better, but it's your story. You tell it. I think you've earned it," I laughed.

"Fine," Matt said. "Remember Jennifer, from freshman year? Well, I sent her a gift for Valentine's Day. She was still home. In high school. And, well, I wanted to send her a gift for Valentine's Day, you know, something—"

"Damn, man, I'll tell it. You can't tell a story for shit," I interrupted. "He must've spent like two or three weeks—"

"More like a day, or two at the most. But whatever," Matt shot back.

"Agree to disagree. So, what he did was, he bought pink, red, and white construction paper, cut it into about a hundred small pieces, and then wrote on each one something different that he loved about her. Then he put it all in a clear glass Mason jar. And he sent it to her."

"Aww…." Natalie said. Though this was barely audible above Chris and Colin's chorus of something in the area code of "You are *such* a pussy."

"No, easy with that," I said. The group looked quizzically at me, wondering why I'd be defending Matt about this. "He wasn't being a pussy. That wound up working out. They stayed together for at least…what, three more weeks after that?"

"Shut the hell up," Matt laughed. "You've got a better

one? Something more manly, I'm sure."

"I once got head on Valentine's Day in Newhouse."

"Get out! Where?!" Chris asked. Part of him had to hope it was nowhere he'd ever been. The chances of that being the case, however, were slim as Newhouse was the main building for broadcast journalism majors, and it wasn't exactly a warehouse.

"You know, I'm not exactly sure," I said, "but it was at night. We were there working on something, Katie and I, and I think it was in the bathroom."

"Now...*that's* romantic!" Matt said.

"I've got one," Chris said.

Pause.

"Well, are you going to actually tell us?" Matt asked.

"Uh, yeah. Sorry. I thought you'd ask. Anyway, it was sophomore year—"

"Oh, yeah, I remember this one," Colin chuckled.

"Let me tell it, okay? So it was sophomore year. There was a girl in a psychology class of mine. She was all right-looking, I guess."

"What are we talking about here?" I interjected, as the resident girl-ogler.

"Uh…I'd say a 6-1-7? Good, not great."

"Okay, sorry. Needed a visual. Continue," I said.

"This girl, we'd talked a few times after class. One day, I'm not sure what came over me, but I just asked her to go to dinner with me on Valentine's Day. I wasn't even thinking about doing it. I just did it. I just went up to her, no lines, and just said asked. She said yes, which absolutely amazed me."

"Eddie, come on," Natalie chided. Chris always tried to put himself down, especially his looks. He was no David Cassidy (dated reference, hi-yo!), but he wasn't anywhere as bad as he'd lead you to believe.

"You know what I mean. I guess I was more shocked at the fact that I just did it. It was like one of those movies about being possessed by another being. Anyway, I invited her to Delmonico's," he said, winking at me. "Twenty, thirty minutes go by, no sign of her. No call, no text, nothing."

"Wow, this is a real pick-me-up. Thanks, Ed," I said, taking a swig of my beer.

"Hold on now; let me finish. You'll see. So, as you can guess, she didn't show. So I left. Not before I had a steak, which is beside the point, but you know how good those steaks are...."

"On with it," Matt laughed.

"When I left, it was around eight, eight-thirty? Point is, around ten-thirty I'm in my room, watching television, and my phone rings. It's her. She's apologizing and wants to come over to see me, and sounds completely bombed. So she comes over and we hook up—but I made it a point not to get in touch with her again. The way I look at it, I had the last laugh. Sure, she stood me up, but I'm not the one who wound up on my knees at the end of the night."

"Thatta boy, Ed!" I said. Not only was it a nice ending, but it was decidedly out of character. Normally, Chris wouldn't even have phrased it this way, let alone not call her again or take sexual pleasure from a girl as drunk as she seemed to have been.

"Okay, now that we're all sharing stories—" Colin began to say.

"Wait—sorry to cut you off—but that's not the end of the story. A few weeks later, some time near the end of the semester, she calls me on a weekend night. Might have been a Friday night. Or Saturday. Either way, we hadn't really spoken since that night, so, needless to say, I was shocked to hear from her."

"'Needless to say'? Who are you?" I mocked.

"It's an expression, you dick. One that doesn't have the word 'fuck' in it—you should try it some time. She calls, all hysterical, crying. For the first bit of the conversation, she's completely incoherent. I can't get anything from her. Eventually though, she calms down enough to tell me she just did cocaine and is freaking out—"

"What the fu—" the group gasped out.

"I know, right?" Chris continued. "And that she's down on Salina Street, and can I come and pick her up? So what was I supposed to say? I couldn't say no, so I spent the rest of that night walking her off her coke high. How's that for an ending?"

"That's it?" Matt asked.

"What do you mean, *'that's it'*? That wasn't enough?"

"No, I mean, what else happened? Did you speak to her after that?"

"Well, like the first time, we didn't speak much after. And since then I haven't had any classes with her, so that was that. Why she called me that night, I have no idea. But that will forever be etched in my mind when it comes to Valentine's Day."

"Wow, my story sucks compared to that," Colin said, sounding deflated.

"No, go ahead, Colin," Natalie said.

"Okay, mine is from high school. There was this Valentine's Day dance for sophomores. It was because we didn't have our own prom yet and obviously juniors and seniors did. Honestly, I had no intention of going. There was a big Celtics game on the night of the dance, so I was planning on staying home."

"Sounds like reason enough to me," I chuckled, and another swig of beer was had around the room. Interjections were frequent and seemed to serve not only comedic purposes but also as a natural point for the original storyteller to have a drink break.

"That year, my gym class shared the room with a group of the, the...uh, the special-ed kids. So this girl from that group, Rachel, comes up to me, and point-blank asks me if I want to go to the dance with her. Mind two things: I'd never spoken to her before, and the dance was two days away. I said, 'I can't. I have to work.' I thought I was in the clear. Without missing a beat, she goes, 'Where do you have to work?' She wasn't even being demanding; I think she was just curious. I completely froze. I had no idea what to say. So I paused for a second, looked her in the face and said, 'I have to work at a factory that night.'"

The room burst out laughing. Matt nearly spilled his beer.

"You told her you had to work in *a* factory? No specification, just *a* factory?" Chris gasped out between fits of tear-inducing laughter.

"Basically, yeah," Colin chuckled.

"And she didn't question this?" I asked.

"No, *that* was the most amazing thing, at least to me. I said it and then she smiled, so I did, too. And then I walked away."

"A *factory!*" Matt howled.

Once it died down, Colin asked, "How about you, Nat?"

"You guys don't want to hear mine," Natalie said. "Dinners with Kent. Roses, chocolate. Typical, romantic and girly. No factories, no cokeheads." She was a girl, after all. Sometimes hearing the word "cooter" from her as often as we did allowed us to forget that fact.

These were the moments, trapped inside our otherwise meaningless days, that we would soon miss. We took them largely for granted. This was the way it went and it had been this way for four years now. Who thought, for more than a fleeting moment, about what things would be like *afterwards?* It just wasn't often considered.

Matt and Natalie and Chris and Colin lived upstairs. I lived downstairs. Rarely were fewer than three of us at home. That was enough for a trip to Chuck's, a drinking game at home, a Mortal Kombat challenge, or even just a bullshitting session about women, food, or sports (the only three things on our minds most of the time). In all of this there arose a familiarity, a comfort. The kind so intrinsic that it only became apparent when it was gone.

20 saturday, february 23rd

The Panasci Lounge wasn't much of a comedy club. Matter of fact, it wasn't much of a lounge, either. Fine, there were a few couches and chairs. That was about it. There were no house lights: simply all on or all off. The Lounge was a high-ceilinged room on the second floor of the student center which sat atop the dining area. No one ever really went up there on their own. It was one of those places on every college campus that were designed by older people and intended to make younger people feel at ease and relaxed. A spot where those young folk can get some work done. The result was something that was likely to fit in better at a senior citizens' center. Hard couches and a single fireplace weren't ideal for relaxation in the minds of many twenty-somethings at Syracuse University.

Tonight, as I ambled up the stairs to the Lounge, I saw that the room was well filled: about eighty-five to ninety people in the audience.

"There you are!" Leah Higgins gasped. "So nice of you to join us tonight."

I had a habit, nay, a ritual of showing up late to these

things. As time went on and I started to realize that I was one of the better members of the group, the lateness became more and more blatant. Rare was it that I showed up before the first comedian had already finished. Tonight was no exception.

"I have you booked to go last," Leah said. She ran the group, emceed the shows, and put up with me. She knew I was one of the funniest in the group. She knew I knew it, too. The reality in all this was that even though people did seem to enjoy me the most, that in no way afforded me the right to act the way I did. Still, no one ever really said as much.

"Can you please show up a little earlier next time? I know you don't care, but it gives off a real 'fuck-you' attitude to the rest of the group," she finished.

"Okay," I said, barely listening. I was trying to scan the crowd to see who was there. The way it was set up on this particular night, with the stage on the far wall and the audience facing away from the entrance, made this endeavor a bit more challenging. Thus, the lack of listening.

"Have you picked out the lucky lady yet?" she laughed.

"Aw, shut up," I smiled. "Not just yet."

"Good crowd tonight. It seems like we're getting bigger each show, don't you think?"

"Yeah."

"Okay, I can tell you're not listening to me. I've got to go and remind Adam that he's going next. You're up after me, three more, all right?"

Tuning back in to her, I said, "Can you make sure to—"

"Yes!" she smiled. "I know, promo your show that you have yet to actually set up. You tell me every show. I've got it down pat."

She was right. For some reason, I had no issue remembering and reminding to promote the show any place I could. Actually meeting with people to get it off the ground? That, for some reason, eluded me.

Tonight's pattern was a familiar one, with regard to my preparing for the show. I wasn't so nervous in the fifteen to thirty minutes before going on. For whatever reason, the nerves were at their worst several hours before a show. It was almost as if, once it got too close to back out, I *had* to do it.

All right, everyone, thank you for staying for tonight's show. We really do hope you enjoyed it this week!

I looked around. *Was she fucking with me?*

Look at the look on his face! Just kidding—we have one more comedian left for you. He's such a big deal, he's doing his own show later this semester, "I Hope God's Wearing Earmuffs." He's also so lazy, he has yet to figure out a date or time. Without further ado, give it up for Nick...Alexander!

"Thank you for the warm introduction, Leah. Real nice," I began. "Glad you could use me to get a stronger laugh than anything from your own material." I was ruthless on stage, not one to let someone get away with making fun of me. The crowd laughed, and so did she. I was in the clear.

"One thing that's not talked about a lot is pornography," I started right in. "We all know that basically every guy watches it, but ladies, it's not to always to do, well, you know, filthy stuff. Guy in the front, here, do you watch pornography? Honestly, do you?"

A shocked, now slightly embarrassed guy in a grey hooded sweatshirt, likely sitting with his girlfriend to his right, didn't answer.

"You see," I picked up, without waiting for an answer, "no comment. That means he watches pornography."

By this point, the crowd was with me. This was a college crowd; they could only deal with ironic observational stories for so long. Eventually, a dick and vagina set of jokes had to come charging through. I simply got right into it.

"Me? I watch it. I was watching it just recently. I won't tell you who I was watching it with, but he's sitting in the back of the room, wearing a red shirt and jeans," I said, pausing so that everyone could turn and look at Matt, in the back wearing a bright red Polo shirt. "What I like is a porn with a little bit of a story line. I want to be *fully* entertained; it's a film, a form of cinema. The name of this video we were watching, it's a classy title—*Bookworm Bitches*."

The crowd continued to laugh at each succeeding punch line. By this point, I'd caught my wind and was going full speed ahead. Jokes and ad-libs of all kinds were hitting on all cylinders.

"It's a tale of a Midwestern girl. She's got a B-minus GPA and she needs an A to get into graduate school. I felt bad for her," I said, even laughing myself. "She'd gotten a C+ on this paper; apparently she'd worked for two weeks on the bibliography. So, at this point, I'm really pulling for her."

Laughter started to spread on the right side of the room. Then, as more people caught on to the pun, it spread to the whole room. I later would tell Matt that, truth be told, I had no idea I'd even made the joke until someone laughed and I'd simply played off it as if I'd intended for it to be that way the whole time.

"You could not have a dick and still be invested emotionally in what happens to this girl. She looks studious, she's wearing glasses....And so she starts pleading with the professor, 'Come on, I need this A, I worked so hard!' 'You did work hard?' he says back to her. It gets to this point where the script writing just—there's no more script, and it's just a bunch of this back and forth....

"*'So, you want this A?'*
'Oh, God, yeah, I need this A.'
'Show me how creative you are.'
'How creative do you think I am?'
'Show me what you can do.'
'What do you think I'm gonna do?'
'What do you want to do?'
'What do you want me to do?'
...And I'm just sitting there like, GET ON YOUR KNEES ALREADY, JEEZ!"

The room broke up again.

Closing my set, I finished, "And before you know it, their clothes have just vanished. We're suddenly no longer in movie mode, but in a full-fledged porno. And thirty minutes later, wouldn't you know it, with a little hard work, she got that A she needed for grad school! Hard work does pay off."

Almost as soon as the show had ended and Leah had *really* thanked everyone for coming, I got up from my chair, giving the room a once-over. Off to the right, I spotted someone who looked like Lauren. She had brilliant blonde hair, but she was at the far end of the room, so I couldn't be sure since I'd left my glasses at the house. Sophia was also here with a few friends of hers, as was Allison. Sophia was closest.

"Hey, you! Great job tonight," Sophia said, grabbing me by my sleeve as I tried to walk past her.

"Oh, hey! I didn't even see you here. How did you know about this?"

"You told me about it, last weekend...." she said incredulously.

"Sophia?" a voice said from behind me.

"What up, girl?" Sophia said back.

It was Allison. The two hugged. I sat back and waited. I wasn't quite sure how I'd get out of this. Granted, I'd only hooked up with Sophia, not Allison or Lauren. But if it was known that I was hooking up with Sophia, then I had shot myself in the foot with the other two. That I didn't want. So I decided to keep quiet.

"You were...all right tonight," Allison joked. She really thought she was a riot.

"Very funny. Thank you for coming, though. Both of you. Very nice, and on a Saturday night. I'm sure you guys have plans?" I was praying they'd say they did. We were having a party for Matt at the house later and I wanted to ask Lauren to come over, not them.

"Nope, free," Sophia said.

"Complete losers," Allison joked. They were hoping I'd have something in mind to do.

"Wow, well, I guess you are," I said, nervously fidgeting in my pocket. I pulled out my cell phone as the two girls went back to chatting.

Furiously, I punched into my phone:
Matt's cell:

Get me out of here!

Looking over, I saw Matt grabbing into his pocket. Help was on the way.

"—yeah, I can't wait for that class on Monday, either," I said, just as I felt Matt's hand slap my back.

"Yo, dude, we've gotta get going. Mike's already there," Matt said.

Great job, Matt! Vague! Great job!

"Oh, he is? Shit. Ladies, if you don't mind," I said jokingly. "I must be going. See you all in class?"

They nodded in acknowledgment. As I walked away, I made mental note of a few things. First, I couldn't find Lauren anywhere. Second, Allison and Sophia didn't seem to question where I was going. Third, they didn't seem to have any clue that I was being deceptive and sneaky and a slight slime ball.

Then again, I hadn't been with a woman since sophomore year, so it was more than likely my radar was just that far off.

"Mike's already there? Great stuff. I was scared to death you'd mention something about the party," I said to Matt once the girls were out of earshot.

"What party?" Matt said.

Was he fucking with me, too?

"I'm fucking with you," Matt said. "But I wasn't being clever; I just figured I had to get you out of there. Why wouldn't you want them at the party, anyway?"

I explained everything, and though it reeked of skuzzy behavior, the logic was fairly strong.

Nearly a block up the street, I saw Lauren heading the other way.

Jogging towards her, I caught up and said, "Hey, I wanted to thank you so much for coming tonight."

"I wasn't there to see you," she said in a very matter-of-fact tone.

"Oh. Well, on behalf of whomever you were there to see, then, thank you," I said, my confidence officially smashed to pieces. Why was she acting so hostile all of the sudden?

There was a pause, so I quickly filled it. "Who were you

there to see?"

"Uh, Leah," she stuttered.

"You're full of shit," I said, stepping closer, with a smile on my face. "You came to see me, you came to see me," I sang.

Playfully pushing me away, she said, "You think you can just not call me? What the hell is your problem?"

Whoa, whoa there. Not call you? We went out on a date. One date. I didn't want to freak you out.

"I...uh, I just...I don't really have a good reason. I'm sorry? Why don't you come to my house tonight? We're having a party for my roommate Matt."

"I don't know if I can," she said.

"Well, if you find yourself free, come by. Please, it's going to be fun."

I didn't feel like playing games. I understood her frustration, but not its level. So angry she would make up reasons for not coming to the party, make up reasons for going to a comedy show by herself? It didn't make a ton of sense.

"I'll see," she said, turning around. "I've got to get going."

"All right," I called after her. "See you there?"

She didn't answer, or even turn around.

When I caught up with the group, Matt asked, "How'd that go?"

"I have no...fucking...idea."

***

No matter the situation, parties at school always started late at night. It didn't matter that most students on campus had been free since their last class on Thursday. Parties would generally kick off at around ten-thirty—but that was only so that people could show up "on time" by eleven or eleven-thirty. Thus, it wasn't really a surprise to have your house ready (kegs in place, tables set up, valuables hidden) for nearly an hour before anyone actually showed up. Set up for ten-thirty, expect to be raring to go by eleven-thirty. That was protocol.

Still, having been scarred by the last party we'd had (actually, it was my birthday party last semester and let's just say that it wasn't that well attended), I was always going to be nervous that no one was going to show. Everyone else's parties had their own fond memories, usually involving extreme (and funny at the time, although, in retrospect, likely dangerous) alcoholism. Having a bad birthday party—without any honest memories, without enough people—felt comparable to social suicide.

Outside of the other particulars (which, if you've ever been to any generic college party, aren't *too* particular), the detail of note was that Lauren never showed. I didn't make a big deal of it. For the first hour.

"Should I text her? Maybe she's not sure where the house is?" I asked nervously.

"Relax. If she's coming, she'll come," Lotfi said.

"What the…Obviously, if she's coming, she's coming. What the hell does that even mean?"

"Would you go, already?" Chris shouted from the other side of the table. We were playing beer pong in the living room, in the middle of the now-packed party. Colin and Chris had won three games in a row and Lotfi and I were challenging. I couldn't quite recall where I'd last seen Natalie, but I knew that Matt was at the flip cup game going on in the kitchen.

"Quit yer crying," I shot back.

"She's not coming, so just shoot, already!" Colin laughed.

"You shut your mouth," I said, releasing the ping-pong ball. It landed squarely in a cup in front of Colin. "Drink up, bitch."

"All I was saying was, just relax. You don't need to text her. She knows where you are and what's going on. Nothing else you can do," Lotfi said before his shot.

"I suppose," I said.

"You're going to text her anyway, aren't you?"

"Yes. Yes, I am."

"Fine, but I don't support the move," Lotfi called out after me.

The text I sent was entirely regrettable and yet completely forgettable. Something about where the house was, and an *"if you're not busy."* Or it might have been a *"not sure if you heard me from earlier tonight, but."* Either way, it reeked of desperation. Not too hard to figure why she didn't show up. Still, she never would get back to me that night, not even to give a half-baked excuse of any kind.

21 thursday, february 28th

Com Law was truly eating me alive. Not in the sense that I was struggling with grades. No, more in that I just couldn't be bothered to pay attention the requisite amount to get those grades in this course.

You see, I never really had to try too hard for grades. I wasn't brilliant, but rather I was naturally intelligent enough and had the sort of verbal skills that meant that for me to get by, effort and grades didn't always have to go hand in hand. Which is to say, I was a supremely skilled bullshitter. I was good at studying, had a good memory, and didn't like to let work get in the way of having a good time. This had been my attitude for the first fifteen years of school. You can imagine what it was like with the finish line clearly in sight, only a few short months left in my life of a college student.

In past semesters, I'd probably stopped doing the assigned readings by mid-semester, having already figured out when I had to pay attention in class, who I could ask for help, and what grades I had to get on specific projects to do as well as I wanted overall. This semester? I got my books after the first few days of class and I stopped reading a week or two later. The only action seen by the thick law book I had bought was when I took it from under my bed to my desk during the class. I made a point of wiping any dust off of it before getting to the actual lecture hall.

However, unlike many other courses I took where I could pay attention during lecture and be fine without reading, I wasn't even able to focus in the Com Law class. There were women to think about, there was...well, anything other than class.

Sitting down with Natalie, I again found myself daydreaming. I took my book out, turned on the school's desktop computer in front of me, and realized that Nat and I, once again, were the last two people to have sat down in the nearly-filled hall.

Edington had already begun his lecture.

"All right, everyone, welcome back. Hope you got through today's reading, wasn't a long one—"

"Yeah, only seventy-five pages in two days," I quietly mocked to Natalie.

"The First Amendment, as you know, is the backbone of our freedoms. Of our society. It's what allows us to live in a democratic society, and what allows us to report freely upon said society. Without it, we'd be in a whole shitload of trouble."

I snapped out of a daydream. Professors cursing completely out of nowhere tended to have that effect on me.

"Who can tell me one reason why the ruling in Peterson vs. State Board of Florida was a beneficial ruling for reporters in the digital age? ...Anyone? No one read this, I can only assume from your thrilled response. Okay, I'll tell you one reason. The right to know is the most important—"

Thankfully, my concentration was broken by a flashing on the screen.

You have a message from Allison.Goldin@syr.edu. Accept?

All of the computers in the room, actually in the entire building, were equipped with this program that was used to store class notes, lecture slides, and TV production software. Amidst all of this, of course, was an instant messaging system that could be used with anyone on the computer network at the same time as you. All you had to do was enter their e-mail address into the "To" box and type your message, and it would appear at the top of the person's screen.

Allison.Goldin says: hey! how boring is this?! - Allison

Nick.Alexander says: I know, awful. You don't have a gun on you, do you? Also, I know who the message is from, you don't need to sign it haha

"The thing to remember, folks, is that when it comes to the courts, prior restraint is one of your best friends. Unless any of you bums are reporting on who killed Kennedy, you won't have to worry about the constitutionality of using prior restraint as a defense. Kennedy's too old a reference? Fine, John Lennon. Kids today, you know nothing of history, nothing."

Allison.Goldin says: ok, ok. very funny. do you know what he's talking about at all? i have no clue haha

Nick.Alexander says: no, I have no idea. none. that could be explained by not doing any reading though...

Allison.Goldin says: hahahaha, no reading? you're just too cool for school, I guess?

Nick.Alexander says: you got it

I was being cool. It wasn't something I ever did in person, but when I didn't have to actually speak and could take my time before each word, I didn't have a ton of trouble being the flirtatious, confident guy I wanted to be.

"When did I say the First Amendment journals were going to be due? A week from Thursday? Push it back a week. I'm not going to be around that weekend, so let's push it back...if that's okay with you guys? I thought so."

Where is Allison going with this, I wondered. I hadn't really talked to her much since finding out from Melissa that she was into me. Frankly, I wasn't all that attracted to her. She was skinny, in shape, and fair-skinned, but I couldn't really handle being around her personality for too long. She always tried to make jokes about everything, and that bothered me. Odd, I know, considering how I was the same way. Even so, she never stopped. It was always some sort of wisecrack.

When I hadn't gotten a message for a while, I began to question whether it was really her typing. I turned around and confirmed that it was in fact her.

Allison.Goldin says: what are you doing saturday night?

Nick.Alexander says: not sure, why?

I knew exactly what I was doing that night. Nothing. But again, we go back to the power of the typed word, where I was allowed to mask my normally patently visible desperation.

Allison.Goldin says: i want to go to see this movie...

Nick.Alexander says: don't let me stop you

Allison.Goldin says: very funny

Nick.Alexander says: I wasn't being funny

She didn't respond for a few minutes.

Nick.Alexander says: Okay, I was being funny. I guess not, though. Are you asking me if I want to go to this movie with you?

Allison.Goldin says: Yes, pick me up at 7?

You have a message from <u>Rebecca.Friedman@syr.edu</u>. Accept?

"Remember the Miller case from a week ago? It's because of that case that we see, in Smith and Sons vs. Wade, that the reporter has the right to shield laws. Anyone want to tell me what a shield law is?"

I had no idea what the fuck a shield law was. I accepted the message from Rebecca. My screen was now more filled with messages than actual work.

Rebecca.Friedman says: I heard you met my friend Sarah last weekend? She asked you about the show at Funk N' Waffles?

Nick.Alexander says: Yeah. Wow, she's friends with everyone, huh?

Rebecca.Friedman says: Yes, she's sooo popular haha...i know you're doing that show, but I wanted to know if you would be interested in doing the Relay show at the Dome?

Wait a minute, the Dome? As in, the Carrier Dome? Was I

being asked to perform in the same building the men's basketball and football team played in? I couldn't believe this. She had to be fucking with me.

Nick.Alexander says: You're fucking with me...

Rebecca.Friedman says: hahahahahaha...no, no. its the relay for life show at the carrier dome in a month or so. we'd have to put your name up for board review, but that shouldn't be an issue. i just wanted to see if you'd be interested in that.

Allison.Goldin says: Well?

Amidst the effort of talking with Rebecca about the show and trying to pretend like I wasn't blatantly not paying attention, I'd completely forgotten about going to the movies with Allison.

Nick.Alexander says: Yes. 8 o'clock. That sounds great.

"Before we close for the day, I want to talk about opinion columns. All semester thus far, we've debated the libel suits. That's probably a bit strong. I've debated, to myself. You just sat there and listened. Regardless...libel. We all know what it means, what it is. The question I ask of you fine, upstanding, budding young journalists that sadly will be running our country in a short time: Can opinion columnists be charged with libel? Remember—"

Allison.Goldin says: No, not at 8. 7. the movie is at 7:30...

Nick.Alexander says: It would be an honor to do that relay show. Honestly. I'm flattered you even asked me. That would be awesome.

Rebecca.Friedman says: Great!! I'll let you know what comes of the meeting. Its in a week or so, I think. And don't ask about whether or not you can promote your show haha. Sarah and Leah told me, it's all good.

"No one in this whole room writes an opinion column? No one? I find that really, really hard to believe. Really? No one, huh? Let's see...Nick—"

"Yes!" I piped up, as if Edington was taking attendance. I snapped to attention upon hearing my first name. It could have been a reference to Nicholas Cage; I'd have had no idea. I heard my name in the midst of all the legal babble, so my brain turned on again.

"You're not in trouble; relax. I want to know, do you know anyone that writes an opinion column? I know you've been paying close attention all class, but for those of your classmates that weren't focusing as closely with their books closed as you seem to be doing, I'll review what we're discussing. We're talking about whether or not opinion columnists are subject to libel charges. So, before we get to just that, do you know anyone that writes an opinion column?"

"Um," I began, "I'm not—"

"Wait a minute! Don't you write an opinion column?"

It was an odd duality. I loved the praise I'd get from the column, loved people noticing me, loved all of that. But despite all of this, I became extremely self-conscious when it was brought up by other people. If I wasn't asked directly about it or questioned repeatedly, I'd probably have pretended as if I didn't write it.

"I do. I write a...uh, a humor column, for the *D.O.*," I said, trying to be as quiet as possible, hoping Edington would take that answer and move on.

"I've read it."

That was all he said. Nothing more. I could feel the room looking back and forth between us. I wasn't sure what to say.

"Okay," I mumbled. What else was I supposed to say?

"Do you think you should be able to charged with libel? You do know what libel is, don't you?"

"Yes, I know what it is [you fucking jerk-off]," I said, giving back the sarcasm Edington gave me. "I haven't really thought about it, but I guess I *could* be charged with anything. But I don't think I should be able to be charged with it. What I'm writing is clearly, in my case, done in jest, and is obviously my opinion."

"So that means you can just say whatever the hell you please, then? What of journalistic responsibility? What's to stop you from writing your next column about how your Law professor is a pedophile?"

"Well," I said, stumbling, as I wasn't prepared for the having-sex-with-kids reference, "What would stop me is that no one cares about you and I doubt that people would find it particularly funny."

"Touché, Mr. Alexander."

"I guess that there has to be some guard against it. I can't just say anything and simply say, *Well, it's an opinion column, so that's that*; but I'd imagine I'd have more leeway than actual reporters."

"Well, you'd be correct. Xaron vs. Fanhouse proved that opinion columnists certainly have more—"

Allison.Goldin says: I live on Windstrom, it's over on the hill past Deke. we're the building with a little front yard and something that was supposed to be a deck

"—because, as Mr. Alexander astutely pointed out, people know, when they go to his column, when they read his column—or any like it, for that matter—they know exactly what they are—"

Nick.Alexander says: alright, i'm sure i'll find it.

"—Isn't that right, Nick?"

"Yes, yes," I said, lifting my head from my screen.

Edington chuckled audibly, knowing full well I hadn't heard a word of his question or his explanation of libel with regard to opinion writing. The class ended shortly thereafter and as I was packing up (which is to say, turning off my computer and picking up my closed book from the desk), I heard Edington's voice coming towards me.

"Do you enjoy not paying attention in my class?" he chuckled.

"What?" I said, hoping to play it off.

"Oh, come on, don't bullshit me," Edington said. "I know you're talking on the messenger and pretty much doing everything other than listening."

"That obvious?" I said.

"Yes. Yes, it is," he said.

We regarded one another, not saying anything for a moment. In this moment, I knew I'd either forged a further connection with him, or started a war.

"I must be going," Edington said, as he turned to head up the stairs to the exit. "But thanks for being a good sport today." Before reaching the door, he turned back and continued, "I've been reading you for the last few months. You do a good job. Very funny. Keep it up."

"Thanks a lot," I said, turning to look at him again, but he'd already left.

22 saturday, march 1st

I wasn't exactly sure what was going on, in any respect.

For starters: Why was I going on this date with Allison in the first place? Was I that desperate? Why didn't I just hang out with Sophia more, or call Lauren back? I actually enjoyed their company.

And how about: Why was I driving to her house, and to the movies, in this horrible weather? Yes, it was March, but that had no effect on the incessant snow that was heaping up all over the campus. It was freezing, it was snowing, and I was driving twenty minutes out of the way with a girl I wasn't that attracted to, to see a movie I wasn't allowed to choose. Why else would I be going to see *Definitely, Maybe*?

With Akon's "Don't Matter" playing in the background, I found that I couldn't answer any of these questions. Well, there was one explanation I could figure. I'd explained it earlier in the week, when I was grilled by Matt and Chris in the living room upon telling them of my plans.

"Let me get this straight," Matt began. "You don't really like this girl—"

"Not much," I said.

"You don't know what movie you're going to go see?"

"No, I know that. She picked it, though."

"Whatever. You're still seeing Sophia and now you're going to start dating Allison, and they're friends and they're in the same class with you?"

"Yes."

"And you're going to go driving in this weather?"

"Yes."

"You care to explain any of that?" Chris said, laughing.

"I don't know, really. It's not like she's ugly," I said, ignoring most of the questions I'd just received. "Chris, you've met her...."

"No, I think she's cute, actually," he said.

"So yeah, she's not *unattractive*, but I don't know. I guess I'm attracted in response to the fact that she's into me. Is that so wrong?"

No one really answered. It was true: there was an attraction, unquestionably, when an at least mildly appealing woman was openly attracted to you.

I continued. "Let me put it to you like this...for the last few years, I've been at the back of the bread line. When it's my turn to get to the front, for some reason they've already ran out of everything. It's all gone. This time, now, I get to the front of the line and they've got a ton of stuff. So fuck it. I'm going to take as much as I can. If that means double portions, then fuck it. Honestly, why not? It's not like I'm *really* dating Sophia or Lauren. Hell, I barely know what to make of any relationship I may or may not have with either them."

"That's a fucked-up analogy," Matt said.

"How? How is that fucked up? What is fucked up about that?" I retorted.

"Comparing these girls to bread rations? That doesn't sound messed up to you? These girls aren't food, man. They have feelings. I know you know that, but don't be stupid here."

"Why don't you just stick with one of them? Actually just try hard and see what comes with one of them? You seem to get along with Sophia, don't you?" Chris said.

"Doesn't matter," Matt interjected before I could answer. "That's not the issue. The truth is that Nick doesn't really like any of these girls. That's the truth. He doesn't *actually* like any of them, yet he's afraid to give any up. This isn't a goddamned buffet line, dude."

"What the hell? Whose side are you on?"

"There's no sides," Matt shot back. "It's you. But what you're doing, you know it, is fucked up. You're going to get burned. It's going to come down on you and you're probably going to wind up losing them all. This isn't the movies. These things never work out."

As my car skidded around the street leading to Windstrom, Matt's words bounced around in my head. I hated that Matt had come down on me, but I could barely say anything back. Matt was right. I knew it. But I was going, anyway.

I didn't look at what I was doing as any sort of sin. It wasn't like I was having an affair. I'd only hooked up with Sophia a few times, never with Lauren; and who knew what would happen with Allison? Okay, I had an idea but thus far there hadn't been any sex anywhere. And there hadn't been any talks of exclusivity, or anything even remotely related. I felt that I was in the—

Bapppp! Bapp! Bapp!

"Hey! You're late!" Allison said from outside the window of my car. She was waiting at the foot of her driveway. Good thing, as there was no way my car was making it up that hill in this snow. Still, though, she'd scared the shit out of me.

"You scared the shit out of me," I said. "Were you trying to break the glass?"

"Shut up and drive," she said as she slipped into the car. I had to say, I was impressed. Even in this heavy snow, she had managed to wear something both functional and sexy. She had her hair done up, too, at least more than the pony tail she wore at school. I was wearing a sweatshirt and a baseball hat.

"You must really like me, if you're driving in this weather to come and see me."

"You have no idea," I laughed.

We chatted all the way to the movie theater off I-81, which was normally ten to fifteen minutes away but took us closer to thirty to reach tonight because of the weather. More accurately, she talked and I listened, occasionally adding something along the lines of "Really?" or "Yes, I agree." It was a combination of not really feeling like talking and not being able to talk, as my concentration was focused on keeping the car on the road.

"You want any candy or popcorn or anything?" I called after her as she headed towards the bathroom before the movie started.

"Get whatever, I'll have some of yours," she said.

That pissed me off. Why couldn't she just tell me what it was that she wanted? Not only that, but now I had to share? Have you seen the size of the movie-theater bags of Sour Patch Kids? They're not really two-person bags.

As we sat down, I had a choice to make. Did I try to put my arm around her? What about arm rests? I had no idea what to do. I was attracted to her, if only physically. But if I was too forward right off the bat, especially with a girl I knew liked me anyway, I might give her the wrong impression. I didn't want her to get too caught up, too emotionally involved.

Just as the previews were coming on, I realized that what I actually wanted was a solely physical relationship. Not a novel concept, not by any stretch. But, while everyone else around me seemed to be saying it, I hadn't admitted it to myself. I had rationalized that I was testing things out, that taking a girl out for a date took me off the hook for my ultimately selfish and devious motives.

Despite the movie's near-alarming amount of appeal and enjoyment (I'd have to pretend, of course, that the film sucked when anyone asked me), I hardly had a good time. I was nervous about whether or not Allison was looking for the same thing, and now, all of the sudden (I could still hear Matt and Chris) I didn't want to hurt her feelings.

"What did you think?" she asked, grabbing hold of my

arm, pulling herself closer.

I smiled a weak smile at her. "I liked it, actually. More than I thought I would."

"Yeah? You don't sound like you liked it...."

"No, I did. Why don't we get going, okay?"

The ride home was similar to the ride there. She talked a lot and I kept my focus on the road. Thankfully, it had stopped snowing at some point during the time we were at the movies and the roads had been cleared away somewhat. It was marginally drivable.

"Which house are you, again?"

"That one, right there," she said as the car pulled to a stop. She was about to lean in, but, noticing that I wasn't even looking at her, she pulled back. "You okay?"

"I'm fine."

"No, you're not. You've been acting funny for a while now. I thought at first, when I got in the car, that you were just worried about the movie, or the roads, or something. But even now, you're acting strange. What's the matter?"

"Nothing. Nothing's the matter," I said tersely.

She paused. I welcomed the break in the noise: no music, no movie, no Allison.

"Well, are you at least going to walk me to my door? Our railing is broken...." It was her last attempt and she didn't think for a second I'd give enough of a damn to take the hint.

I turned the car off and looked over at her. "Of course," I smiled.

As I walked her towards her door, I had no idea what I was doing. Which head was doing the thinking? I couldn't tell at this point. At some moments during the night, I was thinking rationally, thoughtfully, carefully. At other points, like this one right now, I was thinking only with my penis. I had no expectations, at least not sexually, but I knew what was going on when I got out of the car.

Getting inside the house was a warm relief from the freezing winds and the sort-of broken heater in my car. As I plopped down on a couch in the living room, Allison disappeared into the kitchen.

"You know, getting into the house wasn't nearly as dangerous as you'd have led me to believe," I called out after her. "What, with all the *icy* walkways and...*gosh!* No railing!"

A moment or two later, she returned with two beers, wearing nothing but a long nightshirt.

"I think you—" I started.

"Don't say it," she said, sitting down in my lap.

"I was just going to say—"

"Uhhttt!" she laughed, putting her finger up to my lips.

"—that you sheem to have mishplaced your pantsh," I said, putting my hand on the back of her head, gently moving it closer to mine.

"I knew I forgot something," she whispered, smiling.

As I moved closer to her, I inhaled deeply, smelling her sweet scent. *She must use a lot of shampoo*, I thought. *She smells great.*

She pushed me back so that she was now fully on top of me. I looked into her eyes and couldn't think of anything but her lips, her scent. I closed my eyes and went towards her. She met me.

A few minutes and changed positions later, I could feel my phone vibrating from atop my crumpled jeans, which were now on the floor.

11:25 PM
You have a new text from:
Sophia's cell

23 sunday, march 2nd

"How did she not notice?!" Natalie exclaimed.

"I have absolutely no idea," I responded. We were standing around the island in the kitchen. It was around ten-thirty in the morning and I had just gotten home and begun to tell the tale of the previous night to Natalie. I'd hoped to make it in unscathed and simply get back into bed without an interrogation. Not that I didn't want to talk about it. No, not that. I was exhausted and just didn't *feel* like talking about it. But my intended move of stealth—to come in through the rarely-used back door that led into the kitchen—wound up backfiring. It turned out that Natalie was making herself some coffee.

I poured myself a glass of orange juice. "I can't drink coffee," I said. "But I really like how important it makes you look when you have a cup with one of those cardboard things around it. Makes it seem like you're a real adult."

"I don't think I've ever looked at it that way," Natalie said, gulping.

"One time, I actually had them put the orange juice into one of those cups, and I even got the cardboard thingy to complete the look, even though the cup wasn't warm at all.

Every once in a while I'd even take a sip and make a face like, "Oooh, this is hot!"

"What the hell is wrong with you?"

"I'm not quite sure myself," I said.

"I know I asked already, but how on earth did she not notice that your phone was vibrating, and that you checked it?"

"Well, the first part, the vibrating, I'm not really sure. I mean, my...uh, my....my pants were already off at that point, so...." I said.

"Oh *yeah!*" Chris said from the top of the stairs. I knew Chris found Allison attractive. It was almost like he was fucking her vicariously.

"It's not like that," I said, smiling. Actually, it was exactly like that. We didn't have sex, but just about everything other than.

"She's bangin'," Chris said, now having reached the kitchen. As usual, he was wearing nothing but a ragged Chicago Bears Super Bowl XX championship shirt and boxers. No pants, of course, but no one even looked twice at this point.

"You tell that to Erica?" Natalie smirked, her nose practically in her coffee. It was that cold, both inside and outside the house.

"No, I mean, let's not get crazy. Allison's hot, I'll say that much for her, but Erica is...."

"Gorgeous?" I offered.

"Perfect," Chris answered. He was truly happy. The girl in his life, the girl he had been afraid to call or text or Facebook message or e-mail or do anything with, he was now regularly having sex with and, to the dismay of the house, telling everyone about it. We were happy for him regardless.

"Well, for those of us that don't have the perfect situation," I said, smiling at Natalie, but then quickly realizing that I was the only one in the room not dating someone I actually liked. "Fuck it. For me, I'll say this: she's a good looking girl, yes. We wound up having a good time last night."

"How was the movie?" Chris asked, pouring out some

cereal.

"Eh, not great," I said, motioning for Natalie to keep quiet. I'd admitted to her that I loved the movie as soon as I'd gotten inside.

"What's this about you getting a text while you were over there?" Chris asked.

"Nothing really, just that I got a text from Sophia mid-make-out," I laughed. "I know, I couldn't believe it myself. Allison didn't seem to notice and I didn't really check it until I left this morning."

"Well, what did she want?" Natalie asked.

"Just wanted to know if I was going to be at Chuck's," I said.

"Oh, yeah?" Matt said, appearing out of nowhere.

Why aren't they fucking sleeping? It's Sunday morning, I thought.

"Yeah, that's all she said," I said to the newest member of the Breakfast Club.

"That's funny," Matt began, with a look all over his face like he had something quite damning to say, "because we saw her there last night."

"Really?" I said, not paying much attention at first. "Wait, you saw her down there? You guys never go down there on Saturday nights."

"We were bored. Is it okay that we went without you?" Chris said.

"Ha, ha," I mocked. "Did you say anything to her? Did she come up to you?"

"Dude, it's not that big of a place. Of course we saw her and talked with her," Matt said.

"Well, what did you talk about with her?" I said, getting closer.

"Come on, hell if I know. Normal bar shit, nothing important," Matt answered.

"Did she ask you guys where I was?"

"Yes."

"What did you say?"

No one answered. Matt looked at Chris. Chris took a big spoonful of cereal and looked towards Natalie. Natalie gulped her coffee and looked at the ground.

"Well, what the hell did you tell her?" I yelled.

"Dude, people are sleeping," Matt shushed.

"I don't give a fuck. What did you to say to her?!"

"We weren't going to lie to her. That's your shit; I'm not about to step in it," Matt said.

"What—the—hell—did—you—say—to—her?"

"Just that you weren't coming," Matt said.

"Is that all? Did you say anything about Allison or the movie or any of that shit?"

"No, no. Just that you weren't going to be coming down tonight. For some reason, she didn't ask why. But she didn't seem too surprised," Matt said.

"Who could blame her?" Chris mumbled.

"What's that supposed to mean?" I asked.

"Nothing. It doesn't mean anything," Chris said quickly. He clearly hadn't thought I would react to the softly-uttered side comment as harshly as I did.

"You must've meant something by it," I pressed.

"Take it easy," Matt interrupted.

I took a breath. I believed them; they wouldn't rat me out. There was no reason for me not to believe them, and in fact, at no point during the mini-argument did I doubt what they were saying. I was feeling a little paranoid and that can mess with your mind.

The fact was, Matt and Chris liked Sophia. So did Natalie. They liked it when she came over, they liked me with her. As such, they weren't enamored with the idea of me treating her like a third wheel. Four years of friendship, however, trumped the previous sentiment so ultimately they'd all cover for, side with, or stretch the truth for me.

All things considered, I didn't expect a phone call, or even a follow-up of any kind (e-mail, Facebook, letter in the mail, whatever), from Sophia. It was this indicator of the level of our relationship, as I saw it, that allowed me to still see Allison or try to see Lauren. Of course, as Matt and Chris and Natalie and Lotfi and (you get the point, don't you?) would remind me any time I brought up this point: "Did you ever consider the idea that she only acts casual like that because she knows *you* don't want it the other way, when in reality *she* actually does?" Inevitably, I'd say I hadn't considered the idea, which would be followed by an I'm-really-happy-with-myself-sounding "I thought so." It pissed me off, but they were right, so I didn't argue.

The only thing I had left to do that day was to go to a radio station meeting. They'd been held on Sunday nights for at least the last three semesters, yet I rarely remembered about them (granted, I was in London for one of those semesters, but still). It was for this reason that whenever I saw Lotfi ambling up my lawn at around eight-thirty at night on a Sunday, I could feel the wheels turning in my own mind....

...What is he doing here?...Oh, wait...what day is it again?...What time is it?...Do I need to change out of these sweatpants?...I should probably at least start to get ready by getting my hands out of my pants and putting these potato chips away....

I normally (read: always) detested these meetings. I was getting tired of them, of the familiar tune they always seemed to carry. Everyone from the new freshmen, who mostly sat silent for fear of pissing anyone off with their existence, to the sophomores, who probably had a bit too much confidence, to the juniors, who seemed to want to get into any sort of sports debate to prove their dominance, to the seniors, who, by and large, were numbed to the whole process.

The meetings were held in the basement of the radio station, in a carpeted rectangular room outfitted with a circle of comfortable chairs and a host of foldable chairs. You can guess who sat where.

Funny thing was, these guys were my kind. They were my brethren, my friends. Sports junkies, loudmouths, jokesters. Yet it was precisely for that reason that I dreaded these meetings. There was a feeding-frenzy vibe to the whole proceeding. The head of the group would start a topic of discussion, maybe a critique of the most recent post-game show. Someone would make a comment. Then someone else would interject with a wisecrack of some kind. Joke here. Disagreement there. After a while, it began to sound like amateur auditions for some horrible ESPN show. And soon after that it turned into little more than white noise. I wanted to be the center of attention and even though I was recognized as "the funny man," I still wasn't at the group's center as much as I'd have liked. And that bothered me. But I still went to the meetings, if only because they were where assignments for upcoming shows were given out and I wasn't about to let my ego get in the way of that.

"You ready to go?" Lotfi asked, upon letting himself into the house. He knew I wasn't ready yet. I had barely begun Step One of the hand-in-pants/potato-chip plan.

When we were finally a few steps outside the house, Lotfi asked, "What do you think of West Virginia?"

"What do you mean? As a state? An institution of higher learning?"

"No," Lotfi chuckled. "Basketball."

"Well, I guess I'm not really sure. They've surprised me this year. I really didn't think Ebanks would be as good as he's been, but they've always been able to shoot the—"

"No, I mean going to West Virginia, for the game in a few days."

"Any reason you didn't just say that off the bat?"

"Dunno," Lotfi answered without pause.

Satisfied, I mulled it over for a bit. "When is the game?"

"Next weekend. Saturday. We'd be leaving Friday mid-day. Originally, Parkins was supposed to be going with me and Chris and Colin, but something came up for him, so he had to back out."

"When would I have to let you know?"

"Tomorrow."

"Wow. Okay, thanks for the advance notice," I said.

"I do what I can," Lotfi answered. He had a habit of saying things that, if read instead of heard, might come off as smug. But trust that there was innocence in the tone.

By this point, we'd entered the building and were a few steps away from the glass door to the basement where the meeting would be held.

Downstairs, I assumed my normal position in a chair just outside the circle of seniors and kept my mouth shut for most of the meeting. Not that I would've been paying much attention anyway, but today my concentration was squarely on the possibility of the upcoming trip.

24 thursday, march 6th

Everyone turns into a doctor when I'm sick

For quite some time now, one of my secret wishes has been to have a raspy, deep, sexy, sore-throat voice. The sort of voice that sounds like you've been smoking Lucky Strikes since you were eight.

Over the past few days, my wish came true. I have a sore throat. Or at least that's what I call it. I'm surprised they've had enough time to come up with a name for an illness they have no idea how to treat. At this point, I might as well have polio, as at least there's a cure for that.

I've tried those lozenges, the Chloraseptic sprays. None of it works. Recently I purchased lozenges from a brand I'd never heard of before, Sucrets. Here's a Sucret: you can only take one every two hours, they numb your taste buds, and oh, by the way, they don't help at all.

I guess it's my turn to be sick, though. It's that time of year. If you don't believe me, stop what you're doing and listen to the sounds of your classmates for one minute. Sniffles, loogie snorts, coughs. Everyone's got it.

Still, when whatever bug is popular that month does catch you, you act not only as if you are the first person ever to have a sore throat, but as if you have the worst case ever documented.

"Can you believe this? I'm not only coughing, but my voice is sore too!"

My favorite is the clever, original response to your illness you'll hear from your friends. Even as I write this, I'm embarrassed to admit that not only have I been given this suggestion, but I've made it to others as well.

"You know what you should do? Go down to the health center."

I've tried all sorts of methods to clear up my throat. Hot water with salt (that one makes very little practical sense, but my mom told me to, so I couldn't tell let her down), orange juice (for the vitamin C, though ironically, at this school the dining hall orange juice is disgusting), and tea. Lots and lots of tea.

I don't particularly like tea, nor do I know how to make it. I get the general gist - hot water, bag of leaves. Still, there has to be some technique to it, because the cups I've brewed have been wretched. There's nothing worse than tea that's either warm or (gasp!) cold.

As if the lack of enjoyable taste sensation weren't enough, now the value of hot liquid has vanished. At this point, I'd like to drink lava. It's thicker, and, from what I read, it's incredibly hot.

As painful as it may be, the key to the whole "sore throat" routine is the raspy voice. Without it, no one believes you. If you "hurt" your leg, you better pray you have a limp. Otherwise, you're just another college kid with a Harvard medical degree and a propensity to exaggerate your own illnesses. Join the club.

Things had proceeded fairly quickly since that weekend

radio station meeting. Let's fill you in.

First of all, as you have just read, I got sick. I probably picked it up from Natalie, who seemed to have had some sort of throat ailment for nearly the duration of her collegiate career.

Second, I decided shortly after the meeting that I'd be taking Parkins's spot and going to West Virginia that weekend with Lotfi, Chris, and Colin.

On top of that, somehow Matt got worked into the mix. An enormous WVU Mountaineer fan (by virtue of the fact that his father had gone there, and the two of them loved hunting anything with four legs that didn't bark or meow) who had never actually been on the campus, Matt saw it as an opportunity to do something fun.

I sat towards the back of the room, reading the paper (more specifically, my column), in the cafeteria of the newest Newhouse building. Cleverly, it was called Food.com. The cafeteria, that is, not the building. The food was just all right: sandwiches and some weak stir-fry on occasion. But it was generally quiet, it accepted the student charge card (which meant I could get away with having my parents pay for it while making it look like I was buying groceries), and they had a surplus of newspapers.

Just as I put the paper down, I could feel someone approaching my booth. My suspicions were confirmed by a quiet "Excuse me."

I turned to discover a fairly tall, rather motherly-looking girl standing across from me.

"Are you Nick Alexander?" she asked.

"I...am?" I said, not so much asking her, but wondering how it was she knew who I was.

"This is really weird, I know, but I read your article in the paper today," she said.

Article...column, whatever, I thought.

"Oh, wow," I said, still surprised whenever anyone I hadn't met before told me they'd read it. I'd usually ask what they thought, but for some reason, this time I didn't. Instead, I asked her if she'd like to sit down. She wasn't too attractive, a little too tall and large for my liking. Not to say she was fat, but she just had a bigger build, something an athlete might have a better time handling. After initially hesitating and looking at her watch, she decided that she "did have a few minutes" and asked to "let me just go and grab an orange juice."

I was bored and didn't have class for the rest of the day, so I really was in no rush.

When she returned, sitting opposite me, she unbundled herself from the winter weather outside. Scarf unraveled, winter cap taken off, jacket shoved into the corner of the booth.

"So, yes, I read your article today," she began. "Oh, I'm sorry. My name is Meredith. I don't think I introduced myself."

"No, I don't think you did. Nice to meet you, Meredith."

"Well, as I was saying, in your article you had talked about being sick, which I can tell you still are by your voice," she chuckled. "I wanted to tell you, I had an idea that might help you out."

"Oh, really?" I asked, almost doubled over with incredulity at what was occurring. Here I was, having a conversation with an absolute stranger about a sickness I had talked about in a column that just came out earlier *that day* about the ways people tried to help sick people by giving advice. And now, she wanted to help me.

"Yes."

"Would you like to tell me what you had in mind?" I half-croaked, half-chuckled.

"Oh, yes. Sorry. It's just that there's this girl sitting over there," she began, motioning with her eyes to a position towards the front of the room, "who seems to be staring over here at, I'd imagine, you."

"That's quite flattering," I smirked, realizing I was being punked.

"I'm not kidding," she deadpanned.

"Okay, listen. If you did or didn't read what I wrote, that's fine. But if you came over here to just bust my balls, tell Matt or Colin or whoever sent you, message received. I get it, I'm not as cool as I think. Okay?"

"I don't know who Matt and Colin are."

"Do you have any tips for my throat?" I said, returning what was originally supposed to be the main point of this "chance encounter."

"I do," she said, still looking in the direction of the purported girl, who, as yet, I hadn't looked over at. I didn't want to look over, have Meredith say something like "Sucker!" and then leave. I didn't want Matt or Colin to win. So I stared straight at Meredith, who continued, "I work at Starbucks, and I'm a firm believer in the 'Refresh' tea. It's minty, so if you don't like peppermint it might not be up your alley, but you can either put honey in it, or, if you like chocolate, have them put a pump or two of mocha in it. If you get a tall or a grande, ask for two tea bags. That will help with the 'wretched' taste you described in your article."

Maybe she wasn't kidding around. I looked to my right, to where this girl was supposedly staring at me. And, as I'd originally expected, there was no girl there.

"What is this? Did they really go to the trouble of making up some ridiculous back story about you working at Starbucks? That's really some effort. Neither of them ever, ever goes there, so to even use the word 'mocha' in a sentence would require some inside intelligence," I said.

"Listen, I don't know what you're talking about," she said, getting her stuff from the corner. "There was a girl over there. She's not sitting there now; I think she may have left. But I have to be going. I really like reading your articles; they're very funny. I hope you feel better."

"Thank you," I said, still suspicious. Her story seemed to check out, but this mystery girl?

After she left, I mentally reviewed my itinerary for the trip.

We'd be leaving from luxurious Hancock International

Airport in Syracuse at approximately noon the following day. I'd already arranged to get out of my morning class tomorrow, but considering that Colin and I had nicknamed it "Going Through The Motions 102" (yes, we'd had the 101 version a year back in another elective course), I now decided that I'd go, and then head to the airport with the crew.

"Who was that girl?" a voice asked from behind me. As I turned to see who it was, the voice was gone. I faced forward, just about to launch into a mumbled "What is up with all these people appearing from out of nowhere today?", but then I saw her sitting across from me.

"Who was that?" Lauren asked.

"Are you jealous?" I asked.

"No. I just want to know who she was," she said, setting down her wrap and soda bottle in front of her.

"A fan," I laughed. I realized immediately that my laughter implied that I was kidding, which would in all probability elicit another inquisition.

"Oh. So you're going to be a funny guy?"

Ignoring that, I said, "It sure is great to see you, too. I'm doing well, thank you for asking. I'm glad you've had the time to get back to my voicemails. Really appreciate it."

She didn't respond to the sarcastic jabs, instead opting to take a bite out of her wrap. I had given up on her a bit in recent times, not that anyone could really blame me. Hell, I was volleying back and forth between two far more agreeable (albeit less attractive) girls and frankly had gotten fed up with the mind games involved in seeing Lauren for anything, sexual or otherwise.

To this point, it should be remembered, I hadn't really done anything other than take her to a basketball game, hug her awkwardly, and see her a few other assorted times outside of class (read: Chuck's). I'd tried to get her to come to Matt's party and I'd tried to call her to see how she was doing and to see if she wanted to grab dinner one night. Most times, I had been met with either no response at all or, even worse, a non-committal wishy-washy response that only meant a further

"No."

All things considered, from where I'd started—not having spoken to her for the better part of three years—I'd gotten pretty far. For some reason, I still was attracted to her. And, for some reason, I hadn't fully given up and wasn't upset to see her. Normally, within a day or two of a girl not returning a phone call, I'd have gone off on some wild, curse-filled rant to anyone who would listen:

You know what, fuck this girl. Fuck her. She doesn't want to call me back? Fuck her, then. Who the fuck does she think she is? Fucking....

You get the point.

But I hadn't done that. I might not have shown it, but I was happy to see her.

"I mean it, she was a fan. Sounds ridiculous, I know."

"What do you have fans for?"

"I guess for that column in the *D.O.*," I said.

"What column?" she laughed. She knew about the column and she knew that people liked it. She read it every week. Apparently, like a lot of people did.

"It's not that I'm not happy to see you. I really am. But I'm curious," I began, realizing that what I was about to say was almost certain to be taken the wrong way. But I went on anyway. "What do you want?"

She seemed taken aback by this. "What do I want? You call me and want to do stuff, so now I run into you here, and it's *what do you want?*"

"No, no, no. That's not what I meant."

She looked me over once, smiled, and took another bite out of her wrap, a sip of her drink. She paused, the previous look of confidence replaced by a trace of hesitancy.

"What do you like about me?" she said. "Why do you want to see me so often?"

I didn't really know how to answer that question. Well, that's not true. I knew how to answer it, but besides feeling completely ambushed, I didn't want to freak her out by sounding like a deviant. *Because you're fucking hot and I like being with women that I want to have sex with?*

"I...I'm not really quite sure how to answer that."

"You don't have to answer that. I'm sorry, that was really weird. I'm gonna go and get some chocolate pretzels. You want something?"

"No."

I let her get up, which allowed me a minute or so to think.

She soon returned, as promised, with a small bag of white-chocolate pretzels. Staring at them, I thought of how stupid I had been in saying I didn't want any.

"I don't know exactly what it is that I like about you. I mean, I think you're beautiful. But there's something about being around you that I really enjoy and I want more of. I guess that's it."

She smiled. "What are you doing on Saturday?"

"You have to be kidding," I said incredulously.

"Why? What's wrong with Saturday? Plans with another girl?" she laughed.

"No," I said, not necessarily lying but, shall we say, skirting the truth. "I'm actually not going to be in town this weekend. I know, Mr. Big Shot, *not in town*. I have business to attend to on the coast, so I'll be back on Sunday night."

"Business? The coast?"

"Kidding. I'm going out to West Virginia for the radio station."

She responded with something like "Oh, okay," sounding slightly down at the news. She wasn't too used to having people, specifically me, say no to her.

"Well, why don't you try to return a phone call or message of mine? That way we can do something with more than a day's notice. I'm usually...actually, other than this weekend, I'm always free. This shouldn't be so hard," I said.

"Maybe next weekend, then," she said, not really asking. She seemed to be giving up on the future already.

"Okay. I'll talk to you when I get back. I'm doing a show next Saturday. You should come. This time, though, actually stay around. We can do something afterwards. I mean, if you'd like. Whatever."

"Have a safe trip," she said, as she got up and began to leave without answering the question—if it even was one. Without meaning to, I'd flushed away a perfect opportunity to take control of whatever there was of our relationship. She'd put herself out there, actually asking me to do something and instead of capitalizing on it, I'd played it off with a joke (shocker) and then allowed her to regain control by putzing around about doing something the following weekend. Not my smoothest performance.

Just ask her to commit. Be a man, goddammit! What the hell is your problem? She wants you to like her, she wants you to take control and tell her you really want to see her!

"Hey, Lauren," I called out. She stopped a few feet from the table. As she turned just her head to look back, I was taken aback by her beauty. "You, uh...you forgot your pretzels. You mind if I have the rest?"

"No, Nick. Not at all."

25 syracuse at west virginia, the weekend

Once inside the airport, we headed to the one and only "terminal." There were a closed pizza place and two vending machines. Both were drink machines. In short: no food.

"This place really stinks," Chris said, plopping his bag down in front of him as we all settled into seats in front of our gate.

"I'm just curious," Colin said, looking at Matt, "but how did you get tickets on such short notice? For the game and the flight?"

"Don't worry about it. Anyone want a soda?" Matt answered, laughing.

No one was quite sure how he did get the tickets, or why he was being so reserved about his purchase of them.

"Does anyone get that?" Colin asked, once Matt had gotten up.

"Better question, does anyone care?" I laughed. I took out my iPod and Game Boy. It was music and Tetris time. "Let me know when they call us."

"You know it won't be on time; it never is here," Chris

lamented. He hated the Syracuse airport. While most of the house would agree that Chris had a habit of complaining about things that weren't nearly as bad as he made them out to be, this was one area where he had a legit gripe. No matter what, Chris always had something go wrong at the airport. Almost inevitably, his flight, either leaving or arriving, would be interminably delayed: *"We're sorry, folks. Flight 815, nonstop from Syracuse to Chicago, will be delayed. We do not know the cause or length of the delay, so don't even bother asking. Thank you for your patience."*

There was something strange about making a trip of any kind away from school while it was going on. That is to say, leaving college for any reason other than a break. It just didn't feel right.

Any time I (or any of the radio station members at 125 Clarendon, for that matter) was asked to go on a trip, there were always second thoughts involved. Sure, the food and airfare would be free but I would be missing out on something. Without question, even before the weekly debauchery at Chuck's became a regular life staple, there would be something missed. Maybe it was something as regular as basketball. Maybe it was a birthday (I once missed Chris's for a trip to Louisville). Whatever it was, there was the chance that *it* was the next great story that you'd have missed out on. Whenever it was retold, you'd have to laugh along, knowing full well that everyone else knew as well you did that you weren't there.

Trips from earlier in my college career had two major differences from the one I was currently on. The first was that on past trips, I had no concept of my college mortality. What was one weekend in Louisville or West Virginia or Boston? I'd be back for the following weekend; no big deal. The other thing was that on past trips, it was mostly people I wasn't particularly friends with. If I was lucky, Chris or Colin would be along. Never both. Now, I not only had both of them, but I had Lotfi and Matt as well. It wasn't exactly Syracuse, but it could pass for a traveling road show.

I was able to follow my normal routine. First off, I hated having to turn off my iPod during the first few minutes of the flight—so I didn't. *If this iPod being on is going to crash the plane, then we're in big fucking trouble*, I thought. The plane never crashed, though the risk/reward of it having a possible effect on the flight for the sake of my spiting of the rules obviously made little sense.

Finally, and for no real reason, I felt the need to listen to music that applied to the city in which I was landing. Considering that I had no idea on earth where we were, outside of the key words "Morgantown" and "West Virginia," there wasn't much in the way of musically appropriate selections. So I settled for "Homecoming" by Kanye West. The song was about coming home to Chicago, which I figured had to be in the general vicinity of West Virginia.

By the time we got settled in, all we wanted was their version of Chuck's. The bar we found was called "Bent Willy's." Maybe Charles and William were distant cousins.

"This bar is so much nicer than Chuck's. It's really unbelievable. Look at this," I said, lifting my feet off the floor. "Doesn't stick. How about the fact that we all could get a seat...at our own table? I actually hope West Virginia kicks the shit out of us tomorrow, just to stick it to us."

"You would say that," Matt said.

"What's that supposed to mean?"

"That you're a spiteful s. o. b."

"He's right," Chris said. "Remember the time you wouldn't let us watch TV because you couldn't find the remote? You said it was to spite the TV. So none of us got to watch it and you blamed that on the remote."

"Or," Colin shot in, "the time you nearly returned the PlayStation you'd bought two or three days earlier because you lost the first few times you played it?"

"I wouldn't call that spiteful. More like a sore loser," Lotfi chuckled.

"Yeah, you're probably right. I got a bit ahead of myself there. I felt there was a roll going, just wanted to be part of it."

Eventually, the drinks came. And came. Round after round were purchased, some two at a time so as to avoid any possible delay.

Blonde hair. Blue eyes. Long legs. Skinny with curves. She walked into the bar, flanked by two attractive (admittedly less so) female friends/guard dogs. Even a self-proclaimed brunette man like me was impressed. She was a 10.

"God damn," was all I could muster. Since my seat was facing the entrance, I was the first person to notice the young lady. The rest of the group soon took notice, quickly halting any pre-existing sports or Syracuse-girl-related conversation.

"That," Lotfi said, referring to the girl, who by this point had taken a seat with her friends at the bar, "is just unfair."

Gulping down his current beer, Matt asked, "What's unfair about that? She's hot. So what?"

"'So what?'" I asked.

"Yeah, so what?"

"'So what?', he says. The big tough guy here says, 'So what?' He talked to one girl at one dining hall, what...two fucking years ago? And now he says, 'So what?'"

"A year and a half ago," Matt corrected.

"Here's what's so...I mean, here is what is 'so what.' What's 'so what' is that girls like that know they're impossible to approach. They come with other girls, always to some degree uglier than they are, to ward off all predatory gnomes like us. They won't even talk to you unless you've been a rower since you were seven and wear a size 12 shoe. Fuck girls like that."

"That's some deductive reasoning there," Chris laughed. "Have you ever thought about becoming a detective? You broke down that whole girl—matter of fact, the entire female race—by just looking at one girl for about a minute. I can't imagine what you'd cook up if you had some real hard evidence. You might be able to solve the Kennedy assassination, you know that?"

"Fuck yourself, pal," I said, taking a chug. "Not all of us are happily ever after with the girl we were originally afraid to talk to from class."

"Maybe not," Chris answered, sitting up straight. He

wasn't offended, but it wasn't entirely a joke any longer. "But not all of us are too busy fucking around with three hot girls to actually give a damn about their feelings or the one that actually cares about him."

"Easy, boys, easy," Lotfi said, smiling. He had no real reason to be smiling, but he knew that if he did, whatever mounting tension there might have been was more likely to cool.

"Did you ever stop and think that maybe those girls feel the same exact way? That no guys come and talk to them because of exactly what you're saying?" Matt said.

"Yeah, I'm sure they're just waiting for me," I said. Turning towards where they were sitting, I half-shouted, "We're coming over, honey!"

"Shut up, dude, you know what I'm talking about. I'm not saying that all you have to do is go over there and talk to her and she's going to sleep with you. What I'm saying is that you'd be surprised how much women just want guys to talk to *them*. They might look like they're putting out that vibe of 'stay away,' but really, they're just protecting themselves. They don't want to look desperate. They want you to come and talk to them."

"And you got your doctorate in love when?"

Matt stared straight back at me, put his beer down, and gave me a look that said, *Really? Honestly? How do you think I know this?*

Oh, two sisters, one of them a twin. That's right, I thought. "Okay. But still, why can't they come and talk to us? Why do we always have to be the ones that go up and talk to them?"

"Because that's just the way it goes, dude. Sucks, I know. But some things just are. And that's one of them."

"What does it matter to you, anyway? You've got, what, three girls?" Colin chimed in. It was known throughout the group that Colin, despite his humor and boyish looks, had been unable to pull in many (if any) women during the college years. His passivity when it came to women made me look like a rapist.

"Don't start with that, now," I said, pausing to check my suddenly buzzing phone.

11:15 PM
You have a new text from Allison
where r u???? come to Chuck's!!

"Who could that possibly be? You have no other friends that aren't here," Matt mocked.

"Who do you think it is? It's Allison. She's drunk. She wants me to come down to Chuck's."

"Well, I guess that answers whether or not you told her you were going to be around this weekend," Chris said, motioning to Linda, our server, to get another round for the table.

"What did I need to tell her for?"

"No reason, really. You don't owe her anything. But be honest...did you tell Sophia or Lauren?" Lotfi asked.

I pretended I didn't hear him. "Who paid for that last round? Am I up?"

"Okay, so at least you told Lauren. I'll guess you didn't tell Sophia, though," Lotfi finished.

Again there was a buzzing from my phone, which was now on the table. Lotfi grabbed it.

"Nope. He didn't tell her, either," Lotfi said. Reading from the phone, he said, "From Sophia. I believe this would be pronounced 'Hey-yo'? Anyway, 'Hey-yo, you comin' out tonight?' she asks. You going to get back to either of these girls?"

As Lotfi began punching in his own answer, I grabbed back the phone. "Yeah, I'm just going to say that I'm not coming out tonight. It's not a lie, but it's not the full truth."

No one was buying the possibility that it was just a coincidence that only two of the three girls had texted me. The group knew better. They knew that, despite the advances of both Sophia and Allison (sexual and otherwise), I still wanted Lauren more. Likely, it was not being able to have her, after seeming so close and having waited so long, that made me want her even more.

Then came another vibration. This time, Matt grabbed the phone before I could. The violent lunge nearly knocked over the pitcher of beer, a certain party foul.

"Oh, shit," Matt said, a look of real surprise on his face. "Looks like someone's got a text from his dream girl! 'Hope you're having a great trip! Can't wait to hang out next weekend.' Damn, dude! This girl wants you. You're in. I don't know how, but you did it. Somehow, you've tricked these girls into liking you."

I smiled a coy smile. I knew I had it pretty good. I also knew my arrogance was nearly toppling the whole thing over on itself.

Re-energized by the recent texts, I looked right at Matt and said, "All right, let's figure out how we're going to get Colin to go home with that girl over there."

"Oh, no, I don't think so. Why don't you do it? You're the one rolling in girls, big shot," Colin said, sitting back in the corner of the booth.

"Lotfi, tell him why I can't do it."

"I....Why can't you do it?"

"Stop playing around. Tell him."

"Oh, that's right," Lotfi said, clearly confused, but trying to play along anyway. "Well, Nick can't do it because he's spoken for. Same with Matt and Chris. And me, well, I just think she looks like she's more your type than mine. What else is there to say? That about does it."

"I'm not going over there. That's all there is to it," Colin said weakly. But we saw that he could be turned.

"Linda! Can we have a round of shots, whatever you want? Get yourself one if you'd like. And another round of beers. We're celebrating," I shouted to the waitress.

I passed the shots out, giving Colin mine. Lotfi followed suit. Now Colin had three shots in front of him. We all knew he wouldn't go over there without having a bit more of a buzz on and we were happy to oblige him.

As expected, he continued to put up a meager fight. No, he wasn't going over there. No, he wasn't going to take all those shots. But soon enough, he relented. He took the shots, he finished his beer, and he let Lotfi push him out of his seat towards the bar.

"This is going to be embarrassing," Chris laughed. "I mean, this could be bad. Real bad. Like, me-freshman-year-on-the-way-to-that-basketball-game bad."

I broke up laughing, Matt joining in. Freshman year, on the way out of our dorm, Chris had slipped on the stairs. He was in a rush to get to the Carrier Dome to get good seats in the student section for the game. But he forgot that it never stops snowing or raining in Syracuse. The stairs were icy as could be and he went up in the air like Lucy had pulled the football out from in front of him.

"We were sure your clothes were going to come off from that one," Matt laughed.

"You know what though, Matt, you had one freshman year, too," I started. "We were walking back from the dining hall in that underground bunker connecting the two halls. Remember that? You and I and Chris were talking, walking side by side. I was in the middle and you were on my right, next to the wall. Looking at me, you walked right into this metal box sticking out of the wall. The edges of that box were like little knives. You went down like there was a sniper in the room."

"Oh, my God, I remember that!" Chris laughed. "Matt, you were so fucking angry. I remember thinking, 'Don't laugh, just don't laugh.' And then I looked over at you, Nick, and you were rolling on the floor, howling with laughter. I knew you had to be good friends with Matt if he wasn't beating the shit out of you for that."

"Come to think of it," Matt said to me, "you always seem to be there laughing at everyone when they fall down or do something embarrassing….Why is that?"

"Great timing?" I said, smiling and raising my glass. No one raised with. "Hell with you guys," I said, gulping down.

"Okay, I've got one for you, Nick," Lotfi said.

"I think I know where you're going with this one," Chris piped in.

Lotfi paused, looking at me as if to say, *You ready for this?*

"Go ahead; do your worst, sir."

"Junior year, we're all at my place. Spurs were playing—"

"The Kings! That was a fucking foul. I can't believe they didn't call that for Duncan!" I exclaimed.

"Obviously, you remember this night," Lotfi joked. "What you may choose to forget, at times, was the little bet we had with you. We'd ordered two pizzas for the group and we had each bought a 40 of this malt liquor called 'Wailing Wench.'"

I groaned, the memory nearly causing a gag reflex.

"There you go—some memories never fade," Chris cackled.

"We bet you that if you could chug one of them, you'd be off the hook for paying for any pizza. For some reason, you said yes. I think, honestly, it would only have been about five or six bucks on your end. But you pounded that Wench, and said—"

"*How's that for a Wailing Wench?!*" Chris, Matt, and I said together, laughing.

"It didn't make much sense at the time, and it still doesn't. Anyway, you were fine for a few minutes. After the pizza got there, though, we looked back at you and you were white as a ghost. You finished your pizza, then promptly threw it all up. That was a fun night."

It had only been about fifteen minutes since Colin had left, but he was already back and he seemed to be in an immense hurry. Before he even started talking, he grabbed his coat and motioned for the rest of the group to do the same.

"Well, she was a bitch. You were right, Nick."

"What the hell happened? What's going on?"

"Get your stuff and let's go. I'll tell you as we walk."

"Why are we leaving now?" Matt asked, picking up his coat. None of this made any sense. The sudden exit, the frantic look on Colin's face.

"Well, I went over there. Actually, first I went to the bathroom. But then I went over there and introduced myself, asked if I could buy her a drink. She told me, No thank you, I have a boyfriend, and I wouldn't take drinks from you anyway. So I bought the drinks, and then I spilled them on her."

"Holy shit!" Chris exclaimed.

"So, yeah, we'd better get going," Colin said.

"Holy shit!" Chris repeated, both stunned by the recent turn of events and at the same time laughing uncontrollably.

Grabbing our belongings, we quickly ran towards the exit, ducking into and around groups of students in the now-packed bar.

Once outside and waiting as Lotfi called the taxi service a block down the street, I smiled at Matt. "What did I tell you? Bitch. Fucking...bitch."

26 friday, march 14th

After we returned home from West Virginia, there was only a week left before Spring Break. Even though the first day that classes were "officially" cancelled for break wasn't until the following Monday, people all over campus were trying to figure out ways to get out of town earlier.

Having Spring Break the following week ensured that the weekend itself was shot. No one was going to be around come Saturday night. Maybe, just maybe, Friday night at Chuck's. But that was probably wishful thinking.

I had to think wishfully in this instance, as I'd have to stay in town to do the comedy show at Funk N' Waffles that I'd promised Rebecca's friend Sarah I'd do. Without realizing contextually what the date of March 14th actually meant, I'd committed to the worst Friday of the year. Still, it was all going to charity (although I was convinced no one would be there to donate) and I was a man of my word in these areas.

Besides trying to get my own show idea off the ground, the only issue I had to consider was Lauren. Fortunately for me, she wasn't leaving town until Saturday night. She had a midterm on Friday and couldn't get out of town, so in Syracuse she stayed. Fueled by her text from the weekend, I took some initiative and called her up to make plans for the weekend. I had originally planned on leaving Saturday morning with Lotfi. But once I found out Lauren would be in town, I convinced him to stay the extra night. He didn't actually argue, but it was clear his preference was to leave Saturday. It didn't matter all that much to me, as I was the one with the car and could pretty much do what I wanted.

Not surprisingly, I asked Lauren if she wanted to go to dinner at—here's the surprise—Delmonico's. I picked her up from her apartment, and as I did, I realized that this was our first real date. Sure, we'd gone to the game together and had hung out a bunch of times, but this was a real date. A non-alcoholic, semi-adult date. Matter of fact, I realized, I hadn't done something like this in a long time. Maybe since I dated Katie? I couldn't quite remember.

"Hey there, you," I said as she stepped into my car.

"Hello, sir," she smiled. "How was the show?"

"It was fine," I said. I wasn't thrilled that she hadn't come, but I tried not to let it show. Obviously, I wasn't doing a good job.

"I'm so sorry I couldn't make it. I really, really wanted to go, I mean it. But I just couldn't make it. Here," she said, handing me a twenty-dollar bill.

"What's this for?"

"I feel bad—I know it was for charity. I know that you take that seriously, so here, I want you to have it. I really did want to go."

"No, I appreciate it, but I can't take that," I said, both shocked and pleased by her offer.

"Well, either I'm going to give it to you," she said, "or I'm going to throw it away."

"Ha," I said. "I say that all the time to my friends. They think I'm nuts."

"You don't normally throw it away, though, do you? I'm not kidding—I will throw it away."

"Okay. Jeez. Thanks a lot; I appreciate it. I'll give it to Sarah when I see her next."

"Sarah?"

"Wow. You know, for a girl that doesn't call me back all the time, you seem to get pretty jealous whenever I mention any girls. Her name is Sarah Schultz, she's the one who put the show together. That okay with you?"

"Yes," she said smiling a coy smile she knew would erase any annoyance.

There was a pause in the conversation. I took the money and, surprising even myself, I didn't ask her why she wasn't able to come. For once, I left it as was.

"So, tell me a joke you used!" she said.

"Come on, you know how much I hate that," I responded. "Do I tell you, do...I don't know...what are you good at, again?"

She didn't say anything.

"Oh, that's not so funny, huh," I laughed. "Okay, fine. One joke I used, actually, I think was funny because it was completely unplanned and off the cuff. I was talking about women—"

"Shocker," she said.

"And," I said, pausing to faux-glare at her, "I was talking about women, and someone in the front yells out, 'Yo, dude, get over it. We read all your shit, you hate women, we get it!'"

"Get out of here!" she laughed.

"No, really. That's what he said. So I go, 'Sir, first of all, I'm proud to know that you can read. Second of all, I don't hate women. Women are the reason we're all here; they brought us into this world. I love them. I'm here tonight because of a woman.' Then I paused for just a beat, and I said, 'Well, my roommate is a girl and she drove me here, but that's neither here nor there.'"

"You thought of that right then and there?"

"Yeah, I was pretty happy with it. They seemed to relax at that point, the crowd. Laughed at that, gave me some leeway."

"Good, I'm happy to hear that," she said, rubbing my arm.

What it was that was going on here, I couldn't tell. We hadn't so much as kissed, yet when we were around one another we often acted as if we were dating. Well, more accurately, she acted that way. At times. At other times, she'd be cold, wouldn't return phone calls. Then she'd go out with me, loving talking to me and being with me. Touching me and being flirtatious. Beyond the difficulty of putting a label on it, I had no idea what was going on.

Once we sat down at the restaurant and ordered (I firmly suggested we share the East Utica Greens), the conversation returned in earnest.

"Sooo, how was the weekend in West Virginia?" she asked.

"Well, the team got their ass kicked—"

"Yeah! I know. What happened?"

"They didn't score as many points as the other team, so...."

"Shut up," she said.

"Nothing big. Same old, same old. Boeheim was miserable; the players weren't too thrilled, either. Most of them weren't wearing clothes, maybe a towel if I was lucky. You'd love it in there, though—finally, some tall guys for you to hang out with, make you feel at home amongst your kind...."

"What's that supposed to mean?" she asked.

"Oh, good, the food's here," I laughed.

As she ate, I checked my phone. I'd switched it to silent so I wouldn't be bothered. When I'd decided to do that, I'd realized that no one was going to be calling me, anyway. But, just in case, I wanted to avoid having to do the old "Excuse me, I just need to check this" routine. I hated when people texted in front of me. *People don't realize how rude that can be*, I thought.

I saw that I had a missed call from Lotfi, without a voicemail or text. Not a big deal. I snapped the phone shut and put it back into my pocket, where it would stay for the rest of the night.

Though the conversation on the way to the restaurant,

before the meal, during the meal, and after the meal was virtually without pause, everything dried up once we got back into my car after dinner.

We'd each had a few glasses of wine, so you'd think that, at the least, we'd both be a little *more* chatty. Not so. I asked her, for the third time, if she'd liked her food. She said, for the third time, that she had and thanked me, for the third time. I asked why she couldn't get a flight out until Sunday, for at least the second time. She answered. It was slow-moving, repetitive, and awkward.

Stopping in front of her house after driving through an obviously barren Syracuse University campus, I couldn't think of anything else to say. I knew what I *wanted* to say. I wanted to say something smooth, I wanted to lean over and kiss her, I wanted to wish her a safe flight.

Grabbing the door handle, she paused, as if waiting for me to say more. I didn't, so she continued out, thanking me again for the night.

"Hey!" I shouted out at her. It felt like someone had taken over my body and shouted for me.

One foot already out the door, she turned back. "Yes?"

"You want to, uh...go back to my place," I said, pausing, "and maybe watch a movie, or something?"

"What movies do you have?" she said.

This was what I didn't understand. *Why would she say that?* I wondered. *Here she is, basically begging me to ask her to do something, to make a move. Finally I do, and now she wants to know what kind of fucking movies I have?*

"Uh...well, what would you like to...I mean, whatever you want."

"Whatever I want? Are you running a Blockbuster over there?" (writer's note: for you young bucks reading this, Blockbuster used to be a place that men and women would actually leave their houses to go to, in order to rent hard copies of VHS tapes).

Firming up a bit, I countered, "I'm sure I can find something you'll like. You want to come, or not?"

"Yes," she smiled, coming back into the car, "I do."

I knew the "let's watch a movie" move all too well. It was how I nabbed my first girlfriend and I'd used it many other times with great success in the past. The principle behind it was simple: if a girl was willing to watch a movie with you alone, all that was left was for you to make the move. However, that was also where some difficulty came in. Did you make your move at some random point in the movie? Did you wait until the end? How about at a particularly romantic part? Was that too corny? I thought about these things.

"I'm going to go to the bathroom," she said. "Pick something out, would you?"

Now she doesn't care? Before, I was on trial about the depth of my film collection; now it's pick something out?

"Sure, no problem," I answered. My first inclination was *Goodfellas*, but I nixed that idea for a number of reasons: too much gore, too long, too Italian, too serious. After rifling through a number of choices, I settled on *10 Things I Hate About You*, with Joseph Gordon-Levitt and Heath Ledger. Funny, light, romantic. I hadn't seen it in a while, either, so it worked.

I sat down on the couch, waiting for her to emerge from the bathroom. Purposely, I sat on the far side of the couch, wanting to see where she'd sit. As she walked from the bathroom towards me, it was like a scene from a movie. Slowly, I cocked my head away from the screen, towards her. She seemed to glide in my direction, her hair blowing in the imaginary wind.

She sat down, right next to me, without touching me.

"What movie did you pi—"

I kissed her.

Pulling back, I said, "*10 Things I Hate About You.*" I realized how awkward that sounded, given what just happened. "I mean, that's the movie—"

She kissed me.

I grabbed her, pushing us down on the couch, passionately kissing her. Keep in mind, folks, this was nearly four years in the making. You ever wait that long for something like this? For anything at all?

She pulled off my shirt and I almost literally tore hers off.

"Easy, killer, I like this shirt. Here," she said, sitting up, reaching behind her back, and unclasping her bra. She threw it on the ground and slowly lifted her shirt over her head.

Holy shit, this is happening! This is fucking happening.

As we continued to kiss, to pet (okay, fine, grope) on top of one another, I knew I had to get off this couch. All my friends sat on this couch. We played Donkey Kong on this couch. I couldn't do anything real on this couch. That I was thinking of this, instead of, say, her supple breasts or her pretty face or her soft lips or the fact that she smelled like a bouquet of flowers, should at this point be no surprise.

"Do you want to, uh...."

"Yes," she said, without letting me finish.

"I was going to say, do you want to finish the movie?" I joked, pulling away from her to grab the remote.

She pulled me closer back towards her, slipping her hand underneath my jeans. "Let's go into your room, okay?"

"I think that's okay," I smiled. I let her walk in front, leaving all our stuff behind. No one else was in the house; I could do what I wanted.

Once inside my room, we continued where we'd left off.

I had watched enough porn that I thought I had an idea of how these things went. Make out, swapping of oral sex, then actual sex. There was no room for much else. Obviously, I had much to learn, but that would come later. Right now I knew where I wanted to go and I knew that getting my penis involved, outside of its denim prison, was key. Exactly how to do that, I wasn't sure. Again, as if she was reading my mind from on top of me, in a sort of moan, she asked, "Do you have any condoms?"

No, no, no! This isn't happening. This isn't fucking happening!

"I...I...I don't know. Let me check," I said, knowing full well that I didn't. I got up quickly so as to hide my blatant hard-on as I walked around the room. Why I was embarrassed about it, I wasn't sure. She was the reason I was that way; it was essentially proof of a job well done on her part.

"Well...." she half-whined, half moaned, "I want you inside of me...come on, already."

Think! Think, goddammit! She wants you inside of her. She said she wants you inside of her!

"Hold on one second, okay?" I said, bursting out of the room. I didn't wait for her to answer, knowing Colin had condoms somewhere in his room. I got up the stairs and into his room in what must have been record time (if time was kept for such a dash). Several rummaged drawers later, I found the box of Trojans.

Coming back into my room, I announced that I had the condoms. Before getting back into the bed, I looked down at her from where I stood. After all this time, here she was. Finally. Lauren Parker, girl of my dreams, was now naked in my bed, waiting (nay, wanting) to have sex with me. I smiled.

"What is it?" she asked, noticing my smile.

"Nothing," I said. "I'm just happy, is all."

27 saturday, march 15th

Like a scene out of a movie, when I woke up the next morning she was gone. The only difference was that she didn't leave a note. Not a big deal, I figured. She had to catch a flight early; I wasn't sure when.

Getting my stuff together for Spring Break, I took a mental inventory of what had happened. No matter how many times I passed by my garbage can while packing, I couldn't help but look at the condom wrappers and smile. *Maybe I should hold on to those wrappers as a keepsake. Would that be weird?*

I'd told Lotfi we'd leave around noon and it was after one at this point, so I gave him a call.

Straight to voicemail.

Hmm, I thought. *Odd he wouldn't have his phone on, or that it would die. Maybe he sent me an e-mail?*

A quick check revealed that he hadn't. I texted him something like "ready to go when you are." After about twenty minutes with no response, I called again. And again, the call went right to voicemail. Now I was starting to get worried.

The only thing I could think of was to see if he was at either his apartment or the radio station. I checked the apartment first, but no one answered the buzzer. Upon arriving at the station, the only person I saw was the receptionist.

"Vera, have you heard from or seen Lotfi?" I asked, although it could also have been categorized as a demand.

"Oh, why, yes. I have," she said in a quiet tone, looking down at her desk.

"Well? What's his deal? I'm looking for him. We were supposed to go home for break about an hour ago. I can't get in touch with him."

"No one told you?"

"No one told me what?"

"What happened to him...."

"What? What happened to him?!"

"I just know what I heard from the boys, but apparently he was walking down to Marshall Street around dinner time last night, and...." she said, pausing.

"And? And?"

"And, he collapsed," she said. "He was walking, and his legs gave out, and he fell down on the sidewalk."

At that exact moment, I stopped listening. I realized that that was why Lotfi had called me. He was in trouble and needed my help. It immediately dawned on me that my selfishness had prevented me from helping my friend.

Vera continued, "And so they took him to the hospital, and the last I heard was that he was en route to another hospital back home in New Jersey."

Sitting down, I couldn't think of anything to say. I was really upset. I was upset at myself, but I was also upset at Lotfi and at my friends. Why hadn't they called me more than once? Why hadn't anyone sent me a text or left a message? I missed one phone call, and that was it?

Vera finished the story, explaining that although he was sick, the word was that he was going to be fine, eventually. His back and legs had given out, a symptom of the condition he'd had for years. No one really knew what the condition was, but they knew that it had this potential to flare up in dangerous ways. Lotfi had actually told me about a time in high school when he had encountered this same issue, except that time he was actually crossing a street. Remembering his story, I took some solace in the fact that at least he was on a sidewalk.

I tried calling a host of people who might be able to get me in touch with Lotfi, or just help me find out more about what had happened. It was all to no avail. By the time I'd given up, it was close to six o'clock. I called my house to let my parents know why I wasn't home yet, and that I'd be leaving the following morning.

Staying in Syracuse that night, I felt about as lonely as I had in a long time. Maybe ever. Accompanied by only my own guilt and anger, I drifted off into a fitful sleep. I'd leave for New Jersey, alone, by eight in the morning on Sunday.

28 spring break: march 17th-23rd

Already two days into it, Spring Break was shaping up to be a real hoot. My high school friends all had their breaks other weeks, one of my best friends from college was in the hospital with a mystery back illness, and I'd missed the first two days of the break because I had stayed in Syracuse.

The weather in Millington, New Jersey was nicer than it was in Syracuse, though that wasn't saying much. The temperature hung around forty-five degrees, just cool enough to make it no fun to be outside for too long. Both of my parents worked, none of my friends were home, and my brother was in high school. It was pretty bleak.

I'd spoken briefly with Matt and Chris about Lauren, and at more length with Natalie. But for the most part, I watched TV. A lot of *Price is Right* and *Law and Order* reruns (is it ever not on some channel out there?). By Wednesday, I was so bored that I sat down to write my next column, even though it wouldn't be coming out for another week.

Everyone stop with the crazy e-mail signatures

Honestly, my fingers are too fat to text.

Call me Nickward Sausagehands, if you like.

Nowadays, there isn't much space for freaks like me. Most of my friends are wizards with texting. I'm sure you're familiar with the telephone, that old thing that people used to speak to each other on. Why call, when you can text?

As was the case with other new forms of technology upon their popularization, there are newfound etiquettes that come attached to texting, e-mails, and instant messaging. Even the ol' Facebook has its rules.

Why do people feel the need to sign off on Facebook messages? As if the bolded name on top of the message wasn't enough, the large picture should do the trick. You could get a driver's license with that many forms of ID.

More than that, what bothers me are e-mail signatures and the silliness that ensues when someone is done writing.

The worst are those lengthy signatures that include everything you could ever want to know about the person. Name, date of birth, place of birth, social security number, siblings in college, favorite quote, GPA and complete address.

From now on, I'm going to use my own signature, one I've devised in light of the way e-mail signatures frequently appear.

Nick Alexander
Favorite Pre-Internet President: James K. Polk
Favorite Tori Spelling Show: 90210
"Ain't nothin' but a gangsta party" - Tupac Amaru Shakur

The first time I saw one of those, I wasn't sure what to do with it. Initially, I thought it was a checklist, as if I was supposed to see if I knew

those things about the person and then report back
to them. Signatures on e-mails should be what they
are everywhere else - a cursive version of your
name, not a biography.

Of course, when the Pony Express speed of e-mail
won't suffice, there's only one alternative: instant
messaging. I struggle with IMing because my
deadliest tool, sarcasm, is shot right in the foot.
Though I must say, when typing an instant message, I
often feel like the world's fastest typist. I think
that if there were some sort of Olympic competition
to see who could most quickly communicate their
thoughts via instant message, I'd have to at least
represent our country, if not the hemisphere.

My major issue with IMing, which I'm 100 percent
guilty of, is the incessant need to correct typos.

A little while back, I messaged someone, "I'll be,
bathroom." Almost instantaneously, I felt the need
to make sure that person knew I meant, "I'll be
back, bathroom." As if the person on the other
screen was looking at that, thinking, "He'll be
bathroom? He'll be bathroom?! What the hell does
that mean? He had better correct himself soon, or
I'm going over to make sure he's all right."

My ultimate hope is that someday, in the near
future, we'll be able to just do away with talking
face to face or even via phone. Maybe you could even
donate your voice boxes to people who can't afford
iPhones. Who knows what the futur holds?*

*future holds, my bad.

I was particularly proud of this one, if only because I put
some real thought into it. Most times, I'd sit down and write
as things came to me. That's not to say it wasn't an effective
strategy. I didn't like doing revisions, felt my best stuff
typically came on the first draft. But this particular column
was the product of a discussion I'd had with the editors at the
D.O. What had started as a riffing session eventually turned
into a column. Actual thought, actual brainstorming. It
flowed, it was funny. I liked it. Most importantly, I was happy
I could write a full column without mentioning anything about

women. It was a step in the right direction.

Other than the forty-five minutes that took to write, I was still bored.

I called all of my roommates at least one time during the week, went over to my grandmother's house for lunch a few times, and even put together a K'Nex rollercoaster. Yes, K'Nex.

The only semi-interesting thing that occurred the entire week happened on Friday morning. I got a text from Allison, telling me about a party she was having at her place that night because her parents were out of town. At first, I had absolutely no desire to go. She lived about an hour from my parents and the boredom of the week had completely sucked the life out of me. Lack of activity begets boredom, which in turn begets sloth-like inactivity, which ultimately begets things like wearing sweatpants for days on end and rarely showering.

Eventually, though, the power of female persuasion (read: the realization that if I went down there I might get some ass) got me into the shower and, finally, out of sweatpants. I hadn't asked to sleep over, though I knew that was in the offing, considering I'd be drinking.

It almost goes without saying that the party was an awkward time, doesn't it? Here's the college friend, hanging out with this girl he doesn't really like that much anyway, in front of all her high school friends. Not to mention that my showing up on account of possible sexual activity no doubt continued to fuel any (now certainly) misplaced notions she might have had about our relationship.

She'd opened the door when I'd arrived, and as I tried to take a step into the house, she pushed me back out with her, closing the door behind us. Once we were both outside, she turned around and forced herself on me.

"Whoa, whoa," I said, half-enjoying it, half-freaked out by it. "Let's cool it, okay?"

She frowned at me, grabbing my genitals.

"For now?" I compromised.

"Come on in! I want you to meet my friends!" she said,

immediately darting inside.

It was that sort of night. One moment she acted like she wanted to film pornography, another moment she was giddy, at other moments quiet. In other words, not too out of the ordinary for a drunk girl, especially one that was horny.

While I wasn't *that* drunk, I did have enough that I wasn't going to go home that night. And while I may not have been *that* into Allison, I still was a man. A man who liked having sex with women. Attractive women, no matter how annoying they might be. So I stayed. (Trust me, I realize how pathetic this reads for us. And by us, I mean men in general.)

"You're going to stay tonight, right?" Allison cooed from the far room. She was cleaning up some beer bottles, making more of a mess than she was eliminating by spilling just about every fourth one. I was in the bathroom.

"Yes, I'm going to stay," I said, now leaving the bathroom. Looking around the corner, I couldn't find her, but I continued, "I can just clear off that couch there; I should be fine. Actually, if you have pil—"

She came up behind me and grabbed me by the waist, turning me toward her and pressing me close. Not one to wait, she kissed me, again playing the role of aggressor. The make-out session soon progressed from the hallway to the kitchen to the stairs to the upstairs hallway to, finally, her room. Making out while taking off your clothes and trying to figure out where you're going, and doing it while walking backwards, is much harder than it might outwardly appear.

As I ran my hand across her naked body, grabbing every curve I could find in the dark of the room, I realized that, again, I didn't have any condoms on me. It was likely a presumptuous thought, based on the fact that we'd never really done anything more than kiss, touch, and take each other's clothes off. Nothing more than your typical "high-school make-out sesh," as Natalie would say. Still, one can normally tell when sex is in the offing and I got that feeling. Pretty loud and clear.

"Do you want to have sex?" she asked.

"I don't have any condoms," I confessed sheepishly.

"You don't have any condoms?" she said, in a tone of both anger and confusion. It was as if she couldn't possibly imagine why I *wouldn't* have condoms on me when I came down for this party.

"No, I don't really keep them on me. I feel like it's bad luck, like it's going to jinx it or something."

"Well, that's pretty stupid," she said.

"Trust me," I said, looking down at my penis, "I'm well aware of how stupid it is. Believe me."

The mood was clearly blown. She wanted to have sex, and so did I, but neither of us was so into it that we were going to forget about the condom. I took a shot in the dark, after a moment of awkward silence (writer's note: is there another kind of silence in this type of moment?): "You wouldn't happen to have any condoms, would you?"

"What do I look like, a whore?" she asked.

I didn't answer. That one backfired, no doubt.

"Why don't you go and get some? There's a 7-Eleven about five minutes from here. You can get me a Slurpee."

Truly, I was a man at a crossroads. Did I take the ordering around, the possible DUI ticket, all in the name of getting some ass? Or did I stand my ground, both morally and chauvinistically, and simply call it a night?

You know, if it's not really that far, I can probably drive and just focus real hard on the road. Squint, if I have to, I first thought.

Is a fucking DUI worth it? You don't even like this girl that much and you just had sex with the girl you really do like, so why would you risk messing that up and maybe getting in some actual trouble just to have sex with this girl? I continued to think.

"How do I get there?" I asked.

Fifteen minutes after I'd told her I wouldn't be getting her a Slurpee and made her promise to not fall asleep, I returned. On the bed she lay, almost a déjà-vu from the night with Lauren.

While I certainly didn't feel the same level of satisfaction and joy as I climbed into bed with Allison as I'd had with

Lauren only a few days prior, I did have a moment of "what the hell is going on". I tried my best to cover it up and as far as I could tell, she didn't seem to notice. As I climbed on top of her, the thought of what was taking place, the randomness of it, the fortune, the success, were remarkable. Here I was, about to have sex for the second time in less than a week, and with a new girl, no less. And both were attractive. This may not seem like a big deal, and to a normal socially-equipped college male, it may not have been. But I had gone nearly two years without sex. For men of my age, that's an eternity. The thoughts and feelings of these women, what I might or might not be screwing up with Lauren, when or whether I planned on actually getting back in touch with Sophia: these were all things that I'd put on the back burner for the time being. Now, my penis was in charge. And my penis was an aggressive field general.

Although I wasn't as attracted to the girl involved this time, I certainly enjoyed it more. I'd forgotten what it felt like to be that connected, on whatever level you please, to a woman. To make a woman respond, to touch her in a way that lets you know you're doing something right. The feel of it all, the smoothness of firm breasts. Okay, that's enough. You get the point.

I left the following morning, after we went out for breakfast. Spring Break, outside of the party, concluded uneventfully. The ride up to school was a particularly dry one, as it was my first in a while without the company of Lotfi.

I had gotten to speak to him over the phone and in his typical fashion, he said that everything was peachy. Except, of course, for the fact that he was basically Grandpa Joe from the beginning of *Charlie and the Chocolate Factory*. And he wasn't sure when he'd be coming back to school. Except for that, everything was fine. As infuriating as it could be for my negativity to deal with someone as positive as Lotfi, it was this perspective that made the difference in situations like this. Never would Lotfi allow someone to feel sorry for him. He didn't present his situation, desperate as it may actually have been, as anything other than unfortunate. He'd come through, he knew it, and he wanted you to feel the same way. I wasn't exactly sure how to feel, as I'd always been somewhat wary of so much positivity, especially in the medical field. But I knew I didn't feel bad, because at the least, that wasn't what Lotfi wanted.

Over the course of the Spring Break week and the ride back to school, I'd spoken with Lotfi a few times. I'd obviously seen Allison, I hadn't contacted Sophia at all, and I had chatted on the phone with Lauren once or twice. My priorities, in no particular order, were getting the comedy show up and running, re-establishing contact with Sophia, and somehow managing to balance the other two. Not even four and a half hours of sports talk radio, mushed with Montell Jordan and Notorious B.I.G., could keep me from thinking about those things and the weeks to come.

29 thursday, march 27th

The meeting with Jennifer Gagliardo was supposed to be on the Tuesday after Spring Break. Of course, she wasn't free then and had to reschedule and the only other time she had available for that week was on Thursday—right during my Com Law class.

Oh, yes: who is Jen Gagliardo? I wasn't exactly sure myself—Matt had asked me that question earlier in the day. All I knew was that Leah Higgins told me she was the woman I'd have to talk with to get everything cleared for the show. Why it had taken me this long to actually get my shit together to see this woman, I have no idea. I'd love to lie to you and tell you it had to do with the girls or with classes or with radio work. I mean, I'm sure those things had something to do with it, but let's be real: there's one word at the heart of my lack of action, and it rhymes with schlazy.

"She's waiting for you," a person I couldn't even fully see behind the desk said as I walked into the office.

"What?" I said at the desk.

A small, dark-haired girl picked her head up. "You are Nick Alexander?"

"I am."

"You're here to meet with Jen?"

"I am."

"You're late."

"I am?"

"You are."

I hadn't even realized it. Great start.

"Come on in, Nick," a voice I assumed was Jen's called from the room on the left. "You're not that late. Yet."

I did that quick I've-got-to-go-to-the-bathroom walk into the room and sat down opposite this woman I had yet to get a visual of. She had her head buried in the school paper. At least two minutes passed; nothing was said. She flipped a few pages—still nothing. Then, out of nowhere, she quickly folded the paper in half, then again over itself.

Jabbing a stubby finger at my picture over my column, she said, "So this is you, huh?" She was a middle-aged woman, tan with straight dark hair and dark eyes. She looked like she wasn't happy to be working at a college, to be reminded of the fact that she was no longer as youthful and carefree as the people who surrounded her.

"Yes, it is," I said, unsure whether I should be proud of that or not given the way she said it.

"You do stand-up comedy, I've heard."

"I do." Looking around, I shifted in my seat, unable to figure out what was going on.

She stared at me some more, visually interviewing me, as if whether or not she'd approve the show had only to do with whether she liked my outfit.

"I'm sorry, is this a bad time?" I said, interrupting the silence.

"No, fine time. Fine time for you, right?" she responded, still not smiling.

"I just figured, you'd told me it worked for you, so I'm here."

"Listen here, you," she said sitting up in her seat, "You think you're the first person to come in here, thinking, 'Oh, I can do what I want'? 'I'm popular because I'm in the paper'?

'I want to do my own show'?"

"Uh...."

"Well, do you?"

"I...I don't know what you're talking about."

"You think you're a big shot? You think you're funny?!"

"I guess so," I said. *What is going on?!* I was thinking.

"Well," she said, her face relaxing, "You are."

"What?"

"I'm just kidding with you, Nick," she laughed, reaching out and playfully touching my shoulder. "Relax, okay? Leah told me you were a little nervous about this whole thing. She told me to mess with you."

I exhaled, deeply. "That was some joke."

"I know, right?" she grinned. Her whole countenance had changed by this point. The miserable woman I'd seen before had vanished, and in her stead was a joyous, salted-nuts-eating ("You want some?" she asked, mouth full), joke-cracking young lass. Maybe "lass" is a bit extreme. But either way....

The conversation went, surprisingly, quite smoothly from there. I explained what I wanted to do and how I wanted to do it, and asked what I needed to do to make that happen.

"Well, how many people do you expect? You sure you don't want some peanuts?"

"I'm fine, thank you. I expect...I don't know, really. I guess we could have anywhere between twenty-five and a hundred and fifty people. I know that doesn't help at all. But I really don't know."

"No, that does not help at all," she smiled. "Here's what I'd suggest. I'd suggest an on-campus auditorium. They're much smaller, but could fit at least two hundred people, most of them, and are usually more available than the bigger venues."

"How about collecting money?" I asked.

"You're going to need security there. Not because we think people are going to steal—it's more of a precautionary thing, you know?"

I said I did, even though I didn't.

"Call this number and ask for Sergeant John Wallington; he's a friend. Tell him I said that we'd take care of the cost of keeping a man there."

I didn't even realize that it would cost money for this service, so obviously I was stunned by the gesture. "Really? Wow, thanks."

"Not a problem. Anything else?"

"Yes," I said, pausing. I was nervous about this part, but I knew I had to ask. "I know what you're going to say to this, but—"

"Don't say that yet; you haven't even asked."

"Okay, fine. Would I be able to have a poster for the show put up in the student center in one of those life-sized kiosks?"

"You're serious?"

"Yes…?" I said, actually asking, because I had begun to doubt it, too. I couldn't expect her to say yes to that. The only things I'd seen in those kiosks were giant posters for people like John Mayer and Dane Cook when they'd come to the school.

"Well, obviously, *that's* not going to happen," she said. "Anything else?"

"Uh, well, no. I guess that's it," I said, clearly dejected. It was a pipe dream, sure, but before I'd gotten there, I'd somehow imagined she'd say yes.

"I'm kidding! Come on, Nick. For a comedian, you know, you really need to work on picking up sarcasm."

I really had no idea what was going on.

"Let me guess," she started. "You probably thought those kiosks were reserved for big names. Huh?"

"No," I lied.

"Yes, you did," she laughed. "All it costs is money, not fame. You need to show me the design, of course, but other than that, it's not a problem."

"How much?"

"You know, off the top of my head, I'm not sure," she said, stopping to look through a pile of papers. "Heck with it.

I'll take care of it."

"You'll what?"

"Don't worry about it—it's paid for. Just get the design to me as soon as you can, so we can have it approved."

I was confused. First she berated me, then she told me she was kidding. Then she was a snack-food-eating fiend. Next, serious. Then, back to joking. The whole time, she was donating and giving me things for free that I didn't even ask for.

"Is there some sort of catch to this? Are you kidding around still? Am I not allowed to curse in the show, is that what this is about? Why are you doing all these nice things for me?"

She laughed. "Of course you can curse. You wouldn't have much to say if you couldn't, would you?"

"I mean, I curse sometimes...okay, I curse a lot. How did you know?"

"Leah told me," she said. "And listen, there's no catch. You seem like a good kid, pretty humble about this. She told me what you were trying to do, and how much it meant to you. I get that, I really do. I have a nephew with CF, so I get it. I also was a college student in the last...the, uh, recent past, so I know what it means to not have money to shell out. I want to help you get this off the ground, so it's really no problem."

Blown away by her sincerity and generosity, all I could muster was a simple "Thank you."

"You are quite welcome."

My phone vibrated in my pocket and without even thinking, I knew who it was. Glancing around the room, I couldn't find a clock.

"It's one-thirty," Jen said. "You have a date?"

"Actually," I started, "I did. At one, but that was before I scheduled this with you, and I completely forgot, and now I'm late, and I really, actually more than you could imagine or I'd care to explain, need to get there. Like, now. So, thank you very much and I'll be e-mailing you, okay?"

"Sounds fine by me," she answered. "You sure you don't

want some peanuts?"

I was already out her door by that point, doing my best not to get winded while sprinting out of the building and over to the Student Center cafeteria. Earlier in the week, I'd asked Sophia to meet up with me for lunch on Thursday. Not surprisingly, I'd put something in front of her and, even more predictably, forgotten to mention it to her at all.

Despite the second-rate treatment I seemed to constantly afford her, Sophia still stuck around. She couldn't quite explain it herself, but there was something about her that actually liked me. She saw past my bullshit, somehow, and seemed to truly enjoy my company, although I might not be as forthcoming with the same sentiment. There'd been some disconnect between us lately. We'd talk in class every so often, see each other out fairly regularly, but the sleepovers and hook-up sessions had stalled, especially over the two weeks prior to Spring Break.

"Good, you're still here," I huffed as I reached her table.

"You run here?"

"Yes. Please, let me explain. Can I explain myself, why I'm late? I'm really sorry. Please, just stay for a bit longer, let me explain."

She didn't get up, so I told her to hang on so I could grab a soda.

"Get the fuck out of here."

"Kidding," I said, smiling. She tried to hold back a smile, but couldn't. *Okay*, I thought, *all's not lost.* I proceeded to go over the comedy show idea I'd hatched while at Notre Dame, the time-sensitive nature of it all and how I absolutely had to take whatever meeting I could get with this woman. I apologized again and tried my best to make it seem as if I had no other choice but to double-book myself. True as that all may have been, the bottom line remained clear to Sophia: I didn't seem to make her a priority when it came to basically anything else in my life.

"Well, good luck with all that," she said.

"You're going to come, right? It would obviously mean a

lot to me."

"Of course I'm going to come," she said. "Of course."

This time I did go and get a drink and when I came back, she was ready for me.

"What's been your problem lately?"

"What do you mean, *my problem*?"

"What happened to you—your phone break? I see you around, in class, out sometimes, but you barely look at me anymore."

"Nope, works fine," I said, taking out my phone.

"Oh," she smirked. "Now you're going to play me? Is that it?"

"No, no. I'm not playing you. I don't know what to tell you. What do you want to hear from me?"

She didn't answer.

I took a sip out of my cup and kept going. "I don't know what to say. I haven't called. I'm sorry. We can hang out more—"

"Oh, thanks for fitting me in," she said.

"Come on, now, that's not what I meant. You know that. Listen, what are you doing tonight?"

"Tonight?"

"Yes, tonight. Don't act like you've got plans. And don't, I see you thinking right now, don't pretend like you can't come because you don't want to make it seem like you'll just give in to me right away."

"Shut up," she said.

"Okay," I responded. After a silent moment: "Well, are you free?"

"I am, after a meeting at around eight or so. But I don't want to go to Chuck's, if that's what you're thinking. I don't feel like doing that tonight."

"Fine by me, fine. Why don't we get dinner or something? How's that sound?"

"You? You're going to take me to dinner?"

"What's that supposed to mean?" I asked. I soon realized that despite having taken the other two girls out to the movies or to dinner or other things, I'd never done anything other than bring Sophia back to my room. The other two girls who didn't seem to care about me as much as she did, the other two girls who weren't interested in what I truly cared about, the other two girls I'd had sex with. I took them places. I didn't take Sophia anywhere.

"Nothin'. It's just, the most date-ish thing we've ever done was meeting at Chuck's."

"Let's do it, then."

"What?"

"Let's go on a date. Let's fucking do it, tonight," I smiled, putting my hand on top of hers on the table.

"You're so sweet, you know?"

"That's why you like me, isn't it?" I said, leaning in to kiss her.

"Nah, don't try that. You've got to earn it back. I'm not that easy," she said, getting up.

"Oh, it's like that?"

"Yeah, it's like that," she said as she walked away.

"All right then," I called out, "I'll pick you up at eight-thirty, then?"

"Sounds good," she answered back. And then she was gone. I didn't know where I'd take her, but I figured that if I wanted to play my past odds, taking a girl to Delmonico's had worked pretty well so far.

Later that night....

Far as I was concerned, the formula was pretty simple. I took a girl out, be it to the movies or dinner. I drove to the place, paid for everything, let them talk more than I talked, and then took the girl back to my place, where we hooked up and maybe even had sex. Not too difficult, or so I assumed. Naturally, I had this plan (or more accurately, exactly what I'd done with Lauren right before Spring Break) in mind when I picked up Sophia to go to Delmonico's.

Things progressed as you'd expect, just as I'd planned.

The meal tasty, the conversation easy and interesting, the wine flowing. It was a nice evening. I got into the car with her to drive her back to her place, figuring I'd score big-time. A good night was at hand.

Obviously, if you're reading at higher than a fifth-grade reading level, you've probably assumed that it wouldn't go as planned. If so, you'd be right.

Parking my car outside her place, I leaned in to kiss her. Unlike earlier in the day, she didn't back away, but instead leaned in on top of me. We kissed for a few minutes, during which I pulled her close with my right hand, my left hand caressing her breasts. After those few minutes, with both hands on my face, she pulled back.

"Thank you so much for dinner," she said, and almost as suddenly, she unbuckled her seatbelt and hopped out of the car.

"What the—" I started to say, alone in the car. *—hell just happened?* my thoughts finished. Rolling down my window, I yelled out, "Yo, what was that?"

"Good night, Nick!" She turned and smiled.

"Good night? That's it?"

"Yeah, that's it. You expecting something more?"

"Umm...I'd say so," I said.

Coming closer to the car, I could smell her perfume. She leaned in to kiss me through the open driver's-side window. "Good night, Nick."

I pulled away from her face. Turning my car back on, I muttered "I don't have time for this shit."

"Hey, you just going to leave? That's it? You're ghost, you're leaving because I won't let you fuck me after one dinner?"

"One dinner? You just don't know, do you? You just don't know," I said, putting the car into reverse, backing up.

"You know what?" she screamed after my car as it took off. "Fuck you, Nick Alexander! Fuck! You!"

I don't recall any of the drive home, thoughts running through my mind at a million miles an hour...

This fucking girl, after a dinner and all that, she won't even invite me back to her place?...How many times have I taken her out, and all we've done is kiss? What the fuck do I have to do to get some from this girl?...Why did I react like that? She seemed really mad at me. Did she tell me to fuck off?...You know what, who gives a shit about her anyway? Fuck her. If she thinks that way, I don't fucking need her....

As I stormed into the house, I walked past Natalie in the kitchen. There were other people in the house, too, I could tell, but I wasn't sure who. At the moment, I didn't care.

"Early night, huh, stud?" she said.

"She said 'Fuck you' to me. Twice, I think. Loudly," I said, collapsing onto my bed.

She was doing something in the kitchen but came into my room almost instantaneously upon hearing what I'd said. Closing the door behind her, she asked if she'd heard me right. Talking into my pillow, I muffled out something that said she had.

"Are you going to tell me *why* she said that to you?"

Something more muffled, from face-down in my pillow.

"Can you turn around, sit up like a big boy, and tell me what happened?"

"Fine," I said, following instructions. I proceeded to tell her what had happened, at least as I saw it. "You know that we were going out to dinner tonight, right? I took her to Delmonico's—"

"Shocker," Natalie interrupted.

"Sue me, I like that place. There aren't that many good places around here."

"There's more than one," she said.

"Does that really matter? You want to let me tell this story?" I asked. She said she did. "So yeah, we're there. We eat dinner, we have a great time, I pay, we leave, go back to her place. I park right outside, we start making out for a little bit and then, in the middle of nowhere, she just gets up and leaves."

"And..."

"And then she says good night," I said. "Can you believe

the nerve of that fucking girl?"

"Oh my God! She said *good night*? You're right, she is a bitch. Some nerve on that girl. Do you have her phone number? I need to give her a piece of my mind."

"You want to cut it out?"

"Can I ask you a question?" she asked, her tone changing from the sarcasm of a moment earlier to complete seriousness.

"Go ahead."

"What the fuck is your problem?"

"My problem?"

"You barely talk to this girl for a few weeks because you're too busy screwing around with other girls. You never do anything with her and put her off until it's convenient for you. Finally, you take her out. Once. And now you're mad because she didn't have sex with you *immediately* after that?"

"It's not like that," I said. "We've hung out a number of times. She's slept over a bunch and we've hooked up before. I've bought her dinner, bought her drinks, bought her—"

"So because you bought her stuff, you have the right to have sex with her?"

"No, that's not what I'm saying," I said, starting to get a little angry now at Natalie. "Don't put words in my mouth."

Getting up from the chair in front of my computer, she said, "Then what is it you're saying?"

I sat up straighter on my bed. "What I'm saying is…I'm saying that I don't think I'm being ridiculous, being overbearing if I want to…I mean, isn't that what people do? We've hung out a bunch of times. How many more times do I have to…"

"I love you, Nick, I do. But, you're an asshole. I can't have this conversation with you anymore. I know you look at me as one of the guys and I'm fine with that. But I'm still a girl. I can't handle how you treat her, like she owes you sex because you bought her a beer and pasta. I know you don't care, but this girl likes you. For real. I can see it in the way she looks at you, when she comes around."

"The heck are you talking about?"

"How about a little while back when you called her after her awards dinner? She was tired from the whole day and still came over here anyway. She wanted to see you. And what did you do? You made fun of her for wearing a dress, you said—"

"I said she looked nice. I did say that," I clarified.

"But that's not all you said. And that's not how you said it. You made fun of her, Nick. And for some reason, even though she was angry, she didn't leave. She stayed. I saw her that night and other times. The way she looks at you, she likes you. And you still treat her like shit. Now, if you don't like her, that's fine. Just cut her loose. Stop stringing her along, pretending that she's more important to you than she actually is. You don't have any problem being nice to Allison, even though she bothers the hell out of you. Or Lauren, even though she won't get back to you for weeks. But this girl, because she won't sleep with you, you treat her like crap. You're not this big of a dickhead, but you're acting like it."

I was pissed. Really angry. But I knew she was right, so I didn't say anything and neither did she as she left the room. Alone with my anger, frustration, and questions, I stayed in my room for the remainder of the night, hoping that something would come to me. Nothing did.

30 thursday, april 3rd

Can you trace back to the moment when you realized you were going to be friends with someone? Actual friends? The one I'm thinking about with Matt was during our freshman year. I came back to our room to see candy scattered all over his bed. "What's up?" I said. "You rob the CVS? What's with all the candy?"

"My mom sent me a package," he said. "You want any of this?"

Inspecting, I settled on the Peeps. I was hesitant to ask, because I only liked them in a particular way. Texture is an important, often underplayed aspect of eating. It was because of texture, for instance, that I hated eating scallops...*They feel like marshmallows, but from the ocean. That's gross,* I'd said to my mom when she first made me try them. Texture, as it concerned the Peeps, was very important. I only liked them, odd as it seems, when they were a bit crunchy. And the only way to establish said crunch was to let them get a little stale Open the packaging up, let them get a little fresh air, and devour in a few days. As much as I loved them this way, I recognized the oddity in such a request.

"Yeah, I'll, uh…I'll have some of those Peeps, if you don't

mind."

"No…no problem. I offered, didn't I? How many do you think you're gonna want, though? Because I'd like to leave the rest out for a bit. I like them a little crispy."

"Dude," I deadpanned.

"What?" Matt asked.

"Did I just say that out loud?"

"Say what out loud?"

"That I like them crispy."

"No, I just did."

"Holy shit. I love them like that. I always thought I was the only one."

"Nope," Matt chuckled, "that's the way to eat 'em. You're in good company, homie."

Later that night, we were watching TV from our respective beds before going to sleep. Matt had the TV remote. We'd been watching a re-run of *Sports Center*. Matt flipped around through the channels, settling on a music video show while we discussed something from the *Sports Center* Top Ten Plays list.

"How could a three-sixty dunk over Shaq not be the number-one play?" Matt asked.

"Eh," I said, "he's only seven-three. It's not really *that* impressive."

Matt laughed. "All right, dude. I'm going to bed. You can change this if you want."

Looking towards the screen, I saw an 'N Sync video dazzling on the screen. Bright colors, boy bands, frosted tips, teeny pop.

"Nah, your call."

"I'm fine with it if you are. Just going to sleep over here."

"Okay, fine here. Me, too."

Ten minutes later, another similar song (maybe the Backstreet Boys?).

"You still 'just going to sleep' over there?" I asked.

"No, you?" Matt piped up.

"Nope."

"Aw, who the hell are we kidding?" Matt said, getting out of bed and turning on the light. "We both love this shit. Admit it."

It was an odd moment to bond over, but when you're eighteen and living on your own for the first time, how much do you really need to find a friend?

Now, from the living room, Matt asked me: "Where are you going?" He had this habit, originally deemed obnoxious and eventually accepted as just annoyingly nosy, of asking everyone about their plans. If he was around and you were leaving, he wanted to know what you were up to. Rare was it that he did anything with the information, but it seemed to make him happy to know everyone's whereabouts.

"Ah, sorry, sir," I said, popping my head back into the TV room through the saloon doors. "My apologies. I'm heading out, actually, to take a look at the venue for my show. You see, venue is a word that refers to a location, a place where—"

"I got it, dick," Matt shot back from his seat on the couch.

"I assume you don't want to come with, so I'm going to head out."

"Normally, you'd be right. But I don't want to see you get hosed. Plus, if I'm going to be running the door for this thing, I want to know the place. Get the lay of the land. Hey, maybe I'll get lucky and you'll teach me a new vocabulary word."

I had convinced Jen Gagliardo to allow me to have my friends run security and she ultimately relented because the on-campus security people simply didn't want to be bothered. Matt would work the door as a bouncer. Colin and Natalie would be ushers, handing out the programs I would make, and Matt's girlfriend Jamie would be in charge of collecting the money. She was an accounting major, so it was really the only thing I could think of for her. As for Chris, he was in charge of making sure the whole thing got recorded and sent out to the campus television station.

At this point in the semester we didn't have much choice, but we still scoped out the Gifford Room. It would hold a good number of people, had gradually inclined seating, and featured a small stage in the front. Afterwards, as we sat down on a bench outside the lecture hall in the main lobby of the building, I saw a pair of blonde-haired girls reading the newspaper, giggling.

"Do you see that?" I said. Matt didn't answer, so I continued. "I think this is the place. What do you think?"

"I like it," Matt said.

"That's it? That's all you have to say?"

"I *really* like it? I don't know what else you want me to say."

"Anything, really. Any comments or thoughts would be appreciated."

Matt punched me on the arm. Conversation over. He would've told me if there was something wrong.

"See what?" Matt asked, belatedly.

"Those two girls laughing over there. I bet they're laughing at my column."

"You really are losing your mind, dude. I'm glad this whole thing has made you feel like you're not the loser you really are, but cool it a bit, huh? They could be reading the comics; who knows?"

"Have you ever read the comics in our paper?"

"Fine, maybe not the comics."

"Here, let's make this interesting. I'll bet you they are reading my column. I've got..." I said, taking out my wallet, "...I've got...twenty-five bucks on me."

"Easy, killer," Matt said. "I don't want your money. How would you suggest we prove this, if we were to do it?"

"Just go over there and ask."

"Why don't you?"

"Duh, you idiot. If I go over there and ask, they're going to lie. They're not going to tell me they read it; that's embarrassing for them. Would you like me to go over there with a pen to sign the paper, too?"

"Holy shit, you are an egomaniac," Matt laughed. "Put your wallet away. I don't want the money, I don't. I just want to shut you up."

As Matt walked towards the girls, I picked up a copy of the paper and flipped to my most recent article, about hot-dog-eating contests and how disgusting they actually are. Basic premise: Could you imagine trying to explain the idea of a hot-dog-eating contest, or any eating contest, for that matter, to someone living…anywhere else? Hey, I thought it was a funny idea.

I could tell how the encounter went just from the way Matt was walking back towards me. But, to have fun with it, I pretended like I had no idea.

"You know what happened, don't you?" Matt asked. Obviously, I had to work on my hiding skills.

"No, no, what did they say?" I laughed.

"I'm going to pretend for a second like you don't know," Matt started. "I go over there and I say, 'Excuse me, I know this is a weird thing to ask, but what are you reading?'"

"Points for being blunt," I said.

"Get this, though," Matt said, sitting down. "She says, 'The newspaper.'"

"Bonus points for a college education," I said.

"I know, right? After I asked her to be a little more specific, she asked why, and I said, just tell me, and she said, 'Why?' So I said, because I just want to know, and she said—"

"Good Lord, get to it, already," I said.

"Your stories can take hours, but mine can't go over a minute?"

"No, they can't. You don't know the rules by now?"

Ignoring me, he continued, "I didn't want to tell them I knew you. I just wanted to see what their honest answer was, so I didn't tell them. Eventually, though, they told me they were reading your column and I explained to them why I asked."

"Which was because…" I prodded.

"Because you're my friend and you're an arrogant egomaniac."

"You said that to them?"

"Yes, I did."

"Oh, great. Two hot girls who like reading my column and think I'm funny and you go and lie to them about me?"

He didn't say anything back. The look said it all: *Really?*

31 wednesday, april 9th

The e-mail from Professor Edington, the one regarding the job in L.A., was fairly serious as it turned out. I'd put it off for a while after I'd first read it, a month or so back. Even when I'd responded to it, I'd given it half-attention. In typical professor fashion, Edington took his time responding. He was going to dictate the pace of these proceedings. If I didn't want to take it seriously, the least Edington could do was to make me sweat a bit. The whole thing was, at the very least, mature.

For those of you who don't care for the silly back-and-forth, the bottom line was that we'd settled on this Wednesday to meet up and discuss the whole thing. That's where I was heading as I left the house, on this brisk day in early April. Sunny, but extremely chilly. The sort of day that would trick you into wearing shorts if you used only your eyes, from inside your room.

Approaching Edington's small one-windowed office, in the building I'd been taking journalism classes in for the past four years, I caught myself wondering why I'd taken so little care in attending to this. *What if I've thrown away a great job opportunity? Wouldn't Edington have stayed on me if it was really that important? Then again, who knows with Edington, right? He's not my dad; he doesn't have to stay on me. But wouldn't guilt set in at some point for most people, the kind of thing that would make you want to see a young guy you'd gotten along with over the years succeed?*

"Professor Edington," I said after two sharp raps on the closed door. "It's Nick Alexander."

No answer.

I took a step back and leaned up against the wall opposite the door, figuring Edington had to be on a phone call or something.

Leaning in to knock again, I said, "Hey there, I can come back if you'd like. Just wanted to let you know I'm here. Sorry for being late."

"I'm not shocked to hear that," Edington's voice said from behind me.

Whirling around, I was surprised to find him standing there, but tried to play it cool. "Not shocked to hear which part?"

"That you were late."

"I suppose I'm not the most prompt person…"

Sitting down at his desk while I took a seat opposite him, Edington said, "Cut the shit, Alexander. You're always late. You and I both know it. You're late to class, you're late to meetings. You don't get back to people on time. You probably show up late to dates and to your comedy shows and in responding to people about them. Don't you?"

"No," I said, smiling.

"Why do you act that way?"

"You seem to have all the answers, so why don't you tell me?" I smarted back.

"Don't be a wise-ass," Edington answered. "But, since you asked, I'll tell you why. I think you act that way as a defense. I think you act that way to protect yourself, to give off this sense that nothing is important to you—because that way, you can't be let down. This idea that you're *too fucking cool*, that you can't be bothered with getting to class on time or showing up to something that you deem important—or, say, getting back to a professor about a job: I think, quite frankly, it's all a front."

I took a breath, looked around the room. Unlike most professors' offices, this one wasn't decorated with degrees. There was one behind him, but that was it. There were several shelves, each packed to the absolute brim with various tapes and recordings, most seemingly homemade. In each of the far corners, there were stacks of magazines and newspapers, most of the latter yellowed by the powers of time and coffee stain.

"Well, do you have anything to say for yourself, Mr. Alexander?"

"Not really," I said, noticeably slumping in my chair.

"Sit up. Let's go. It isn't like any of this is damning stuff. And, let's be honest, if you'd ever stopped to think about it for a minute, you'd have drawn the same conclusions."

"I guess, but I've never really thought about that stuff before." Ready to move past my own dissection, I changed topics as swiftly as I could. "So, about that job...."

"Smooth," Edington chuckled. "Real smooth. Well. The situation with the job is fairly simple. A former student of mine, Ethan Kroner, works out in Los Angeles as a producer for the NFL Network. Now, I know you've made quite clear your distaste for producing and for television—"

"Sorry to cut you off...I mean, I guess just did, but whatever...but, that's not entirely true."

"I believe your exact words were 'I have no desire to work in television' when Phillips asked which members of the class would be needing to make a reel."

"You heard about that?"

"I hear about everything."

"I'm gathering that. I meant that I don't want to be on TV. I'd rather be on the radio."

"I'm going to be real with you. Radio might be your profession of choice, might be something you'd love to do and be great at. But it's a dying industry."

"I know that," I said confidently.

"I hear you say that, but I don't know if you really understand what that means. But that's okay," Edington said, folding his legs as he sat back in his chair. "When I was your age, I had no fucking clue, either. I thought I was going to graduate, get a job right off the bat, work it for a little bit, and then be doing the nightly news by the time I was twenty-six. Turns out, it didn't work that way. Things rarely do. I got a job in TV, working in the control room. Eventually I was able to move into producing segment pieces for the weekend news and from there to actually being the talent. It went forward, but it took a while. My specific story is irrelevant. What's important is…don't pigeonhole yourself. You're a talented kid; you know it, I know it. I know that in an ideal world you'd love to be talking sports on the radio, but those jobs are not only quite difficult to come by, but they don't pay well, either. Now, you've known me for a while. And you know that I'm not one of these stuck-up professors here who are trying to steer you away from radio because I worked in television. You want to go and try radio? Go ahead, be my guest. I know you could be successful. But what I've heard from this connection with the NFL Network is that this job will not be around for much longer. I'm not saying give up radio, I'm just saying, give this some serious thought."

"Okay," I said, still processing.

"'Okay'—that's all you have to say?"

"Yes, okay. You just threw a lot out at me, you know? I mean, I can't really argue with anything you're saying. But right now, my head's spinning a bit."

"Fair enough."

"Well, let's say I wanted to pursue this, what would I do next?"

"You'd let me know."

"Okay, I'm letting you know."

"Just like that? You were spinning a second ago, now you're ready?"

"I'm ready to find out what I'd have to do to pursue this. Isn't that enough?"

Ignoring my last question, he said, "I'll e-mail him and tell him you're interested, ask him if it's even still available, which I think it is. From there, I'd suggest you get in touch with him: cover letter, e-mail, resume. You know that whole drill, I assume."

"Yes, quite familiar."

"Listen good, though, Alexander," Edington said, now sitting forward, smile vanishing from his face. "If you're going to do this, actually do it. Don't half-ass it. Don't e-mail him once and then not get back to him for a week or two. Take yourself seriously, for once. I know you like to joke about everything, that you think joking is what gets you attention, what people like about you. I'm sure it's what people enjoy about you, no doubt about that. But if you don't take yourself seriously, no one will. Don't be a tight-ass, either, but take this seriously. You never know what could come of it, on any level."

I paused, letting that sink in. "I'll wait to hear from you, then?"

"Sounds good, Mr. Alexander."

I left the room simultaneously confused and contented. Happy because I might have a job possibility, happy because I enjoyed my talks with John Edington. Bewildered beyond belief because I'd been, in a matter of moments, called to task on all of my bullshit. And accurately. But what might have been worse was that Edington was probably right about my career choice, too. Maybe the most troubling thing of all was that I had some thinking to do.

32 saturday night, april 12ᵗʰ

I'd thought about what this night would be like for a while. A real long while. Matter of fact, even before I'd been asked to do the show, it had been on my mind. Any time I'd gone to the Garden (that's Madison Square, for those of you not from New York City) to see a game or a concert or a show of any kind, I'd imagined what it might be like for me to be on that kind of stage. To have my name in lights, to have that whole crowd there, brimming with excitement to see me perform. To have everyone know my name, to have all those people take time out of their schedules so they could pay to see me do my thing. To make a whole crowd of strangers laugh. It was a hell of a daydream, no doubt about that.

Nervous, excited, anxious, proud. I was all of these feelings and more on Friday as I prepared for my set later that night. The Relay for Life, which I'd been invited to be part of earlier in the semester, took place in the Carrier Dome, the forty-thousand-some-odd-seat arena where the university played its basketball, football, and lacrosse games. I didn't expect the place to be filled, or even close. Then again, I really didn't have much of a clue what to expect. *Won't people be walking around and not have time to stop and listen to me? How's the stage going to be set up? Where will it be set up? How about the lights?*

With all the questions I had, I did manage to secure a few answers from the people running the event. First off, I knew I'd be going on between midnight and one on what technically was Saturday morning. Second, I knew I had pretty much free rein to include whatever I wanted in my act.

As I did for most shows I performed in, I waited as long as I could to finally prepare. My pre-show routine was fairly consistent, albeit likely to lead to more nervousness. I'd have a set of ideas, things I had jotted down in previous weeks or days. Once I had the ideas I wanted to use, I'd usually volley them back and forth with a friend. Sometimes it was Matt, sometimes Chris, sometimes Colin. But most of the time, it was Lotfi. The conversation would almost always go something like this:

Lotfi (after listening to the first joke/idea): It could work.

Me: It could work? What does that mean?

Lotfi: It depends on how you do it.

Me: I know that it depends on how I do it. Obviously, it depends on how I do it. Do you think it's funny?

Lotfi: It's not bad. What do I know, though?

I hated when people said that. Lotfi might not have known how to tell a joke, how to "be a stand-up comic," but he certainly knew how to laugh. Everyone did. And that was my point. It didn't matter to me who it was; the point of what I did was to make people laugh. That meant Lotfi, that meant you, that meant her and him and this guy and that guy. All of them, or at least as many of them as possible.

Once that was finished, I'd create an order. I didn't like comedians just telling quick one-liners or really short stories that didn't flow into one another. I wanted it to make sense. For the Relay show, I had the following topics:

Hibachi steakhouses/Fat Americans

Where in the World is Carmen Sandiego?

Golden Girls TV show

Looking the wrong way down a one-way street

Ultimately, I settled on leading off with the hibachi steakhouse and fat American jokes that I used in my last column. From how embarrassed I got by how my family acted at these places, I'd go on to how embarrassed I got from looking the wrong way down a one-way street. From there to the later embarrassment that came from realizing what was going on with Blanche from *The Golden Girls*. Finally, I'd wrap up with the popular (for my generation, the generation I knew would be in attendance) TV show and computer game, *Where in the World is Carmen Sandiego?*

The last step of my process would find me tucked away somewhere quiet, either my room or a lounge somewhere on campus, where I'd basically write out all the jokes. I'd write them several times, over and over, into what would come to look like a detailed outline. The actual jokes themselves, the exact wording, I trusted myself to freestyle once I got there. Some of my best stuff came that way. I'd write it out almost like an outline I'd hand in to a history professor, but instead of bullet points about the impact of the political climate on the Cold War, there would be punch lines about girls and TV shows and anything else I could think of.

All of this—the writing, the organizing, the outlining—I'd done in the day or so leading up to tonight. Due to the odd timing of the event, I couldn't really do much else that night before my set, and since it was a Saturday night, several people were at the house instead of at Chuck's.

"So, you nervous?" Matt asked.

"Not really," I said from across the room. I was sitting at the table reading over my notes while Matt, Colin, and Chris watched TV to my left.

"You look a little nervous," Matt said.

"I'm fine," I said, head still buried.

"I don't know about that," Matt laughed. "Colin? Chris? What do you think?"

"Nervous," Colin said.

"Definitely," Chris laughed.

"Can you guys just listen to this one joke, just one more time?" I pleaded.

The TV group chuckled; they knew this was coming.

"You always do this," Chris said. "And what happens? You get nervous, you worry—'Is this going to be funny?' 'Are they going to get this?' And then they do, and people laugh, and you're fine. You'll do fine."

"Just listen to this one thing about *Carmen Sandiego*. Come on. Don't make me beg."

"The one about how you think it shouldn't be up to you to catch her, but instead the blame should go to the airlines that are allowing this shady-looking woman to sneak items like the Eiffel Tower on board and into the overhead luggage compartment? That one?" Colin said.

"Uh, yeah," I said, embarrassed.

"You told us that one already. And before you ask, yes, it's funny. Just make sure that you—"

"Do it right? Deliver it right? Let me guess…it depends on how I do it?" I laughed.

"Yes," Colin said. "You think you know about this whole comedy thing. But you could learn a few things from pros like us. The secret to comedy? It's all in how you say it. And, what you say. That's important too. Those are the two biggest things. What you say, how you say it."

"Deep, real deep," Matt laughed.

"I'm just trying to help him; he looked nervous," Colin said.

I got to the Dome about twenty minutes before midnight. I had to get out of the house. My friends were trying to get my mind off of it, but they were all drinking and there wasn't much I could do other than think about the show. So I just got going.

Walking through the empty stands to the football field, I caught my first glimpse. Spread across the field were all sorts of blankets and tents and pillows. Honestly, it looked like something out of the Hurricane Katrina relief videos. People in matching shirts were all over the place, either walking around the field in groups, playing catch, napping, joking, eating, or doing any number of other things. At around the fifty-yard line, pushed up against the side line, was the stage, where a band that was trying way, way too hard to sound like Fall Out Boy was "playing."

At around two in the morning, a little later than scheduled, I hopped on stage. The group near the stage slowly formed, closer and more compact, and my light poking at various people in the crowd eased the tension.

"Few days ago, I did something I hadn't done in a while. Something I really love doing. I went to a hibachi steakhouse. God, I love those places. I'm not sure what the fascination is with these places, though. Food's good, no doubt about that. But I have a stove, I have an oven. I cook for myself every night. I don't get what people get so worked up about, having people who 'aren't Japanese' do it for them," I said, mocking it up around the "aren't Japanese."

"I always get the guy that's basically a moron. Almost sets himself on fire with that onion inferno, flipping shrimp tails in your drink. The other table, mind ya, has Jackie Chan. He's cutting vegetables with his feet, he's making jokes."

The crowd laughed hard at the Jackie Chan part, which gave me some reassurance. Leading up to that punch line, I wasn't so sure.

"Worst is the part when this guy turns into a hockey goalie, starts shooting stuff at the people at the table. *Open up, you fat Americans!* And what do we do? We open up. It's FREE FOOD! And it's not even the good stuff; it's the uncooked zucchini that no one even wants. I missed the first four times they went at me; it was bad. My dad gets up, he nabs it right out of the air like a golden retriever. Just—snatch! It's just the worst, though, watching this. I'm embarrassed to be a fucking American. We all just open up our mouths— uhhh, give it to me!"

Another laugh, specifically at the way I opened my mouth, hands wide at my sides and mimicking the food being thrown at me. I continued on through my set, facing only a minor hiccup with the one-way street bit. Later I'd ask someone what they thought of it, and their exact response would be, "What one-way street joke?" Exactly.

It wasn't until three o'clock that I got off the stage. I got carried away. People were laughing, there wasn't much in the way of further entertainment after me and so I just went with it. I did most of the jokes I'd planned on doing, forgot a few, went back and did some more. I joked with the crowd, made fun of them, made fun of myself and the event. I did some older material. Once I'd run out of funny things to say off the top of my head, I ended with something I'd wanted to say all along.

"I just wanted to say," I said, wondering why I always felt the need to clarify that I was speaking when I was, well, speaking, "that you guys are the best." Pause for some self-congratulatory clapping. "You're way better than the selfish prick that I am. I haven't done this event and it's been going on for four years while I've been here and I'm sure my high school did it, too. I got to come here for a little bit and try to make you laugh for an hour or so. You guys put your money and time into this. For that, I say to you, thank you. Honestly, what you're doing is great. Thank you for letting me be a part of this."

The crowd wasn't sure exactly how to react at first, unsure (after having laughed for the better part of the last forty-five minutes) of how to respond to this random, albeit well-spoken and appropriate, bit of seriousness. Waiting a beat, they clapped and whistled. Walking off the stage, I could have sworn I heard someone shout, "You fucking rock!" Somehow, none of the people I bragged to about it later had heard.

33 friday, april 18th

Things had really picked up for me, at least in the past few weeks. Speeding towards graduation, I had too many things going on to even take notice of how close I was to the end. I'd nailed down Saturday, May 3rd for *I Hope God's Wearing Earmuffs*. I'd gotten two of my comedian buddies to open for me (read: bring their friends and hopefully their friends' friends). I was either writing a column or getting my show together or trying to figure out ways not to run into Lauren and Allison and Sophia at the same time on a given night at Chuck's.

Speaking of the trio, things had definitely cooled with Sophia. Matter of fact, they'd cooled on all fronts except Allison. Sophia, as you can quite rightly imagine, wasn't dying to see me any time soon and though I fully knew I was wrong, I couldn't admit it. Stubbornness getting the best of me, I refused to budge. She didn't, either.

So far as Allison was concerned, I'd see her in class and despite my best efforts to only have sex, I often found myself in the mind-numbing reality of making conversation while at dinner or on the way to a movie—before I could then have sex with her.

Finally, of course, there was Lauren. I'd seen her a handful of times since Spring Break, but without much story to tell. There was the time at Chuck's when we started sucking face outside the back entrance. But a friend of hers needed help, so she left, promising to call but of course never following through. Back and forth I went on how to handle her and I wasn't sure that she even wanted a relationship. But did I? She *was* moving to New York—this I'd found out recently over lunch with her at Syrajuice—so if I stayed put, I figured to have another chance with her.

Quite simply, I had no idea what was going on with Lauren. I'd pretend, to anyone willing (or unwilling) to listen, that I had a clue, that I had some sort of control in the situation. The reality of our entire "relationship" (however you choose to define that word is mercifully up to you since you've gotten this far) consisted of the following:

1. I really liked her. As far as I could tell, Lauren really liked me. At least some of the time.
2. Sometimes we'd get drunk and make out, or worse, make promises about future dates that inevitably would never happen.
3. We had sex once.
4. Just when I'd think I'd seen or heard the last of her, she'd get in touch with me, almost angrily curious about why we hadn't seen each other in a while. For purposes of clarification, let's just repeat that despite my infatuation, it was always Lauren that came back, only to vanish once more.

Really, number three was what fucked everything up. If number three hadn't occurred, and especially in the way in which it had occurred, I'd never have thought anything of this. She was hard to figure. In sharp contrast to Allison, who had no brain matter so far as I could tell (but a willing vagina), and Sophia, who actually had morals and a backbone (and also a willing, but principled, vagina), Lauren seemed to have no rhyme or reason. My initial confusion after our first "date" at the basketball game regarding her feelings towards me didn't seem nearly as silly now as I had originally imagined. I'd thought I'd been overanalyzing, looking too deep. Probably not. Then again, maybe? I had no idea.

***

Laughing as Natalie and I strolled down the dairy aisle, I picked up a loaf of bread, examining it as if there were divine secrets contained within its packaging.

"Speaking of that," Natalie said, causing me to look at her in confusion since I hadn't said anything, "how is Lotfi?"

"Oh, I get it. The bread is huge. His head looks like this loaf. His name sounds like the word 'loaf.' You're on a roll, you know that?" I smiled.

"I know," she cooed. "How is the Lof-meister?"

"From what I last heard, he's doing all right. He's out of the hospital, so that's good. He's not sure if he's going to be able to walk with us at graduation, though. But it seems to me like he's just being overly cautious. I think he'll be back fairly soon, but I don't know for sure. He won't put a date on it."

"That's good to hear, though, that he's doing better," she said. Lotfi, although he started out as *my* friend, had become an extended member of the clan. He was hard to really dislike. That rubbed off on my housemates and though they rarely hung out with him alone, they had gradually begun to hope he'd come to parties and various events.

As we packed our purchases into my trunk, I knew I wanted to chat with Natalie about the conversation with Edington about the job. I couldn't really talk to Matt about it, as he just didn't get it. He already had a job with General Electric, working in South Carolina. His field, while infinitely more complex than mine, was far easier to get a job in. People actually came to the school to recruit him. Not so for me. And, with that in mind, I didn't really love talking about that sort of stuff with Chris and Colin. It wasn't that there was any real competition between us, but I still didn't want to complain to them about having a job opportunity when I couldn't say for sure whether they had anything at all yet. So I vented to Natalie.

"I know I'm not supposed to complain about—"

"Don't worry about it. If you weren't allowed to complain, you wouldn't have much to say. I'm glad you complain. It keeps you entertaining."

"Thanks?" I retorted, then went on. "I told you about the whole L.A. thing, right? The NFL Network and Edington and maybe having a job out there? Well, Edington got back to me this morning and told me that his contact out there still wanted to hear from anyone interested in the position, so he sent him my name, and then we exchanged an email or two, and I'm going to call him sometime next week."

"And…where is there a complaint in that? What's wrong with *any* of that?"

"Well, nothing. On its face, it's great, right? I mean, a job, NFL, fun L.A.? Sounds exciting, right? But I'm a little—"

"Scared? You should be."

"Well, I am. Shitless. I have no shit. I'm so scared, I am devoid of feces. None left."

"Got it," she snickered.

"Yeah, it's scary. I'm not sure I want to move all the way out there. And what about being on-air somewhere? Do I just give up on that?"

"Didn't Edington tell you to consider that?"

"Yes."

"Well, did you do any considering?"

"I did, but I shouldn't be settling, right? At least not this early. It's my life. I know this is a big deal and I'm scared to make a choice here. All I keep thinking about is myself years down the road, looking at this one choice as the reason why I wound up being miserable and wondering what else could have been if I hadn't taken the job."

"All you're doing is calling him. It's not like he's going to offer you a job on the phone. I say just call him and get a sense of it. Nothing bad will happen. You want to keep your options open, right? Call him next week, keep it going."

"You're probably right."

"I am right," she said, as she skipped off to return the cart. Returning to the car and plopping down in the passenger seat, she continued right where she'd left off. "Definitely call him. I get why you're nervous. I'd be nervous, too. But you're not committing to anything; you're just following up. Who knows, you might love it. Either way, be glad you at least have something cooking."

It had been a while since we had all gone down to Chuck's. How long, exactly, I wasn't sure. There had been Spring Break and the trip to Notre Dame, and then various nights spent with Allison or Sophia or Lauren. There were moments, brief though they might have been, when I wondered if I was spending enough time with my roommates. I was usually snapped out of that thought by the more powerful memory of the most recent hook-up, whichever of the girls it had been. It wasn't like I was *never* around. I stayed at the house nearly every night, so I was there most of the time. So what if I didn't go down to Chuck's every single Friday and stay the whole time with the group? I was convinced that all the other guys in the group would've done the same if they were in my spot.

"You coming out with us tonight, punk?" Matt called out to me from the living room. Natalie and I were still putting our groceries away.

"I don't know," I responded, mocking Matt.

"Funny, really funny," Matt said, his voice getting closer as he walked towards the kitchen, beer in hand.

"I'm going to come down, definitely. Jamie's going to let you go down there tonight?" I laughed.

Matt half-smiled, enough to give the solid impression that he was as angry as I was kidding. Which is to say, for each, a little bit.

Between men, at least between us, there rarely was actual anger. Displeasure, sure. But most frequently, everything was masked with kidding. It was easier, by and large, to deflect it with humor and then let it pass.

"You've got some nerve to talk," Matt said, laughing nervously. Were we arguing? Neither of us could tell, but it certainly was reaching an uncomfortable level of contentiousness.

"You want to say something, say it," I said, sitting up and putting my beer down.

Matt turned off the TV.

"Hey, I was watching tha—" Chris started to say. Matt shot him a look that said, in no uncertain terms, *Shut the fuck up*. He turned to me.

"Listen, man, no one's mad about you going out with these girls. You want to do what you want to do, go ahead and do it. But don't bust my balls about Jamie or this and that, because you haven't been around much lately, either. I'm not mad at you—"

"Neither am I—" Chris interjected, before Matt shot him another one of *the* looks.

"No one's mad," Matt said.

"It sure as hell seems like it," I said. "Don't you say shit either, Chris. You're always gone. Fuck, we're all doing our own things. Don't make it like I'm the only one that isn't around as much."

"I never said that," Matt said calmly.

"You're making it seem like that, though," I said, looking around the room for some backup. Chris looked away purposely, not wanting to get involved. Colin, who had just entered the room, also said nothing.

I sat back in my chair, taking a last look around the room before staring at the television—which had just been turned back on to ESPN. After several big gulps of my beer, I got up to get another and took a few more healthy sips.

The TV was blaring and someone in the house was playing music, but the silence in the room was deafening. Matt, Chris, me, Colin. No one said a word to anyone else, and it was become quite unnerving. Silence in this house, amongst these friends (particularly whenever I was around), wasn't a common occurrence, you see.

After what seemed like an eternity, Colin cleared his throat and began to speak. "You know what Disney character I think would be the most enjoyable to have sex with? Jasmine, from *Aladdin.*"

As if on cue, everyone turned to Colin. He stared back at us with a plain look and slight smirk, indicating that he was aware of the bizarre nature of what he'd just said, but confident in its validity.

"How can you argue with that?" he tried again, after no one had said anything.

"You know who I'd choose," I began, smiling. "Nala, from *The Lion King.*"

The air had been let back into the room. Everyone started laughing, mercifully, loosening it up once again.

"That's messed up," Matt laughed.

"No, no. Come on, give me some credit," I said, "Not the younger Nala. The older one. That teenage one that's in love with the Matthew Broderick version of Simba."

"Well, that's a load off," Chris laughed, "because we were worried you were into underage animals. That's a line not even *you* will cross."

The crisis, if you can even call it that, had been averted. That was probably the most Matt and I had ever fought in the four years we'd known each other. Sure, there were stupid basketball and sports arguments over the years, but as far as real-life arguments go, this was about as far as it had ever gone. I knew that the group wasn't particularly enamored of the way I was juggling the girls. This had been discussed before; they'd told me this. I didn't care then, and I didn't care now.

As we headed down to Chuck's about an hour or so later, Matt slowed his walk down to the crawling pace that was my gait. Out of listening range behind the group, Matt said, "We're cool, right?"

I smiled. "Come on, you don't even have to ask. Let's go get trashed."

One of the benefits to being a guy—easy makeups with friends.

That, and no pregnancies, I thought.

Chuck's, later that night

Besides being packed almost wall to wall with people, Chuck's was already unseasonably hot inside. Every so often, the weather had a way of throwing a curve at the inhabitants of Syracuse. Just when they thought they wouldn't see the sun for months, it would suddenly be hot again. Mind you, not *actually* hot but when you compare it to weather that makes the phrase "bone-chilling" commonplace amongst twenty-one-year olds, anything warm is a welcome diversion. In any case, it was warm and a little muggy. Wearing shorts, we were prepared— though you can never completely avoid that sticky feeling of wet heat, can you?

Things don't change at a place like Chuck's. It was a Friday, it was after five p.m., and college was still in session so that meant there were a lot of kids either there already or on their way down. We were now in the former group, having grabbed a table in the far back near the pool table.

"You know, I always thought that Belle looked like Anne Hathaway," Chris shouted from across the table.

"What are you talking about?" Natalie asked.

"Earlier," he said, now pointing at Colin and me, "they were talking about what Disney characters they thought were hot."

"Are you on a time delay? That was hours ago," I laughed.

"I know, but I just thought of it now. Doesn't she, though?"

"Wait," Colin said as he poured another round from the only pitcher with beer left in it, among the several at the table. "Are you saying Anne Hathaway looks like Belle, from *Beauty in the Beast*, or the other way around?"

"Either one. What difference does it make?" Chris said.

"It's *Beauty and the Beast*, moron," Matt mocked.

"Whatever," Colin answered, while still gulping down a

beer.

The conversation continued, Chris insisting that Belle did, in fact, looking like Anne Hathaway and Colin arguing that the comparison was ridiculous. Probably not as ridiculous as the issue being debated itself, but I digress.

My ears were invested in the conversation, and so was my mouth, as at one point I added that Ariel, from the end of the movie when she has legs, certainly merited consideration in this discussion (for the record, Natalie agreed). My eyes, however, were in scan mode. Who was here, what girls were with what guys. It was a lazy and usually futile effort.

Thus far, I hadn't really seen much. Which is to say that Lauren, Sophia, and Allison were nowhere to be found. So far, at least.

Sitting down back at the table after having picked up a few pitchers, I was happy to discover that the whole "what Disney character would you have sex with?" conversation was over. Still, everyone at the table (in particular Natalie and Matt) had smiles on their faces. Wider than usual, wider than four pitchers into the night.

"She's here," Natalie said, revealing the reason behind the smiles.

"Where?" I asked. I tried to play it cool, but before Natalie could answer, I turned quickly to look for Lauren. Nothing. I even got up and took a few steps in each direction. Nothing. Sitting back down in my chair, still looking out towards the crowd, I began again. "I don't sss—"

I stopped cold. Sitting right next to Natalie, right there in the flesh, was Allison. Natalie could barely stop herself from laughing. Watching me squirm and try to wiggle my way out of this one was truly a delight for the lone female of the house. Actually, they all seemed to be enjoying the hell out of this.

"Hey, Allison," I said, with as much excitement as I could muster.

"Hey, you! I haven't seen you in a while. What happened? Did your phone break?"

I smiled at the déjà-vu.

"Did it?"

"Yes, actually," I lied.

"Oh, I'm sorry to hear that," she said.

"Ha. Don't you feel like a jerk," I laughed, now easing into my chair. The tables had turned a little bit, I was back in control.

"Oh, come on, Nick, stop joking around. Your phone wasn't broken," Natalie said.

"It wasn't? Maybe it wasn't," I said. It wasn't smooth, but I couldn't think of anything else to say. Fortunately for me, Allison didn't seem to care much what the answer was. She had moved her chair away from Natalie and was now immediately next to me.

Her hand now on my thigh, she leaned in. "You going to be here late tonight?"

"I hadn't really thought about that yet," I said, not interested.

"Well, we're not staying. I'm going home pretty soon. You should come."

"I don't know," I said, not returning her gaze. "I don't want to leave my friends." *Wow, that is so weak*, I thought. *Just go back to her place. You can put up with her for another hour or so.*

She play-slapped me on the shoulder, got up, and said, "Text me when you're leaving. I'll be home."

When she was out of earshot (which, in that bar, was a step away), I glared at Natalie. "What the hell was that for?"

"Oh, come on. Have a sense of humor," she laughed. "That girl is a moron. She wouldn't know she was being played with if you...if you...."

"Good one."

"Quit being a bitch, will you?" Matt said. He always thought Allison was attractive, so despite his distaste for my juggling acts, this was the one girl he didn't seem to mind me going all in on.

An hour or so later—I wasn't sure how long it had been, since time had a way of slipping away at Chuck's—I felt a vibration from my pant pocket.

11:05 PM
You have a new text from Allison
When r u commmmming?

This girl was an idiot, even over text. She had to put in those extra M's, but no extra G's or, for that matter, any other letter in the word.

About thirty seconds later:

11:05 PM
You have a new text from Allison
I want you...

This went on for a good ten minutes more, with me sending generic texts back and Allison sending increasingly sexual texts begging me to come over. At one point, she even typed (drunkenly? I wasn't sure) *I need you inside me.* Maybe she meant *I need you*—but no, she couldn't really have meant anything other than that, I eventually reasoned. Then, sexual innuendo or not, the bathroom bug hit me. Anyone that's ever been out drinking, even once, knows that unless you're willing to accept a urinary tract infection, you have to go the bathroom immediately.

Squeezing between and around the groups of friends on my way towards the front door, I realized that I had left my phone on the table. I didn't care—my only concern was making sure Big Steve remembered that my hand was stamped so I didn't have to wait in the line when I came back. As I held my hand up, the enormous bouncer nodded and waved me out to my outdoor, dumpster-themed bathroom. Not so much themed as it was just a dumpster. Either way....

The freeing sensation of urinating into the night having passed, I ambled back into the packed bar. The transition from cooler (relative, of course) outside weather to sweaty hot inside weather was quite an experience. The second I passed through the first set of doors to enter the bar, the warmth smacked me in the face, literally making me stagger back. It could have been the heat, or the alcohol.

Or, more likely, the hand of Big Steve across my chest. I showed him my stamp.

"Oh," he bellowed. It truly was like he was a sad giant from another planet, brought here as an experiment.

Getting back to my spot at the group table wasn't going to be easy. From where I stood, right in front of the entrance—the only semi-clear spot in the place—that table seemed like it was at least three or four miles away. Never one to push or shove to get through a crowd (or be the guy who lightly taps everyone on the shoulder and says something like "'Scuse me, bro"), I wove my way in and out of pockets of people by tailing a group of girls. For some reason, women didn't seem to have as hard a time getting around.

As I got closer to the table, I couldn't believe what my eyes were seeing over at the bar. Staring ahead, I saw Sophia. Sophia, *talking with Allison*. What the hell was Allison doing back here? Why was she talking to Sophia? My head felt like it was in one of those Gravitron machines at the fair.

"I have to go home," I said to my friends without taking a seat. "I can explain tomorrow morning, but Chris, can I borrow your hat?"

"What for?"

"Can I, or not?"

"Why?"

"Can I fucking borrow the hat, or not?"

"Sure, fine," he said, tossing the worn blue Cubs hat in my direction.

"If anyone asks, I left because I have to get up early for the radio tomorrow morning." With that, I turned away from my friends and pulled the brim of the hat as low as it would go over my eyes while still allowing me to see my feet. As stupid as I felt, I knew that wearing my glasses and this hat were the best disguise I could muster. I had to get out of there right away. What was Allison doing back at the bar and would she tell Sophia about me? Would Sophia tell Allison about me?

What if they both came over to the group at the table? How long could they hold out before one of them gave me up? I didn't feel like staying to find out the answer to any of these questions. Cheaply disguised, I snuck out of the bar undetected and slipped into the Syracuse night.

The walk home was a quiet, lonely one. No one was on the roads—they were all still out at parties or the bars. I didn't care. Tonight wasn't going to be my night and to sacrifice one night for the good of any in the future was better than what might have met me had I stayed at Chuck's.

As I fell asleep to the TV in my room that night, two thoughts were still racing through my head: *What was Allison doing back at the bar?* and *Man, Sophia looked really good tonight.*

34 saturday, april 19th

Before anyone else in the house was awake, I was already at the gym. Rarely, if ever, did I work out on the weekend. Even rarer was it that I worked out so early in the morning. But I couldn't sleep and couldn't conceivably spend any more time hitting the Refresh buttons on Facebook and my school e-mail account.

By the time I got back, now dripping with sweat not so much from the workout as from the heavy moisture in the air, it appeared as if most of the people in the house were gone.

"Anyone here?!" I shouted, opening the door.

"I'm upstairs," Natalie yelled back. Coming out of her room to the edge of the stairs, she said, "Where were you?"

"I couldn't sleep," I said from the foot of the stairs. "Last night was a fucked-up night. I just got up early and went to work out."

"Did you eat yet?" she asked.

"Nope, you want to go get something?"

"Sure," she said. "Let me put on pants. We'll go to Bruegger's?"

That's right, I noticed, she's not wearing pants. Was it strange I didn't notice? I couldn't tell at this point; these things had become so stamped into my subconscious that reality held little consequence.

Chomping on bagels while walking back to the house (both now wearing pants, mind you), Natalie asked, "What got you so spooked last night?"

"You didn't see what was going on?"

"No," she said, smiling.

"Come on. You saw them there; don't act like you didn't," I said, looking ahead.

"I did. But what's the problem? They've been out together before when we've been there, haven't they? And aren't they friends?"

"I think so."

"What are you so afraid of, anyway? It's not like you really like these girls anyhow. And haven't you and Sophia broken up?"

"We weren't dating."

"Easy, easy," she chuckled. "You know what I mean. I thought you weren't talking any more. And why didn't you just go home with Allison? What's wrong with her, now?"

I didn't answer, still walking alongside.

"Well?" she continued to probe.

"You know why," I said, voice noticeably lower than before.

"Oh, my God," she said, sounding like the cream cheese in her bagel had gone bad mid-bite. "*Her?* You need to move on from her. She's using you, Nick. Come on, already."

"I don't think so," I disagreed. "Lauren and I had a connection. We had something that night."

"You sound like such a pussy," she said. "I can't believe I'm even saying it, but you are acting like a woman. *We had a connection.* Jeez. Get over it. You guys have been all over the place. She only seems to call you and want to see you when it's convenient for her."

"What are you saying?"

"I'm saying that she's using you. Not necessarily that she's with another guy. She might be; she might not be. But she clearly doesn't consider your schedule important in the relationship. When she has spare time, when she's free, that's when she comes a-callin'."

"You really did just say 'a-callin', didn't you?"

"I did," she smiled.

Changing the subject, I said, "What I can't figure out is why Allison came back down to the bar."

"She probably read into one of your texts the wrong way," Natalie said.

"I don't know about that. I thought I went out of my way to make it clear I wasn't too interested. Certainly not interested enough to warrant her coming back."

"You sure about those texts?"

"Uh, yeah. I don't think there was much room for—" Suddenly, it all hit me. Natalie had been fucking with me. I'd left my phone at the table when I'd gone to the bathroom and she must have taken it and started texting Allison, pretending to be me.

Her eyes filled with tears of hysterical laughter. "Figured it out?"

"Why would you do that?"

"Because I knew it would be fun. And I wanted to see you try to wiggle your way out of it," she laughed.

"Fun? How is that fun?"

"Because I like seeing you sweat. You think you're *sooo* cool with this girl stuff. I remember you, Nick Alexander, when you were too afraid to talk to Katie. Now you're a big shot. You can get any girl—at least you think so. And so, when you left your phone, I decided it would be fun to see what you'd do."

As angry as I wanted to be, I had a hard time sustaining any ill will. Besides the fact that her criticism was quite accurate (not to mention consistent), Natalie had a way of delivering that last little bit with a sort-of smile on her face. Friendship aside, it's hard to get truly annoyed with people who can smile sincerely while delivering critiques.

I could muster up only a "Hmmmph," in response to

which she cooed, oozing with sarcasm, "Oh, Nicky! Don't be mad at me!"

Arm around her shoulder, in a mock-1930's gangster voice, I said, "How could I be mad at you, kid?"

But I had to know everything. "What did you text her? And did she or Sophia come over to you guys?" I asked.

"Let me go get a cup of coffee," she said. "I'll meet you downstairs in a few minutes. Tell you the whole thing."

When Natalie finally came downstairs, I shut off the TV in my room. I sat up on my bed, she took a seat at my desk.

"So, what do you want to know?" she said, bringing the steaming cup of coffee to her face.

"How can you drink that when it's this hot out?"

"Not sure, just can. That it?"

"I think so," I laughed. "Really, what did you text her? I checked my phone, but there were no new texts going out, none coming in. I have to say, well done. You could be a real criminal. Nice job tracing your steps. Very thorough."

"Thank you, sir," she smiled, taking another sip. "But I should tell you: those texts weren't sent from your phone." She paused, giving me time to make a *What the...* face. "I sent them from my phone, told her it was you from my phone, and that you had to use it because your phone died."

"Wow."

"Yeah, I know, right?" she said, clearly proud of herself. "So I still have those texts. Let's see...." Pulling out her phone, she said, "Okay, here it is. After explaining the new phone bit—which, by the way, she didn't even question—"

"Not surprised."

"—I said to her, *I want to see you tonite, bad, but I need someone to pick me up from here... Can u?* I knew that she would say no at first, which she did, so I said, *Fine, I'll just stay here then....* She couldn't stand that. I mean, it was like literally ten seconds later and she tells me that she can come to pick you up, but that you should be outside. I didn't want to let her off that easy, so I shot back, *No, no. Come in here, let's get a drink, then we'll go back to your place and fuck.*

"You said the words, 'we'll go back to your place and fuck'?!" I said with incredulous laughter.

"Yes."

"Those were your exact words?"

"Yes."

"Wow," I said, laughing. "I knew it would get there eventually, but didn't think it would be that fast. Anyway, I get the point with the texts. What happened after I left? Did they come over?"

"Yes, both girls did, actually. Allison came over, squealing about where you were, and if we knew. Sophia didn't really say much; she came over to say hello to us around the time Allison was leaving. Unfortunately, I have no real good details about that part of the story. That kind of just happened. Trust me, I really wish there was something great to tell, like that Sophia asked Allison, how big is Nick?"

"Yeah, I bet you do wish that," I said.

"Nothing happened at that point; they both just left. I know your ego has a hard time believing this, but it wasn't weird for them both to be there on a Friday night. "

"No, you jerk. I know it's not weird that they were both at the bar. I'd just rather not have had Sophia hear or see Allison asking you guys where I was. I mean, it's not the end of the world, but if I had things my way, then I'd—"

"Then you'd be with Lauren," she interrupted.

"Yes, probably."

Getting up from the chair, Natalie said, "Not probably. Definitely. Listen, no harm, no foul, right? Just some fun at your expense. You've had it enough at other people's, so it's all in bounds. I gotta go finish something on my computer."

"Okay. Well, thanks for the bagel."

"You paid."

35 tuesday, april 22nd

Most weekdays, I daydreamed my way through class. I'd doodle, I'd instant-message people on the computer, I'd think about girls in the class. Sometimes I'd listen to what was being talked about and occasionally I'd even venture to raise my hand, if only to prove to myself that I could bullshit my way out of anything.

Today, though, I was supremely focused.

Not on class, mind you. Rather, I was concentrating entirely on the comedy show coming up. Sure, it wasn't for over a week, but there was so much that had to go into this to get it off the ground. I wouldn't tell him so, but I realized Chris was very right: this wasn't easy.

The actual jokes, the stand-up itself, wasn't something I was too concerned about. No, the concern was squarely on marketing and promotion. I'd planned on going on a friend's local radio show that weekend to promote, I'd planned on writing a column on it the Thursday before (as well as including a brief mention in my signoff this week), I'd planned on getting a poster in the student center, I'd planned on posting fliers all over campus.

With class wrapping up, Edington finished the lecture:

"...and that's why you can say shit and fuck after eleven p.m. on TV. So next time you're watching a Comedy Central Roast of someone, make sure to thank FCC vs. Pacifica. Tell your friends; I'm sure they'll appreciate it. Does anyone have any questions about the Final or the First Amendment Journal due next week? Nick, yes?"

"Actually, it's not a question about those two things," I said.

"Before Nick tries to convince everyone to go to his show..." he said, smiling at his student knowingly. *Am I that predictable?* I wondered. As if I were speaking aloud, Natalie looked my way, as if to say, *Yes, you are.* "...does anyone have any *actual* questions?"

No one did, so Edington retreated to his makeshift desk in the corner of the room. "Mr. Alexander, the floor is yours. Everyone give him a second, please. That means you, too, Army folks. Hold on a second. Thank you."

I was used to doing comedy shows, to performing in front of fairly large audiences, but the sudden shift in the gaze of seventy-some-odd pairs of eyes from professor to student threw me off a bit. For the next few moments I stammered along, explaining the details of the show: time, location, performers, and charity. I put it all out there and passed out a few fliers, leaving the rest in the front of the room.

"Do you think they were into it?" I asked Natalie on the way home.

"I couldn't really tell," she said. "You didn't seem that into it."

"I am, I *definitely* am. This is all I can think about, all I have been thinking about. Tomorrow I'm going to go to every dorm and building and put these suckers up. It's just, I get a little self-conscious when I have to do that sort of self-promoting. It's one thing for someone else to talk about me. I can say things like, "Oh, come on, stop" or, "Please, please, cut it out" when everyone knows I'm really loving it. This—this is a bit different."

"I understand, but if you want people to come, you're

going to have to get over that. You have a ten-foot poster in the Student Center, for cryin' out loud."

That poster, by the way, would grow by at least a foot on each side every time someone made fun of me for it.

Talking with Lotfi later that night, the same sentiments were echoed. Get over it, this isn't only about you so don't feel like you're being too self-promoting. "What you should do," Lotfi's deep voice boomed through the phone, "is go down to Marshall Street and hand out the fliers there. Get down there, do it to it."

"You'd be good at that," I smiled. "That's not for me. I don't like that. And people usually throw those fliers away right after they get them. I do, at least."

"I'm not most people. I keep them," he answered.

We agreed that Lotfi wasn't "most people." I asked him how he was doing; Lotfi, unsurprisingly, said he was doing fine. To which I asked, if he was fine, then when was he coming back and would he be walking with us at graduation? Dropping his normal bravado, Lotfi answered, in a much lower than normal voice, that he wasn't sure.

We spoke on the phone every few days. I had been keeping him up to date on the comedy show and the various bumps and bruises along the way with putting it together. The general Lotfi response? "You, you're pretty, you...you know that?" I was frustrated that I couldn't see my friend, but realized that on the other end of the phone line there was even greater frustration.

36 friday, april 18th

For all the drunken debauchery we had collectively taken part in over the four years of college, there was one thing we'd never done together: drugs.

That needs clarification, doesn't it? Nothing too serious. We're talking about smoking weed. I had fooled around with it when I was in Amsterdam; Chris once hotboxed his car on the way to getting Brazilian food at home. Natalie may have tried it a few times, same with Colin. I couldn't say for sure. I did know that Matt hadn't and wouldn't because he was worried he might get tested for work.

It wasn't something we often (really, ever) thought about. Actually, it just sort of came up. Middle of the week, the lot of us (minus the engineer) went to see one of those stoner comedies that seem to be mass-produced from some stoner-movie warehouse in Los Angeles.

Walking out of the movie theater, I said, "You know, we should do that."

"Go to White Castle?" Natalie asked.

"Yeah, that would be great," Colin said. "I could go for that, after watching that movie. They don't have White Castle in Massachusetts."

"No, not that," I said. "You know…"

"What? You know…what?" Chris asked.

"Weed."

No one answered; it was a thought that had never been tossed around much within the group. Those who had tried it on their own were obviously fans and those who might not have didn't need much convincing. We had all reached the point in the semester (if we hadn't already been there for months) where we just didn't care much about anything other than having fun at all times.

It was decided right then and there that I would get the merchandise from one of my friends who dealt (in college, no one was more than one degree away from a guy who sold weed), and that in the coming days, we'd eat brownies and have a swell time.

Walking down Ostrom Ave with a Tupperware box of brownies like I'd just come from a bake sale, I could have been the most excited kid in the entire 13201 zip code. The last time I'd had pot brownies, I'd laughed so hard I had nearly lost consciousness, thought a real person was a mannequin, and slept soundly for twelve and a half hours in a hostel. Truly a glorious experience.

This, of course, would be a little different. In Amsterdam, nearly everyone I ran into either was already high, was en route to getting high, or was extremely aware of the fact that everyone around them was one of the first two. Not exactly the same in Syracuse. Sure, people smoked; Syracuse had its fair college share of that. But getting drunk was the more popular method of brain-scrambling. We would be doing both. The plan was simple. Eat the brownies at around four or five, let them set in, and then go down to Chuck's and have an absolute whale of a time. There were only a couple of weeks left, no time to be wasted. (Ironic word choice, no? Man, I need a drum set.)

It took a while for the brownies to actually take effect. No one was quite sure how long we should expect to wait, but when it came, there was no denying it.

"And so I told him," I said to Chris, "that I'd stay in contact. I mean, obviously, moving to L.A. is a scary thought, but it's something I'd be willing to do. At least at this point. For a job like that, right out of school...with the NFL. What is so funny, Colin?"

He was laughing so hysterically that he could barely catch his breath to say he didn't know. "There's just something that is very funny about that story," he gasped.

We then knew: it had gotten Colin. We all fell in short order. Before long, Colin and I were fashioning ourselves in a GAP ad as Plain Jane and Plain John, Chris was claiming to see pinwheel figure-eights in the carpet, and Natalie was inhaling Cooler Ranch Doritos by the bag.

"So how were the brownies?" Matt asked once we'd gotten down to Chuck's.

"Still going," I said. "Still going."

"Wow, good for you," Matt laughed. "What's up with Chris?"

"Him?" I asked, pointing at our mutual friend of four years.

"Yes. Chris. Chris Gordon. Why is he so white? His face looks like computer paper," Matt said.

That must have been the funniest thing ever uttered, because Colin and I completely lost it.

"What's so—oh, never mind," Matt chuckled, remembering who he was talking to. "Nat, you had a good time with the brownies too?"

"Oh, yeah," she said, head buried in her phone as she texted furiously.

"Wow, good talk, guys," Matt said. No one was in any state of mind to have a serious conversation, at least not yet.

All the fun, all the good times instantly evaporated for me once I saw Lauren walk into the bar with some guy I didn't recognize. No, maybe I did recognize him. The more I thought about it, I probably did know who that guy was, but that wasn't the point. The point was, why did he have his arm around her? Normally I'd have stayed away, sulked, and complained to everyone later in the night or the following morning. But not now. I was high and I was drunk, so I felt free. But it was more than that. I'd been drunk and high before and I'd kept to myself. The last few days, it had begun to close in on me. The frustration and pressure associated with the comedy show and the fliers and the ending of school and whatever happened to Sophia and everything else. It was all mounting up to the final moment, that "I just don't give a shit" moment we all come to at some point. Sometimes that's a give-up-on-everything moment. Not here. This was more of a clarifying moment.

She saw me before I could say anything. "Nick!" she shrieked, hugging me. "How are YOU!"

"I'm fine," I said, weakly hugging back.

"I haven't talked to you in so long. Where have you been?"

"I've been around," I said.

"Hey," she said, manically changing the subject. "This is Guy Connington. He's a friend of mine from home."

"Hey," he said, visibly uninterested in matching her unfounded enthusiasm.

"Can we talk?"

"Sure," she smiled. "Let me just grab a drink. I'll be right back, okay?"

"No, now. I know you; you won't come back for an hour." I grabbed her by the arm. "You don't mind, do you, Guy?"

Before he could answer, I led her towards the door so we could go outside to talk. Walking down the alley, away from the bar, I let go of her arm.

"What was that about? What do you want to talk about so bad?"

"Us. You. Me. What is going on?"

"What are you talking about?"

"Don't pretend like you have no idea what I'm talking about. You call me all the time, then you never do. I call you, you get back to me right away sometimes, and then other times not at all. We have," I paused, looking around and lowering my voice, "we have sex, and then we don't even kiss in a month."

"You are sounding like such a woman right now, you know that?"

"What is your problem? Do you like fucking with me? Is that what this is?"

She got closer to me, pushing up against my side. "You know it."

"Stop that. Stop doing this. I can't handle how much I'm frustrated by you," I said.

She backed off and we stopped walking for a moment. She looked up at me in the light and I couldn't stay angry. I did my best to maintain my dark look, but she was so stunning that I couldn't hold it for long. Her blonde hair cascaded down to her chest, framing her face. She was one of the prettiest girls that I'd ever been with, that I'd ever seen. As frustrated as I was, I had a hard time ignoring her beauty. And, of course, she knew this.

"How can you stay mad at me?" A slow smile curved across her face.

"Stop doing that," I said, looking away.

She took a step closer and stood on her toes. Turning my face towards her, she kissed me. "I'm sorry," she whispered. "I've been acting really shitty lately. You don't deserve that."

I kissed her back, then pulled away. "You say that now. I feel like you always say things like that, and then nothing will change. You'll go back in there with me, then I'll turn around and you'll vanish with that guy—Guy. What kind of name is Guy, anyways?"

Chuckling, she said, "I don't know. He's just my friend, honestly."

"Listen, you don't owe me that. You don't owe me anything; we're not dating. I know that, I do. But I'd like a little consistency—is that so much to ask? I know, the semester is ending and all that, but it's not over yet. I want to have fun these last few weeks, not have to deal with this bullshit."

"Me, too," she cooed. "I want to have fun. I'm sorry. I'll be better, I promise," she said, sliding under my arm.

We walked back to the bar and before she left me to rejoin her friends, she grabbed me close and said into my ear, "Guy is staying at a hotel, just so you know…sweep me away in a few hours, please." She kissed my cheek and slipped into the masses.

…the next morning, at breakfast with Lauren

"I'll have the deviled eggs," she said to the waitress.

"I hate deviled eggs," I said.

"It's a good thing I'm ordering them, then, wouldn't you say?" she smiled.

"Guess so," I said, still unhappy with her choice. "I'll have a chocolate milk. That's all for me."

Last night, we had gone back to her place and had sex again. It wasn't as good this time as it was the first time, but that was to be expected. That first time had been nearly four years in the making. Still, saying it wasn't good would be a stretch—kind of like saying your girlfriend isn't as hot as Jessica Biel. That's not necessarily a knock on your girlfriend, you know?

Though I was happy to be with her again—having sex with Lauren, being with her sexually at all, really, satisfied me more than anything else—I was still unsettled regarding what was going on between us. Watching her eat breakfast, I tried my best to remember how great she could be. How charming, how sexy, how pleasant. But despite that, I couldn't put away the distraction that clouded my mind. I couldn't forget how distant and schizophrenic she'd been.

Maybe it was the poorly mixed chocolate milk, or maybe it was seeing her with bits of egg and such in her open mouth as she spoke. Maybe it was that I was sexually satisfied. The morning sun, making the vinyl seats of our booth sticky, finally had a sort of cleansing effect on my brain. I was finally clear that this wasn't going to be clear. That isn't to say that I was okay with this reality, but more that I'd finally begun to accept it. She wasn't someone who was going to commit to anyone. Whatever the case was, I was comfortable with whatever it was that we were. Which, in all honesty, wasn't much.

37 thursday, may 1ˢᵗ

The show was only a few days away and despite all of the "Oh, yeah, we'll definitely be there!"'s I'd been hearing from people across campus, box office tickets sales were still at just under fifty. Matt and Chris assured me that a lot of people were going to come and that most of these promised attendees would be buying their tickets at the door—as I had repeatedly made it clear that they were allowed to do. Still, I was nervous. So I drew up a column, in one final effort to shamelessly plug my show.

Spare a buck: If you don't give to another charity, give to mine

Guilt is part of my life. There's really no way around it.

Italian guilt, from my dad's side, tends to be angrier. Jewish guilt, from my mom's side, tends to be more subtle, with the purpose of making you feel bad about yourself.

"Listen, if you don't want to call your grandma for her birthday, I guess it's not really a huge deal, but what if she died tomorrow? Then how would you feel?"

One of the worst forms of guilt comes from when people ask you for donations. I could be a billionaire and it still wouldn't matter; I feel like I'm always inventing excuses to avoid giving to these people.

Is that horrible? Does that make me a terrible person? Probably, but in fairness, if you're reading this and you're human, there's a strong chance you've been in the situation I'm describing.

"Sir, excuse me. Sir, could you spare a dollar for Ronald McDonald House?"

I could have just come from the strip club, pockets filled with singles.

"Mmmmm...wow...you really did catch me at a bad time, I'm sorry."

How about the "do you have any spare change?" people? First of all, let's give them credit. They're not stupid; they know that every single person they're asking has some form of change, because they just came from someplace where change is given.

So when you say, "I'm sorry, man, I don't have any change," is this person actually going to believe you just bought something with exact change? My grocery bill, for the first time ever in the history of groceries or money, came out to a whole number. Sorry, too bad.

All this being said, I'm about to pull the move I've been railing against for the last 400-plus words.

"Excuse me, public of Syracuse, could you spare three dollars?"

Not bad, huh? My pitch is pretty similar to those other guys', but the difference is that I'm offering something tangible in return for your money. Normally, all you get for your change donation is a good feeling that fades as soon as you remember you haven't called your mom in a week.

Here's what I'm offering in exchange for three dollar bills: a comedy show with me, Andrew Cohen, and Mark Samson.

Advance tickets are available at the Schine Box Office. You can also show up to make donations at the door and all proceeds will go to Cystic Fibrosis, a condition that's affected a cousin of mine.

Actually, correction: the donations will go to fighting Cystic Fibrosis, not just to Cystic Fibrosis.

Not to make a sob story of it—she's doing all right. We talked about putting her face on fliers all over the campus. Surprisingly, she didn't go for that.

All of this said, I'd be lying if I said arrogance had nothing to do with it. I'm puffing up my ego to an absolutely unmanageable size. Truth be told, I'm having trouble sleeping at night, as my bed won't support the new weight.

There are fliers all over campus with my ugly mug on it. In Schine, I actually convinced people not only to photograph me, but also to print out a larger-than-life poster with me on it. You want to talk about a freak-out moment, I had one when I went to pick it up.

"Uhhh, I'm here to pick up the poster with...my own giant face on it."

Arrogance mixed with a bit of desire to do something good for someone else. Now that's not the worst combination in the world.

38 friday, may 2nd

Walking towards my familiar pre-show thinking spot, it suddenly hit me. College, this life I was leading, was rapidly coming to a close. How much longer did I have? A week, two weeks? No, it was definitely at least two weeks. It hadn't sunk into me at any point in the past few months, at least since that first conversation I'd had with Lotfi. Things had picked up; I'd gotten carried away with the house and my friends and my girlfriends and my columns, and now with my show. But I'd always, if only subconsciously, associated the comedy show with the end of the year. I looked at this show as not only literally occurring at the end of the semester, but as figuratively being a culminating event in my college life. I'd worked my way to this point and now it was here, only a day away.

As I'd done many times, and almost identically to the run-up to the Relay for Life show, I got down to preparing. Making my lists, jotting down jokes, chatting them over with friends. Though this time, there wasn't so much of that last part. You see, this was by far the longest set I had ever prepared for. The Relay show had gone long and wound up lasting for forty-five minutes, but that wasn't what I'd planned for. It just happened that way. Knowing I was going to have to fill at least a half-hour of time was a more daunting task. And so, in my preparations, I went back to all of my notes and started cobbling together an act from many of my previous sets. There would be some tweaks, some new material here and there, but, by and large, this was a recycled show.

In the past, people had come to see me, but this was the first time that these people, friends and strangers alike, were actually paying specifically to see me. Without question, that heightened my already elevated sense of responsibility to deliver. Newer material was always more fun to do, but this wasn't really the time or place for all that exploration. I'd still be able to ad-lib with my older material and creatively rove around, only this time it would be confined to the spaces I'd already explored in previous shows. I owed it to the people who were paying to see me, I owed it to myself, and I owed it to my cousin. This had to be a great show. Period.

After a few hours of messing around and piecing bits together, this was what I came up with:

> To Catch a Predator
> the c-word ——> differences btw men and women
> men and women
> talking about boyfriends
> crying
> taking girls on dates/to movies
> eating out at restaurants
> graduating from school
> ——going to miss:
> ——registering for class
> ——watching TV all day
> Toy Store Sweep
> Legends of the Hidden Temple

getting in fights...with women...
end of marriage fight at airport...you didn't
happen to call her a c? Did you?

Leading off the show would be a bit on the TV program *To Catch a Predator* that I'd worked on a few weeks back at a Woo Hoo comedy show. I'd tooled around with it a little bit and decided, based on the reactions I'd gotten, that it was strong enough to lead off with. From there, I decided, I'd go into my older bit about the C-word. Those jokes weren't that funny, I knew, but they served a greater purpose: the story I planned on closing with—matter of fact, the line I planned on closing with—would bring back one of those jokes to tie a nice little comedic bow on the whole evening. In between, I'd talk about taking women on dates, eating at restaurants, some of my favorite TV shows, and graduating from college. Every topic pretty much flowed into the next, just liked I'd wanted.

By the time I'd finished, it was close to eleven. The house had been at Chuck's for hours at this point and drunken texts had been flowing in for quite some time.

> **Matt:** *hey pussy get ur ass down here!*
> **Colin:** *engaging in consumption of alcoholic beverages at alarming rates*
> (Note: Colin did an incredible impression of a robot and, when drunk, would often text as one. Read in normal inflection, it wasn't particularly funny, but if you could imagine someone speaking like a robot and saying those things....)
> **Chris:** *what time is your show tomorrow night? people are asking me about it here. you should be down here for it, give the people what they want haha*

A few texts later, I discovered that Allison truly was hounding them to find out where I was after I'd been ignoring her *where are youuuu* texts. Once those went unanswered, she asked Matt and Chris and they both told her my location.

Never one to let me off the hook easily, Matt lied and said they hadn't told her anything. Now, it wasn't as if I wanted to be hidden, but I certainly wasn't looking for any distractions tonight. If I was, hell, I'd have gone to Chuck's with them, no?

Leaving the Student Center through a side door, I headed up the hill back towards the campus and my house. From behind me I could hear the sounds of loud music and people shouting and screaming. The bars were just a stone's throw away—ironically, a mere block or two from the campus and school buildings. I trudged back to the house, slightly upset that I wasn't having the same fun as my roommates (who wants to give up fun, no matter the cause?), but confident that I was making the right choice. After a few steps in the slightly brisk air, I pushed all that away, shoving headphones into my ears and cranking up the volume. Sublime's "Santeria" would be my soundtrack. Sue me—I was feeling nostalgic.

About a half minute or so later (just about the time Bradley Nowell's soul would have to wait), I was nearly tackled to the ground by someone jumping on my back.

My iPod jarred from my hand and my headphones yanked out, I spun around to see Allison, grinning like a fool.

"Are you fucking insane?" I said, not returning her joviality.

"Oh, come on, Debbie," she whined.

"Debbie?" I said incredulously. "Debbie Downer? For not wanting to get surprise-tackled at night? Yeah, I'm a real loser. What's wrong with me?"

"Oh, please—you know you liked it. Where were you tonight? How come you didn't answer any of my texts?" she said, grabbing at my pockets to try to get my phone.

"I got them," I said flatly.

"Why didn't you answer them, then?"

"I was working. I don't have time for...for this," I said. "I have the show tomorrow. The one I've told you and everyone else about, at least a million times. It's important to—"

"I know, I know," she said, sounding annoyed I was taking it this seriously. "I told you, I'm going to be there."

"And you're going to—"

"YES!" she laughed. "I'm going to bring my roommates. What do you think I am, stupid?"

I smiled, opting to let the smirk speak for itself. She was too tipsy to give a damn.

"Well, then," I said, putting my headphones back into my ears and beginning to turn around. "This was fun. I have to get back to my place. I'll see you tomorrow. Thanks again."

Without waiting to hear her response, I began walking away. She waited until I had taken a few steps to call out after me.

"Really?"

I turned.

"Really?" she asked again. "You're just going to let me walk home? By myself?"

"Yes, I am," I said. "You seemed like you were fine to come and tackle me, so I'm sure you can make it home."

"Come on, Nick," she whined. "Just walk me home. Let's go." She took a few steps towards me, finally getting close enough to where I could smell the beer on her breath. Besides that fact, her proximity wasn't the worst thing in the world. She was wearing some sort of loose beige tank top and tight black jeans.

Damn it, why can't I just be drunk right now and not have a problem with her? This would be a layup if I were just a little drunk I thought. Taking another look at her, as she continued to push for accompaniment on the walk home, I reconsidered: *No, this is still a layup, even without anything to drink. But do I need to do this? I'm up by thirty, the clock is winding down, why rub it in?*

The analogy didn't wholly make sense, but even my innermost thoughts couldn't escape sports clichés. Eventually I relented, unsure whether I wanted to have sex with her or was simply tired of hearing her whine, or whether it was a combination of the two.

The fifteen-minute walk from campus to her apartment consisted largely of her drunkenly but intentionally grabbing my ass, trying to hold my hand, and basically trying for any other form of contact that was publicly acceptable.

How doesn't she get how standoffish I'm being right now…and for the last month or so? Maybe she does get it, and doesn't care. Is it possible that she just wants the same thing I do? I mean, not to be sexist or anything, but I just feel like she's more into me than I'm into her and that if I left it up to her, we'd be dating.

So we've now established that my inner thoughts not only were filled with sports clichés, but also were slightly sexist, a little conceited, and totally neurotic. Then again, whose aren't?

By the time we arrived in her room, my mind was completely on the fritz. I wasn't sure what to do. My options (disregard my moral compass and have sex with her, or simply leave) would appear quite simple in print. But, to paraphrase Jack Nicholson in *The Departed*, "I ask you, when you're staring down the barrel of a naked woman, what's the difference?"

I knew damn well what the "best" option was—hell, Matt and Natalie had repeatedly made that clear to me. But I was a man and Allison was an attractive woman. Was that a good enough reason? I couldn't decide.

Lying down on her bed, we started to kiss as she slowly took off her clothes. With a naked girl on top of me, I still couldn't think of anything other than why I should leave. Yet, despite all of my internal protests, I couldn't get up, couldn't stop her from taking off my clothes, item by item.

Ripping off my belt and shimmying my pants off, she moved her mouth to my now exposed penis.

"I know you want this," she cooed.

I did, I knew that much. But just as she was about to take me in her mouth, I pulled back.

"What's wrong?" she asked, staring up at me. I looked like I'd seen a rodent in the room, spooked beyond comprehension, as far as she was concerned.

"Nothing," I said, easing a bit. "I just...."

"Don't say anything else," she said, moving her head back down.

"No, I can't do this. I don't want to…I mean, I do want to do this, but…" I paused, not sure exactly how to phrase this. Normally, I would never pull away from this situation. But I didn't like this girl and I was tired of taking advantage of her.

"But what?" she asked, now sitting up, covering herself with a nearby pillow.

"But…I just don't want to do this…" I started, and then, lowering my voice considerably, I finished, "with you."

The last two words hung in the air for what seemed like an eternity, sloppily sobering up the reality of the room. She sat in the same position, blankly staring towards me without saying a word.

"I'm sorry, I just don't want to keep—"

"It's fine," she said curtly. "Please leave."

"But I…"

"Leave, please," she said, slipping off the bed and putting on her clothes. She opened her door and repeated, "Please, just leave."

"It's just, I have my show tomorrow," I said, unsure of why I felt the need to explain myself or why I was blatantly lying.

Still holding the door open and looking towards the floor, she whispered, "Stop talking and please leave."

And so I cut myself off and listened to her directive. Walking home, it was just like I'd planned: I'd be going home, alone and sober, to get a good night's rest for my upcoming show. Only I didn't feel nearly as happy about it as I had prior to running into Allison. I put my headphones on, my iPod still tuned to "Santeria," but it just wasn't the same. I didn't feel the same boppy cheer I had felt when I'd been listening just under an hour ago. That had left and in its stead was a confused sense of having done the right thing, but at the wrong time.

39 saturday, may 3rd

For all the jabbing I would do to people who worried about the weather, making fun of them for concerning themselves over something they had absolutely no control over, I was just as guilty as the rest. When it was in direct conflict with something that mattered to me, I was terribly preoccupied with the weather. Today was no different.

Even though the entire show would be taking place indoors, even though the weather really didn't have any effect on how the show would go or attendance would be, I still wanted a nice day. (Who actually doesn't want a nice day on every single day? Let it be known that I wanted it *more* than on most days, if that counts for anything.)

For the past few days I'd compulsively checked the weather forecasts on dubious sites like weather.com and accuweather.com and hadn't been happy with the results.

"It says it's going to rain," I had moaned to Chris the first day I checked.

"What day is it today?" Chris asked.

Thinking, I said, "Monday. Why?"

"And the show is on what day?"

"Saturday."

"You're checking weather.com on a Monday and you're actually worried about what they say it's going to do on a Saturday?"

"Well, yes. I am a little worried about it," I said.

"What does it say it's supposed to do today? Chance of something, right?"

"Uh," I had said, clicking towards that day's forecast, "yes. Forty percent chance of rain. There's a picture of a storm cloud."

Getting up from his seat in the living room, Chris had peeled back the blinds to reveal a sunny day outside. "My point exactly. And why is there a picture of a storm cloud? It's just to get people, normally people like me and not you, worried about this stuff. If there's a forty percent chance of rain, then there's really a sixty percent chance of no rain. So why not a sun?"

"I have no answer for that," I said. I had left it at that. We both knew what would go down. I would continue to check the weather, moaning about anything that was less than a glowing report for that Saturday. Whoever was "listening" would either ignore or insult, whichever took less effort. That was how it would go until it was time for the show.

On Saturday, I woke up and was immediately depressed by the lack of sunshine I could feel coming through my bedroom window. Barely dressed and hoping it was just cloud cover, I hopped outside to discover what my window had already previewed: it was not a nice day out and it was probably going to rain. In fairness, had it been a gorgeous day, I would've found reason to worry over every single cloud that popped into the sky. Nothing would have totally satisfied me.

It was only ten in the morning. I had enough to do, but not enough to completely occupy my mind and (more importantly) calm my nerves after the previous night's events. At first, I had trouble figuring out what to start with. Should I go over my routine now? How about making sure each roommate knew what they were supposed to do? What about calling the people who were going to be recording the show? I also had to get in touch with the other two opening comedians. Then, I'd have to rehash all that had occurred with Allison the night before to any or all of my roommates (as if living it once wasn't enough, there would always be a second pass. This was enjoyable when the story was fun; not so much the other way).

Without cutting out too much of the story, suffice it to say that I pretty much squandered the whole day, drifting back and forth from task to task without feeling confident that I'd completed any of them. Before I knew it, it was six, an hour before the show, and we had arrived at the auditorium. Everyone would soon be in their proper places, ready to go. Jamie sat at a desk outside the entrance, ready to collect tickets and money, while Matt would guard the doors to make sure people didn't sneak in. Natalie and Colin would be inside the theater, ready to hand out programs and seat people. In a funny twist, the pair had gone to the Salvation Army store on Erie Boulevard to purchase 1920s-looking vests and matching knit caps. As nervous as I was, when they'd arrived at the auditorium I'd had no choice but to break out laughing.

"Where is everyone?" Natalie mockingly asked me.

"Very funny," I said, pacing in front of the entrance to the auditorium. I wore a blue v-neck t-shirt and jeans, plain and simple clothing on maybe the most important night of my life to date. "It hasn't rained much today, so that's good news."

"Are you expecting roofing issues?" Colin asked. The group chuckled. It was easy for them to be light. They knew people would show up; they knew this would all turn out fine. And, most importantly, they didn't have to go on stage.

"No, I'm not," I answered unnecessarily. "But I feel like if it's not raining, more people are likely to make the trip here, right?"

No one answered. The logic wasn't flawed, but it wasn't strong. After a minute of silence, I spoke up. "Everyone knows what they're—"

"Yes," the group answered in unison. I'd gone over responsibilities at least fifteen times and they had all been clear on what they needed to do even before I'd done it once.

"Sorry, I'm a little nervous," I said, waiting for someone to take the softball-esque potshot about stating the obvious. No one did. "This weather better hold up, honestly. It's been fine all day. Just give me another hour. Come on."

Almost on cue, it started raining. For a minute it was a light pitter-pattering of rain, nothing too noticeable. Then, without warning, it went from drizzle to Noah's Ark-type rain. A complete and total deluge, the likes of which I hadn't seen in four years at Syracuse.

Turning around and around to stare blankly at the rain through the glass walls surrounding the entrance to the building, I had only one word to say: "Really?"

Matt and Chris bit back laughter. I was too angry even to take notice. "I can't be up here," I said. "I'm going downstairs to get ready and prep for this. I can't stare at this rain; there's nothing I can do but get angrier. This is fucking insane. When the other two guys get here, just tell them I'm downstairs if they need me. If not, I'll be back up at seven."

I'd stuck to my word, holing up in a classroom underneath the auditorium where, a full floor beneath the pavement, I could still hear the rain pounding down viciously. The other two comedians never showed up downstairs, so I assumed they'd just gone inside. As was the case with most shows, my nerves about actually performing had dissipated as the start time for the show crept nearer. Sitting in one of those little half-chair, half-desk contraptions that never seem to have quite the right balance to either half (but that's neither here nor there), I could only think about my family. My cousin and my mom and my dad. I knew they were all proud of me, waiting to hear from me as soon as it was over to find out how it went. I felt an enormous amount of pressure, self-imposed though it might have been, to make this night a success. This event, everything from the idea for it to the planning to its eventual occurrence, had taken a lot of gall. To pull this off, to get people to pay to see me do comedy and put on a good show for this long: these were things that, though no one had asked me to do them, I felt pressure to prove I could do. Maybe not to anyone specifically; maybe just to prove it to everyone in general. Or maybe just to myself. Before I headed up the stairs to face the evening, these were the last thoughts that went through my mind.

At the entrance to the auditorium, I saw only Jamie, sitting outside at her table. The doors were closed and all my housemates were presumably inside.

"Before you ask," she smiled, opening the cash box to her right, "it's a great crowd. You pulled it off."

"Wow," I said, looking down at the box. "That's...that's incredible."

"I know. Now all you have to do is go and be funny," she laughed.

I thanked her again for helping out and opened the door to see an auditorium filled to capacity with people: both sides of the room packed, every single seat filled. I was so excited, so happy, that I could barely contain myself.

"Excuse me, sir, but I'm afraid we simply don't have any more room. You should have come earlier," Natalie said, still playing the part of usher. She smiled and we hugged. "There's someone special here for you," she said.

"Special?" I said, wondering what could top what I'd just seen.

From behind her, an enormous head rose out of the last row. A head I knew as only one man's.

"What are you doing here?!" I nearly shrieked.

"I wouldn't miss this," Lotfi said, now out of his seat and leaning on pair of crutches.

"Once you told me what day you were doing this, I told my doctor that I had to be up here by then."

"Get out of here!" I said. "I can't believe you're here. I cannot believe it! You're feeling better? I guess so, you must be, I hope so? God, I can't even speak," I smiled. I took a step forward, embracing my friend. "I don't know what else to say. I'm absolutely stunned. This is just..."

"Go, do your show. We can talk later," he said.

They told me later that once I was out of earshot, Natalie

looked at Lotfi and said, "You didn't really give your doctor an ultimatum like that, did you?"

"No, but it made it sound more dramatic," Lotfi said.

My elation was now replaced by complete shock and awe. Matt and the other two comedians were the only people sitting in the room's front row of seating. I sat down next to Matt, who had a Grinch-sized smile on his face.

"Can you believe all these people?" Matt asked. "And, how about that he not only came, but brought his friends from the team, too?"

"I am stunned," I said, staring straight ahead.

Not getting the reaction he wanted, Matt tried again. "I have to tell you, buddy, I didn't think you could pull it off," Matt said. "Not only did you fill up the room, but you got Jonny Flynn and the rest of the team to show up."

"I told you I could do—*what?* Jonny Flynn? What the...." I turned around in my seat to find the hoops star and his friends. Considering that they were the only six-five and taller black men in the room, it wasn't too difficult. "Holy shit. Holy shit. Holy shit."

"Calm down, dude," Matt laughed. Pausing a beat, he continued, "It is pretty cool, though, isn't it?"

"Hell *yeah,* it's cool. I thought you were talking about Lotfi. I thought he was the one you were saying had brought friends."

"He doesn't have any friends," Matt laughed. We chatted a few minutes longer, until I remembered that I was the one who had to introduce the first comic and open the show.

Hopping onto the makeshift stage at the front of a room I had once fallen asleep in while in class, I looked out for the first time at the massive crowd. I'd performed in front of a large crowd at the Carrier Dome, but nothing this packed, nothing this dense. Nervous as I got closer to the microphone, I thought, *Relax, these people can't all be here to see you. Some are here for Mark and Andrew. You can do this, you've done it before, just calm the fuck down and don't stutter or fumble with the mic.*

In an effort to dodge that last warning, I ripped the

microphone so hard from the stand that the cord detached, leaving me talking into an unplugged microphone.

"Speak up!" someone from the back of the room shouted.

"Can't hear you!" came another call.

Realizing what had occurred, I fixed the issue, then spoke to the crowd for the official first time.

"Why, hello there," my voice boomed through the room. "Whoa, let's tone that down a bit. There...there...there we go. All right, everyone, welcome to I Hope God's Wearing Earmuffs. Thank you so, so much for all coming out tonight. This is just incredible." I paused, and people applauded. "I know some of you may know this already, but you are all doing a great thing tonight. Taking time out, coming to this show, donating to cystic fibrosis...it means a lot to me, so thank you. This is going to be a fucking incredible show. Yes, I said it," I laughed. "A FUCKING GREAT show. Let's get it started!" Another pause, more cheering. After introducing the opening comic, I went back to my seat.

Approximately thirty minutes later I was back on stage, this time ready to deliver my own closing act. Closing not only the evening, but my Syracuse career (comedy and otherwise) as well.

The nerves hit me again and though I didn't rip the plug out of the mic this time, I wasn't exactly rolling in laughter to start my set.

"Just wanted to thank everyone one last time. Thank you so much for coming out," I said. I paused, looking out into the crowd again; the sheer mass of people in the dark distance overwhelmed me. For the first time in my brief comedy life, I stood silent. A light from the back of the room snatched me away from my brief lapse. Looking towards the door opening in the back of the room, I said, "You guys want to come in?"

The room turned to see what I was looking at.

"I'm just kidding; I wanted everybody to turn around."

As they had all uniformly turned, so too did they uniformly laugh at my offhand remark. And with that, the show started. All it took was the one laugh to calm my nerves, and before I knew it, I was off and running.

"You know, I'm sorry, but I have to point this out," I said, stopping in the middle of a joke about hibachi steakhouses. "They're probably not going to love me for doing this, but, for those of you that don't know, those enormous men sitting in the back of the room—are the Big East-leading men's basketball team!"

Most of the crowd craned their necks to catch a glimpse while the team stayed seated. Once they all saw what I was talking about, a loud cheer went up.

"All right, all right. Let's not forget who you came to see," I chuckled. "I'm glad to see that you guys came. To be honest, I wasn't sure if the guys on the team could read, so I'm glad that the posters all over campus actually worked."

More laughter.

"And Jonny Flynn is here," I said, another cheer rising up from the crowd. "See, they love you, Jonny…Why leave here for the NBA when there's tons of eligible college girls right here in sunny Syracuse?"

More laughter. Flynn stood up halfway. "Hey yo, fuck you, Nick!"

Even more laughter.

"The men's basketball team, folks!" I said, raising my hand to the group in the back. We weren't friends; all I knew was that Flynn had read my column at least once. But they came and that was cool, far as I was concerned. And they were good sports.

The show really rolled from there on. The laughter came frequently and fervently; people really seemed to be feeling everything I was trying. At one point, I completely veered off topic again (something I hadn't been so sure I wanted to do at the show's outset) to talk about the creepy IT guys that worked in the various campus buildings. Instead of going for thirty minutes, I went for a solid forty-five and there didn't seem to be much of a letup so far as crowd enjoyment was concerned.

Having made my opening jokes about the c-word, I closed with the following:

"I need to get into one of those fights, you know? One of those, I hate you! and you hate me! type of fights, the kind you only have with people you're having sex with." I paused. "You know, women." People chuckled, mostly men. I continued, "So, yeah, a few semesters ago, I actually saw one of those fights. I went abroad—to London, great time. Really, just very inexpensive over there, very easy to exist. So I'm in line, waiting to go through Customs. Right in front of me is the fight; I walked in right in the middle of it. Man's name is, shit you not, is Nick, woman's name is Mary. Two little girls, the two of them are married—-not the girls, the man and the woman. The two girls are the byproduct of their marriage...via...sexual intercourse. Sorry, makes me uncomfortable," I said, feigning uneasiness.

"I get there and I'm doing my best to make it like I'm not listening to their fight, I'm just..." I said, pausing, as I pantomimed myself staring blankly ahead, mouth open, eyes fixed on where this fight would be taking place.

More laughter.

"I'm not even faking it at all, just being blatant. The woman's whispering, 'Why would you say that about me, Nick?' He's like, 'Mary, would ya please shut the hell up? Please!' 'But why, why would you say that?'" I said, volleying back and forth in the fake conversation.

"It was the sort of fight where, fifteen years down the road, ten years down the road...thirty minutes down the road...those two little girls are going to say, 'All right, that was the moment when our parents decided to get a divorce.'"

"I witnessed it. An end-of-marriage fight, courtside seats to the end of a relationship. Now the fight has been going on for so long and I've been there so long, that I feel like I'm actually part of the fight. As if it's my place to say something. Part of me wanted to jump in and go, 'What the fuck? Why *would* you say that?' I didn't, though," I laughed.

"But what I *did* say was—I leaned in, and I said—'You didn't happen to call her a cunt, did you?'"

The room erupted. It was a perfect ending, just long

enough and reprising a joke from earlier in the evening. That ending tied it all together and allowed me to leave on a loud laugh—every comic's dream.

As I stood at the front of the stage with the other two comics, the room in full applause, I scanned the crowd. Unsure of who I was looking for, it was more of a glazed look, just a content man surveying the land he'd just conquered. Afterwards, a group of people came forward to offer either congratulations or good wishes. It was at this point that I got a clearer view of the audience (mainly because the lights were turned on, not because of some new perspective). Listening to the various people and thanking them in turn, I began to take stock. No sign of several of my radio or *Daily Orange* friends, or of Allison or Lauren. Asking Jamie later, I'd find out that my surveillance wasn't off base. My housemates obviously showed up in full force, not only attending but donating their time to help out as well. One friend from the radio station, Jason, showed up, and that was particularly big news because this kid was the biggest Rangers fan on the planet. And the Rangers had a playoff game that night, which he either skipped or DVRed (likely the latter, but still shows effort, no?).

Just as I was getting my final pats on the back from what remained of the now-dwindling audience, she appeared.

"Nice job today," Sophia said.

"Hey, there," I said, undoubtedly surprised to see her. "Uh, thank you. I'm really surprised to see you."

We hadn't spoken more than a few passing words in or out of class since my blowup about a month or so earlier. I'd wanted to see her again, to apologize, but could never bring myself to. When I did see her in class or on campus, pride would get the best of me. *I'm not that into her,* I'd "reason". *I shouldn't have to apologize to her for anything. We're not friends anymore; so what?* You can see why the word reason is in quotes.

"Nah, I was planning on coming to this show before I found out you were a jerk," she laughed.

Nervous, I had no choice but to chuckle. In a normal situation, I'd defend myself, try to reason with the person calling me a jerk, but I knew I had no recourse. I was a jerk and if she wasn't being so pleasant, I was sure she could easily have settled on a more hurtful word or phrase.

"You come by yourself?" I asked.

"Yeah, I couldn't get anyone to come," she said. "I've got to get going, but I just wanted to let you know I thought you did a great job, not just on stage, but with this whole thing...this was really a good thing." She moved in to hug me and we embraced.

"Well, I'm glad you came," I said. "It means a lot to me, really."

And it did. I meant that, truly.

***

In college, you never really need a reason to celebrate. In a universe where anyone with a pulse drinks beer heavily at the very least two nights a week (and more often three or four), it didn't actually seem as if my roommates and I were celebrating anything other than it being Saturday night. Sure, the show had just ended and it had been a great success. We were all happy, no one more so than me, but it wasn't about me after the round of car bombs at the house. Together we went down to Chuck's and, for once, together we all returned, at around two-thirty in the morning.

Lying in my bed, I thought about the day. These were the sorts of things that showed you who your true friends were, I decided. When something truly important came up, who would be there? Who would say they were coming, and mean it? There were intramural basketball games and parties and flip cup games and radio shows and newspaper articles and favors and lunches and dinners. But this was the one thing, above all, that truly meant something to me. Those who got me, who understood what I was about and why I was doing it, knew that, without having to ask why. And if making a commitment in this instance meant showing up for an hour and giving a few dollar bills to a good cause, then that was all it took. Some people, I realized that night, just weren't worth the hassle. When it came down to it, the people who cared about what you cared about, who made the effort, big or small, were the ones worth keeping around.

40 monday, may 5th

This particular Monday represented a day that we'd all been looking forward to for at least a year and half. The first Monday of May, for the last few years, had become a sort of campus-wide bash loosely known as May Fest. Its origins were humble (and, might I add, more academic); it began as a day for students to display work done over the course of the semester at various venues throughout the university. Naturally, this day would have to be a school-wide off-day, and even more naturally, many of the students who weren't participating in the world of academia took it as a chance to engage in that favorite of youthful pastimes: day drinking.

Over the years, it had devolved into what it had been the past few years: the type of party you've come to expect in wild college movies, with lots of sunshine and people spilling out from their lawns into the streets and drunken debauchery and basically anything else you can imagine. For example, last year Colin had nearly gotten a concussion while sparring with Matt with a foam spear atop a trampoline. Matt had delivered a crushing blow to Colin's side, knocking him clear off the tramp and onto the small grassy hill on which the house resided. From there, he rolled down the hill and just barely missed smashing his head into a parked car at the curb. That close to serious injury—but also, what a great story.

So, as you can imagine, this was something we'd all been excited about. Colin had joked that he was going to get up at seven a.m. for it, kind of like you did on Christmas morning in anticipation of a day filled with presents and food. Well, on this beautiful Monday, he and I did just that. Sort of. It was actually closer to ten; but still, that's got to count for something on a day when you didn't need to be up for anything in particular, doesn't it?

The plan we had mapped out took us to about two in the afternoon. On second thought, calling it a plan is probably a disservice to the word. It was more like a routine, which would simply be to purchase several thirty-racks of whatever we could afford, set up the beer pong table and grill in the front lawn, and continue until we finished the food and beer.

It was the sort of day that made outgoing seniors forget about all the assorted, for lack of a better term, shit that they had to take care of. My correspondence with the NFL Network (which had gotten to the point where an interview was almost a certainty), my few finals (which at this point I obviously didn't care about), my few girls (who at this point I could barely call "mine"), and any number of other worries that one might associate with leaving behind "the best days of your life" in only a week's time: all of these things were put on the back burner. There were no worries like "Man, I should enjoy this, because who knows when I'll get to do anything like this again." It was simply get drunk early and sustain it. And don't pass out. That was about it.

Once the front lawn partying had run its course, we splintered off towards various parties taking place along the school's main drag, Euclid Street. A suddenly crutchless Lotfi and I began our trek from his apartment, about a block or so up the street.

"You're not going to be drinking anything today, are you?"

"Yes, today...today is the day I've been waiting for my

whole life to drink," he said. He was feeling feisty today.

"Funny. I meant water. Are you going to be carrying a water bottle?"

"Oh, got it…no, I don't believe so."

"Okay, then hold this," I said, handing him my bottle. The only rule the school police had that day was that students didn't drink from open alcohol containers. Put it in a red cup and you were fine to walk the street as you pleased. So I decided I'd double-fist and have Lotfi hold onto the water bottle so I wouldn't get too drunk or dehydrated.

From outside Lotfi's apartment, I could see groups of people walking around, partying and having fun. It truly was a gorgeous day out, not a cloud in the sky. Oddly, it had been this way the year before. Maybe there was a God in Syracuse after all.

The sights and sounds of the day were hard to ignore, and as we came around the corner, they came into even clearer view, at higher volume. Up and down Euclid, there was a mass of humanity unlike anything we'd ever seen before. In front of every single house, people were pouring out onto front lawns and sidewalks, playing beer pong and flip cup and basically any other drinking game under the sun. And those who weren't playing drinking games were simply drinking and talking to friends. Music blared from stereos at each house, to the point where each location's musical choice was audible only if you were directly in front of said stereo. From the street, or walking the sidewalks, it all sounded like noise. But somehow, despite the cacophony of the day, there was a distinct clarity to it all. Even though we'd taken part in it the year prior, as juniors, we felt as if we truly belonged this year. We'd worked hard enough; this was almost like a university-hosted celebration in our honor.

Walking down the street, Lotfi and I had no particular plans. We were simply going to amble our way down Euclid and see where the day took us. I knew I'd run into friends, either those who lived on Euclid or others who were partying at their friends' places on Euclid. Seeing as how it was a nice day, I had donned nothing other than a Tim Duncan jersey and shorts, and Lotfi a Syracuse Lacrosse t-shirt and jean shorts.

I could go into the various stops we made along the way, but honestly, what do you really care about that? So let's cut to the chase, shall we? (editor's note: I'm sure you were desperate for that sentence about two hundred pages ago…but you're still reading this, so you need to either find something better to do, or stop complaining and finish this thing.)

There were trampolines and kegs and flip cup games and beer pong and (insert crazy college stuff, à la Jell-O wrestling). That was all fun to see. Lotfi and I didn't take part in any of it. I (and, by extension, Lotfi) was simply happy to accept a beer from whoever was throwing the party, drink and observe, and move on.

"Hey! Are you Nick Anderson!?" a blonde girl screamed at me from a few feet away.

"Yes, I am," I admitted, rather shyly. I'd never gotten used to the idea of people recognizing me outside the house.

"Hey, Liz," the girl said to her friend. "It's Nick Anderson, from the *Daily*—"

"Alexander," I corrected.

"Oh, sorry. It's Nick Alexander, not Anderson, from the *Daily Orange*," she said as she listened to her friend ask a question in the vein of *who the hell is that?* "The guy that writes those funny columns for the *D.O.* You know?"

At first Liz didn't know, but eventually she came around and the two started chatting me up about what I did and how I did it and why I did it and basically anything else they could think of. Externally, it seems like all fine and good, no? Well, at first, sure. But eventually it got to a point where it wasn't so fun anymore. That point arrived a moment or two later.

"Hey, we have an idea for you for your column!" one of the blondes exclaimed. They were both exceedingly attractive, but I still failed to remember either one's name.

"Really?" I said, trying my best to sound uninterested. Obviously, I wasn't doing a good enough job.

"Yeah! It's about when you were—"

"Hey, you told Xavier we were going to be at his place by four, didn't you?" Lotfi interrupted.

"Uh…yes!" I said, checking my cell phone when I realized what Lotfi was doing. "I'm sorry, but we have to get going. I told a friend I was going to be at his place for a beer pong tournament."

"Oh, okay," they said.

"It was nice to meet you," I said, turning to walk away before waiting for their response. "Xavier?" I said to Lotfi. "Really, Xavier?"

"We're out of there, aren't we?"

"Yeah, we are. Thanks. But that's some name to pull out of your ass," I laughed.

Just as we started to walk away, I heard a female voice calling my name from the house on our left. It was Lauren and she was, not surprisingly, drunk.

"Hey!" she shouted out towards me as I continued to walk away. I had nothing to say to her and, frankly, I was surprised she had anything to say to me.

Catching up to me, she tugged on my arm and whirled me around to face her. "Didn't you hear me shouting for you?"

"Yes, I did," I said, motioning to Lotfi for a sip of water.

"Listen, I want you to know," she began, her gaze leaving mine and now glancing towards the pavement. "I want you to know that I'm sorry I couldn't make it the other night. It's just…"

"Don't worry about it," I said, looking to simply move on and rid myself of the conversation.

"Really?" she said.

"Yes, it's no big deal," I replied.

"You sure?" she asked again. "I mean it, I'm sorry. You believe me, don't you?"

I took another sip from the water bottle and looked at Lotfi, who gave me a *Relax, it's not worth it* look.

"No, I don't," I said, watching a look of shock come over her face. "But I don't really care, you know? I just don't care."

"What are you—"

"Don't do this," I said. "We're both having good days today, right? I don't care why you didn't come; that doesn't make a difference to me. I've got to get going. There's a party—"

"Our friend Xavier," Lotfi interrupted, "is having a beer pong tournament we've got to get to."

"So, yeah, I'll talk to you later," I said, and again turned to leave.

As I walked away, I heard her mutter, "Xavier?"

"Again with this ridiculous name?" I laughed. Turning serious for a moment, I looked at Lotfi and asked him, "You thought I handled that right, didn't you?"

"You know me," he started. "I'd have just said nothing and gone on my way. But you don't do that. But you didn't blow up or insult anyone, either. I think you did what you felt was right, what you felt you had to do."

"I did. I feel good about it. Let me get that beer," I said, taking a huge swig and tossing the cup into a nearby garbage bin.

The rest of the day raced by and before we knew it, night had fallen over the proceedings. Of course, that didn't really stop anyone. There was a concert scheduled for that night and while the crowd had thinned (slightly), there were still parties vomiting out of every house on Euclid.

Despite my wishes to the contrary, Lauren wasn't the last problem I ran into. About an hour or so later, I ran into Allison and Sophia in quick succession. A situation that just a few weeks ago had me running for the hills now left me calmer than ever. There was something different, something missing from the relationships between us. I wanted to scream at Allison, as I'd wanted to scream at Lauren, but I held back in each instance, opting instead to politely move forward and put it behind me.

Where Lauren had stood almost dumbfounded, though, Allison wasn't so easily left behind.

"What the hell does that mean?!" she screamed as I walked away. I'd just told her that I didn't care why she didn't come to my show and wasn't interested in hearing her try to explain herself. She stomped a few feet towards me and again shouted, "What does that mean!?"

I stopped and turned around to face her.

"You didn't seem to mind me when you were *fucking* me!" she shouted at a volume that, in any situation (campus-wide party or not), was far too loud.

"You shut the hell up," I said quietly, so only she could hear.

"What?!" she continued shouting, trying to get anyone around to listen to her. "You don't want anyone to know *you had sex with me?* Are you *embarrassed?* Mister funny guy, *mister big shot can't be seen with me?*"

"You're drunk," I said, still quietly. "Just watch yourself, before you say something stupid," I added, knowing full well that she already looked exactly that way.

"You're a fucking asshole, you know that?"

I didn't say anything.

"An ass-*hole!*"

With all my might, I was biting back an extreme urge to tell her off. To tell her to shut her mouth, to tell her I never really liked her, to tell her I was only with her because I knew I could be, to tell her I didn't care about her and never really had. But I kept that all inside. There was something about being next to Lotfi. Or having drunk beer for nearly seven straight hours.

"I'm sorry you feel that way," I said, walking past her. She continued to shout after me, but as we got farther away, her shrieks were replaced by the noise of music from the next house we'd come to.

"Jesus, this was supposed to be a fun day," I said to Lotfi, taking another sip from the water bottle. "Wasn't it?"

"Well, it's about to get just a bit more fun," Lotfi laughed, handing me the red cup filled with beer. "Here you go; you'll need this."

"Sophia," I said, sounding exasperated.

"You sound beat. Rough day?" she laughed, tapping my

cup.

"You could say that," I laughed, eying Lotfi, who at this point had taken enough steps back from the action that it appeared as if he had purchased courtside seats.

"You ready for finals? Graduation?" she asked.

"Already? We've run out of things so quickly, we're talking about that?" I laughed.

"Oh, my bad," she said. "I forgot you're too cool to talk about something everyone else talks about."

"Maybe that's why I don't want to talk about it," I mumbled.

"What's that?"

"I said, I forgot you're too boring to come up with anything else to talk about."

"Ha, ha," she mocked. "I'ma get going. A pleasure, as always."

"All mine," I said, smiling as we parted ways. A step away, I called out, "Hey, listen, if you're not doing anything, hit me up. We're gonna be grilling and all that at my place, if you're around."

She paused before answering, still mulling over what to say. A smile came over her face. "No doubt."

"That didn't go nearly as horribly as I'd hoped," Lotfi said, now joining me.

"Hoped? Whose side are you on?"

Laughing, he said, "No side. I just love seeing you try to squirm your way out of those things."

The night would pass and Sophia wouldn't come over. But it didn't bother me. Again, it just wasn't the same. I was happy to be with my housemates and friends, drinking and barbecuing and laughing with them. Sophia and Lauren and Allison's whereabouts were no longer my concern. In the last few days, I'd been able to fully let go. The peace I'd made with them had manifested itself in how I'd handled myself throughout the day. I was over it. As much as I could be.

41 saturday, may 10th

Whatever the exact date of infection was, it was clear: the apathy bug had hit graduating seniors. If grades in high school served the purpose of getting you into college, and grades in college served the purpose of keeping you in college, then what did that say for real life, for getting a job? Not much, was what I was now realizing. What difference did it make how I did on my Com Law final? Was I either going to get a job or be turned down for one based on the outcome of my Baseball Cards final? No, probably not. Barring some unforeseen, cataclysmic academic collapse, I'd be walking with my friends on the tenth of May…

…which was also known as today.

How had that happened so fast?

It was an ironic thing, to look past graduation towards the ensuing partying. On one hand, no one wanted the weekend to fly by, but on the other hand, the family and friend barbecue seemed like a whole hell of lot more fun than the actual ceremonies.

"This is so boring," Colin groaned.

"God, tell me about it," I said. I sat in between Chris and Colin, while the keynote speaker droned on about never leaving any opportunity behind.

"Who the hell is this guy, anyway?" Colin asked.

"Bob Woodward, the guy from the Watergate thing. Deep Throat, you know?" I answered.

"No, it's Bob Wood*ruff*," Chris corrected. "He was on ABC, went off with the troops in Iraq. Got injured over there. You don't remember that?"

"Nope, never heard of him. You sure it's not the Watergate guy?" I said.

"Do you pay attention to anything?"

Ignoring that last question, I switched gears. "I still think they could've done better than one of the Watergate guys."

"It's not..." Chris started, before quickly realizing that it was a fruitless effort. "Who would you want, smart guy?"

"Don't say Jay-Z," Colin laughed.

"I wasn't going to say Jay-Z," I started. "I was going to say...Shawn Carter. He's not just a businessman, he's a business...man."

"What is that? A line of his?" Chris asked.

"Why, yes, my good friend, it is indeed," I said, ramping up the inner "whitey" as high as possible. Going back to a normal voice, I continued, "At least that's a guy we all care about and would like to hear talk. Who gives a shit what this guy's talking about?"

"You're right. A journalist who risked his life in the field in the preeminent war of this era...what relevance does he have here?"

"Glad you're coming around," I smiled, putting my arm around Chris's shoulder.

"How much longer?" Colin continued to moan.

The answer to that question would wind up being only another twenty-five minutes, but boy oh boy did it seem like a lot longer.

Shortly after Woodruff had finished his remarks, the procession part of the ceremonies finally came. The only reason I was aware of this part was that it signaled the end of the whole wretched thing. That, and the fact that my mom had texted me ten times to remind me to look towards where they were seated once I shook the Dean's hand.

There were over five hundred people from my college in the graduating class, so it was a while before my walk from seat to Dean was complete. As I walked towards the stage, my steps as a college student now literally numbered, I expected to have some sort of flashback. You know how it goes in the movies: the past four years, memories and laughs and fun times all flashing through the mind's eye. And in the background, a mid-'90s rock song crooning something like "Those were the best times of my life." That's what I expected, but that's not what I got.

Instead, I was blank. The more I tried to think about Chris, Colin, Natalie, Matt, Lotfi, classes, basketball games, the radio station, girls, drinking, video games, the quad, the bookstore, Syrajuice, the late nights, Chuck's, the newspaper...the more of a blank I drew.

Finally, I took a step onto the stage, only four people left between me and my diploma. To my right, I took in what was a pretty crowded scene. The stage had been set up at midfield, with students seated in folding chairs on the field in front of it. Parents and family sat in the actual stands. I could now see my mom and dad under the sign for Section 112, just as they'd said. I flashed a smile, not just to appease them but because I truly was proud. I never doubted that I'd graduate, but I was still aware that it was an accomplishment. In a few short steps, I'd be the first Alexander ever to graduate from college.

"Does that say more about me or about how pathetic your gene pool is?" I had joked with my dad.

...*Nicholas Alexander, Broadcast Journalism*...

With that, I took steps forward. Right hand extended for a shake, left hand for the diploma, as Matt had reminded me. It's odd. This moment you've been waiting for, expecting, playing out in your head: it's over in a second. A blink later, I was walking off the stage—walking away from college.

On my way down, I caught my mom and dad again. Both were grinning from ear to ear, my brothers pointing at me, my sister raising a thumb with her daughter sitting jubilantly on her shoulders. I put my head down for a brief second, caught my breath and then looked again. Smiling, I pointed back at the group.

Shrugging my shoulders, smile still aimed in their direction, I mouthed, "What's for dinner?"

42 sunday, may 11th

Most of the underclassmen had left campus a few days back, but my friend Aaron, the Chinese food buddy, was still in town for the graduation, as a number of his friends were outgoing seniors.

"You still mean what you said?" Aaron said as he found me in the quad prior to the second day's ceremonies.

"About Myanmar?" I joked, knowing full well what he was referring to.

"Yeah, about Myanmar," he sighed. "No, you ass, about graduating. You ready for this? Ready to leave all this behind?"

"I…I'm fine," I said.

"Doesn't sound that way to me," he said.

"No, no," I started, "I am. I'm really good, dude. It's all good. This is what happens, right? Listen, I had a great time here, but it's time to move on. That's what you do. Everyone's saying congratulations for a reason."

"No, you're right. But don't you find it funny that at the same time everyone's saying that, they're also saying how they wish they could go back?"

"Not in my family. They weren't smart enough to stay in college in the first place," I laughed.

"You know what I mean," Aaron said.

"No, I do," I said. "That's just a part of it, man. I mean, of course I'm going to miss this, but there is no 'best time of your life.' It doesn't end here," I said.

"How can you be so sure of that? How do you know that?"

"I don't know. But, in a way, that's how I'm sure."

Aaron wasn't sure he believed me when I said that, but it was my day, so he let it slide. "Well, man, I'm gonna get moving, but let me be another on your list. Congratulations."

"Thanks a lot, man. Much appreciated. It's cool of you to still be up here. You do know that I'm not going to come back up here for yours…" I said.

"Wouldn't expect anything less from a guy like you," he laughed.

The routine for the day was basically the same as on the day prior. My alarm was so loud, I could have slept across the street and I'd have been fine. I'd showered, gotten dressed, and walked over to the Dome with my housemates. We all went in together and sat in a row.

Unlike yesterday's proceedings, Sunday's graduation went by in an instant. There was barely any time for idle chatter about the merits of the speaker, plans for drinking the rest of the time in Syracuse, whether anyone was naked underneath their gown, or any other sort of inane conversation fostered by situations where boredom runs rampant. Before I knew it, I was taking pictures with everyone. Natalie's dad had one of those "I'm really serious about photography but not good enough to be a professional" cameras, so everyone looked at his lens when the photos were being taken. There were group shots and individual shots, silly poses and serious stances, smiles and arms around, mortarboards on and in the air.

From the Dome, we met with our parents and headed back to the house, where a few people had already gotten things started with a spread of cold cuts and veggies. Make-your-own Italian cold-cut sandwiches, with burgers and hot dogs on deck…could life get any better? Probably not.

As soon as I possibly could, I tore off my shirt, tie, and dress pants and changed into jeans and a plain red t-shirt. The red part isn't really important.

My roommates and I were desperate to get outside and soak up the sunny day. There was food, there were friends, there were families. And it was barely three o'clock. This would be going on for a while, we all knew, and that was decidedly a good thing.

Sitting down in a folding chair, I was flanked by Matt and Colin. Chris and his girlfriend played beer pong against his parents, Nat hovered near the food, where her family was chatting with my family. All told, everyone had a group.

"You know what this means, right?" I asked.

"What's that?" Matt said, taking a swig of his beer.

"No more papers. For us, at least," I chuckled. "I won't have to bullshit for six or seven pages anymore."

"God, were those a joke, or what?" Colin asked. "If professors on this campus were only half-aware of the stunts I've pulled. They think they're *so smart*, looking for plagiarism. Come on, who is that stupid?"

Matt and I laughed. We knew a kid from playing basketball who actually was that stupid.

"What sort of stunts did you pull? This I'd love to hear," Natalie said, grinning and grabbing a seat. "I can only imagine what sorts of shenanigans a real wild card like you got up to."

"Well, you're going to laugh at this one, but," Colin started, "I always bolded my periods. And any punctuation of any kind."

"You cannot possibly be serious," I said, laughing hysterically. "How long did that take you?"

"Better question is," Chris shouted from the beer pong table, "how much of a difference could that actually have made?"

"First of all, it made a huge difference. We're talking at least a full half-page added on. And—"

"Get the hell out of here," Matt said. "There's no way that's true. You're saying bolding punctuation added half a page? That can't be right."

"It is," Colin said. "But it was a real time suck. It took me," he paused, knowing how everyone would react, "at least an extra forty-five minutes."

Everyone did laugh, as Colin expected. The idea that he would spend more time than it would take to write that half page was nearly as comical as the idea of bolding periods.

"I'd ask how you thought of that idea, but I'm actually more curious to hear what else you pulled," I asked.

"This one is legit, I swear. If you ever have to write a paper again, definitely use this," Colin said.

"Kerning? Is that your big secret?" Matt asked.

"Uh, yeah," Colin said, slightly disappointed that his story had been ruined.

"Oh, come on, everyone knows about that," Matt said. "I've written maybe five papers in four years and I knew about that. Nat? Chris?"

They both agreed that they knew. I had absolutely no idea what they were all talking about, but I didn't want to look like the dunce, so I played along. Matt noticed.

"Nick, you don't know what kerning is, do you?"

"Yeah, man, of course I know. I've kerned on all papers," I said. I knew my cover was blown. "I got so good at it, my nickname among the professors here was Kid Kerner."

"That's so fucking stupid," Matt laughed. "Just say you don't know."

"I don't know," I answered, while grabbing myself a sandwich and beer. "Dearest Matthew, would you be a doll and enlighten me?"

Matt explained that kerning had to do with the space assigned by your word processor to go between all of the letters you type. By simply going into the computer's settings, you can adjust (read: increase) all the spaces by a fraction, which won't be noticeable to the naked eye but will add at least a half page, sometimes a full page, without much effort.

"I have no words," I said. "How come no one ever told me about this? You all knew about this the whole time?"

"Yeah, dude," Matt said.

"It's not as if we were keeping it from you," Chris laughed.

"It was in the SU student handbook," Colin joked. "That's how I found out."

"Wow," I said, truly dumbfounded. "I feel like I could've graduated at least a semester early had I known about this."

It was the sort of day where the only thing on earth that you could possibly desire was to be outside. Whatever you do from there is completely arbitrary. In our case, it was a barbecue with family and friends. But it could just as easily have been anything else. The air held a faint smell of grilling. Women were wearing shorts and sundresses again and those kids who would have been hippies had it been about forty years earlier were playing hacky sack in the quad. You get the idea. Not necessarily hot, but warm enough where you don't question yourself for dressing for the warmth. That guy who wears shorts too early in the season is a real ass, isn't he?

Sitting with my friends, I couldn't have been happier. Slowly, of course, the party died down…at least in terms of attendance. My parents had to leave because my grandma needed to get some rest. Colin's parents were heading back home to the Boston area, so they wanted to get a head start on the drive. Natalie's folks had the same issue—substituting Florida for Boston and the drive with a plane ride. Either way, by eight-thirty, all that remained were the housemates and Natalie's boyfriend Kent, who had very little else to do as he'd graduated from UNC a week prior.

"You want to chill here?" Matt started, "Or do you want to go to Chuck's?"

"I'm not sure," Chris said. It was clear that he was looking to stay with his girlfriend for the night. No extraneous adventures were necessary, so far as the success of his evening was concerned.

"Anyone other than Lady Gordon? Nick? I know you're in. Anyone else?"

"Why am I automatically…" I said, trailing off.

338 |

The rest of the group agreed, so to Chuck's it was. It didn't take much longer for Chris to be coaxed into going. Though I'd sworn I'd never do it, I used the classic "this could be our last trip to Chuck's" line to ultimately rope him in.

As it would turn out, this would be our last night at Chuck's and this reality slowly dawned on us as we walked down from the house.

"I don't know if I'd tell my parents this," I started, "but the thing I'm almost definitely going to miss most about this school is Chuck's."

"Oh, no question about it," Colin said. "Chuck's and you guys. Probably in that order."

"Really, though," I said. "You could come down here, have dinner, get drunk, buy a girl drinks all night, maybe even leave with her, and not spend more than twenty-five bucks doing it. That's fucking nuts."

"Yeah, won't be like that once we leave here," Matt said.

We all agreed: the booze was cheap in Syracuse. But it was the sort of unison agreement that simply signaled a shift in conversation, not so much recognition of that soon-to-be problematic reality.

"I'm going to miss the music," Chris said, filling the silence. "Great '90s rock. I want a Chuck's CD. Maybe they can make me a mix?"

"Yeah Eddie, I'm sure they could," I laughed. "When they're done using your iPod, I'm sure they'll burn you a CD."

"Oh, so funny, big guy. Listen, when I think about Chuck's, I'm never going to forget about that night when you snuck out because your two girlfriends were there," Chris said. Erica began to ask what he was talking about. "The specifics of the night aren't that important, but does anyone—other than Nick—remember what it was he used as his 'disguise' to get out of the bar?"

Chris noticed Matt raising his hand foolishly and called on him. "Matt?"

"What is...a baseball hat?!" Matt laughed, grabbing me around the shoulder.

"Judges?" Chris mocked. "Well, we can accept that, but that's only part of the answer. He also donned glasses. That's right, a baseball hat and glasses. Regular reading glasses. That was your idea for a disguise?"

"I never said it was a good idea," I laughed. "But I had to book it. Couldn't have been there any longer than I was. That had bad news written all over it."

"How about the time when Nick—" Natalie started.

"What is this, a roast?" I piped in.

"No, it's just, you probably made the biggest ass out of yourself time and time again down there, so it's more fun to remember those times," she laughed. "Now, how about the time when Nick thought that there was a whole table of girls looking to buy him a drink, and it turned out to be a bunch of dudes?"

"Yeah," Matt laughed, "That was great."

"I'm never going to forget going out back by the dumpsters and taking a piss," Colin said. "I doubt I'll ever feel that free again." All the men agreed.

"Totally," Natalie joked.

"You know, I've heard that people were crying at Chuck's the last few nights," Colin said.

"That's fucking pathetic," I said flatly.

"Wow. Nice, real nice," Matt said.

"Oh, come on. Really? Crying? I'm going to miss this place, but I'm not going to cry. Jesus. Get a hold of yourself. If I see any of you crying tonight, I'm leaving. Don't come up to me and—"

"All right, Ebenezer," Matt said. "Just get your ID out so we can get in. First round, mind erasers. Let's go."

And so we went. The drinking started out heavy, with two quick rounds of mind erasers. But, for whatever reason, it sputtered after that. Occasional beers were had, but no more rounds, no more shots, no more bombs, no more erasers. The fact that we'd been up and drinking all day likely had something to do with it.

I (and the housemates) never did wind up crying before

leaving that night. But I did recognize what might make someone cry, as I left. There was nothing particularly charming about the place. An outsider would have described it as dingy, overcrowded, too hot, and even dirty. But it was precisely those qualities (and others, such as the innumerable markings on the walls from outgoing seniors) that made the place feel like a home away from home. And, considering how frequently we'd all been there, it was just that. Walking away from the bar at two a.m., I realized this. Eyes dry, I bid the bar farewell.

43 the next few days

After that Sunday, it was all a deconstruction. There was a lot of beer in the fridge that needed to be drunk, there were clothes that needed to be packed, beds that needed to be sold to juniors, pieces of furniture that needed to be either junked or left at the curb, holes in the walls that needed to be patched, and a whole mess of cleaning.

None of it was fun. Aside from that first one—but even that couldn't be fully enjoyed, with all the other chore-like activity that had to be taken care of. Everyone had their own crap to handle, but in addition to that were the housecleaning chores Matt had divvied up so that we could attempt to recoup as much of our security deposit as possible. Not to ruin a (boring) story, but despite our hours of cleaning and money spent on things like spackling paste and paint, the realty company that owned our house would only give each of us back $50.86 of our security deposit. For the record, our initial deposit was $750.

Once the posters had been taken down, the refrigerators emptied, the TV and video games packed up, it all started to officially sink in. This was over.

"Lotfi left yesterday," I said to the group. We were all

sitting outside on Wednesday at around noon, waiting for my dad to come. He'd rented a U-Haul to bring up to Syracuse and drive me and my stuff back to New Jersey. That reality was now seriously setting in.

"Oh, I didn't get to say good-bye to Lotus," Natalie said.

No else one had gotten to say good-bye, either, but then again, at that exact moment no one else really felt like making conversation. It was fairly hot out, which made the day all the more depressing. A full four years, a weekend of graduation ceremonies and parties, a final night at Chuck's. And after all that, all it took for the final sobering reality to set in was the empty house. What finally made it real was that there was nowhere to go home to in Syracuse any longer.

Twenty agonizing minutes later, my dad pulled up in the mid-sized moving truck. We all hugged and they helped me move my stuff out and take that one last picture. It was pretty much how every last day of every other semester had gone in the past. Except that now there was a hollowness to the words "See you later," or any other expression tumbling out of our mouths.

No one was quite sure how to end it, exactly. Was this the end? Not really, but for now it was and that was how I chose to handle it. I tried my best to say with confidence and certainty that we'd see each other soon. That day would come, that we were sure of. But exactly when, no one knew. So, one by one, we said good-bye. Hugs, handshakes, smiles.

With my dad waiting in the driver's seat of the truck, I turned back to my friends one final time that day. I paused before speaking, which was a rarity. Unsure whether to try to be funny or sentimental or some odd combination of both, I ultimately couldn't decide. So I just spoke. "Have a safe trip back. I'll let you guys know when I get home."

From the truck, I lowered the window as my dad began to pull away. Smiling, I stuck my head out and yelled, "Hey!" They all turned. "Don't forget me! Don't ever forget! I love you guys...and Matt."

No one laughed, and not because it wasn't that funny.

44 at home

Talk about culture shock. Within only a few short weeks of coming home from school for good, I'd developed a pretty set routine. Because everyone in my house was asleep by ten-thirty at night during the week and eleven-thirty on the weekends, I fell into a similar pattern. During the day I might see a few of my high school friends, but since most of them had jobs, I usually just dragged around the house. It got so bad during one stretch that I didn't sleep in my room for a three-day period because it was upstairs and the TV was in the living room. On the first floor.

I've never been a really heavy sleeper. You know those people who can sleep until two in the afternoon? I was never one of those. Like most kids, I got up (extremely) early to watch cartoons and later on I got up for *Saved by the Bell* reruns. Anyway, since I was going to bed earlier than I had at pretty much any time in the past four years, I was up even earlier than I had been in those four years. Which was great, you know, because of all of the things I had available to do. The irony was remarkable, truly. At school, where I had no shortage of activities, I woke up lazily and lounged around. At home, where I was so bored I was literally DVRing live TV shows so

I would have something to watch later (it's every bit as idiotic as it seems), I was awake almost all day.

When I wasn't watching taped episodes of *Lingo* from the Game Show Network, I rode my bike to the YMCA where my family had a membership. Why did I bike, you ask? Because it ate up more time than driving my car, honestly.

Predictably, home didn't offer nearly the number of good-looking girls as school did. The YMCA workout room was no different. I would go days between seeing women within even four years of my age. Four is probably being kind, but I've been told it's bad form to ask women their ages.

I wish I had some sort of great story for you about how I ran into a friend of mine's mother who wouldn't stop telling me about how great her son was doing. About how I had to lie about what I was up to. About how I had to pretend my "car" was double-parked so I could get out of this horrific conversation that made me feel so pathetic and out of place in my new, albeit old, surroundings.

Well, I'm sorry. I don't really have any of those. I did run into a friend's mother who worked at the bank. But, seeing as how I didn't have a job, you can imagine how frequently I ran into her.

No, more often at the gym I just kept to myself. I'd keep my headphones blaring as loud as they could go without freaking anyone out. I'd look at the people working out around me and wonder how it was that I could not know any of them. At school, I'd recognize at least one of every four faces at the gym or the bar or the supermarket. Here, I was lucky to even kind of remember a face. It was like moving back into the town you grew up in only to find that everyone you knew had moved out and all that remained was your house and a few Italian restaurants.

All of these people—guys in their mid-forties on lunch breaks, women getting in a workout while their young kids were at daycare, and even kids who were my age and in similar situations to me—they all seemed like they had somewhere to go. Even within the gym, they moved from machine to machine with purpose, as if each workout had only a certain allotment of time before it had to end. To these people, it seemed, time had value. The gym was what they fit in between the rest of the events in their busy days. For me, it was what I used to help fill some of the vast empty space that was my day.

So much for not having a pathetic story, I guess.

Sometimes, when I was bored and looking for a pick-me-up, I'd reread some of the nice e-mails I'd gotten about my *Daily Orange* column. There was someone who identified herself only as "Creepy Freshman Fan," another girl who Facebooked me, a cute junior Poli Sci major, and even the mother of a student. No matter how far removed I was (either geographically or chronologically), it always felt amazing to hear or read strangers saying glowing things about me.

Matt, in short order, had moved down to South Carolina to start his first job with General Electric. Natalie, Chris, Colin, and I were all in similar boats. Which is to say, we didn't have jobs. I still was in contact with the NFL Network, but I grew more and more pessimistic about something coming of it as the days wore on and nothing concrete was settled.

"What's going on with the NFL Network? We haven't heard you talk about that in a while. Are you staying on top of it?" my mom would ask nicely (read: as a bother).

"Yeah," I said, pushing my food around on my plate. I wasn't depressed; far from it. Just bored. Very bored.

"What's wrong? You've been a mope the last few weeks, since you got back from school," my dad said.

"Nothing, nothing's wrong. Just bored. I need to get a job, do something," I said.

"Yes, you do," my dad said.

"Thank you for that," I smarted.

"How about we have a graduation party for you? Would you like that?" my mom asked. "I know we talked about it, but I forget what you said you wanted."

"That's fine," I said.

"Does that mean you do or you do not want one?" my

mom asked.

Before I could answer, my dad shot in, "Answer your mother!"

"Whoa. Give me a second, huh?" I laughed. "I meant, I do. Let's do it. Should be fun."

And it was. Fun, that is. There was a keg and there were friends and family. It was clear: there was a direct attempt on the part of my parents to imitate that final graduation party. It was a noble effort, no doubt about it. My grandma, at one point, even volunteered to do a keg stand. We convinced her that, besides the fact that it wasn't exactly "safe," the beer would almost certainly ruin her hairdo, which ultimately proved to be the winning argument. But, despite the veiled familiarity, none of the major players was there. Sure, it was nice out and there were booze and Italian cold cuts. But there was no Matt, no Colin, no Natalie, no Lotfi or Chris. That was a void that couldn't be filled.

45 sometime in mid-july. or maybe early august? no, definitely late july.

For the first few weeks and months after school, there wasn't a ton of contact among the lot of us. Sometimes Colin would send out an e-mail. Chris might call me, or the other way around. There wasn't a pattern to it. More often than not, the preferred method seemed to be e-mail. And, while the e-mails were often funny, there was something missing in reading Colin quote Billy Madison instead of hearing him do it.

This was the first one we received from Matt, to the whole group:

From matthew.reilly@ge.com
To: cgordon@gmail.com, natalie.vaughn@hotmail.com, josephsen.colin@gmail.com nick.alexander@gmail.com
Subject: What's up ladies?
Long time no see. I'm emailing today to say that just because we're miles apart, it doesn't mean we can't come together and discuss something we all love (no not Captain Crunch Oops All Berries or even that word

acronym game). I'm talking about meeting up in the not too distant future and staying in touch.

I think Homecoming is out at least for me. So I am for saying screw you to our school. "Home is where you hang your hat" (Danielson, Karate Kid II. min 48). Lets try to bang out a time to meet. Possibly spring? Possibly Feb? At school? At a school? I vote for Syracuse at least the first year. What do you guys think? When would be good for you. I'd like after New Years, as I'm a little tied up right now. No literally I am tied up. If anyone knows how to get out of a left hand half hitch without rupturing a spleen, I think this e-mail chain is the perfect place for that information.

If you ever cross the Mason-Dixon Line, turn around. But give me a call while you're turning.
Matt

PS. I had to sign up for a GE email address, and had to enter questions that I could answer if I forgot my password. So I chose the option to enter in my own questions. None of this first teacher's name bullshit. My question: What do douches wear to escape from bars? My answer: glasses and a hat.

From: josephsen.colin@gmail.com
To: cgordon@gmail.com, natalie.vaughn@hotmail.com;
matthew.reilly@ge.com, nick.alexander@gmail.com
Subject: Re: What's up ladies?

Hope all of you are enjoying the real world as much as I am. I'm "working" at a radio station in Boston and unintentionally refusing payment for the time being. I can do a reunion basically whenever as of now. My thrilling life generally consists of hours upon hours of Home and Garden TV, debating whether newlywed couples should follow the conservative route and go for the three bedroom colonial with the fenced in yard, or whether they should go a bit beyond budget and splurge for that two story modern with the great porch. It's in a much better school district and the property value has nowhere to go but up. I mean sure the bathrooms need a little work, but what's more important, closet space or having two sink fixtures? These are the questions that I try to tackle on a daily basis, so for all you 9-fiveers, life's not so bad now is it?

Speaking of which... Matt, still waiting on that video you took of the Greenville Drive mascot dancing on the field. To say that I'm anxiously awaiting that email attachment would be the understatement of the summer.

It's the little things in life that count guys. Such as Chinese gymnasts,
Colin

> From: cgordon@gmail.com
> To: josephensen.colin@gmail.com,
> natalie.vaughn@hotmail.com; matthew.reilly@ge.com,
> nick.alexander@gmail.com
> *Subject: Re: What's up ladies?*
>
> *Hey All.*
>
> *First things first. Matt, amazing work, as always. You delivered and I was cracking up reading that this morning.*
> *Yesterday I was so bored I was debating which 80s/early 90s sitcom had a better theme song, "Who's the Boss?", "Family Matters", "Growing Pains", "Full House", or "Fresh Prince of Bel-Air". Song wise, I decided you had to go Fresh Prince, but they're all so great it's tough to pick just one. Show wise, you all know where I put my vote.*
> *As far as the grand meeting in Syracuse goes, I'm 100% in for it. Since Erica is still there, I'll be in 'Cuse a few times at least in the next year. By the way, I went in to see her Saturday and went to Chuck's Saturday night and it was really weird without all you guys but it was an absolute blast. I wish we had college back so badly.*
> *Anyways, I hope you're all well and I'll talk to you all soon.*
> *Take care,*
> *Chris*

> From: natalie.vaughn@hotmail.com
> To: josephensen.colin@gmail.com, cgordon@gmail.com;
> matthew.reilly@ge.com, nick.alexander@gmail.com

Subject: Re: What's up ladies?

Eddie, take care? That's what we get, after four years? Take care? Real nice.

I would love to meet up with you in Syracuse to see what sort of shit we can get ourselves into. Sometime next semester around March sounds good. I'll probably be in NYC by that time, so it should be pretty easy to get up there. I'd love to go anytime, and it's sounding like this works for everyone, so I'm in for that visit.

Anyway, I have to get back to playing with dolls, a beloved pastime of mine (new job: working at a doll manufacturing factory in town. Gotta love the weight that having a college degree throws around!)

-Nat

From: nick.alexander@gmail.com
To: josephensen.colin@gmail.com, natalie.vaughn@hotmail.com, matthew.reilly@ge.com, cgordon@gmail.com
Subject: Re: What's up ladies?

I must say I'm glad that Matt started this chain, though I'm surprised that he was the first of all the group to send out the "hey, how's everyone doing" e-mail. That security question, I think we can all agree is fucking hysterical. Hope you didn't stay up all night thinking of that one.

I'm generally free, though, as I'd imagine the case is with Chris/Colin/Natalie, a job could come up that moves us elsewhere and dictates availability. I too can wait til next semester if that's what works for everyone. I agree—-fuck homecoming. Fuck it. Someone I was talking to couldn't believe I didn't want to go up for it. I told them, honestly, I'm going to get fucking cold cocked on a Friday with my roommates, and after that, all bets are off. That's about it. Maybe prey on some young gals, maybe some young gents. Maybe steal some shit from the old house. That's all.

As far as what I'm up to...you know when people answer that with "Nothing" but they really mean, "A lot, just nothing new since we last spoke"? Well, I actually mean it as "nothing", or as humanly close to nothing as "nothing" can be. I haven't really heard much from the NFL

Network, though I'd love to move out to LA if only because someone has to make jokes about having vicious, rough sex with Matt's smokin' hot cousin out there.

Yours forever,
  Nick

Lotfi wasn't on that e-mail chain, for no particular reason. However, he and I stayed in similar contact, via phone and e-mail. He didn't have a car, so he wasn't able to drive up to hang out. I had planned on going down there, but as the calendar turned to August, the post-college malaise only set in harder.

46 monday, august 4th

Those e-mails chains came and went. Gym trips were
biked, back and forth. TV watched and DVRed. Facebook
checked and thoroughly reviewed. Finally, after what felt like
(and actually was) months of startling inactivity, I received an
e-mail from my contact at the NFL Network that changed
things:

From: ethan.kronner@nfl.com
To: nick.alexander@gmail.com
*Nick—-sorry for the delay in our conversation. As per what we've
discussed over the previous few months, there are a few PA spots opening
up for this upcoming season. If you're still interested, get back to me asap
so we can move on this.*

-ek

As you can imagine, reading this e-mail was like getting a
bucket of water dumped on me. Immediately I snapped to
attention and reread the body of the e-mail again. *There were a
few production assistant spots available? Was I ready to move to L.A.?
Could my home prison sentence be coming to an end? How would I get out
to L.A.? How about all my stuff? Did I know anyone out there?*

RELAX! I said to myself, snapping out of it. *You haven't even gotten the job yet. Just e-mail him back, see where it goes.*

Where it went, in about an hour's time (amazing, isn't it, that after months of inactivity, this could all go so fast? Try looking for a job nowadays, you'll see), was to having a Skype interview set up for the next morning. If all went well, I'd know within the next week if they were going to offer me anything.

The rest of the day was spent stressing over not only what to wear, but where to position my computer so as to have nothing embarrassing in the background. Ultimately, I decided that wearing a suit was too much, so I went with a button-down shirt and tie (I kept my sweatpants on, no need to be unnecessarily uncomfortable). I found a nice spot in that room in the house where no one but my mom ever spent any time.

Considering that this was my first real job interview since school (I'd met with the fine folks at Marcello's regarding a distinguished pizza deliveryman position, but had yet to hear back), the result was a definite success. Actually, no matter which way you sliced it, it was a success. About twenty minutes into the interview, I was offered the position. They repeatedly told me that they couldn't guarantee me work once the season was over, but that if I did well and proved myself, there was always a chance that something could pop up.

Before I could call my parents, I called John Edington and filled him in on the whole thing.

"So what do you think I should do?" I asked. "I need some advice."

"What do I know? I couldn't hack it out there; that's why I'm a professor," Edington said.

"Are you serious? I come to you, a recent college graduate asking for life advice, and you say—"

"Easy, easy there, Mr. Alexander," he chuckled. "I think you should do it."

"That's it?"

"Yes, that's it," he said, pausing. "Let me ask you a question. And answer this honestly; no jokes."

"Sure."

"What else do you have going on right now? What other opportunities are you turning down by taking this?"

"No, I know what you're saying, but—"

"Just answer those questions," he interrupted.

"I have nothing…else going on right now. No other real opportunities," I said, resigned to the fact that it was real now that I'd actually said it.

"Then what do you stand to lose?"

"Well, I don't know. I want to be on the air and I feel like once you move away from the microphone, it's hard to come back. And what if I go out there and I hate it or nothing happens after the season ends?"

"Then you come back home. You're twenty-one years old. Live a little. Trust me: if this is the worst decision you ever make, you'll be fine," he said.

"No, I know, it's just…" I started to say.

"This is a big decision, I know. I'm not attempting to trivialize what you're about to decide. You called for my advice and that's what I think you should do. Let me know what you decide."

And with that, the conversation was over. The more I thought about it, mulling over what my professor had said, the more I realized how right he was.

At dinner, my parents were surprisingly on-board with my decision to give it a shot. The only sticking point was how I was going to get out there. They were both strongly opposed to my driving out alone and it was too expensive to have my car shipped out. Neither of my parents was going to be able to accompany me due to various work, family, and social hang-ups.

"So what do I do?" I asked.

"Why don't you check one of those drive boards, see who is going out that way?" my mom asked.

Looking at my dad, I said, "Is she serious?"

"I think she is," my dad laughed.

"What?"

"That's insane, that idea. No way I'm doing that," I said.

"Okay," she said, not arguing. "How about...how about Lotfi? He doesn't have a job, does he? We'd pay for his plane ticket back home."

"Just because he doesn't have a job, it doesn't mean he can just get up and do a basically pointless cross-country trek with me," I said. Even as I said that, I knew it wasn't true. Lotfi didn't have a job and if ever there was anything up his alley, it was an adventure like this. Still, that would be a mammoth of favor if there ever was one and I wasn't about to ask him to do it.

"What other choices do you have?"

"I could go out there alone," I said.

"That's not happening. So, outside of that, if it's not him, what else is there? Call him and tell him what we've suggested and that we'd be willing to pay for his flight back to New Jersey and wherever you guys stay on the way out there."

Unable to muster sufficient information to dispute their logic, I made the call. Not surprisingly, Lotfi was in. Once the dates had been discussed (departure in a week and a half) and the financial aspects agreed upon, it was settled: I would drive out to California with Lotfi to start my new job with the NFL Network.

To most people, that might sound incredibly glamorous. And, to an extent, they'd be right. Moving out to the golden coast, working in television and in sports. All good things. But those who know the business know how risky it was. This was a temporary position, not guaranteed past the Super Bowl. That's not to mention that the job itself was an entry-level, underpaid, overworked position.

But it was a job. And that was more than a lot of people I graduated with could claim. So, on a clear Wednesday morning, Lotfi showed up at my house. The routine we'd gone through many times before on our way up to Syracuse had been revived, if only for one more go.

Bags and crates and boxes loaded into the car, I hugged my parents, promised to call each night after we stopped for the day, and hopped into my car. There was still that initial excitement that comes at the beginning of a long car drive. You know, when the music is still fresh, before you realize, "Hey, wait a minute, we have at least (insert absurdly incredible amount of time) left before we arrive at our destination. This is horrible."

"Before we get to White Castle," Lotfi said, excited that this element of the trip was still in play, "let me just say, and I know I've said it to you before and you don't want to hear it but I'll say it again anyway, Congratulations. This is going to be great for you."

"Yeah, thanks. I guess," I laughed.

"No, really, this is great," he said, his big body nearly squirming out of the seat due to his excitement.

"You all right?" I asked, smiling. Lotfi seemed more excited than I was.

"All good," he said, turning up the radio. "Can you believe the 'Niners are going to go into another season with that kid at quarterback?"

"Haven't we had this exact same conversation before?" I asked.

"I don't think so," Lotfi said.

We had, but that didn't matter. After the White Castle had been ordered and finished, gas tank filled and refilled, state lines crossed and left in the rear-view mirror, that's all there was left. Me and my friend Lotfi. Driving together. The former ready to start a new life, the latter simply along for the ride. That was all there was to it and that was all there needed to be.

about the author:

scott spinelli is a stand-up comedian, author, and contributor
to various online publications. he lives in hoboken, nj with a
roommate. this is his first novel.

thank you:

as this is my first novel (or situation in my life where i've done anything even worth thanking anyone), i wasn't sure about the best way to do this. i settled on doing it alphabetically

joseph battiato, jana battiloro, and gwen bernfield for their incredible suggestions and guidance, aaron goldfarb and megan halpern for putting up with my constant stream of questions, bridget lichtinger for pointing me in the right direction, arthur mallet for helping me believe in this, my editor kirstin peterson, lutfi sariahmed and kent stein for being my never-ending sounding boards and my incredibly talented (and patient) cousin allison wolfe

i also would like to thank my friends, family, parents and anyone else who not only supported me but also (knowingly or unknowingly) served as creative inspiration

to anyone i forgot, i'm sorry, but thank you, too. there's always next time

Made in the USA
Charleston, SC
09 November 2012